# ADVANCE PRAISE

*Girls in a World at War*

A lucky reader learns the back stories of history, finding insights that bring events to life, such as in the new book *Girls in a World at War*. Like Walt Whitman in the Civil War tents caring for the wounded, Nancy Ewing Munro endured the hardship and richly remembered people and events of WW II with an observant, caring voice. Sensitively edited by her daughter Peggy Munro Scholberg, the reader will have a deeper understanding of courage and compassion from this vivid human story.

~Jim Wojcik, Co-author of *Bud's Jacket*

A compelling story of women serving in World War 2, it builds from a manuscript of one of them to the story of many of them. From tragedies to celebrations, you won't forget.

~Lonnie Pierson Dunbier, Author, Editor, Historian, and Writer

What an interesting read that tells us about women/girls during war, a subject we don't read about much. The book is based on a true story that makes it even more special. It is important that we read the stories of the women of that time—and how they stepped up to help win World War II. Each young woman had to decide to join the Army (or Red Cross), go overseas, and do what she could do to help others survive and thrive.

~Stephen Anderson, President, Minnesota Eighth Air Force Historical Society

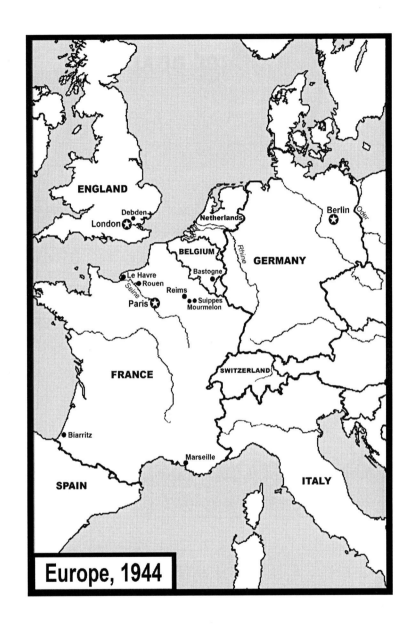

**Europe, 1944**

# Girls in a World at War

Kirk House Publishers

Bonnie + Gina
Enjoy ♥
*

# GIRLS IN A
# WORLD AT WAR

*Peggy Munro Scholberg*

**PEGGY MUNRO SCHOLBERG &
NANCY EWING MUNRO** IN MEMORIAM

First Edition

Printed in the United States of America

Paperback ISBN: 978-1-959681-68-7
eBook ISBN: 978-1-959681-69-4
Hardcover ISBN: 978-1-959681-70-0
LCCN: Pending

Cover design and interior design by Ann Aubitz
Illustrations by David Geister
Photos are from of the collection of Peggy Munro Scholberg
Headshot by Amy Zellmer


Published by
    Kirk House Publishers
    1250 E 115th Street
    Burnsville, MN  55337
    612-781-2815
    Kirkhousepublishers.com

# PREFACE

In 1957, Nancy Ewing Munro wrote about her experience as an Army dietician during World War II. Per Nancy, it is "the story of five girls seeking purpose and meaning in a world too large to grasp. It is a fictional account of women at war, as Kathy (alias) saw it. The story is based on actual experience. In order to give shape and meaning, some characters and events were changed."

Nancy's original 660-page manuscript, captured on a manual type-writer, titled *L'Ange au Sourire,* or *The Angel of the Smile*, was never published. In 2023 Nancy's daughter, Peggy Munro Scholberg, pulled the manuscript off the shelf and proceeded to shorten and edit the book.

Consistent with the original writing, young women were referred to as "girls," Prisoners of War as "PWs" rather than POWs, and "mess" is used instead of mess hall where they ate.

# TABLE OF CONTENTS

# PROLOGUE

**August 3, 1936**
**Olympic Stadium**
**Berlin, Germany**

Adolf Hitler looked out into the vast stadium. This was the time for Germany to show the rest of the world Germany's prominence. It was time to display their rightful place in Olympic history. After years of preparation, building the Third Reich was well underway. Today would again be a day of magnificent celebrations with flags, bands, and parades.

Straight across, buried in the crowds, was Katherine Collens sitting with her favorite uncle. She had celebrated her 16th birthday just three days earlier. As a "Chicago Times" correspondent, her Uncle Fred Babcock was covering this event. Kathy giggled as she and her Uncle Fred continued to practice and learn their "secret" language, German.

At two p.m., a surprise upset shook the world. USA runner Jesse Owens came in first in the 100-meter dash. His time was a record-smashing 10.3 seconds. The crowd leapt to their feet and cheered. In unison they thrust their right arms out and pointed upward, performing the famed Olympic salute, an old tradition of honoring a winning Olympian.

Neither Kathy nor Uncle Fred were able to notice that Adolf Hitler did not acknowledge the Black man's victory. They were also unaware that the Olympic salute was being transformed to instead become a Nazi salute, along with the utterance of "Heil Hitler," a signal of obedience to Hitler.

Kathy would forever remember that day. The time when the world was not at war—the time when the Olympic salute celebrated excellence—the time before she would join the forces to fight Hitler's evil.

# PART I
# SERVICE IN THE UNITED STATES

# CHAPTER 1

# BASIC TRAINING

Kathy opened her alligator-skin purse. No young girl could join the Army without first combing her hair. It was not proper to comb her hair in public, but neither could she walk the length of the car full of soldiers to the washroom. No civilians, no other women, just Kathy and twenty-four soldiers.

The train was due in Camp McCoy, and still she saw only the backwoods of Wisconsin. She combed her short brown hair. She powdered her generous nose the dark shade of powder to minimize its size. Carefully, with modest touches of lipstick, she outlined her very ordinary mouth. Her thickly lashed eyes were her only good feature. What she lacked in beauty she would make up for with her caring personality. *She'd be an angel.*

The train slowed in the thick woods. Kathy stood up to get her overnight case from the baggage rack. This case held the few things that could be brought from home into the Army. She was short, so she stepped up onto the green plush seat, hurrying to grab the case down before one of the watching soldiers might offer to help.

When the train lurched around a curve, she lost her balance. She grasped at the hanging strap and was able find her footing. A soldier whistled, and another and another, until she was surrounded by wolf whistles. She clutched her bag and sunk down onto the seat. She could not keep a smile from twitching on the corners of her mouth. After all, she was single and hoping for romance.

Maybe the soldiers could tell how she felt about them. These soldiers so bravely fighting for their country. She must serve their sick and wounded. She would bring food to the starved prisoners of war. She would carry nourishing hot meals to heal wounds and knit bones. She would make Spam taste good.

Kathy didn't dare look at the GIs' faces, as a smile might encourage more whistles. When the train stopped, Kathy waited. If she got off behind the soldiers, they would not all be looking at her.

As the last one off, she paused at the door, wondering where to go. A small clearing had been bulldozed out of the woods with a three-walled open shelter in the middle. A narrow gravel road was the only opening through the trees. A large green Army bus drove up the road and stopped. Dozens of soldiers from the train moved toward the bus. That must be the Camp McCoy bus.

Kathy started down the train steps. A red-nosed soldier in an unbuttoned jacket with a single stripe on his sleeve reached up for her suitcase, saying, "I'll take that for you."

Kathy hesitated. She did not want to hurt his feelings. Officers were not supposed to be too friendly with enlisted men. Yet how could he know that just yesterday she had been sworn into the Army as an officer, a Second Lieutenant, for she still wore her tailor-made black traveling suit. Would it be proper to let him carry her case? She just didn't know.

The soldier did not wait for an answer. He grabbed her suitcase and rushed off, away from the bus, toward the dark woods. Kathy decided she did not want him carrying her case, certainly not in the wrong direction. She would take it back. She started after him, walking as rapidly as a Second Lieutenant's dignity and inch-high heels on rough ground would permit.

She noticed he was teetering. All thoughts of rank and dignity vanished. Kathy ran after him as best she could, till the soldier neared the wall of trees and bushes. Nothing in the suitcase was worth following him through that wall. She stopped, a little girl, small and helpless, only five feet, one inch tall, 115 pounds, in an Army of big men.

A long-legged, broad-shouldered soldier strode past her. "I'll take that, Private!" he commanded. The thief dropped the suitcase, and vanished into the woods. The hero picked up the case, and returned it to Kathy. He smiled down at her with friendly blue eyes. His jacket, with two stripes on his sleeve, was neatly buttoned.

She looked up to him. "Thanks! What would have happened without you?"

"If I hadn't, any one of these men would have helped you." He waved his arm toward the men clustered near the bus. That's why most of us are in the Army, to protect women and children."

He offered Kathy his arm. Almost skipping to keep up with his long legs, they made their way towards the bus. The group of soldiers separated, making a lane to the bus door. As they boarded the bus, the sun shone gloriously. Even bands playing and flags waving could not have made a more magnificent welcome into the Army for Kathy.

Seated next to her on the bus, her rescuer told her his name was George. He was a Corporal, marched in the infantry, spoke five languages, and had a master's degree in International Relations. Never again would Kathy be concerned about rank. Men were men, and women were women; even the Army could not change that with stripes and bars.

A soldier with a white-helmet with an "MP" painted on it walked down the aisle, checking papers. George said, "'MP' means Military Police. He's checking for passes."

The MP stretched out his hand to Kathy. "Your pass?"

"I don't have a pass, just my orders. Will they do?" She handed him her mimeographed paper. He read it, nodded, and returned it. He glanced at George's pass, and went on to the next seat.

Kathy handed her orders to George. "Maybe you can help me again. Where do I go? This just says to report to my commanding officer at Camp McCoy. It doesn't say who he is nor where he is."

George read the paper. "You are a dietitian? You'd probably report to the hospital. I'll show you where to go." He returned the paper. "It takes hours to sign in. Would you like to eat lunch with me first?"

Kathy accepted with pleasure.

The bus emerged from the woods and stopped at a gate flanked by two guard houses. White-helmeted soldiers with pistols on their belts and rifles on their shoulders stood guard. Jeeps full of soldiers drove by. Troops of soldiers marched along the road and in the fields. "Hup, two, three, four."

In the distance, four tanks lumbered and thundered powerfully. Behind them ran soldiers with their rifles leveled. In the field opposite were straight rows of olive-drab green tents and small white-walled buildings. It could have been a movie set.

When the bus stopped at a large brick building. George said, "This is the hospital. We can eat in their PX, or Postal Exchange."

The PX was a large room arranged much like a small-town drug store. It was filled with patients in wine-red pajamas, white-uniformed nurses, and uniformed men. Patients with no signs of illness other than the wearing of pajamas sat on stools at the soda fountain. Thumping on a walking cast to a juke box, a patient inserted a dime to play "Praise the Lord and Pass the Ammunition." Two patients in wheelchairs raced to the door, one ramming the other. Kathy chose a table in a corner, and sat facing the room so she could observe. "It's not what I expected," she said.

"Patients in the Army stay in the hospital until ready for active service. They must be able to hike 25 miles," said George.

"I'd ask you to dinner but I cannot date you. You are an officer. I am an enlisted man."

"I'd accept if you asked."

"Even if you wanted to break regulations, there would be no place we could go. You couldn't go to the enlisted men's club and I can't go to the officers' club," George shrugged.

After lunch, he took her to the hospital door. He said, "Good bye, good luck," and left.

Kathy pushed against the brass rail on the heavy glass front door and entered the hospital. In the green-tiled front hall, she asked both a young nurse and a Captain where to find the head dietitian. Neither knew. She walked down the hall and looked at white signs hanging over office doors. Commanding Officer, Executive Officer, Chief Nurse. None said Dietitian.

Kathy asked a Corporal with a tray of blood pipettes and slides. He didn't know. She asked a nurse carrying an armload of charts. She gestured, "I can tell you where they eat—that is their mess—and it's right around the corner, together with the kitchen."

The mess with gleaming stainless steel serving counters and long tables with piles of white china plates looked even cleaner than Chicago's newest civilian hospital. Evidently there was not an acute shortage of help in the Army. When she saw the shining modern mixers in the kitchen, she knew why Chicago's Cook County Hospital had been unable to get any new equipment. It was all going to the Army. This kitchen was a delight.

The white-uniformed dietitians, one with silver bars and the other with gold bars on her shoulders, were in a glass-walled office in a corner. They smiled cheerfully to welcome Kathy. Both were so charmingly feminine that the men working in the mess must have been wanting to please them rather than grudgingly obeying orders.

"I'm a new dietitian reporting for basic training," said Kathy, presenting her orders. "Might one of you be my commanding officer?"

The girl with silver bars shook her white-capped head. "Not me. I know of no basic training for dietitians. I've been here for six months without it and haven't missed it." She read Kathy's orders. "They do specify basic training. You might take it with the nurses."

They took Kathy to the nurses' office in the small wooden building next door. The nurse Captain finally accepted her because she didn't know where else to send her.

She asked Kathy to fill out several forms. On the first she wrote out her name, her Army serial number: R1340, and birthdate and age, 23. The next blanks were for corps, unit, regiment, and division.

"What corps am I in?" she asked the nurses.

One nurse answered, "You're not in the nurse corps." Another said, "I don't know." A third answered, "Dietitians do not have a corps. You're just in the Army."

"What regiment? Division?"

"None. You are just in the Army."

"I don't belong to anything? How can I get an esprit de corps without a corps?"

"You are in the sixth service command. You can wear our shoulder patch."

"Who gives me my orders?"

"The chief dietitian in Washington. She's a Major."

When Kathy finished the payroll forms, insurance policy, will, and other required forms, Lieutenant Perkins offered to show her to her barracks.

Outside, a Captain stepped in front of them on the sidewalk and saluted Lieutenant Perkins, which surprised Kathy. After he passed, she asked, "Shouldn't you salute him, a Captain?"

"Femininity outranks his Captain's bars here," she explained to Kathy. "Nurses here are treated with respect. When the shooting starts, nurses are put on pedestals. Just in case any wild soldier wants to knock one off her pedestal, nurses are well guarded. MPs are assigned at all nurses' doors and in every situation." As they entered the barracks, Lieutenant Perkins returned the salutes of the alert MPs at the door.

Inside, Lieutenant Perkins introduced Kathy to a girl with smooth and rosy cheeks and starry eyes. "Lieutenant Darlene Robins, meet your roommate, Lieutenant Kathryn Collens, hospital dietitian."

Darlene was turning in front of the mirror that hung over the chest of drawers, looking at herself. "Glad to meet you. Don't you just love it? Our uniform. Imagine me, Darlene Robins, in a Schiaparelli suit! She designed the most gorgeous uniforms in the world! I don't look like a cowgirl." She turned to face Kathy. "I'm a lady in a Schiaparelli suit!"

"Pretty as a recruiting poster!" said Kathy. "I'm a country girl too. From Libertyville, Illinois, just outside of Chicago."

"I'm from Cheyenne, Wyoming!"

Lieutenant Perkins stood in the doorway. "That's the spirit. Stay proud of our uniform. Look sharp! Lieutenant Robins, please show Lieutenant Collens to the officers' mess at 1700 and explain the schedule. You both report to the quartermaster at 0900 tomorrow." She saluted Kathy. "Glad to have you with us," she said and left.

"I'm glad the Army has dietitians now. The food is wonderful, not at all the awful food the books say." Darlene looked at herself in the mirror again. "Do you have any mascara? With a Schiaparelli uniform, I must have mascara!"

Kathy put her suitcase on the upper bunk and opened it.

"No, I have no need to wear mascara. Your lashes are long and dark enough by themselves. I've tried. Boys just ask where I bought my lashes."

"Why did you join the Army, Kathy?"

"I joined the Army because, well, because one night I visited Eddie, the boy who gave me my first kiss. I was home from my internship that weekend and went to a friend's house. Eddie was there with a brace on his back and neck. He couldn't move. He was a Seabee in the South Pacific. He was shot, and he'll wear that brace for years, maybe all his life. He may not walk again. He said, 'Kathy, if there's anything you can do for the poor devils who get shot, do it.' I could not sleep that night. I knew I could never sleep until I was doing what I could. So, the next morning I volunteered."

"How about you, Darlene?" asked Kathy.

"A ticket out of Wyoming!" Darlene exclaimed. "I want to see the world! I want to see men in uniform. I hope to never see a pair of cowboy boots again!"

That evening, Darlene and Kathy double-dated at the officers' club. The unattached men they passed on their way to a table grinned broadly at Kathy and Darlene. When they were seated, Kathy and Darlene were asked, "What do you want to drink?"

Darlene didn't answer. Kathy said, "A Coke." Darlene nodded.

"Anything in it?"

Kathy grinned, "You ask me, a girl in an Army of brave men, if I want to deaden my nerves with alcohol? I should miss any part of this? A plain Coke is fine, thank you."

"I just want you to have a good time. Liquor helps."

They danced, and handsome young officers cut in. When the Army was so smilingly glad to see her, what could she do but smile back.

The next morning as Darlene and Kathy stepped outside the mess into the sunshine, a passing Jeep veered over the center line and screeched to a stop directly in front of them. A Captain swung open the Jeep door. "Hop in. Captain Bradley at your service. I'm going your way."

"Uh… How do you know which way we're going?" asked Darlene.

"Whichever way you ladies are going, that's the way I'm going. Not to worry girls. I just want to show off this Jeep."

"I've never ridden in a Jeep," said Darlene.

"Neither have I. This could be an adventure," said Kathy. "Let's go!"

As they got in, Darlene said, "We are due to the quartermaster at 0900, if you please."

"No problem," Bradley responded. "First a tour of the camp. You are in the latest 1943 General Purpose vehicle, or GP, or Jeep—fresh off the assembly line. In this, we can go anywhere and do anything. This can tow artillery, carry the wounded, and deliver ammunition. When fitted with a machine gun, it can be a weapon itself. What you ladies might like the best is that this windshield folds down and becomes an operating table. I heard this vehicle has even been nominated to receive a purple heart."

They zipped around corners with the wind sweeping through their hair. Men shouted and waved from the back of trucks as they passed. Right on time they came to an abrupt stop in front of the quartermaster's building.

"Thanks Captain Bradley! Next time please show me how to drive this myself!" Kathy yelled.

"Anytime I can be of service, please let me know." He saluted, revved up the engine, and sped off.

In the quartermaster's warehouse, a GI gave them fatigues. A tailor would be adjusting them.

"Tailor-fitted fatigues!" Darlene exclaimed.

The tailor explained the buttons on the sleeves and ankles. "These fold and button snugly at the ankles and wrists, like this, so poison gas and bugs can't get in. These are chemically treated to keep out gas. Your combat boots are impregnated too."

"I thought all we needed was gas masks."

"Depends on the gas. You'll learn about your gas masks."

Heavy steel helmets were placed on the counter. The GI also brought in several other hats, including white nurses' hats and overseas caps.

"What's the fish netting on the helmet for?" Kathy asked.

"It's intended for camouflage. I suppose you nurses could stick flowers in it. The inside rope liner is a shock absorber for when you get hit with flying debris. You can use it to store toilet paper."

The GI chuckled as he brought in his next load. "I've been offered $25 cash for this duty, but I'm keeping it. What we have here is the slinkiest thing in underwear." He held up a drab olive-green knit slip. "Sorry, girls, no lace."

"Just when I'd decided the Army wanted us to be glamorous. Why that awful color?" Darlene asked.

"You nurses have a habit of washing your undies and hanging them out to dry. A Kraut pilot a mile high could spot dainty pink things on a line. Poof! There goes your hospital."

Darlene held up olive-drab long-sleeve undershirts and knit long john underpants. "These look like my grandmother's. I won't wear these."

"Oh, you certainly will. If it gets cold enough. And it will get cold enough."

The tailor looked at Darlene's jacket. He pinned a tuck in at the waist. "Take off your blouse," he said, grinning again.

"I will not!"

"In the Army, a jacket is a blouse, for both men and women. I need to tailor it." He was now beaming.

Nine pairs of shoes were issued. This included two pairs each of heavy marching boots, white duty shoes, and sturdy brown oxfords, in addition to a pair of high combat boots with buckles, and both rubber and four-buckle overshoes.

Class A uniforms were provided in both summer and winter weight. A one-piece wrap-around summer dress made of brown-and-white striped seersucker was furnished. Overcoats, raincoats, trench coats, field jackets, and combat suits with wool liners were issued. A musette bag was given, a smaller alternative to a full pack that could be worn on the back or over the shoulder. All articles were put in a footlocker, along with a bed roll, for delivery to barracks 10.

Standing tall with her best posture, Kathy gazed in the mirror at the new finished product. She looked at the shiny gold bars on her shoulder and the helmet on her head.

That evening, at the Officers' Club, Kathy was wearing the same brass-buttoned Class A uniform everyone else had. Kathy was part of the gang. Every soldier was her buddy.

Their training films displayed the facts of war. They saw actual combat: a pilot crashing in a burning plane, a soldier in an African village shot by snipers, a man in a muddy trench bombed and frozen. Then the Army demonstrated techniques for treating burns, bandaging wounds, typing blood, giving plasma and transfusions, and injecting morphine.

Kathy listened intently, taking precise notes.

"You're a dietitian," said Darlene. "Why bother to learn about morphine?"

"When I was a dietician intern at Cook County Hospital in Chicago, there weren't enough nurses, due to the war. If there are not enough in a war zone, maybe I'll be needed."

"You wouldn't give injections. Only nurses do."

"I did at County. I gave injections, changed bandages, fed babies, took X-rays, even assisted in surgery. It wasn't proper, but either I helped or the work wasn't done." Kathy stopped talking to watch the demonstration of bed-making according to Army regulations.

On their way to chow, Darlene said, "I bet you'd even make beds."

"Of course. Why wouldn't I?"

"I thought maybe college-educated dietitians wouldn't stoop to that. And you know medicine and first aid."

Kathy knew she had a friend.

For two weeks, they learned, rode horses, bowled, swam, and danced. Kathy had even driven a tank. That was a mistake because she was not strong enough to pull the brake. Fortunately, the field was large and empty, so she could steer it around it until the tank finally lost momentum. She decided driving a tank was one thing she would never attempt again.

Saturday, March 15, 1944 would be their final day of training. From there, they could be sent almost anywhere in the world. The Germans continued to occupy most of Europe, but their Luftwaffe no longer ruled the skies. The Allies, flying out of England, were reaching Germany and bombing day and night to weaken the Nazi might. In the Mediterranean, after rough fighting through Africa, Allies were working to gain access to the continent up through Italy. Japan still occupied much of the Pacific, yet the Allies were "island-hopping," slowly taking back territories while making headway towards Japan.

At their commencement ceremony, the Chief Nurse stood on the stage before the crowd of girls. "Silence!" she yelled. "Your orders will be distributed upon exiting the auditorium. This afternoon at 1400 the second Army will give a camouflage demonstration. Your attendance will be good for the soldiers' morale. Dismissed."

As they walked out of the auditorium, Kathy and Darlene each opened their orders. Kathy was assigned to a dietitian's replacement depot at Riley General Hospital, Springfield, Missouri; and Darlene to a station hospital at Fort Knox.

"Kentucky!" Darlene shouted. "What has Kentucky got that I didn't see in Wyoming? I want New York, or Seattle, or England."

That afternoon the girls donned their olive-drab rubber raincoats and black overshoes and walked across several fields of mud to the demonstration area. As the girls approached, some 100 civilians and officers on the bleachers stood and cheered. How heroic were the nurses to come out in this downpour.

They sat, waiting. Nothing was happening. There were no signs of preparation. On the field there were only shoots of green wheat growing in the brown stubble—and a few buttercups blooming. The splashing rain was noisy on their rubber hoods. The wooden seats were hard. Still, they waited.

Suddenly there was a loud "Bang!" At the sound of that signal gun shot, 200 wet camouflaged soldiers popped up from unseen fox holes. The field suddenly came alive. Leveling their guns as they ran, groups of soldiers charged at an enemy. Orders were shouted. Men were running everywhere in the sludge. Explosions thundered in the nearby woods.

Alarmed, the crowd on the bleachers watched intently. Kathy and Darlene looked over at each other without words. Indeed, their training was complete. It was apparent that war training for soldiers was distinctly different than that for nurses.

# CHAPTER 2

# A FRIEND FROM HOME

Kathy's duty at Riley General Hospital in Missouri was simply to wait for an assignment. She visited the town, but there was not much to see or do. At the hospital, from a glass-paneled observation room she watched the miracles of plastic surgery restore chins and noses blown off by war. In the medical library, she read about diet and bone growth. She played bridge with other dietitians.

The war raged on. To end the war, the Allies needed to land a powerful force in German-occupied Europe. There were rumors about a potential invasion, but no one seemed to know where or when that might happen.

For Kathy, it could be several weeks before she would be reassigned. She began to wonder if she could have been more useful in civilian life rather than joining the Army.

During her second week at Riley, Kathy recognized an old friend from Illinois in the mess.

"Rhys! I'm surprised to see you here! Last I recall, you were at basic training for medical officers in Oklahoma."

"Yes, and now I'm about to be shipped overseas. I haven't seen you since we were both at Cook County Hospital in Chicago. You were so helpful to me at County."

"I completed my dietician internship there, and now I've decided to join the war effort."

"I see that. I cannot even believe this, Kathy. You are the last person I would have expected to join! You won't fit in!"

"Oh, who does?" she replied. "Are you just here for lunch?"

"My flight leaves at 1400. We have some time to catch up. I've thought of you and your family. Whenever I couldn't stand the hot sand in Oklahoma and wanted to think of something fresh, I thought of that picnic at your place when I fell into the creek. Sorry, but what could have persuaded you to leave your magnificent home for a barracks room?"

"Oh yes, I love my family and all the trees and creeks. But I want to see something new and exciting."

"Kathy, your good life has not prepared you for the Army. You won't like it."

"You've tested your strength, Rhys. I haven't. You pushed against life and know what you can do."

"And that's good? Kathy, I'm struggling to get what you already have."

"I've never pitted my strength against anything."

"Why should you? With four servants to do the work! Your father has everything! Seven cars, a yacht, and carved oak furniture," Rhys said.

"And I had a fur coat plus a dressmaker and a hair stylist, but I did not earn them, and they didn't buy me more dates."

"You had them. What more could you possibly want?"

"Rhys Jones! You think better than that. Because I had them, I know how unimportant they are." She attempted to change the subject. "You are going to be a doctor! You will be a fabulous doctor! I know how much you care for your patients. Tell me about your training."

"I'm certainly not much of a doctor now. I'm assigned to a medical outfit. I completed my initial training in Oklahoma—a hell hole if ever there was one. The camp had just so much sand that was blowing into the barracks through every crack. The saying goes that one could be up to their waist in water and still have sand blowing in the face. Goes against all rules of cleanliness I have learned for the past two years. All that seemed to matter was that our beds were made right. My first day my ex-prize fighter commanding officer came at me twice. First to tell me to make my bed, and I wasn't even out of it yet, and later to tell me it was not made right.

"We were assigned to the 329th searchlight outfit. We don't get to fire guns. As part of the medical staff, we just have flashlights. Can you believe it? On the battlefield without a gun! What will I tell my kids I did in the war? I'd rather tell them I played piano in a French brothel. I can just see it. Our flashlights waving conspicuously in blacked-out England. Then, if a Kraut drops a bomb on a light, the doctor will survive to sew the soldiers back together. So, I asked the ex-prizefighter who would sew the doctor back together? I got no answers. He doubles up his fist with one arm, and points to the door with the other. I need this job so I just try to go along.

"Which brings us back to your joining the Army. Are you ready to fight the Germans?" Rhys asks.

"I don't hate the Germans."

"I didn't think so. You never hated anyone. However, you might think we should fight the Nazis that are attacking us."

"I don't believe the Germans are attacking us," Kathy said.

"Ha! There is a war on and people are being killed—but no one is attacking? Explain how Germany has taken over most of Europe. How about the genocide of the Jews? Their concentration camps? Their massacres in Poland? Holland? France? They aren't trying to hurt us! Just kill us!"

"My brothers are fighting but they don't want to hurt the Germans. They volunteered because there is a war, and so we have to fight. The Germans might be trapped in the same way."

"Yeah, right! The Nazis are really kind and gentle?" His voice was tense. "You just finished basic training. Didn't they teach you about the elite German SS? The Schutz Staffel? They are the most vicious soldiers in the world. They are also the best armed, best fed, and best equipped. Each SS guard is hand-picked. His "Aryan" pedigree must go back 200 years. His eyes must be a certain color, and his build must fit specific qualifications. The SS, in any situation, are ready to immediately unleash their fanatical brutalities.

"There are newspaper stories written to get us into a war. I went to Germany. You know that. I heard and saw for myself what a great country and people they are," Kathy says.

"Ah yes. You went on that German propaganda tour to see the 1936 Olympics. What other countries were included?"

Kathy said "England, Belgium, France, and Switzerland."

"The Nazi propaganda machine." Rhys said. "Especially in Germany, you would only see exactly what they wanted you to see. Hitler's military might was well-developed by then—and also well hidden. Back in 1933, Hitler was named Chancelor, and when the president died, he just took over the presidency, pronounced himself "Fuhrer," and ruled the country. Secretly, he began developing one of the most powerful military organizations in the world, disregarding WW1 reparations. No one stopped him. How do you suppose he was able to take over country after country in Europe so quickly, with just England now still standing," said a frustrated Rhys.

"I cannot explain this war," Kathy said.

"You just don't want to believe anything bad," he said.

She tried to change the subject. "It's a beautiful day. Do you have time to go for a walk?"

"In the year I've known you, you've pronounced every day and every night beautiful. Rain and snow and fog and sun are all beautiful. Kathy, I know I sound cynical. It's just that I've been in long enough to know how the Army works. Actually, I'm not all that surprised.

"Long ago I learned not to be too disappointed about what doesn't work out." He sighed. "Once I expected a watch for my high school graduation present. Mom was a teacher and I worked after school in a drug store. I knew how little we earned, with my father blind and unable to work, and I knew Mom could not buy me a watch. So, I saved my tips for three months. When I gave Mom my pay check, I added the tip money saying it was a bonus. I expected her to buy a watch for me.

Mom and Dad were proud of my diploma, and my being valedictorian, but they did not give me a watch. I was too big to cry but I had to stand outside in the dark for a while. I learned not to expect watches, and I'm not disappointed. When the war is over, if I survive…"

"Of course, you will survive! And you will help others to survive along the way."

"Oh my gosh. My watch has stopped. I cannot miss my flight! I gotta run!"

After Rhys left, the first thing Kathy did was go over to the PX and buy their best watch to send to Rhys. She could do nothing to make the Army let him practice medicine. Yet she could fulfill his dream of a good watch. Maybe he'd believe some dreams do come true.

She received one lonely letter from Rhys. "You would be so nice to come home to," he had written. She wrote him three cautiously warm letters, but received no answers. Why, she did not know.

One month later the watch was returned, unopened. It had been forwarded to another Army post office address. Finally, it had been rubber stamped "Return to Sender."

Kathy refused to believe Rhys had been killed. She went to the PX and bought a bottle of Taboo perfume.

# CHAPTER 3

# ARMY REGULATIONS

It was early in June, 1944, when orders finally came for Kathy to report to Castoria General Hospital. Kathy took the bus through the rolling hills of northern Ohio. Newborn calves and red barns were nestled in the black earth—indicating regenerative signs of spring. Here a wounded soldier could heal his wounds and restore his soul.

As the sun sank and shadows deepened, Kathy descended from the bus into a cluster of low wooden buildings. This was the time for which she had been waiting. All had been preparatory for this. Now she could contribute, not directly to the war effort, but to the healing of its wounds.

Kathy reported to the officer on duty at the headquarters. He said she could find the head dietician in room 21 of barracks 30, the third building on the right.

Using the street lamp, Kathy found the building. There were no MPs guarding the door. Evidently in this peaceful country no MPs were needed to guard the nurses.

Kathy opened the front door and stepped into a dark room. If it was like the day rooms of other barracks, the light switch would be on the wall to the left. She fumbled along the wall for the switch.

A commanding female voice shouted from the dark, "Don't turn on the light! Wait!"

Kathy froze.

After a minute came, "OK. Turn them on."

Kathy found the switch. At a glance she saw three couples of nurses and officers on the floor. One girl clutched her unbuttoned shirt together; another straightened her skirt. One officer, his arm in a cast, was fumbling with his pants. Bottles and glasses were on the table and floor. Without pausing, Kathy hurried straight through the day room and out to the hall.

As she closed the door behind her, she heard, "Turn off the light."

What had she just seen? It was too late now to go back for a better look.

In the hall, bare light bulbs hung from the ceiling on black wires. She found Room 21 and knocked.

"Come in," a gruff hoarse voice summoned.

Kathy opened the door. On the bed was a frumpy woman, maybe 30. She held a bottle by its neck and waved it toward Kathy. The woman's faded red chenille bathrobe hung open almost to her waist, revealing folds of flesh. "Have a drink," she invited, pulling her bathrobe into almost decent shape.

Kathy had never tasted alcohol. "I, uh... No, thank you."

The woman snorted. "Come on, girl. This is Southern Comfort." Her tone implied that Southern Comfort was a drink not to be lightly refused. The woman sat up, poured some into a glass on the table beside her bed, and handed the glass to Kathy.

"Thank you." Kathy looked at the smeared lipstick on the rim of the glass. This must be the wrong room. Every head dietitian she had known wore an immaculate uniform and insisted on clean dishes. Kathy faced the woman, "I am Lieutenant Collens. If you are the head dietitian, I am to report to you."

The woman made a futile attempt at smoothing her hair. She stood, tall and heavy. She arranged her bathrobe properly and tightened the sash. "I am the head dietitian, Lieutenant Groot." She spoke quickly, hurrying to assume the composure of a head dietitian. "Enjoy your drink. It's Southern Comfort. I'll show you to your room. I didn't expect you until tomorrow. That's all right. Glad to have you early. We need you for therapeutic diets. Well. Where did you get your training? Sit down."

Kathy sat on the edge of a straight chair. The table, the two chairs, the chest of drawers and the bed were all plain wooden GI furniture. She didn't say she was reporting on the day her orders specified, but answered the direct question. "Graduate of Iowa State College and dietician internship at Cook County Hospital in Chicago. I am most interested in therapeutic diets, so that will be a happy assignment."

Lieutenant Groot pulled her robe together again around her neck, and retied the sash more tightly. "I didn't have an internship, didn't even major in nutrition. I majored in textiles and clothing." She spoke with pride. "Wonder how I can be head dietitian? I have pull. Yes, I have pull in Washington. I have ten years' experience in hospitals." Her massive jaw jutted belligerently, demanding that Kathy be impressed. "Drink, girl, drink. That's Southern Comfort."

Maybe Kathy could get by with a little sip and then put the glass on the table. She sipped. It tasted so bad she grimaced. She explained, "I don't know much about drinking."

"Learn, girl, learn. No one survives Castoria without drink. Come on. Bottoms up. Then I'll show you your room across the hall."

Kathy's training against drinking was not easily dismissed. Her family and friends never drank. The few students that drank at Iowa State had been kicked out of school. She had, however, seen some of the charity patients at Cook County with delirium tremors and cirrhotic livers.

Lieutenant Groot took Kathy to her door across the hall and gave instructions to be ready for duty at 0550 in the morning, and left. The room contained the same GI furniture. Red-and-white flowered drapes were the only concession to femininity.

Kathy assured herself that Lieutenant Groot drank only at night, and by morning would be a perfect model of competence. Kathy hung in the closet the few uniforms she had carried with her. She showered down the hall. She opened her window, and once in bed, fell asleep.

She was awakened a few hours later by a slapping sound outside. Then, a thumping sound. A man's voice, in a loud whisper, "Wake up, Bosco. Wake up!" Slap, slap.

Alert now, Kathy sat up and heard a car door slam shut. Thump, step, drag, thump. Out her window, by the light of the street lamp, she saw an officer pulling a nurse on her back on the sidewalk. Thump. His walking cast made the thump. He stood on his good leg, and balancing himself with the cast, dragged the nurse.

He pulled her up to the front step. He hoisted her head and shoulders up the step. Her large, rounded hips blocked movement up the step. He tugged, to no avail. He dropped her arms. She lay, her back arched over the step. Her massive breasts thrust up, catching the light of the street lamp.

He slapped her cheeks. "Wake up, Bosco!" She slumbered on.

He banged on the front door. Silence. With his head down, he looked helpless. Someone had to help the poor patient. Kathy slipped into a bathrobe and walked down the hall. From the other end of the hall, came a small, gray-haired woman in a blue flannel bathrobe. She opened the front door.

"Get up, Bosco." The lady spoke as a school teacher to a naughty child.

The patient said, "She passed out. My first date in a year, and she passed out."

"I can see that." The lady's lips were set in a straight, prim line.

Together they helped get Bosco on her feet, and draped her arms across their shoulders.

Bosco revived a little, enough to bear some of her weight. They managed to get her into her room and beside her bed. There Bosco sighed and collapsed. She knocked Kathy down on her back onto the bed, burying Kathy's face in her massive breasts. Bosco reeked of alcohol.

The gray-haired lady grabbed Bosco's arm and pulled, but could not move her. "When I lift, you try sliding out."

The lady tugged. Kathy could not move. The lady went next door to recruit assistance. Finally, they were able to pull Kathy out.

They laid Bosco lengthwise on her bed. Kathy took off Bosco's shoes. "Shouldn't we take off her girdle?"

"She doesn't wear a girdle or panties." The lady's thin, straight mouth twitched with a wry smile, and her blue eyes snapped. "Disgusting," she said. "I'm Lieutenant McClain. Maxine McClain. Feel free to refer to me as Mac the WAC…everyone does. I was one of the first from the Women's Army Corps, or WAC here, and the name just stuck. I'm the head nurse here. You must be the Lieutenant Collens we have been expecting."

"Yes, I am."

"I wish I could assure you this doesn't happen often, but it does. Don't let it upset you too much. Tomorrow morning at 0800 Lieutenant Bosco will be in the operating room, clear-headed and efficient, an excellent surgical nurse. I don't understand how she does it, nor why, but she does. Well. It's late. I'm not clear-headed if I miss my sleep." Before Mac went down the hall to her room, she said, "Welcome to Castoria General Hospital. Good night."

"Good night." Kathy returned to her room, but not to sleep. She had seen drunks before. Cook County's wards had filled with them on Saturday nights, but she had associated drunks with destitute old bums who were unable to manage their lives. Then it occurred to her that this was the first useful service she had given since joining the Army. She had wanted to help the sick and wounded, yet she had had brave soldiers in mind. Basic training had not included treatment of someone drunk.

From across the hall came sounds of a door creaking open and of someone, probably Lieutenant Groot, shuffling into the latrine next to Kathy's room. Kathy heard Lieutenant Groot, if that's who it was, throw up, and throw up again. When there was nothing left to vomit, the retching continued, painful and revolting.

At dawn, at 0550 hours, Kathy answered a knock on her door to greet Lieutenant Groot. "Good morning. Come in. I'll be ready in a minute."

"Good morning," said Lieutenant Groot, in a voice that found nothing good about the morning. She looked better in her starched white uniform and cap, though the wrinkles under her eyes sagged. She did not come in, but stood in the doorway.

Kathy fastened her white nurse's cap at the most glamorous angle with bobby pins. She pinned a gold bar on the left tab of her collar, and the caduceus with the HD, for Hospital Dietician, on the right tab.

Lieutenant Groot smiled condescendingly. "The bar goes on the right, the caduceus on the left."

Kathy forced a smile. "Oh. I get them mixed up." She exchanged the insignia.

Lieutenant Groot looked at her watch. "It's 05:55 hours. You are late."

"I'm ready." Kathy took her fountain pen from her purse and her notebook from a drawer.

Lieutenant Groot led the way out the door at the end of the hall to the ramp that connected the hospital buildings. Lieutenant Groot was proud of this hospital, and pleased with her role of guide. She pointed out the various wards, messes, barracks, and warehouses, "We are really self-sufficient. I haven't been to town in months."

"You'll eat here in this mess with other officers." Lieutenant Groot continued, "I eat in the special diet mess, for my colitis."

"Is there a chapel?"

"I was coming to that. The chapel and the Chaplain's office are at the other end of our ramp. We are a 1,000-bed hospital, 80 officers, and 50 nurses. We have five medical specialists, 300 enlisted men and 100 WACs." She recited the personnel with clipped precision. "Not counting the civilian help. Our office is here."

They entered a large room with eight wooden tables and a long steam-heated serving counter. The kitchen area was obviously for large-quantity cooking, with a giant range and a suspended rack of huge spoons and dippers. Few civilian hospitals could boast of such clean, modern equipment. What misgivings Lieutenant Groot's lip sticked glass had roused Kathy the night before now vanished—she did keep a clean kitchen.

With her head high and her jaw pushed out in a gesture that asserted command, Lieutenant Groot said, "Here you will supervise the preparation of the therapeutic diets. You will visit patients and write special diets. I write the main menu. You will use regular foods as much as you can for the specials. I do the requisitioning."

A slender blond with Sergeant's stripes on the sleeve of her white uniform, hustled over to Lieutenant Groot with two cups of coffee. Lieutenant Groot introduced them, "Lieutenant Collens, meet Sergeant Leiben, our mess Sergeant." They went into a small room with three desks.

"Call me Sarge," she smiled timidly.

While Kathy and Lieutenant Groot looked at the forms for diets, Sarge worked silently at her desk. She treated Lieutenant Groot with subservience—or was it fear? Afraid to speak to her unless spoken to?

Lieutenant Groot handed Kathy a stack of papers from her desk. "Check the diet trays on the carts."

Checking involved simply seeing that each tray contained the food listed. One paper was marked "408 – Diabetic." There was no list of specific foods and the gram weight of each.

Kathy returned to Lieutenant Groot's desk. "I don't have this diabetic patient's diet list."

Lieutenant Groot barked, "We don't write individual diabetic diets. The women know which foods to dish up."

"Are all diabetics on the same diet?" Kathy knew all diabetics could not be on the same diet. Doctors ordered specific amounts of carbohydrates, proteins and fats according to each patient's size, activity, and metabolism. Foods have to be calculated to provide just those amounts, no more and no less.

Lieutenant Groot snorted and stood up, bigger and taller than Kathy. She thrust out her jaw defiantly. "I have trained the women. They know how to serve diabetic patients."

This was, if not impossible, highly improbable. Kathy doubted that these women knew food values well enough to determine the serving size. And evidently, no one had bothered to make a record of patients' likes and dislikes, especially important for a diabetic who was ordered to eat all the foods served him.

"I haven't time to write 17 different individual diets. There's a war on, you know." Lieutenant Groot's massive jaw refuted any further discussion.

Kathy considered that Groot's major in textiles and clothing had not taught her how to calculate diets. Kathy returned to the carts.

When Kathy had finished checking, Lieutenant Groot said, "Today you watch me check the ambulatory patients' special diets. In the future that will be your responsibility."

Kathy stood at the end of the steam table beside Lieutenant Groot while patients in maroon pajamas and robes filed by, helping themselves cafeteria style to the foods.

Lieutenant Groot greeted each with an animated "And how are we today?" Each patient grunted or answered with a disinterested "Fine." Lieutenant Groot added, "Are we getting enough to eat?" Without listening to the answer, she greeted the next patient with "And how are we today?"

A young, round-faced Corporal, dressed in woolen khaki shirt and slacks, came through the line. Lieutenant Groot explained that he worked at headquarters, and ate an ulcer diet here at the hospital. She changed her tone. "Good morning. How are you?" She spoke with genuine interest. Kathy glanced at Groot's left hand. She had no wedding ring.

He answered with a frown, half-closed eyes, and a half-open mouth.

Groot introduced Kathy, "Joe, this is Lieutenant Collens." Groot turned to Joe, "You were a hoot last night. After that sixth drink, you…" She laughed with a silly giggle.

Joe set his tray down on the counter. "Alcohol and my ulcers don't mix. What a hangover." He patted his head tenderly with one hand, and his stomach with the other. "I have a desk piled high with reports waiting for me. I need coffee before I tackle them."

Kathy noted the coffee and sweet roll on his tray. She smiled to ease the abruptness of her words. "Milk and soft-cooked eggs with toast could ease your stomach."

An upturn in Lieutenant Groot's stiff jaw forbade further discussion. Joe removed the coffee from his tray and set it back on the counter. He took a glass of milk and a poached egg. "Thanks." He smiled boyishly to Kathy and carried his tray to an empty table.

"You may go to breakfast now, in the officers' mess." She dismissed Kathy, carried her tray to Joe's table, and with a giggle, sat beside him.

The Sergeant bustled from the kitchen and went over to Lieutenant Groot. "Ward 4 phoned for jelly for the low-fat, high-carb diets. I sent it over."

Lieutenant Groot shouted across the room to Kathy, "I thought you checked the carts."

Kathy returned to Groot's table. She just couldn't remember jelly on cart 4.

"Well?" Groot asked impatiently.

"Yes, ma'am. I checked the carts."

"I certainly ordered enough jelly. Please be more accurate in the future. You may go to breakfast now." With a look of smug satisfaction, Groot turned from Kathy to Joe.

The officers' mess was almost empty by the time Kathy arrived. She ate alone, and returned to the dietitians' office. Lieutenant Groot looked up from the papers on her desk, and glanced at the clock. "I'll show you how to make the ward rounds, and what foods to order. We'll begin with the ulcer ward."

Kathy, with job experience at Cook County Hospital, didn't feel she needed to be shown. Nevertheless, she obediently followed Lieutenant Groot on her rounds.

Each ward was a separate wooden building. In the first building, they walked into a large open room with a dozen beds along two walls. Near the nurses' station were just four private rooms, used for critically ill, and for high ranks, both rare. Patients in wine-red pajamas bustled about making beds, throwing pillows, and carrying trays back to the kitchen

Lieutenant Groot stopped at the first bed. "How are we today?" The patient was sitting on his bed polishing his shoes. He jabbed the brush into the brown wax. "Fine."

"Are we getting enough to eat?"

"I'm glad you asked that question." He shook the shoe brush in her face. "That's a good question. What do you mean by 'eat'? All I get is milk. Can I eat milk? No, I drink milk. Milk, ten times a day, milk. Moo-ooo." With a determined smile frozen on her face, Lieutenant Groot walked stiffly to the next bed. "How are we today?"

With some dexterity, the patient spread a deck of cards into a fan shape, and held it toward her. "Pick a card, Lieutenant, any card."

She ignored him and walked on to the next bed. "How are we to-day?"

The patient responded, "Moo-ooo."

Groot turned to Kathy. "We haven't time to visit each patient." Head high, she turned around and marched toward the door.

In the next ward, most patients were on their feet and moving around. One man leaned on a crutch. With his other crutch, he shoved his shoe across the floor like shuffleboard. It hit another shoe. He waved his crutch and whooped. Another man, with both arms and legs in casts, expertly wheeled his chair up to Kathy. He offered her a pen with one hand, and gestured to the cast on his arm with the other. "Autograph?"

Kathy bent over and wrote on the cast.

The patient looked at her signature, and announced to the ward, "Listen up! Let me introduce Kathryn Collens."

"We have work to do," snapped Groot. She hustled past five beds, asking, "How are we today?" She passed by, not waiting for responses.

Then, satisfied that she had done her duty, hurried on to the next area, a surgical ward for officers.

Lieutenant Groot stopped at the first bed and smiled her mechanical smile. "How are we today?"

According to his medical chart, Kathy read that this patient had a broken jaw, wired, and a liquid diet had been ordered. His jaw would be wired tightly shut for several weeks. Until it healed, he could eat only what he could strain through his teeth.

He flashed back an equally mechanical smile, showing a space where a tooth had been removed. "Fine," he spoke through his permanently clenched teeth.

"Are we getting enough to eat?" asked Lieutenant Groot.

"No."

"We'll send you more." Lieutenant Groot said as she turned toward the next bed.

"More tea? I'll drown in tea," he said.

Kathy spoke quietly to Lieutenant Groot. "His chart says he's had a tooth removed so he could get in thicker liquids, pureed foods, and small bits of solids."

Groot rejected the advice. "The doctor ordered a liquid diet. That is defined in the diet manual—tea, coffee, bouillon, fruit juice, and Jello."

"Jello!" The word sounded grim as he spoke through his teeth. "Did you ever push Jello through a hole the size of a tooth?"

"I'll talk to the doctor," offered Kathy.

Lieutenant Groot snapped. "Lieutenant Collens, we do not tell doctors what to order!"

Kathy said nothing, but was determined to talk to the doctor. He could order what he pleased, but she would make certain he knew what he was ordering.

Groot continued on to the next bed. "Are we getting enough to eat?"

The patient had a raw red scab where his lower jaw and tongue should have been. Near the top of the scab was a round, moist, dark hole—his throat. Kathy tore her eyes from the raw wound and looked at the rest of his face. His eyes, which were watching Lieutenant Groot, were brown and defeated. He was pathetically thin. He made no response to her question, just looked on, indifferent.

Kathy wondered why they didn't cover the gruesome wound with a bandage. The patient picked up a square of gauze to wipe his dripping drool. She understood why.

For plastic surgery, he would need to get into better physical shape. Yet he was marked for a liquid diet. Kathy intended to do something about that. She'd talk, not to Lieutenant Groot, but to his doctor.

They were met in the hall of the next ward by an angry doctor, identified by the MD on the caduceus. He shook his fist at Lieutenant Groot, and spoke in a loud voice. "Corn on the cob! You gave Sam corn on the cob!" With an effort at control, he lowered his voice. "The man's in an oxygen tent. He needs all his energy for breathing! He cannot manage to hold and chew corn on the cob!" He glared at Groot.

Lieutenant Groot glanced at the diet chart and thrust out her jaw. A regular, low-salt diet was ordered. She pointed out, "There was no salt on the corn."

The doctor threw up his arm. "Use your head, woman. Think! Chart that as a soft low-salt diet."

Lieutenant Groot changed the patient's chart as ordered, and handed it to Kathy. "You finish the ward rounds. I have requisitions due before ten." She stalked out.

"Now I suppose I've irritated Groot's colitis. We'll all get lousy food for a week," said the doctor.

Kathy returned to Ward 2 to talk to the surgical officer. He was making his rounds, so she waited for him in the ward kitchen.

As she waited, she pondered, just what could that patient with no lower jaw eat? She tried drinking a little water without using her tongue, tilting her head back to pour the water down her throat. She tried a ball of bread. Each time her tongue insisted on helping with the swallowing. How could he eat with no tongue or jaw?

"Excuse me, but what are you doing?" a man's deep voice asked.

She turned to face the balding surgical officer standing in the doorway. "It must look silly. I was trying to figure out how the patient in 202 eats."

He looked at the HD on her caduceus. "Hospital Dietician, right? So, you're the new dietitian. I'm Captain Lewis." He stepped into the kitchen, and took two cups from a cupboard. "Want a cup of coffee?"

"Yes, thank you sir. I'm Lieutenant Collens. What diet do you want for him?"

"He may have whatever he can manage. He's the one to tell you. There's nothing wrong with his stomach." He poured the coffee. "Cream? Sugar?"

"Neither, thank you." She picked up her cup. "Then you didn't know that a liquid diet order is only clear liquids?"

"Is that what he's been getting? Hell, no! I'll change that order. Give the man whatever he wants."

"And what do you want for the man with the wired jaw?"

"Anything he can manage. Nothing wrong with his stomach either. I'll change that to nourishing liquids. High calcium and protein and vitamins. You should know what knits bones," he said and hurried out.

Kathy sipped her coffee, working up her fortitude to face first the man with no jaw. She took a deep breath and started toward the ward. The roster listed 202, Robert Austin. With another deep breath, she walked down the hall and across the ward to stand beside Robert Austin's bed.

"I am Lieutenant Collens. I'll be your dietitian now. Do you want me to call you Robert?" She paused. When he did not respond, she asked, "or Austin?" The corners of his mouth and eyes sagged. "Bob?" The corners of his mouth and eyes raised slightly, not to a smile, but not quite as glum.

"Your doctor just told me you could have any food you wanted. I'd like to know what you want, Bob."

He shrugged in a helpless gesture.

"There are special formulas for patients like you. The fellow in the next bed will get a formula; a mixture of all the foods you need, milk, eggs, fruits, pureed with liquids. Do you want your formula hot?" She paused, holding her pencil on a pad of paper, waiting for his response. "Or cold?" No response. "What smells do you like? Most of our taste is really smell. Chocolate? Strawberry?"

His eyes looked a little interested. Saliva drooled across his wound. He wiped it with his white gauze.

She nodded and wrote "Strawberries." "You like strawberries? Can you eat little pieces of bread?" He looked blank. "Want all your food in a thick liquid diet?"

His face sagged wearily. Turning down a corner of his blanket, he uncovered a whisky bottle in the bed beside him. He patted it affectionately and covered it again.

"That's the formula you like?"

He didn't bother to nod. His face showed a little sign that she had gotten the idea.

"Oh." She couldn't blame him. Her words were echoing ridiculously in his apathy. She believed she had important information. "I've just come from a plastic surgery center. They make fantastic repairs. If your body is in good condition, with lots of calcium and protein, the stuff that knits bones, you stand twice the chance of making a good graft. Alcohol won't knit bones. Our formula will."

She had talked too much, pushed too hard. "I didn't mean to preach." She was going to cry. She had intended to talk next to the man with the wired jaw. Instead, with tears welling up in her eyes, she rushed back to the kitchen. When she had controlled her tears, she went back to check on what had been ordered for the two men.

By a quarter to eleven, she had not yet visited two wards. To give the women in the kitchen time to make the formulas, she would have to finish her rounds after lunch.

Lieutenant Groot was not in the special diet mess, so Kathy introduced herself to the two cooks. They were plump, motherly-looking women. "I'm afraid I have extra work for you, but I don't think you'll mind when you know who it's for." She told them about the two patients and the changes.

The shortest cook, whom she had met earlier that morning, dabbed her eyes with a handkerchief. "I'll make it, she offered. "My boy is in North Africa. Maybe… Well, I'll make anything for these boys."

Kathy wrote down the formula for her. "There's also a change in the low-salt diet for A410. He is in an oxygen tent and cannot bite and chew." Kathy wrote a new menu for him.

The taller woman, who had initially appeared grumpy, offered to change it. "I suppose that's the least we can do for them."

I have some calculations to make. Then I'll bring you the diabetic menus for lunch. Kathy watched the cooks for any signs of objection— but there were none.

Suddenly Lieutenant Groot was standing beside Kathy, scowling. "All diet changes must be made before 1000 hours. We cannot have these last-minute confusions."

"Of course," Kathy agreed. "I'll make them myself, and that will be no bother to anyone. If someone will tell me where the milk and eggs are."

Groot asked, "Did you finish the ward rounds?"

"No, but…."

Groot snorted. "A dietitian has no time to do the cooking. That is not her job."

"I can finish on my off-duty time. I don't mind working extra hours. That's why I'm here. Is the milk in the left refrigerator?"

"What you do on your own time is your own affair. Just see that tomorrow's diets are written before 1000." Lieutenant Groot glared down at Kathy, and then left.

Kathy helped the cooks and finished up her work at 1300. She returned to her quarters to change her uniform and clean up for lunch. She never could work in a kitchen without splattering some food.

When she left the barracks by the side door, she recognized Bosco, from the evening before, coming out of the officers' club. This afternoon she stood erect and laughing with her black hair shining and her dark eyes flashing. She spotted Kathy and greeted her, "Hey, are you Collens?"

"You helped me in last night. Thanks." She laughed, not at all embarrassed. "That party was a riot. Hal was so drunk he got into the wrong car," she laughed again. While Kathy thought it was stupid to be so drunk you didn't know your own car, Bosco's laugh made it seem fun.

Bosco put her arm around Kathy's shoulder. "Join us tonight. Party night, every night. Get yourself a man and join us. To show you how grateful I am for your help, I'll spring for drinks."

Two buxom nurses came from the club toward them. Bosco introduced them. "Meet my fellow witches, Lieutenant Boltz and Lieutenant Kincaid. Bosco, Boltz, and Kincaid. We are the three witches. Let me tell you before anyone else does. We may be called the three witches, and get a little drunk, but we're not as bad as some people I won't mention. We drink only with unmarried patients." She put her arms across the girls' shoulders. "Back to the bloodied scalpel. So long." They bounced down the ramp.

Kathy couldn't help liking Bosco, so naturally friendly and exuberant. But, of course, Kathy would not join the witches' party.

In the officers' mess Kathy looked around to choose a place to sit. She saw Mac the WAC sitting with a husky blond girl.

Mac, cup and saucer in hand, stood and came toward Kathy. "I waited for you. Lieutenant Kathryn Collens, meet Lieutenant Bunts Hanson, physiotherapist."

"Glad to know you." Kathy sat across from Bunts who was putting a piece of roast beef into her mouth.

Bunts smiled and nodded. She placidly continued chewing until she was quite ready to swallow. "Glad to know you," she responded with a good-natured smile. She cut another piece of beef and continued chewing.

Mac sat straight and stiff in her chair. "Bunts is one of our more wholesome girls. Her current physical fitness program is softball—as you might deduce from her name."

Bunts smiled and continued chewing. With clear blue eyes, skin scrubbed glowingly clean, and no makeup, she looked healthy and wholesome. She swallowed her meat and spoke to Kathy, "Do you play?"

"I'd love to play. I like all sports. Do you have organized teams?" Kathy wanted to be included.

Bunts considered the question. "No," she said. "We don't have any teams." She carefully, methodically cut her beef with her knife. "Some of us toss the ball around, after supper." She pushed the beef onto her fork and held it up to look at it. She seemed about to say something more, but instead continued eating.

Mac sipped her coffee, raising her cup to her lips, not bending down toward it. She broke the silence. "It seems difficult to get many interested in sports here, or in anything constructive. That's the difficulty in living as well as working in a hospital. You think and talk of patients and medicine. The young people here just sit and talk. Don't you find that so, Bunts?"

Bunts shrugged indifferently.

Mac gave up trying to include Bunts in the conversation, and turned her full attention to Kathy. "Come to the officers' club tonight. I'll introduce you to some of the staff. It won't be an exciting evening. Most of the staff around here are married men. They are too old for overseas duty. The young unmarried men are sent to the front lines. That's the Army's policy. My evenings are spent playing bridge with the executive officer. He's married too. His wife is in Minnesota with their children. Bridge is certainly a harmless pastime."

Kathy agreed. She could not imagine this prim Lieutenant McClain, or Mac, as she says, doing anything not completely proper. The way she held her spoon, how she sipped her coffee, her precise speech, the way each gray hair stayed in place, and her straight back were all completely ladylike.

"Most of the nurses spend their evenings in their barracks. Only the "Three Witches" have much of a social life. Theirs is so wild and lusty that the other nurses have disowned them. They kicked them out from the nurses' barracks over to our quarters, where the non-nurse women live."

Bunts, who had been sitting quietly since she finished eating, rose to leave. "Goodbye," she said softly.

Mac looked after her. "Sometime I'm going to shake that girl, just to see if anything can spur a reaction. She is the most unemotional person!" Her words were strong, but smile lines wrinkled around her eyes. "Who's to say? Maybe she has the best way to face the war's casualties day after day. If she doesn't care, she can endure."

After lunch, Kathy finished her ward rounds, calculated diets, checked supplies, and gave the lists of needed foods to Lieutenant Groot. Kathy checked the food carts for supper and supervised the cafeteria line. She felt useful.

She was impressed by the undaunted spirit of the patients. Some seemed to almost welcome their wounds as preferable to the ever-threatening death at the front. Others couldn't wait to get back to help their comrades. They complained not at all of suffering, but about the food, a healthy diversion. Among the patients, Kathy was at her best, as she understood dietary problems and could handle them well. They responded to her genuine interest. *This was the work for which she had joined the Army.*

It was after 2030 by the time she had eaten dinner, put away the clothes from her footlocker that had just arrived, pressed her Class A uniform, and showered. She stood in her olive drab green slip in front of a sink in the latrine, brushing her teeth. A black-haired man of average height came in. He was dressed in a brass-buttoned Class A uniform with Captain's bars, yet the cast on his arm indicated he was a patient. He carried a tray of ice cubes balanced on a pitcher.

"Hi," he said with a smile. He set the pitcher on the glass shelf below the mirrors, and ran water over the bottom of the ice tray. He grinned admiringly at her figure. "Want an ice cube?"

Kathy's first impulse was to run for a robe. However, since the Captain was not embarrassed, and was, in fact, enjoying seeing her in her slip, Kathy decided to stay. "No, thank you. Water will do." She rinsed the toothpaste out of her mouth.

The Captain sat on the edge of his sink. "I've met you somewhere. You're from Peoria."

"No, I'm from Libertyville, Illinois." She gathered her toothbrush, toothpaste, washrag and towel, turned and left.

Now wearing her Class A uniform, she walked across the ramp to the club. She paused in the doorway to look and determine where to go. On one side of the pine-paneled room was a bar, and the other had equipment for games. The room was bare of any decoration.

On the game side, Mac the WAC was playing bridge at one of the small card tables with the executive officer and the head nurse, both with graying hair, and a balding medical officer. At a slot machine against the wall, a Captain pulled the lever with one hand, holding his drink with the other. A group of men were playing pool and another group poker. A Red Cross girl in a gray uniform pounded on the piano, "Don't sit under the apple tree with anyone else but me." A Lieutenant, leaning against the piano, sang. No one played at the ping pong table. The juke box was silent.

Several officers stood at the bar, drinking and talking. One, a full Colonel, swayed. Could he be that drunk this early in the evening? In this hospital, anything was possible. Lieutenant Groot took her empty glass over to the bar and turned to the Colonel. She said something that must have been funny, for they fell into each other's arms laughing.

Kathy walked quietly to Mac's table, hoping Lieutenant Groot wouldn't notice her and make an issue of drinking Southern Comfort. As Kathy approached, Mac and her friends put down their cards and the two men stood. Mac made the proper introductions. Kathy answered their polite questions about her hometown.

The commanding officer strutted into the room. "I've got an announcement! D-Day has been deemed a success. All beachheads have been secured. The Allies are now actively moving inland into France. It won't be long and we will take back Paris from Hitler! It's been almost four years that France has been occupied. Next it will be on to Berlin!" The entire room stood up and cheered.

About 2200, after drinks and celebrations, the group began breaking up, and Kathy returned to her quarters.

Walking down the hall past the dayroom door, Kathy heard singing. Bosco, Boltz, and Kincaid were harmonizing to the "Three Blind Mice" tune. "Three witches we. Wild witches we. We wiggle for whistles. We swizzle our bizzes. Wild witches we."

Kathy went on past their laughter to her room and to bed. Just as she had turned out the light, the door opened. A black-haired man poked his head in and switched on the light. It was the Captain she had met in the latrine. He asked, "Were you ever in Wichita?"

"No."

"Oh. Good night." He switched off the light, backed out, and closed the door behind him.

It was rather nice to have someone say goodnight to her.

Within a month, Kathy was becoming well acquainted in this hospital community. But acquaintances did not become friendships nor a sense of belonging. Kathy was groping for her place in this world.

After dinner, she walked out of the hot mess onto the area near the nurses' quarters. A group of giggling nurses came out of their barracks, talking of "The Secret Life of Walter Mitty." Kathy walked toward them, ready to say "Hi," and hoping to be invited with them to the movie. They didn't notice her. They weren't rude; they simply didn't see her, but walked on toward the theater.

Don, the Adjutant, leaned against the door of the officers' club, drinking from a bottle of beer, watching the girls walking by. He waved the bottle toward Kathy. "Hi. Want to go to that show? I'll take you."

"No. I told you last night, no. Thanks anyway."

"No to a show? How about a beer?"

"Beer doesn't appeal to me. It's a lovely sunset, isn't it?" The yellow hills rose above the green valleys against the scarlet sky. Beside the solid hills, the barracks and lives of Castoria seemed unreal and temporary.

"A Coke?"

"No thank you. I told you; I don't go out with married men."

Don took a long drink from his bottle. "You went out with me last night."

"That was before I knew you were married."

He twisted the bottle, gazing at the foam. "What has that got to do with going to a show? What's the harm in a movie?"

"No harm in a movie. I simply won't go out with a married man, not if I know it."

"My wife is not here. What she doesn't know won't hurt her."

Kathy stared in silence at the fresh green paint on the ramp's railing, already blistering under the summer sun.

Don took a step away from the door to stand straight in front of Kathy. "You're in the Army now, little girl. Everyone dates, married or not, from the Colonel on down." He pointed his bottle through the open door of the club. "Look. The Colonel is pouring a drink for that girl. His wife's in Kentucky, so why not?"

Kathy held her head high with what she hoped was dignity, too drained to find an answer, and went alone into her barracks.

Bosco, Boltz, and Kincaid were walking side by side down the hall; there was no passing them. Kincaid lifted a tray of glasses toward Kathy. "There's a glass for you. Tonight, any time, any night, all night."

Bosco laughed a deep, hearty laugh. She held up a bottle in each hand. "There's a drink waiting for you."

Boltz stepped back to let her by. "See you later in the day room."

Lieutenant Groot stepped from her room into the hall. She also carried a bottle, but there was nothing friendly or carefree about her. She looked tired, sick, and miserable.

The door to Bunts' room was open. Kathy turned to it, away from Lieutenant Groot. Kathy preferred baseball to bottles.

Bunts lay on her bed, her jaw swollen, tears running down her cheeks. "Come in. I wanted to see you." She mumbled, careful not to jar her jaw.

"You're hurting. What can I do?"

"I'm hungry, but I can't chew. My tooth. "Bunts held her jaw with one cupped hand, "Bring me ice cream?"

"Sure. That's easy. We had ice cream for dessert. I'll just run to the mess and bring you yours."

"No. Bosco just tried that. The mess Sergeant said Groot's orders: no food taken from the mess."

"I'll get you some ice cream."

Kathy walked down the hall to knock on Lieutenant Groot's open door. "May I talk to you a minute, Lieutenant Groot?"

"Come in." Groot stood in her red chenille robe, which looked uncomfortably hot. On the table were three tall bottles. "What can I pour for you?"

"I'd like permission to take a dish of ice cream from the mess to Bunts. She's in bed with an infected tooth.

"If she's sick, she should be in the infirmary."

"That may be. But she's not. Meanwhile, she's hungry. May I bring her some ice cream?"

Lieutenant Groot thrust out her massive jaw. "My orders are that no food leaves the mess."

"I'll dish it up myself. It will be no extra work for anyone."

"Do not question my orders!" Lieutenant Groot pulled herself up to her tallest and looked down at Kathy. "For your information, I have good reasons. I am responsible for the taxpayers' money. Food is expensive. Food could be stolen and sold if it were taken out. I'll not allow it taken out. Last year alone I saved over $3,000 of our money allotment."

Groot stood so adamant, her jaw set so firmly, that Kathy said no more. But she wondered how such savings could be possible with the cheap foods they served. And the ice cream was a part of Bunts' rightful supper.

She went to her room, put on her nurses' cape, made of a large full circle of fine wool. She hoped it did not look too out of place outside in the cool of the evening. She returned to the special diet mess. In the walk-in refrigerator, she put a quart of chocolate ice cream under her cape, along with spoons and bowls. She hid her movements from the mess Sergeant behind the cape.

Kathy returned to Bunts. She carefully closed the door behind her before she threw off her cape. The smooth chocolate ice cream tasted wonderful.

The next Sunday afternoon Bunts slammed open Kathy's door and shouted. "We have a softball team! Two teams! Hurry up. I want you on my team. She looked at Kathy's seersucker uniform. "You'll have to change into slacks."

True enough. The newly issued wrap-around seersucker dresses were not suitable for playing softball. They gaped open indecently over the chest unless modestly pinned closed, and split open to the thigh in a stiff breeze or fast run. Kathy took her seersucker slacks from a drawer.

On the ball diamond, Bunts was a different girl than the Bunts attempting conversation. At dinnertime, making conversation with Bunts had seemed like walking knee deep in mud. Now she ran across the weed field and shouted directions. She named off the teams, a mix of patients and staff. Two patients were in wheelchairs, two in leg casts, and two in arm casts. There were patients with dermatitis, ulcers, and asthma.

A man in a wheelchair wheeled himself into the umpire's position, another rolled himself across the rough ground to an outfield position.

"Kathy," shouted Bunts, "you field beside Pete. He can relay your throws." Kathy agreed. Pete from his wheelchair could throw better than she. She took her position beside him. "Play ball!" shouted Bunts, standing behind home plate, punching her catcher's mitt.

The ulcer patent on the pitcher's mound tossed the ball. A patient with a leg in a walking cast dropped his crutches and grabbed a bat. He hopped over to home plate, and swung to get the feel. He let the first pitch go by.

"Strike one!" shouted the umpire from his wheelchair.

The batter swung at and hit the second pitch. The ball flew past Pete and bounced by Kathy. Her eye was not on the ball, as she was watching the batter, wondering how he could run bases on crutches. He threw down the bat. A patient with a broken arm ran for him.

"Get the ball!" yelled Bunts. Everyone screamed.

Kathy ran for the ball and tossed it to Pete. From his wheelchair, Pete threw it hard and straight to second base. The throw was high. The second baseman simply held up his crutch to knock down and catch the ball. Too late. The runner was safe, resulting in a home run.

A nurse hit a high ball. Kathy pushed Pete's wheelchair under it. He caught the ball. Out.

At the end of the fifth and last inning, with the score tied, five all, Kathy was up to bat. She stood ready, bat poised, dreading the pitch she would surely miss. The pitcher raised his arm, then stopped. He stared past Kathy. She turned and there was Bosco. She wore the new seersucker wrap-around dress, only it didn't quite wrap around her ample figure. Her dress fit neatly around her waist, but not around her breasts. The neck line plunged low and revealing. Every man in the game whistled. Bosco put one hand on the curve of her hip, and waved happily with the other. With a high kick, she raised a shapely leg through the split front, a kick the designers of the wrap around had not anticipated— or maybe they had. That could make the dress very popular.

"Play ball!" shouted Bunts. The teams returned their attention, at least a part of their attention, to the game.

The pitcher's throw was an easy toss. Kathy smacked the ball, bringing in the winning run. With the game over, Kathy hoped for some attention, at least for her game-winning hit, but the men shouted after Bosco and followed her towards the barracks.

Kathy and Bunts picked up the bat and ball. Bunts took a small paper sack from her pocket. "Have a gumdrop." When Kathy had helped herself, Bunts tossed a handful of gumdrops into her own mouth and chewed them thoughtfully. "I don't think they are much interested in softball."

"They liked it. I liked it."

Bunts frowned. "No one said 'Let's play again tomorrow.'"

Kathy said, "Bosco's competition is hard to beat. Bunts, how does she do it?"

Bunts shrugged. "Who wants a dozen men? I'm waiting for one. My Tex. I call him Tex because I met him on a train in Texas." She chewed on another handful of gumdrops, and then with a shy smile, asked "Want to hear about Tex?"

"Sure."

Bunts talked while they walked back to the barracks. "I was traveling alone across Texas, two years ago this next September, on my way back to college. A man sat in the seat next to me. He had yellow skin and yellow teeth and sleek, oily, yellow hair. When he kept talking to me, I didn't like him. He kept talking, and I didn't know how to get rid of him. He drank from a flask. The more he drank, the less I liked him.

"Tex walked down the aisle. I hadn't seen him, but he'd been watching me and the yellow man. Tex was in uniform. He was a buck Private then. He's a Sergeant now. He was six feet tall, and he sure looked strong. He said, 'My wife has a headache and would like to lie down. Would you please leave?'

"The greasy slob jumped right out. Then, of course, to be convincing, Tex had to sit with me. I had to lie down with my head on his lap. He called me "wife," and I called him "husband." For the next three hours we were husband and wife." Bunts giggled. "The conductor was sure surprised when Tex got off the train before I did. He said, "I thought you two were married." Wish we were. I've not seen him since, but we write to each other every week. I write "Dear Husband." He writes "Dear Wife."

Kathy opened the barracks door and followed Bunts into her room. "Where is Tex now?"

Bunts shrugged, "Maybe Africa. Army Post Office, or APO, 619 wherever that is." She tossed the ball onto the bed. It rolled and stopped on the green blanket. "I joined the Army hoping I just might be sent to the same country, or even the same continent. Maybe that will happen." She propped her pillow against the wooden head of the bed, then reached under her bed for her guitar. She strummed it and sang, "I'll Be Seeing You." At the end of the chorus, still strumming, she said, "You see, I don't really care about softball. What does it matter if Bosco does break up a game? It'll just wait. I'll get by." She changed her fingering on the strings, and sang, "I'll get by, as long as I have you."

Kathy had no such guaranteed future. She wanted to belong to someone, or to some group, to share interests and activities—and had no one. The only meaningful part of her life here was her work with the patients.

The next afternoon, the patients who had been playing vigorous ball were flat on their backs in bed, receiving sympathy as bravely suffering soldiers.

Kathy made her ward rounds during visiting hours. She intended to visit only those who had no visitors, and later return for the others. As she walked past Axel Popowski's bed, she saw two men in gray flannel business suits.

"Hey! Kate!" shouted Axel. "Where's my steak?" His deep, bass voice vibrated across the room.

"We're spoiling you," said Kathy, pausing at the foot of his bed.

"Watch what you say. You are speaking to a war hero. These men are reporters, who will tell the world how you treat me."

One of the reporters spoke. "He told us he could have anything that he wanted to eat. We didn't believe that ever happened in the Army."

"Go ahead, Kate," said Axel, with a broad grin that showed even white teeth. "Tell them how I arrived, weak and emaciated after months of starvation in a German prison camp, and you tempted my jaded appetite with steaks—all the steaks I wanted."

"We did give him anything he wanted. He was on a high-caloric, high-vitamin diet. But any day now the doctor is going to notice he's getting fat and put him on a regular diet."

Axel waved grandly toward the bedside chair. "Sit down and listen, Kate. It's a remarkable story. I was just saying that they were looking for an American to send behind the German lines with Tito's guerrillas. I was a natural. Strong and brave. And I look like a Yugoslavian peasant because I am Yugoslavian." He was a tall, big-boned, black-haired, dark-eyed man. "Ma and Pa came straight from the old country. I talk Slav and German because Ma and Pa talked Slav and German.

"And I know radio. In Yugoslavia we lived in a cave in the mountains, fourteen of us in one cave, men and women. The women were tough fighters, and could handle guns and slit a throat as easily as any man. Men slept next to the women on a dirt floor. We were so crowded that if one turned over, everyone had to turn over. Everyone brought me information, and I sent it out by radio from the cave. Then I lived three weeks upstairs in a house where German officers were billeted downstairs. I listened to them. I heard their plans."

"How did you get out?"

"At night when the Germans were sleeping. I walked right past them, wearing my own uniform too. I had an overcoat over it, so if I were caught, I'd be a prisoner of war, not a spy. Night after night I walked out with information."

A reporter said, "We want you to write your story."

"Sure. Glad to. Can you get me a typewriter, Kate?"

"All right."

"You want to hear about how I got caught, and escaped with bullets in both legs?"

Kathy had heard this before. "It is quite a story," she said to the reporters. "He is lucky to be alive. But you will have to excuse me. If the Red Cross has a typewriter, I'll bring it to you, Axel."

"Kate!" Axel's voice was commanding. "6XT and 5QR."

Kathy wrote in her notebook, "6XT and 5QR. Check."

Axel beamed with mystery at the puzzled reporters. He didn't reveal his code for three bottles of ginger ale and two quarts of ice cream, ordered in his best cloak-and-dagger manner.

Dignified old Colonel Wilson sat alone in his private room. His increasing weakness seemed out of place among the vigorously recuperating young men. He sat erect on the straight chair beside his bed, his Class A uniform resplendent with medals for bravery in combat in many theaters.

He greeted Kathy with a sad smile. "Perhaps if I ate my soft-boiled egg, and waited fifteen minutes before drinking warm milk, I might retain them?"

"That sometimes helps," said Kathy. Colonel Wilson's stomach regurgitated all his meals. His talk of past glories and courage made the indignity of an irritable stomach all the more humiliating. She was already feeding him six small meals a day. She'd try something different.

Kathy asked "Why don't you eat in my special diet mess with the other ambulatory patients? It would give you people to talk with. Maybe it could take your mind off your stomach. I'll have my cup of coffee with you there."

"OK. Not coffee for me. Just warm milk."

"Your warm milk will be on the counter." She noted the request in her notebook. "See you at supper."

After receiving so many special requests for food, Kathy had developed a system. Patients hid folded notes in secret places, such as cracks between window frames and walls. After supper every evening Kathy put on her large nurse's cape and went and collected the notes. Requests were for sandwiches, fruit, ginger ale, and ice cream. Many were from patients that had been on nothing but K-rations for months. Who could refuse them? She, of course, could not. She could not refuse anyone. After collecting their notes, she returned to the special-diet mess. With the help of one of the cooks, she filled the orders and then delivered the goods. All were covered under her billowing cape. Kathy walked out past Lieutenant Groot, who didn't suspect that food was taken out right under her nose.

In time, everyone, including the cooks and ward nurses, were in on the conspiracy operation—everyone, except Groot.

Kathy was suspicious about the use of ginger ale that was ordered so often. Since many patients kept a "baby" tucked beside them in bed under the sheets, the ginger ale was most probably used as a chaser. But that was really none of Kathy's business. Actually, maybe they were better off diluting their alcohol with ginger ale and sandwiches.

That evening, it was too late to go to a movie. Mac had her four for bridge in the officers' club. A fifth was a fifth. Kathy returned to her room. Things that usually take up much of a girl's time such as shopping and fussing with makeup were all taken care of by the Army. The Army issued uniforms, and then tailored and laundered them. The Army pre- scribed short hair styles, and even cleaned their rooms. Kathy might have painted the walls of her room, but it was considered a waste of scarce paint. Putting up shelves was unreasonable in an Army that might travel with a moment's notice. Things of beauty were a burden on the war effort.

Kathy put up her hair with bobby pins and put her insignia on a fresh uniform for the next day. She turned out the light and went to bed.

She was almost asleep when the door opened. A man poked his black-haired head in. "Was it Kalamazoo?"

"No."

"Oh. Good night." He backed out and closed the door.

Again, it was nice to have someone say good night to her.

Before starting her rounds the next morning, Kathy went to the Red Cross for a portable typewriter. In her office, she gathered the diet ros- ters, her notebook, and a pile of full-color reproductions of paintings that she had cut from her book of famous art, and a box of thumbtacks.

Lieutenant Groot was at her desk trying to ease a hangover with hot coffee. "What is all that stuff?"

"The typewriter is for Axel Popowski. He thinks he's going to write a book. The pictures are to tack on walls."

"Why would you tack pictures on walls?" Groot looked puzzled.

Kathy explained, "With a leg and an arm in traction, Sam couldn't go anywhere. He just laid on his back. He said the rows of nail heads on his sheet rock walls were driving him crazy like pairs of eyes looking at him from all four walls. So, I sent for a book of masterpieces to give him something to look at."

"You cut up a book for that?"

"He couldn't lift the book or turn the pages. Pictures were made to be looked at. Other patients wanted paintings too. About a dozen now."

"Couldn't you cut pictures from magazines?"

"They look at these pictures a long time. I change them once a week. You can look at a good painting a long time with increasing appreciation."

Lieutenant Groot put down her coffee cup. She stood to look at the pictures, and focused on a painting of purple, pink and white orchids. Just flowers, with no vase and no leaves. "Soldiers look at that and like it?"

"That's a favorite. Sam took it as a joke. Yet each day he showed me something new he'd found. Look at it in a different way, and it becomes something else."

"It's just flowers."

"Look here. A nose and eyes. A young woman's face. Look here. If this is a nose and this the chin, it's an old man's face. Sam found fifteen faces in two weeks."

"That's nonsense," Lieutenant Groot snorted.

"They like nonsense. They choose the nonsensical abstracts rather than sensible pictures. I should have thought they'd prefer something happy like Bruegals' "Peasant Dance," but they did not."

"You're not to be wasting your time on that. You're a dietitian."

"I make up the extra time, and it gives me something to talk about besides food."

Lieutenant Groot said, "Humph." She didn't exactly say to throw away the paintings, so Kathy prepared to go on her rounds with the typewriter and paintings.

Sergeant's blond mass of hair seemed more blond today than it had been yesterday when she came into the office with a list of food orders to show Kathy. "Lieutenant Collens, did you want 75 pounds of mashed potatoes? Orders are usually about 60 pounds of potatoes."

"I'll check. Kathy set down the paintings and typewriter and counted the diets who would be served mashed potatoes. "You're right, Sergeant. It should be 59 pounds. I added wrong." She corrected the order. "Thank you. You're accurate."

Groot stood tall and hulking before Kathy. "Harumph! In case you've forgotten, there's a war on. Priorities do not allow automatic calculators for adding mashed potatoes. And with the food shortage it's a crime, a crime, to order 16 pounds more potatoes than you need."

"Maybe serve potato soup tomorrow?" said Kathy with an appealing smile.

"May I suggest," said Groot through clenched teeth, "that you devote more time to correcting your addition and less time to paintings and typewriters." Her jaw thrust out, defying any argument.

"Yes ma'am." Kathy picked up the paintings and typewriter and left on her rounds.

After rounds, on the ramp on her way back to her office, Kathy was stopped by Major Molina, the motherly-looking head nurse. "I tried to reach you this morning." Her warm smile showed she was not accusing Kathy.

"I'm usually on the wards in the morning."

"I couldn't reach Lieutenant Groot. She had gone back to bed. Is she ill?"

"Sometimes she has attacks of colitis."

Major Molina nodded understanding. "Well, it was you I wanted to see. The nurses are having a party this evening. They don't have much fun here. A party might help their morale. We hoped you might have sandwiches made. And come yourself, if you'd like."

"Thank you. I'd like that. Sandwiches. Do you want cookies too? Something to drink? Fruit punch?"

"Fine. Thank you. In our day room. 2000 hours. Does that give you time? Need some help?"

"Plenty of time. For how many?"

"Just us girls. About 40 will be there. Maybe less."

Kathy asked the special diet cooks if they wanted to help. These three cooks were delighted to be helpful, even though it meant extra work. They were all happily working when Lieutenant Groot came in.

Lieutenant Groot scowled at the stacks of bread, bowls of sandwich filling, and trays of cookies on the work table. "What is this?"

Kathy sliced olives stuffed with pimentos. "Major Molina asked for refreshments for a nurses' party."

Groot put her hands on her hips. "You did not get my permission."

"You weren't here. Major Molina thought you were sick, so I didn't bother you." Kathy put the olive rings on cream cheese sandwiches.

"How often must I tell you? No food is to leave this mess. If the nurses want refreshments, they should get their own."

It was ten miles to town, but Kathy knew from the belligerent set of Groot's jaw that she must not argue. "What should we do with those that are already made?"

Groot ignored the question, looking at her watch. "Is the food on the steam table? It's time for checking."

Kathy put down her paring knife. "Yes, it's all there. Yes, I'll check it." She turned to a cook. "Those chocolate cookies smell done."

Groot stamped her foot. She contorted her face into ugliness. "Lieutenant Collens! Will you please check the steam table!?"

"Yes ma'am." Kathy hurried out to the serving counter where patients were already helping themselves to their suppers. She looked at the food. It was all there. She took her place at the end of the steam table.

Lieutenant Groot took a tray from the other end of the steam table and walked along. She dished up for herself a bland diet of cream soup, pureed peas, and a soft-boiled egg. She was eating more cautiously than usual. Something was irritating her.

The doctor from the ulcer ward came in. He looked around, and walked past Lieutenant Groot to speak to Kathy. "The medical staff agreed to step up the ulcer diets for these men as you had suggested." He handed her a list. "Could you go over the foods with us?"

"Certainly. Anytime."

"If we collect data on their treatments and recovery rates—this research rates publication. Can you keep records of diets? Are you free at 1000 tomorrow morning?"

"Yes. I'm certain I can help. This is the kind of work I did at Cook County."

"Then you might know statistics. Good. 1000? In my office?"

With the meeting settled, the doctor left. Kathy returned to checking trays. That finished, she poured herself a cup of coffee to drink while she visited with old Colonel Wilson. Her company apparently took his mind off his stomach.

Suddenly, Lieutenant Groot shrieked: "Lieutenant Collens!" She tilted a sauce dish of pureed peas toward Kathy. The green puree oozed over the side of the dish and dropped down her fingers. "Sour. SOUR!" she screeched. "You served sour pureed peas!"

Groot stopped. She set the dish carefully on the counter. She picked up a napkin to methodically wipe the green mush from her fingers. She threw the napkin onto the counter. She stood straight and large in front of Kathy. She thrust her jaw with all the authority of a First Lieutenant over a Second Lieutenant. "It's your responsibility to check all special diet foods. You could have poisoned all these patients! Thank God I tasted that." Her voice again rose to a shout, "You would poison me!"

Three cooks came out of the kitchen, looking bewildered. Groot grabbed the dish of pureed peas and shoved it under Kathy's nose. "You are relieved of your duties as therapeutic dietitian."

Groot put the dish down and attempted to assume an officer's stance. "From now on you may not enter this mess. You will be in the ambulatory patients' mess. Lieutenant Johnson will take charge of the special diets." She stalked out of the mess.

Kathy stood, too shocked to move. Patients looked embarrassed. They moved on, carrying their trays to the tables to eat in silence. The cooks walked over to Kathy. The short, motherly cook put her hand on Kathy's arm. "It was my fault Lieutenant, I put the pureed peas out." Tears streamed down her cheeks.

Kathy shook her head. "It was my responsibility to taste all foods."

The second cook smelled the peas. She took a spoon, and with just the tip of her tongue, tasted them. Then, she tasted a full spoonful. "They taste fine to me. I do not understand what just happened."

Kathy said nothing. She could not comprehend the outburst. She thought she had done a good job. She had heard no complaints from patients, nurses or doctors. She started to carry her coffee over to Colonel Wilson. Then she realized she would not be visiting him anymore—nor any of the other patients either. She wouldn't read what Axel Popowski wrote. She wouldn't know if Bob ate and grew strong. She would not know how the ulcer patients got along on better diets. Her eyes filled with tears.

She put down her cup and hurried back to the diet kitchen area. With little left to lose, Kathy took the sandwiches and cookies, and put them on a cart to wheel to the nurses' party.

On her way she took the many secret messages from their hiding places, and replaced them with her new note: "Sorry. No more deliveries."

She walked by two pajamas-clad patients who were leaning against the wall and laughing.

"Lieutenant," called one, "I just broke my leg." He laughed again.

Kathy recognized the boy who ordered a peanut butter sandwich every night, but she didn't answer. She was in no mood for jokes. She walked on by.

The second patient ran after her. "Honestly, Lieutenant." He stood in front of her. "He did break his leg. It's an artificial leg. It just fell apart."

Kathy couldn't help but start to laugh. "OK. We'll get it fixed." She looked for a ward boy or nurse, but no one was nearby. Evidently everyone had gone to supper. She phoned the prosthetics lab to be sure someone was there, got a wheelchair and pushed the patient to the lab. She didn't have the heart to tell him he'd get no more peanut butter sandwiches. He'd given his leg, and all he asked of her was a peanut butter sandwich. It wasn't much that she'd done for him, but it was all he asked.

# CHAPTER 4

# A BOAT RIDE

Two miles from the hospital was a small lake. On weekends it was a popular fishing destination. During the week it was quiet. Kathy put on her red knit bathing suit, and over it, her striped seersucker slacks and shirt. She bought a cheese sandwich at the PX and headed to the lake for a day off.

She left the gravel road and walked through a clump of oaks to the bottom of a hill near the lake. Out here, the air was cooler, sweeter, and without the smells of stale blood and ether. She was surprised to find herself standing up straighter and walking lighter. She had not solved any of her problems, but was surrounded by things in nature that she understood.

Near the top of the hill were five apple trees. Kathy ran up the hill, where she could be on top of the world and see farther. To escape even higher, she climbed up an old apple tree. Halfway up the trunk, the tree had a thick, gnarled limb. She leaned back against the trunk, braced her feet on smaller branches, and surveyed the world.

The scene below showed stylized patterns as her mother might have painted it on canvas. Dark-green apple trees, elongated silver poplars, and drooping willows. The center of the painting would be a lake, blue as the sky above it. Just a little off-center, placed as though to soften the largeness of the lake, was an irregular-shaped bushy island. Small gusts of wind ruffled the water, making rippling patterns that caught the sparkling sunlight.

Kathy watched a robin cheerfully eating a worm from a tiny green apple. This was nature's way. Left alone, nature solved her own problems. When worms grew menacingly numerous, they attracted birds, who restored the balance. The world was made up of cause-and-effect. Problems could be resolved.

If only she could understand her difficulties at Castoria in this simple way. Why had Lieutenant Groot so suddenly rejected her? Kathy had worked hard, capably, along with the cooks, the patients, and the doctors. She should not have been dismissed—and that was as far as her thinking could go. Nurses should not get drunk. Married men should not ask for dates or kisses. The staff ought to be interested in sports. Nothing was as it should be. Kathy could not think of one logical reason why.

Kathy was not one to ponder the unexplainable. Her understandings from her past did not seem to apply to her turbulent present. In the Army, in this world where old values did not work, she must learn new ones. Arts and intelligence and industry were not appreciated in the Army. Sports were not valued. People who got along best at Castoria were those like Bosco. Obviously, the Army would not adjust to Kathy. She was in the Army for the duration. It was up to her to adjust to the Army, to learn a new way…or be miserable.

Done with thinking, she jumped down from the tree and ran down the hill to the lake shore. Standing, she unbuttoned her shirt.

"Ahem!" A man's deep voice startled her. "I should warn you; you're being watched." Turning, she saw a young man lying in the shade of a buckeye chestnut. His hands were padded and bandaged like two bulky white boxing gloves. Stripped to the waist, his chest and arms were tanned and husky.

Kathy took off her brown-and-white shirt. "I swim in a decently modest bathing suit. See?" She hooked her thumb under the strap of her red suit.

"Do you like to row?" he asked

"Love to. Have you a boat?"

"I'll rent one if you'll row." Waving his arms, he said, "This fungus on my hands is a relic of the romantic South Pacific. What a nuisance. You could row us to the island, and we could swim there."

"Sure. Call me Kathy."

"Kathy it is. And I'm Joe. Plain 'ole GI Joe."

They rented a small faded-green rowboat. Joe dangled his legs over the stern, and Kathy handled the oars with the skill of one who had spent all her summers on the water. She could maneuver them precisely. Her easy control strengthened her notion that there was order in the world. Kathy knew how to handle rowboats, canoes, and sailboats. She was proficient in understanding currents, winds, pressures, and balances. She had won races.

She rowed out to the island. The sun was hot, and the water was cool. With her skin sticky from the exertion of rowing, Kathy wanted to swim. But with Joe needing to keep his hands dry, Kathy just stood splashing her feet in the shallow water.

"I too have a decently modest bathing suit under these fatigues," said Joe. He proceeded to take off his pants.

Freed for a swim, Kathy kicked off her slacks and dashed into the water.

"Wait, Kathy," called Joe, "I have a problem. Would you…I'm glad you're a nurse and I'm a patient. A bandage is caught in the zipper. You'll have to fix it."

Kathy cautiously freed the bandage and unzipped his pants. They walked into the water. Kathy swam like a seal, under and on the water. Joe lay cautiously on his back in shallow water, holding his hands up.

Cooled and refreshed, they shared Kathy's cheese sandwich. Joe asked for no help eating, and she offered none. They watched the glorious sunset, and now it was time to row back.

As they floated across the lake in the boat, the colors softened, and the sky darkened. Only vague outlines of the shoreline could be seen. When they reached land, they found they had missed the dock.

"Uh. Oh. I'm lost," said Kathy with a laugh. Really, she didn't feel lost at all. She was at home on the lake. She knew when she returned to the hospital she would be lost. She meant she didn't know which way to head for the dock, "Should we go left or right?"

"I don't really care," said Joe. He had been riding quietly, dangling a leg in the water, lost in his own thought. "Try south."

As it darkened, Kathy rowed parallel to the shore, often losing sight of the land. She was caught in the spell of beauty. She didn't want to return. The lake was a dream world, enhanced by the croaking of frogs. They were in no hurry. Quietly, without speaking, they took in the hazy passing beauty.

Finally, the moon rose large and orange over the hill. From the shore, four or five small lights showed glimmering paths across the water. Overhead, the stars shone bright. To Kathy the stars were old friends. "The Big Dipper is pouring stardust into the Little Dipper now."

"Stardust?" Joe asked.

Kathy laughed, "You sound just like my father. He laughed at Mother's talk of a dipper of stardust. He had more practical use for the Dipper. It was the hour hand of his clock in the sky. We sailed at night, up and down the length of Lake Michigan, and he set watches by that Dipper.

"Well, we're just looking for a dock. The boatman may have left a light burning for us. Or at least for his boat," said Joe. "Try that first one."

Kathy set her course by the light, but just before they reached it, it was turned off.

"That's the story of my life," said Joe.

Kathy pulled on the starboard oar, turning the boat. "We'll try the next one. She rowed on, relishing the cool air, the silver moonlit lake, the peace. She rowed on, heading for a light, and each light in turn went out before they reached it.

Joe pulled his leg out of the water and shifted to sit on the bottom of the boat. He leaned his shoulders and head on the stern seat. "I've traveled half way round the world and back. Who'd have thought I'd get lost on a two-bit lake!"

"Lost? No sailor is lost who can see the stars!"

"You followed stardust across Lake Michigan. Big help that is here."

"Daddy taught us the stars over Lake Michigan because they rotate around the world. Daddy always planned to sail oceans. I can calculate GPs and tell where I am anywhere."

"What's a GP?"

"Geographical position, the point on earth exactly under a star."

Joe tilted his head back to gaze at the sky above. "There are no stars directly above."

She stopped rowing to point to a blue-white star. "Take Vega, there. It's about 30 degrees from the zenith. Multiply by 60. We're 1800 nautical miles from Vega's GP, more or less.

"That is certainly helpful."

Kathy contemplated the familiar, reliable stars. "If we were on Lake Michigan, it would be. The same stars always pass over the same places. I knew which stars rose over Muskegon and Ephraim and..."

"Which star should be over that dock?"

"I don't know. Even the stars don't guide me here."

"Then we are lost?"

"Yes," she said. "We are lost."

One last light continued burning from the shore, with a reflection shimmering across the smooth water. Slowly, relaxing often on the oars to listen to the dripping water and the grasshoppers' song, they followed the last light that guided them to the dock.

"My car is here. I'll give you a ride back," said Joe. He took a fatigue shirt from the front seat, put it on, and stood for her to button it.

On the ride back, Joe said, "It would be nice if I could date you."

Kathy would accept. At least there would be no battle to keep his hands where they belonged. She said, "You can. Just ask."

He gestured at his Sergeant's stripes.

She shrugged. "Sergeants are the back-bone of the Army, the actual leaders of men."

"Oh, I'm proud enough of my stripes. It isn't that. But you as an officer can't come with me to the non-coms club. I can't go to the officers' club where you go. At movies we sit in different sections."

"I enjoyed this evening," she said.

"I wasn't at my best. I couldn't row, couldn't swim, and couldn't even zip my own pants."

Kathy returned to her quarters, tired but encouraged. The evening had been enjoyable. The world was beautiful, the world was right. She didn't know how, but she could learn. Somehow, she would fumble through. Somehow.

# CHAPTER 5

# STEALING STEAKS

Kathy reported at 0600 the next morning to her newly assigned work area, the ambulatory patients' mess. The man in charge was a fat, balding mess Sergeant. For 16 years he had been doing this job, and knew all he cared to know about managing a mess. The mess often ran out of scheduled meat, but he accepted no help with keeping quantity records to prevent that. He cooked asparagus for 45 minutes, resulting in a soggy mess that patients never ate. However, no little girl Second Lieutenant was going to tell him how to cook. Lieutenant Groot praised him highly, and assured him he was doing a fine job. She emphasized her preference by putting her arm around his bulging waist each time they met.

On this ward, Kathy had no authority or responsibility. Very few tasks were assigned to Kathy to be completed daily. She sat at her desk, of no use to anyone. She decided to borrow books from the Red Cross.

Perusing the titles, she came across psychology. If she knew more psychology, maybe she could understand the mess Sergeant, perhaps at least persuade him to cook asparagus less than 45 minutes.

She looked up the pathological effects of alcohol in the Red Cross encyclopedia. She read further about drunkenness. The encyclopedia was describing Lieutenant Groot and her colitis. It did not say what to do about her unpleasant situation.

She found more books in the neuropsychiatric ward. Here there was an enclosure at the end of the hall with a floor-to-ceiling wire fence. Inside several patients were aimlessly wandering around. "Laughing Jack," as he was called, was sitting on the floor, his knees doubled up under his chin, his arms clutching his legs, laughing. She had never seen him in any other position. Only his laugh changed. Sometimes his laugh was low, almost sad. Sometimes it was raucous and maniacal. Today he laughed as though he knew a huge joke. He rocked back and forth, laughing loudly at his huge joke.

Initially Kathy had hoped that she might find a magic key for winning friends and influencing Groot. For two weeks she researched, but found no solutions to her problems. Nothing explained what might be the huge joke Laughing Jack found so funny.

The war was moving slowly. June 6, 1944—D-Day had marked the largest seaborn invasion in history. Troops and supplies poured onto the continent, with plans to liberate France. Yet progress was bogged down. Expecting an invasion, the Germans had fortified the Atlantic coast from Spain to Norway. Further inland, the Nazis were able to use France's natural terrain, with hedgerows, as a barricade. For centuries, French farmers had divided up their fields by growing hedges. Tangled roots and piles of rocks had built up over the years, forming walls as tough as iron and as high as ten feet. Tanks couldn't get through. Germans successfully used the hedgerows to create nearly invisible strongholds, and they dug in for fierce fighting. For the Allies, just crossing a field was a grueling task, often with casualties.

At the hospital, Kathy was feeling useless in the war. She needed a positive force with which to face this world. The Army was not about to adjust to Kathy's ideals. She was determined to adjust to the Army. She must find in it a constructive path. She had to do something different.

Kathy took her first opportunity to change the next afternoon. An administrative officer, whom she suspected was married, invited her out for drinks and dancing. She accepted. Her old values were of no value. She enjoyed dancing. Maybe she could learn to like Martinis. After the club closed, they stood on the ramp near her quarters. He said, "Let's go downtown to the Flaming Flamingo."

Kathy answered, "Are you married?"

"Yes," he said, as though that were not important.

"Where is your wife?"

"Downtown at the hotel," he said.

How could he be talking of taking her downtown when his wife was there?

"Good night," she said, and turned to go.

He put his hand behind her neck, and leaned toward her to kiss her. She twisted away.

"I was just going to kiss you."

Kathy opened the door, went in, and firmly closed the door behind her.

Then she remembered her new determination to adjust. Yet, she just couldn't get involved in someone's marriage. Even Bosco found the unmarried men by looking at their chart.

Axel Popowski was not married. Maybe she could try dating him. A program was developed where a nurse would adopt a patient that remained bedridden. Kathy knew Axel and chose him. Next morning, she found him. "How is your book coming along?" she asked, sitting on his bed.

"Decided to let the reporters write it. I lived it." For the next thirty minutes he talked of parties with the guerrillas, where the women were robust and he was a manly man. How he had gone behind enemy lines and captured war plans. While escaping, the Germans had shot his legs.

"Sounds as though you are now ready for more parties, at the officers club." She stood up, uneasy at her own boldness in hinting at going out with him.

He grinned his broad, open grin. "With you, Kate? You bet. Will you wheel me over? Tonight?"

Kathy, trimly dressed in her Class A uniform, called for Axel a little after 2000. She'd never seen him in anything but his pajamas. He was more impressive in uniform. He had red, white and blue ribbons of honor and magnificent medals slung across his massive chest and rows of ribbons over his pocket. Tonight, his hair was combed back rather than rumpled over his forehead. She helped him from his bed to the wheelchair, a matter of her swinging his heavy casts while he swung his body. He waited for her to push his chair. She knew he was capable of rolling it himself. Tonight, however, if he wanted to be pushed in like a wounded hero, she was willing to play the role of admiring nurse.

More people than usual were at in the club. Bosco, Boltz, and Kincaid and their dates were drinking at tables, and laughing. Kathy wheeled Axel over to a table near theirs.

Axel brought a flask with him. Kathy drank spiked Cokes, which still didn't taste good, hoping they'd give her the desired spirit. She didn't feel different. She didn't think she could kiss Axel. She grew skeptical about his endless tales of bravery. All of these deeds could not have been done by one man. He was probably adding the exploits of the entire guerrilla band to his own repertoire.

Axel finished his flask. Soon, he was having a grand time. He started singing Yugoslav fighting songs in a rich bass voice. Each time he sang a rousing "Ro-he, Rocko - Ho-OOO," which was becoming every other line, he would wave his arm upward in fine-fighting style. He nearly fell out of his wheelchair, but Kathy caught him just in time. It was time to leave.

Kathy wheeled him, still singing, out of the club. She silenced him when they neared the wards, for there were sick patients who needed sleep. In the dimly lit ward, she quietly wheeled him past rows of sleeping patients. She put his chair next to his bed. Since he was so drunk, Kathy decided to find a nurse to help get him into bed.

Searching for the nurse, she looked into the private rooms at the end of the ward, faintly lit by night lights. In the second room, the nurse was in bed with the patient. Could that be? Kathy turned away, maybe she had seen wrong. Maybe the nurse was just adjusting blankets, but Kathy dared not turn back for a second look.

Arriving back at his bed, she saw that Axel had not waited. He was getting himself into bed without help. He was sprawled, chest down, across his bed, his heavy leg casts dangling to the floor as he was sliding off the bed, clutching the blankets as though they could hold him.

Kathy ran to his rescue. She grabbed his belt, and tugged upward. This stopped further slipping, but could not lift him onto the bed. Kathy whispered, "Not the blankets, you dope! Hang onto the head of the bed."

From the nearby bed, a one-armed patient roused himself and was able to lift one of Axel's legs. Kathy got the other, and together they maneuvered Axel onto his bed. They took off his jacket and pants, threw a blanket over him, and left.

The next day, Axel went home for a five-day leave. When he returned, he sent for Kathy. "Got something to show you." He greeted her with his broad grin, obviously pleased with himself. He proudly handed her a picture. "This is Rosabell, my fiancé. We'll be married in three days."

"Well," said Kathy. And then, because it was the polite thing to say, "Congratulations." She looked at the picture. Axel was waiting for her compliment. "She's very pretty."

"Will you reserve a hotel room for her, tomorrow night?" Axel asked.

"I can try, but they say you have to make reservations three months in advance."

"Guess how I met her." He leaned back in his wheelchair, his arms folded across his massive chest, wanting to boast.

"Nothing as ordinary as her being the girl next door, I bet. Tell me." Kathy sat on his bed to listen.

"With all the newspaper publicity, you know, I am quite a hero. Around here a couple of broken legs aren't much, but at home, well," he lowered his head in a mock attempt at modesty, "well, all the girls in town met the train. Banners, bands, parade. I let the girls take turns pushing my wheelchair home. But there were too many. Too many to judge you know. You can't tell what vibrations come from which girl.

So, I had Mom sign them up for fifteen-minute interviews. One at a time, for two days, I gave interviews."

"I can imagine." Kathy could picture him sitting majestically on his polished chrome wheelchair, his enormous chest gleaming with medals, bestowing his broad grin on each girl.

"On the fourth day of my leave I gave the top three girls three hours each."

"In three hours, you could measure those vibrations?"

"An amateur could never have done it, but I've had considerable experience with women. I could tell. When I saw Rosabell, I knew. I gave her all that fifth day. We had a real wingding of a party that night. Now we're engaged."

"Your wedding will be Saturday?"

"Yes. It's all arranged. I've talked to the Chaplain."

"Is the reception arranged?"

"Our mothers will bring the food."

"I could help with that. The officers' club would be the place. I can set up the tables. It would be easier if Rosabell stayed in the nurses' quarters. It's ten miles to town and no rooms there anyway. Bunts is going on a three-day leave tomorrow. Maybe she'll let Rosabell have her room."

Bunts agreed. The next afternoon Kathy guided Rosabell to Bunts' room. Rosabell was thin, but she could out-wiggle Bosco. Where Bosco had the advantage of a rounder figure, Rosabell had the advantage of a full, gathered skirt that flounced. She wore a form-fitting low-necked blouse that was transparent enough to reveal dainty lace underwear. Bosco's wiggle was natural—Rosabell's was practiced. She wore a large, floppy picture hat under which long blond curls hung. It may have given the impression of sweet innocence had she not worn layers of gaudy makeup. She teetered down the ramp on high-heeled sandals that made Kathy's sturdy brown oxfords look terribly sensible.

Rosabell talked continuously. "You know Axel, don't you Kathy dear? Did you ever know anyone so wonderful? He's so considerate and unselfish! He's so modest! Oh!" She waved her arms with unrestrained rapture.

"Did he tell you about our engagement party? It was wonderful. Everyone was there. Just girls. The boys are gone. All the girls all love Axel. Mom loves Axel. Oh, my mom! She was the life of the party." Rosabell giggled with delight. "She was so drunk she had to crawl up the stairs on her hands and knees. What a wonderful bash!"

Kathy opened the door of her quarters for Rosabell and led her to Bunts' room. "This is yours—for three days." She set Rosabell's suitcase on the olive-drab green blanket on the Army bed.

Rosabell dropped her other suitcase onto the floor. "Oh, Kathy dear, this is a wonderful room." She took off her hat and tossed her curls with a charming twist of her head. "You're so wonderful to give all this to little 'ole me. And oh, Kathy, honey, can you arrange something so I can see Axel this afternoon? I can't wait until tomorrow's visiting hours. I just can't."

Kathy took Rosabell to the club and went to tell Axel she was waiting there. She then returned to the mess to helplessly watch the fat mess Sergeant cooking asparagus for 45 minutes.

For reasons that was never explained, the papers did not come through for the wedding. It was postponed for a few days. When Bunts returned from her leave, Rosabell had to move out.

Where could she go? "I'd be glad to have you in my room," said Kathy, "but I have only a single bed. You'd have to sleep on the floor."

"Oh, Kathy, honey, you're wonderful. Just spread a blanket on the floor. I would love to sleep there."

"Oh, I suppose there's room in the bed for us both. If you don't mind, neither do I."

When Kathy came off duty and returned to her room, Rosabell was sitting on the floor polishing Kathy's shoes. She had washed Kathy's underwear and stockings, and hung them on a coat hanger to dry. Her uniform was pressed and spots sponged off, and her bed was made. Now Kathy knew another part of why Axel had chosen Rosabell.

The papers were finally in order. The day for the wedding was set. Kathy arranged the reception, having both the time and interest. She covered the ping pong table at the club with two white tablecloths, arranged flowers, borrowing the best from patients. Lieutenant Groot had consented to letting the dishes leave the mess. Rosabell's father and mother arrived. They brought a carload of wine, ornately decorated hams, jellied fish, molded salads, and an abundance of Yugoslavian food that Kathy could not identify, and a gigantic wedding cake.

This was the work, arranging formal receptions, that Kathy had done often and well at home and in her sorority house. She now had the double pleasure of working, for the first time in a month, and of returning to the values of home. The spirit of the wedding permeated the atmosphere.

Rosabell donned her wedding gown in Kathy's room, with Kathy furnishing such forgotten items as needle and thread for tacking slip straps in place. Rosabell looked happy as a bride should look. Kathy was tempted to adjust Rosabell's makeup by wiping off the too-bright rouge and softening the solid black lines of eyebrows, but decided against it. This was the Rosabell Axel loved, her radiance outshone her makeup, and Kathy should not tamper.

Out of the confused bustle of preparation emerged a serene wedding. Axel, beaming broadly, and resplendent in his brass-buttoned, medaled and ribboned uniform was wheeled into place at the front of the chapel. He had even whitened the ends of the casts that covered his legs, stretched out on his wheelchair. The organ pealed the wedding march. Rosabell, in her pearled and lacey white gown and frothy veil, walked down the aisle. The Chaplain recited the ceremony, and they were pronounced man and wife.

The reception was joyous. Rosabell's mother tried serving jellied eel, first to the ward officer, honoring him as Axel's doctor. "This is my specialty, Captain," she said.

The Captain looked at the jellied mass on the thick hospital china, and said, "I'll try some of your wine." He accepted the glass of red wine Rosabell's father poured.

Rosabell's mother offered the jellied eel to the commanding officer. "It took me three days to make this, Colonel. First, I…."

"The spirit of the occasion calls for a drink," said the Colonel, and took a glass from Rosabell's father.

"Major, would you?" She offered the eel to the chief of orthopedics.

"I would not," he said.

Rosabell's mother waddled around the table to where the Army women were standing. A Red Cross girl rescued her. "It looks interesting. How did you make it?"

Bunts helped herself to ham. "I'll stick to the familiar."

"Cut the cake," said Major Molina, the chief nurse, standing with the nurses from Axel's ward.

Kathy handed the knife to Rosabell and Axel. They poised the knife over the cake, and posed for pictures.

"A toast," proposed the Chaplain, "to a long and fruitful marriage."

The Colonel raised his glass with the others. "To Axel Popowski. May his tribe increase. May his conjugal pleasures never cease."

"The marriage will not be fruitful, nor his tribe increase." said the Captain, "unless we get Axel out of the ward and into privacy with Rosabell. I'll give you a three-day honeymoon leave, Popowski. You can go to the hotel."

"There are no rooms at the hotel," said the Red Cross girl.

"Lieutenant Popowski has just returned from leave," said the Colonel. "He's not eligible for another. That's good wine." He refilled his glass.

"Cut the cake," said Major Molina.

"Mrs. Axel Popowski. Rosabell Popowski. Isn't it beautiful!" Rosabell said, as she cut and served the cake.

The Captain raised his glass.

"To Axel Popowski, the lucky he,
finally found himself a she.
To Axel Popowski, who will see red,
if someone doesn't get him a bed."

He took a big bite of cake, and licked the sticky white frosting from his upper lip. "Popowski's bed in the ward is too public."

"Who would object?" asked the Major. "Not the other patients."

Rosabell pointed the frosting cake knife at the Major. "I would."

"Give him a leave," said the Captain.

"Regulations are regulations," said the Colonel.

The Captain licked his frosted finger. "Where has Rosabell been sleeping?"

"In Lieutenant Collens' room," said the Red Cross girl.

Kathy turned to stare at the plates of ham and jellied eel.

"Really, now," said Major Molina. "I can't allow the nurses barracks for... for that."

"They're man and wife," persisted the Captain. "They must have a bed."

"I don't know what good it would do him," said the Major, "with two legs in casts."

"It's a matter of technique. I'll tell you Popowski, just..."

"I don't need that advice," Axel grinned, enjoying himself. Rosabell giggled happily. Everyone was laughing but Kathy, who focused her attention on eating mints.

The Captain emptied his glass. "I've got it. A private room on the ward. Old Colonel Wilson's room."

The Major nodded agreement. "Wilson's stomach doesn't need privacy as much as Popowski does. We'll move him into Popowski's ward bed."

"That means Rosabell goes to the ward at night, said the Captain. He refilled his wineglass, and waited for the reaction. No one objected. "Looks like you've got yourselves a private room, Popowski. Now, when?"

The Colonel twirled his wine around in his glass, and took a swallow. "We ought to be quiet about this. It could start a precedent, you know."

"The witching hour of midnight, when the patients are decently asleep." So, it was arranged.

In Kathy's room at a quarter to twelve, Rosabell put on a transparent white nightgown with a lace bodice, and an almost equally transparent robe over it. "How do I look?"

"Seductive," said Kathy. "You'll never make it to Axel's room, unless you cover that up." She gave Rosabell her own pink gingham robe.

Rosabell left. She returned hours later to slip, full of contentment, into bed beside Kathy. Each night Rosabell got out of bed in the quiet of the night, left in her transparent nightgown and Kathy's modest pink robe, and returned later to get into bed with Kathy.

With Bosco, Boltz, and Kincaid dispensing free love in the day room, with no meaningful work and no friends, and with Rosabell snuggling beside Kathy lost in her dreams, Kathy was a lonely soul.

After three weeks, it seemed that nothing would improve. Daily she walked past a thousand sick and shattered men—and there was nothing she could do to help them. The Sergeant would sit stolidly in his chair with his arms resting over his paunch forever. Lieutenant Groot's jaw was permanently set in an impassive thrust. Rosabell went on slipping in and of beds. And the heat would bake them all under the dark green uninsulated roofs.

On the last day of August, as Kathy walked toward the medical ward, Lieutenant Kincaid stopped her.

"Do you remember Don and Steve?" she asked.

"Yes." Kathy remembered. These patients had been starved by the Germans in France. Just two weeks ago they had been released from captivity by the Allies. Kathy was getting to be an authority on feeding the starved. Extreme starvation weakens a man that he cannot tolerate any food and initially is fed intravenously. Next a little fruit juice, then cereals and, gradually, more substantial foods. Most of these starved men had progressed to the stage where they could eat by the time they reached Castoria.

Lieutenant Kincaid said, "Don and Steve still don't eat much, but today they asked for steaks. This is the first food they've asked for. Can you get steaks for them?"

"You know Lieutenant Groot's rule. No food taken from the mess," replied Kathy.

"For Don and Steve, you'll get steaks. I know you will."

Kathy went on down the ramp and into the mess, past the table where the cooks were serving mushed asparagus. Three weeks in this mess, and she hadn't changed the cooking of asparagus from 45 minutes.

In his office, the Sergeant sat motionless in his chair. His hands were folded across his bulging stomach. His large face puffed up around his beady eyes, making him look like a comatose beast. He ignored her, staring blankly at the nails on the sheet rock wall.

She stood before him and spoke to his blank face. "If asparagus were steamed in small quantities for ten minutes, rather than 45 minutes, maybe some of the patients would eat it."

The Sergeant went on staring at the wall.

"That asparagus is mush now. By the time it's been on the steam table an hour, it…it will make the patients sicker just to look at it." She was tempted to kick his shins, just to get a reaction. Even if he would disagree, she could have reasoned. Against this immovable lump, she could not make an impression.

The Sergeant stood up. He loomed six feet, 300 pounds over Kathy's sixty-one inches, 115 pounds. He stood before her, looking not at her but past her. He stepped by her with the slow, steady, unemotional movement of a tank.

It would be useless to talk about the steaks. If she could find them, she would simply take them. On the top shelf in the refrigerator, she found seven sirloin steaks. Obviously, these were set aside by the Sergeant for the Sergeant. Kathy took two for Don and Steve, leaving five for the Sergeant. He could not protest her taking them without admitting his greed so Kathy made no effort to hide her actions. She wrapped them in waxed paper, and left.

Kathy returned to the small mess office only to face Lieutenant Groot. Her massive jaw thrust out boldly, and her arm around Sarge's solid mass.

"You took steaks from the mess!" Lieutenant Groot's shrill voice was exultant.

"Yes. For two starved patients."

"You have obviously disregarded regulations." Lieutenant Groot looked scornfully over her jaw. Sarge looked smug.

Lieutenant Groot's voice was cold. "You cannot be trusted in any mess. From now on, you report to me in the special diet mess at 6 a.m. That is 0600 hours, not 0601 or 0602. Then your duties must keep you out of kitchens, so you can steal no more food. You will count exactly the number of eggs in each refrigerator. Every day. Every refrigerator. Report back to me. Maybe this job matches your talents. You can count?" she asked scornfully.

Kathy opened her mouth, realized the futility of speaking, and shut it. She then turned and walked out. This was a matter for someone higher in rank than her. She only knew that Lieutenant Groot was in for a battle.

She marched towards the administration building, wondering which office to go to.

Through an open door she saw Mac the WAC. She would know what to do.

Kathy stood before Mac, waiting for her attention. Mac looked up and smiled. Her friendly gray eyes were warm and sympathetic. "I've been expecting you. Sit down Kathy."

"You've heard? Already?"

"I've heard one side. Now sit down and tell me your version."

Kathy sat on the chair beside Mac's desk. "I took two steaks for two starved patients. Just two steaks. Sarge had five left for himself. What's wrong with giving a starved man, too weak even to get out of bed, steak? What's a hospital for? Fattening Sergeants?"

"I am entirely in sympathy with you," said Mac. "I'll go even further. What was the Sergeant doing with those steaks? Giving midnight steak dinners to his cronies? Ordinarily you should be commended for exposing him, but there is no one in your chain of command who would.

Lieutenant Groot would certainly not. The mess officer would handle this, if he could, but he cannot cope with Lieutenant Groot. How a man with fifth-grade education is a Captain here is beyond me. The war expansion has put men into responsibilities well past their capabilities. The only practical thing you can do is ask for a transfer."

"I've done nothing wrong. I'm not running away." Kathy said.

"Unfortunately, this is not a matter of right or wrong. You must go through channels and request permission to speak to the executive officer. You'll find he knows what's been going on and has known for months. He will arrange your transfer."

"That is not what I want. How can I leave the patients to Lieutenant Groot and Sarge?"

"There are other patients who need you, and certainly other hospitals where you can work more effectively."

Kathy shook her head. "I want to straighten this out. What did I do wrong?"

"The fault is more with Lieutenant Groot than with you."

"But I never contradicted her. I never argued. Why…"

"Never?" Mac smiled. Her eyes were honest and she smiled. "The only thing Lieutenant Groot knows how to do is to maintain order. To rigidly follow regulations. Then you come along with no regard for the order. You tell doctors what diets to order, and that has never been done. You ask the patients what they want to eat, and you yourself carry them what they want. That is certainly disregard for order. You report on duty late. Oh, I know it's only two minutes. To Lieutenant Groot, it's disregard for discipline. You work extra hours, even more contrary to custom. She simply cannot maintain her already shaky position. You upset her foundation, which is order and regulations."

"I suppose I could report on time for duty, if that would help."

"That would not change your attitude toward order. You are oriented toward the patient and his needs, not order. Lieutenant Groot needs stability and obedience. With her fears and lack of intelligence and education, she cannot do otherwise."

"But I never contradicted her." Then she paused. "Why should she…"

"You contradicted her in most of the things you did, just by being you. She conforms. You are different. She could not comprehend, for example, how a dietitian could combine diet rounds and hanging art masterpieces on the walls. You disrupt her pattern. You threaten her. You must go. Ask for a transfer."

Kathy accepted her advice without saying a word.

Mac reached across her desk and patted Kathy's hand. "You have earned the respect of many here. You're not without friends. When you were taken off the wards, the patients gave Lieutenant Groot a bad time. Fortunately, it is the head nurse that gives you a rating. I am certain Major Molina will rate you as excellent. You'll be happier almost anywhere else, and be more effective."

Kathy requested a transfer. The executive officer accepted her request. It would take several weeks or months. Kathy now resigned herself to enduring the wait. Each morning, she counted eggs, walking from ward to ward. Not once did she find a refrigerator overstocked with eggs.

# CHAPTER 6
# LET'S DANCE

It took less than three hours to check the eggs, even after adding time to visit nurses, doctors, and patients. It didn't seem right to retire to her room during working hours. She spent her time in the officers' club, shooting pool and playing ping pong. She even became an expert poker player. But who wanted her contribution to the war effort to be a good game of poker?

One night after Rosabell had awakened Kathy when she left on her nightly visit to Axel, Kathy could not go back to sleep. The cool fall air came through the window as she stood to look at the night sky bright with stars.

The stars made her homesick for her father, who had taught her the constellations, and for her mother, who had taught her Greek mythology so well that Kathy had almost believed them—perhaps believed parts of them.

There were the zig-zagged stars that the Greeks had called Cassiopeia's throne. Beside her were the three stars of her daughter Andromeda's shoulders. Poor Andromeda was chained to a rock, with no escape from the sea monster that was to devour her. But Andromeda had Perseus who could rescue her. Perseus would take the Medusa head, just captured, from his pouch and turn the sea monster to stone. Perseus would fly through the sky, rescue Andromeda, marry her and raise a family of three fine sons.

Kathy easily found Andromeda in the sky, but where was Perseus? In all the millions of stars, where was Perseus?

Kathy wanted Perseus, with his winged shoes and his magic head for herself. She wanted him to slay her monster and unchain her from her rock. Among these millions of men, who would he be, and how would she know him?

Nonsense. That was ancient Greek mythology. God's universe was wonderful, and surely in his scheme of things, there was a place for Kathy. There must be a reason for Castoria. She continued to dream of her Perseus.

Kathy put on a wrap-around dress and walked outside to the chapel. The chapel was quiet and dark, lit only by a bank of small candles before a statue of the Virgin Mary. Kathy did not understand lighting candles; this was not in the Episcopalian services she had known, but she lit a candle and prayed. The candle burned hopefully in the darkness. She prayed to God, prayed for someone to love, prayed for her Perseus.

The next morning Rosabell announced she had found a room for herself and Axel in town, and with grateful thanks, moved out. It was peaceful to have her room to herself. Though she was now alone, her loneliness was not directly contrasted to Rosabell's blooming romance.

After her round of egg-checking was completed, she went as usual to the officers' club. A red-headed patient, a Lieutenant, asked, "Play you a game of chess, Lieutenant?"

She looked at his clean-shaven face. Was he her Perseus? "Sure. I'll play."

In just a few moves it was apparent Kathy could win too easily. Should she protect his ego and let him win, or should she be honest and beat him? Anyway, he wasn't her Perseus. Her Perseus would have to be smarter and stronger than she was in order to rescue her.

As she waited for the patient to think out a play, she watched a tall, black-haired infantry Captain enter the club. He looked at her, and at the patient, and he studied the chessboard. His blouse hung loosely from his broad shoulders. He must have once been a large man, yet now thin. He rubbed a bony, long-fingered hand over his chin. Though it was afternoon, his chin was dark with his thick-growing beard. He grinned at Kathy, and winked a deep-set brown eye, saying, "I'll play the winner."

The Captain swung out a chair from the next table. He set it backwards beside their table, threw a long leg over the chair and sat down, making himself welcome without an invitation.

Was he her Perseus? He was too thin to swing a sword—but he had a confident look about him, and he had the air of a man who had a powerful Medusa's head in his pouch, and wings on his shoes. So, Kathy moved her queen to put the king in check, and ended the game.

The Captain jumped up from his chair, and made a little bow to the patient. "Thank you," he said, as the patient shrugged and walked away to the slot machine.

The Captain swung his chair around to sit opposite Kathy. "I was irresistibly drawn by your luminous eyes, their sweeping lashes, your enchanting smile, and by the fact that you're a dietitian. I could use some good food."

Kathy sorted the chessmen, "Nice try. It's a shame to waste that beautiful flattery, but I am out of favor with the powers that be and couldn't scrape up a cracker. I'm waiting for a transfer."

"I should have guessed. No one as charming as you could be responsible for such unappetizing food." His long, bony fingers placed the black chessmen on the board." I am Roger Rockford, Rocky to my friends. He paused, seeming to wait for a reaction to his name, but Kathy didn't recognize it. "You're not from the east coast?" he asked.

"Just a few visits to New York with my father on his business trips. I'm Kathryn Collens from Chicago. Not really Chicago—we live in the farm country forty miles north."

"And we live north of New York, Westchester County. Never heard of the law firm Rockford and Rockford?" He sat with his hand under his chin, massaging his neck.

Kathy shook her head. "Sorry, no. Am I displaying my ignorance?"

"Well, it's all part of my past history before I abandoned law for the infantry."

"Are you a patient, or new on the staff?" He wore, among other medals, a purple heart and three overseas stripes, showing eighteen months overseas duty.

"Patient," he said. "Do you have a diet for fainting?"

"Depends on what causes the fainting."

"Nothing causes it."

"Running miles, I didn't faint. In the worst battles I didn't faint. Wounded I didn't pass out. Playing a quiet game of solitaire, I keel over."

"I leave diagnoses to doctors," said Kathy

He massaged his neck. Perhaps the rubbing eased tensions. "One hundred and one doctors and two hundred and two psychiatrists have not diagnosed my fainting. Thought I'd ask a dietitian."

"You look healthy."

"I am healthy. That's what's frustrating. "He loosened his necktie and unbuttoned the top two buttons of his shirt. He looked at her khaki shirt and necktie. "Loosen your tie, unbutton your shirt. It improves your circulation. I want to see more of you."

Kathy was proud of her uniform, and wanted to wear it correctly. She could think of no answer, and so merely lined up her chess men.

"An ambiguous statement, unworthy of a lawyer. See more of you…numerically? No. Chronologically? Maybe. Anatomically?" Rocky said as he smiled and raised his bushy eyebrows.

Maybe her shirt did feel constricting. She loosened her tie, and un-buttoned the top shirt button.

"Just as I thought. Under that drab shirt lies a beautiful neck. It im-proves my circulation, too."

Kathy began the game with the old four-play move, the only tradi-tional planned moves she knew. She brought out her queen to work with her bishop—a joint attack on his king in four moves.

"Aha! I am not so easily trapped as that." Rocky jumped his knight out to disrupt the bishop's attack.

From here on she would have to make her own plays, use her imagination. Kathy played with her queen, bishops and castles, moving along straight open lines. He played almost entirely with his pawns and knights, which could jump in unpredictable ways, and could not be blocked, cornered or trapped.

Kathy had never played with a man who used his horses so effectively, so devastatingly. She planned her moves slowly. He moved quickly, and was impatient waiting for her. He straddled his chair like a horse, slapping the beat of the music on the back. Always, without appearing to plan, he knew what his next move was. He attacked, chasing her queen and her bishop round and round the board. He was brilliant; a far more expert player than she. By the time the music had stopped, he had cornered her queen.

"CLANG! CLANG! CLANG!" Suddenly, the fire alarm pierced the air. They rushed to the door. An ambulance clanged and shrieked by. Kathy and Rocky ran up the side ramp to look down the main ramp. The overhead sprinkler system sprayed water over the middle section. A doctor with three bottles of plasma and dangling rubber tubes ran into the ward. Men ran by carrying stretchers. Soldiers shoved through the gathering crowd with fire hoses and axes.

Rocky lifted Kathy onto a ledge at the end of the ramp and stood behind her. They watched from a distance. This was a real emergency. Fire in these wooden buildings, in explosive oxygen tents, in ether-filled operating rooms, was an ever-threatening horror. She turned to ask Rocky, "Do you think..."

Rocky was laughing! His head thrown back, his even white teeth glistening. He was laughing! "You were with me all afternoon. You know I had nothing to do with it."

"Nothing to do with what?"

"That slipped. Don't tell a soul! I just said, all I said was, 'Would the heat of a booming match start the sprinkling system?!' Well, I guess it did."

The commanding officer, standing in the puddles shouted, "Turn off the sprinklers! Turn off the sprinklers!"

"Anyway," said Kathy, "It's nice to know our hospital is quick in an emergency."

Rocky lifted her down, his hands on her waist strong and sure. "I'd better get my laughing face out of here. May I join you for dinner, say in an hour?"

"Love to have you, but the rules say the patients do not eat in the staff's mess. Lieutenant Groot is fussy about rules."

"From what I've seen, she must be the only one that bothers about rules. I'm hoping the food in your mess is better than that on the wards. How about we dine at your mess. Sounds delightful? I'll call for you at six."

Kathy showered and dressed with special care. She brushed her uniform, subtly blended her makeup, and dabbed just enough Taboo perfume on her wrists and behind her ears.

As she left her room, Rocky opened the door at the other end of the hall, stepped in, and whistled a piercing whistle. A man in the hall was no novelty, but his sharp whistle was. Twenty girls popped out from their rooms to look.

"It's dangerous to be so handsome in this man shortage. I should never have come in with my hair combed." He rumpled his smoothly waved black hair. "There. That's safer. Now girls, calm down. One at a time. I came for a little girl who just fits under my chin, well stacked, Kathryn Collens. Oh, there you are." Holding out his elbow in a gallant gesture for Kathy's hand, he opened the door and guided her out.

He led her into the mess and over to the cafeteria line. They looked at the food, the dry, strong-smelling fish and greasy fried potatoes. "Seven doctors and five psychiatrists have not been able to figure out why I lose weight. This meal should make it obvious. Well, shall we go out to dinner?"

They went outside to his car. It was a Mercury automobile, a brand-new blue sedan. On the hood was a small silver statue, a man poised for flying, with silver wings on his feet: Mercury.

Rocky drove his powerful Mercury to a little country inn on the edge of town. A fire burned in a giant stone fireplace. Candles flickered on tables with red checkered cloths and bouquets of flowers. There were no soldiers, and only a few civilians sitting quietly at their small tables.

The smells of cooked chicken were the smells of Kathy's home. This place was so much like the little log cabin near their home. Kathy told Rocky of the parties there, of swimming and sailing along the shores of the fresh water of Lake Michigan. In the winter there was ice skating, hanging mittens to dry, and singing songs in the cool moonlit evenings.

Rocky talked of his adventures of sailing a ketch from Puget Sound to the coast of Mexico, and through the Panama Canal. Some day he would sail to Hawaii with moonlight nights and peaceful beaches. As he talked, he finally relaxed and rested his fingers quietly on his chin.

With the last bite of apple pie now eaten, Rocky put a dime in the juke box, and they danced. He held her firmly, with a subtle strength that easily led her. He guided her through his complicated steps so deftly that she could not have done other than follow his lead. When he swooped, she swooped. When he held her close, cheek to cheek, his chin was scratchy, a tough, masculine scratch. His body was tight against hers, lean and hard. Then with a fling, he swung her out and back, to hold her again in his strong arms.

Kathy had always considered herself a graceful dancer, but never had she felt more beautiful. Rocky was an expert. He lifted her up and around, one minute floating, the next twirling, the next swaying back over his knee. Sometimes touching only his slender fingers, sometimes his intent dark-eyed look keeping the bond between them. Ah! The man could waltz! He held her close, and together that they glided and swirled as one.

Gone in the pleasures of the dance were all thoughts of war, Lieutenant Groot, mutilated patients, and unappealing food. Living in the moment, there simply were no problems.

At midnight, Kathy reluctantly said, "It's late; after all, you are a patient. Though I could happily dance all night, you should be sleeping."

"I pass out when I lie down. Never when I dance. For the sake of my psyche, let's dance all night."

She didn't quite believe him, but when he put another dime in the juke box, she danced again without a murmur, and they danced until two when the candle-lit inn closed.

As they were leaving, he took the vase of orange mums from their table and paid for them along with his bill. He handed the flowers to Kathy. On the drive home, even the Mercury danced. He braked it in little jerks that rocked the car with the radio's music as it rolled around curves.

Late as it was, Kathy walked around to the side door rather than risk walking through the dark day room. Bosco, Boltz, and Kincaid might be with their men and bottles. Bosco's parties, which yesterday might have seemed somewhat fun, seemed only dismal now. The country inn, with chrysanthemums and candlelight and dancing was far lovelier than that dingy day room.

Rocky opened the door for her like a gentleman. He simply said, "Thank you and good night."

He did not ask her to go dancing again, and she wished he would. So, she also simply said, "Thank you and good night."

The next afternoon when Kathy was, as usual, playing pool in the officers' club, Rocky came in. "You shouldn't be here on a sunny day like this. Go watch the football game. The rehabilitation patients of Castoria are playing State's varsity. Now there's a game to see: the sick against the well."

"I don't go off duty until 15:30."

"What duty? You're not working. Come on to the game. There's no point in sitting here. The world outside is full of sunshine."

At the field, Kathy sat with Rocky on a bench. Their brass buttons and the large eagles on their caps gleamed in the sunlight. On the field,

Castoria's patients wore red football uniforms and the college team wore gold. The hospital's cheering section, in wine-red pajamas and bathrobes lined the field. They yelled from wheelchairs, and waved crutches and arms in casts. Rocky whooped and hollered, and Kathy caught his enthusiasm. That afternoon Castoria beat State varsity 12 to 7.

After the game they walked together into the mess for dinner. Again, the food was unappetizing. Again, Rocky took Kathy to the little inn.

Once more Kathy tried to tell him her troubles with Lieutenant Groot—but Rocky would not get serious, and turned everything into a joke. They danced until midnight, when Kathy suggested they go home. Rocky insisted he could sleep till noon. Kathy, though she would have to be on duty at six, could not, yet didn't want to resist the pleasures of dancing. She was now following him more easily, less self-consciously.

The next noon Rocky was waiting for her in the mess when she came in for lunch. He was dressed as always in his Class A uniform, but today he had added two extra rows of ribbons and now two purple hearts.

"My, you do look impressive, General," she said. "Where did you earn all those?"

"That's the idea, to impress the head waiter." He patted his chest. "The top row are mine." He took her hand to lead her out the door. "Tonight, we'll drive into the city for dinner. This display will get us a table. After, we'll see *Oklahoma!* OK?"

It certainly was OK. Though she had intended to take a nap that afternoon, sleep could hardly compete with Rocky or *Oklahoma!*

As they strolled across the street to his car, Rocky said, "Walking out is too easy. It's a lot more fun to outwit the authorities with a legal ruse."

"If you enjoy a battle of brains, please figure out some regulation that will make Lieutenant Groot let me work. Can you outsmart her?"

Rocky opened the Mercury's door for Kathy; then walked around to get behind the wheel. "It took me two minutes to understand Groot.

'Groot the Brute' lives by the regulation. I make the regulation serve me. That requires intelligence, like mine, and knowledge. If you know the manual you can find things that legalize what you want. Groot serves the law. The law serves me." He sang the phrase to an upbeat tune. The melody pleased him, and he sang loudly.

"All right, Caruso. Tell me the law that will make Lieutenant Groot let me work."

"I said I made the law serve me. Kathy, I do not want you to work. I want you to spend every minute admiring me," he said.

He started his Mercury, "Come fly with me in my flying machine." He gazed at her with dark intensity. "Doesn't that resonance tingle your spine?"

"It does indeed." She sang, "I'll fly with you in your flying machine and I'll never work…."

Rocky joined her song. Together they sang all the way to the city.

Rocky did, as he planned, duly impress the head waiter. Even with a group of people waiting for tables, Rocky and Kathy were shown immediately to a central table. Amid the admiring glances it wouldn't have been surprising if the diners had broken out in applause. Kathy was simply embarrassed. Her war record to date counting eggs did not merit any special favors. Rocky was smiling as though this admiration were only his just due, which it was, even if only by the row of medals that did belong to him. Rocky held her chair. He ordered tenderloin steaks, rare in these days of meat rationing. The head waiter presented a red rose in a bud vase to Kathy.

After dinner they hurried down the street to the theater and found their seats just as the curtain was rising for *Oklahoma!*

This was a story of the life that Kathy believed in. The hero was handsome and good. The villain was dirty and bad. The heroine is rescued from her troubles. All with a happy ending. True love triumphed over all obstacles. This was real life as Kathy had lived it before she joined the Army.

As the curtain dropped and drama came to an end, Kathy smiled.

"Why the smile?" asked Rocky. "What are you thinking about that makes you look so pleased?"

"All stories should have happy endings."

His face clouded; his dark brows scowled. "Yes, it would be nice if life furnished happy endings. Do we go home now, or dancing?"

"Home. It will be late enough when we get there."

On the ride home they sang songs from *Oklahoma!* The moon flooded the world with a silver light. The stars were bright and clear. Kathy found Andromeda, but could not find Perseus. "Do you know where Perseus is?" she asked.

"Who? Oh, the constellation. He's right under and a little to the left of Andromeda right there." He pointed. "Did you get the sequence in the dream waltz in the show? He got the effect of love with just a walk and a look and a leap. We'll try that tomorrow night."

"That doesn't sound like a lawyer talking."

"*Dare pondus fumo. Deceptio visus. Ad captandum vulgus. Ad nauseum.* Is that the way a lawyer should sound? Actually, a good lawyer speaks so clearly that every fool on the jury can understand him."

"There's one thing I've often wondered about lawyers. How can you defend someone who you think is guilty?"

"I don't judge guilt. My job is simply to present a case," said Rocky. "Every man has the right to the best defense I can give him. The courts decide the legality."

"And if you know he's wrong?"

"I'm not concerned with right or wrong. A smart lawyer can usually find a legal loophole that gets his client off, or present a case so a jury gets a legal angle. But I'm a corporation lawyer—or was. I spent my time telling corporations what they could or couldn't do legally. I'm a good lawyer, a smart lawyer. I know the law thoroughly. That's where the money is, in keeping business legal. That's what pays for cars and yachts. That's where the excitement is. It's business that's arming the Army; and it's business that will rebuild the world. I intend to be right in the middle of that business, as soon I'm out of this Army."

Kathy understood. For years she sat beside her father as he talked of business cycles with his friends. She sat beside her mother as she graciously served at dinners. She could picture herself with Rocky on his yacht fishing on calm sunny waters, or battling a storm.

They returned to the hospital. They both sat in the car, reluctant to have the evening end.

"It's been a magic evening." Kathy sighed as she put her hand on the door handle.

Rocky put his arm across her shoulder, reached his other hand to her waist, and pulled her toward him. She relaxed against him, her head on his neck. He loosened her necktie and collar. He tilted her chin up, held her face toward his.

Kathy shook her head and sat up. "I don't know you well enough to kiss you." She only knew him well enough to relax in his arms. What worried her? She needed to be certain. "I don't even know if you're married…or not."

His face turned haggard, and then sagged. He held his breath a long moment; letting it out slowly. With a taut voice, and with an effort at a light tone that wasn't light, he said, "Not more than five or six wives."

"You are married."

"Yes."

Kathy fumbled for the door latch, found it, opened the door. She turned to Rocky. "I thought you were..." I thought you..." Her eyes welled up with tears. "I am so disappointed!" She could say no more. She opened the door and moved to get out of the car.

"Wait! I can explain."

She waited, keeping her hand on the open door. The chilling air blew in. A married man could have no explanation she would accept.

"It's not what you think. My wife is getting a divorce." His face was gray in the moonlight. "She is in love with another man. I don't blame her. She was young. She was pretty. I was overseas for three years. There was nothing I could do." His voice was low, almost a whisper. "Nothing I could do. She's getting a divorce."

His face was tragic, his story tragic. Marriage was sacred. How could his wife be so disloyal to so wonderful a man as Rocky? How could she ignore Rocky's love? Love was forever. Rocky's story was heartbreaking. She must comfort him. She closed the door.

He put his arms around her, and kissed her, a soft kiss. She stroked his temple, across his warm skin to his thick hair. There was nothing she could say that would help. She said only, "I'm sorry. Good night."

He held her arm as he walked her to the side door.

The next morning when Kathy had counted the eggs in the kitchen of the officer's medical ward, she decided to read Rocky's chart. With no one in the nurse's office, she went in and helped herself to his chart. She lifted the aluminum cover, and read in a doctor's scrawl: Roger R. Rockford, 0-456-328. Captain. Infantry. 28 years. Parents: 1; Married: Wife: 1; and Children: 2 boys.

She read on. He did faint. Neither doctors nor psychiatrists had found any reason for it. He was perfectly healthy. His flesh wound had healed without complications.

She dropped the lid over the papers. All his family, including two boys, were living and well.

From the ward came the sounds of breakfast trays being collected. Lieutenant Boltz came in. "Hi, Kathy. Why don't you and Rocky come with us to the Flamingo tonight? In Rocky's car. He'd drive if you asked."

Kathy slid the chart into its slot. "Not tonight."

Kathy left to look into refrigerators on the other wards. When she was finished, she had no idea how many eggs were in which refrigerators, and she didn't care. Neither did anyone else.

Kathy left the hospital, walked past headquarters and across the parking lot. Anyone could see her go. It would make no difference to anyone in the hospital that she was going.

On the rolling hills before her, a combine was cutting the golden wheat, shooting out a spray of straw over the windrow. Horses grazed nearby. Kathy rolled a handful of the hard wheat in her hand, separating grain and chaff. She blew the chaff from her open hand, and looked at the tiny miracles.

"Kathy!"

She turned to see Rocky crossing the parking lot toward her, looking puzzled. "What are you doing out here alone?"

"Contemplating wheat."

He glanced at the tiny grains in her outstretched hand. "Not much to look at."

"You forget. I went to Iowa State College. You don't graduate from there without understanding wheat. This, ground up, makes bread, good brown bread. Chew it. Tastes like nuts." She held out her hand to him.

He took three kernels and gingerly put them in his mouth. He grimaced. "I'll buy you bread in the finished form if you'll go to dinner with me. I'll buy you cake. Glenn Miller's orchestra is playing in the city. We can leave at two."

She picked an ear of wheat, carefully rubbed it between her palms and blew off the chaff. So easily the grain separated from the chaff. "Rocky, do you have any children?"

His face turned gray, his shoulders sagged, and the corners of his eyes drooped. "One boy."

"I read your chart."

He lowered his head to gaze at the ground. "I don't know if the second boy is mine."

As they stood before the field of wheat, the great combine clattered by. Rocky lifted his head and looked straight at Kathy. His eyes were deep and dark, and the hurt in them was exposed.

She reached for his hand. "I'll go to the city with you. We'll swing and sway with Glenn Miller."

He straightened his shoulders and the corners of his eyes lifted with almost a smile. They walked hand in hand to his car, the winged Mercury.

She wanted to spend every moment with him. Where they went or what they did were not important. Rocky delighted in swinging and twirling her around, and she was captivated. He now danced holding her close, and in dark corners his hand sometimes slipped below her waist.

One evening late in August when Rocky came to pick up Kathy, he said, "Did you hear the news? Paris has been liberated! The Allies marched in the same path that Hitler took down the Champs Elysee when they invaded in 1940."

"Hooray! Finally! I suppose Eisenhower announced that we would be home by Christmas?" she asked.

Rocky said, "Ha! We've heard that before. Since the beginning of this war, the strength of the Germans has been underestimated. Now on to Berlin, but it won't be easy."

On the last day of October, Kathy woke up to find the world had been transformed during the night with snow. Rocky declared this spectacular snowfall an event for celebration at their favorite place, the inn with candlelight. Only tonight instead of mums there were yellow roses.

There were only four other customers. Rocky seated Kathy at a corner table, sat across from her, and gave her an intent, solemn look.

"You're serious tonight," Kathy said, not sure whether he was happy or sad. He just looked serious.

He said not a word. He took a rose from the vase, pinched off the stem, and gently set the rose in her hair. After dinner, Rocky ordered red wine. Silently he poured wine into two stemmed glasses for their first drink together. He held up his glass, waiting for her to join him.

He patiently held his glass till she responded with hers. His eyes gave the toast—and Kathy knew. The feeling was there, in the air, between them, in his look. Without a word, without a touch, it was there.

Rocky stood, held out his arm in an invitation to dance. She held his hand with tingled touch as he turned on the juke box to *Stardust*. They danced cheek to cheek. Certainly, stardust was pouring from the Big Dipper and the Little Dipper all over Andromeda and Perseus.

His mouth was at her ear. "I love you."

Love! Rocky loved her! Love flowed from her ears to her mind to her heart.

His voice was low and throaty. "I love you." All along the length of their bodies, from cheek touching cheek to leg gliding with leg, the stardust tingled.

Kathy responded, "I love you."

When the music stopped, they lingered on the dance floor in each other's arms. Someone put another dime in the juke box to play "Always." *"I'm in love with you, always. With a heart that's true, always. When the things you plan, need a helping hand, that's when I'll be there. Always."*

This was the love of romantic dreams, the red flame of passionate love, the enduring love that would last forever. Always. Kathy could never hurt him as his wife had done, for this love was truly heaven-made. This was the answer to her prayer, her lighted candle.

They danced on. This man, holding her so close, belonged to her, and she to him. Her life was now dedicated to serving him, to making him happy.

Her passion for Rocky grew. Kathy welcomed her passions and desires. She thought of marriage and children and fulfillment.

Rocky kissed her a fervent good-night kiss. It held the promise of a durable relationship against the loneliness and rigor of life. She left him reluctantly, and went into the side door of the barracks.

As she walked down the hall past the dayroom door, she heard Bosco, Boltz, and Kincaid's usual giggles and the clank of bottle against glass. How much more beautiful was Rocky's solemn glass of wine than the drinks splashed from bottles into glasses on the splintered floor. The three witches sought the same love Kathy sought. They would not find it on the dayroom floor, not a love that would last always. Lust led to unwanted babies and abortions.

Bosco, Boltz, and Kincaid were nurses and certainly should know better. Any nurses who had worked on the OB ward at Cook County knew there was no such thing as a reliable contraceptive. At County, half of the fifty babies born each day had no fathers to support and love them. Twenty-five girls each day came to this charity hospital to have their unwanted babies. They were forsaken by their families, or too ashamed to return to their homes. Contemplating? No, the only safety lay in chastity.

Kathy shuddered and hurried past the day room door. She wanted no part of the life led there. She got under the blanket in her bed, and dreamt of the time she would marry Rocky.

For the next month Rocky spoke easily of love, reassuring Kathy often of his love. If he spoke only of love, never of marriage and a home and children, it was undoubtedly because he couldn't make promises until he was divorced. If Rocky's divorce were declared final tomorrow, she would marry him the next hour.

Two days before Christmas, Rocky gave Kathy five packages wrapped in red paper with gold ribbons. "I'll have to spend Christmas with my family. I haven't been with my father and mother for the holidays in four years," he explained. "You understand, don't you? You know I'd rather be with you, but you do agree that I owe it to them?"

"I'll miss you—but I'm proud you're the kind of man who honors his father and mother."

"Want my car while I'm gone?"

"No thanks. Daddy never allowed us to drive other people's cars. Anyway, I won't be going anywhere without you. We'll celebrate New Year's Eve together."

The executive officer asked Kathy to supervise the Christmas dinner, to be served at a party in the officers' club. This gave Kathy work to fill the hours while Rocky was gone. She planned menus and discussed with the cooks. She made decorations and checked linens and silverware. She would rather have been doing something for the patients, but serving the officers was a pleasant substitute.

Christmas morning, alone in her room, Kathy sat on her bed beside the bright Christmas presents Rocky had given her. She opened the first. It was a box of chocolate candy. The card read, "I'd like to share this with you." The second was a jar of bubble bath. The card read "I'd like to share this with you."

The third present was a bottle of her perfume, Taboo. The card read "Stardust." The next package was a black lace nightgown. Kathy wriggled into it, a snug fit. Had Rocky imagined her in this? He'd never seen her in anything more alluring than an Army uniform. The card read "XOXOXO."

The fifth package was a clear plastic box, with a sterling silver inlay of two doves on a single branch set into a hinged lid. Inside, on a gold chain, was a heart-shaped locket with a ruby center. The card read, "To my love, a red heart set in everlasting gold. – Rocky." Kathy clasped it around her neck. It clinked against her steel dog tags, which she moved toward her back. In the mirror the ruby gleamed red on her throat.

There was no time for dreaming in a tight nightgown. Kathy had to dress in her uniform and hurry to the officers' mess to check on the roast beef, rolls, and pies. Much to do. This dinner of all dinners had to be perfect. She wanted to prove to all of Castoria that she was a capable dietitian. She wanted to serve them all a delightful dinner so that they could honestly say "Thank God for this food" on this Christmas.

The dinner was all she had hoped. Sprays of shiny green holly led across the white table cloth. It framed the silver plates of strawberry and lime molded salads, past the Brussels sprouts baked with chestnuts, around the candied carrots and green beans with mushrooms. The holly circled the platters and platters of crisp fried chicken and stuffed baked potatoes. The holly led on past golden rolls with red raspberry jam to the flaky crusted apple and pumpkin pies, and the rich devil's food cake.

When everyone was served, and the servers were slicing their own roast beef, Mac the WAC asked Kathy "Do you want strawberry or peach salad? By the way, did you get your orders?"

"No. Do I have orders?"

"They came yesterday. The mess officer has them. Do you want strawberry or peach?"

"Tell me. Tell me. When? For where? I won't leave before Rocky returns."

"You can leave now. You get a last pass before you go overseas."

"Overseas? Overseas? Where will I be sent?"

"Top secret. If I knew I wouldn't tell. Now, do you want salad or not? Strawberry or peach?"

"Neither. Both. I don't care."

"I'll give you strawberry because you're lucky to leave here, even to go overseas, and peach because I know how you feel about leaving Rocky. Rocky will be up for a transfer soon, so it doesn't much matter whether you go or stay, as far as he's concerned. Now, if you can collect your thoughts, you might serve Major Molina her apple pie."

With her pass, she could fly to Santa Fe where her parents were spending the winter. She could hitch-hike for free on Army or Navy planes. She could return in six days to celebrate New Year's Eve with Rocky.

She caught an Army plane early in the morning. The plane soared over fields and rivers and towns. From the sky everything Kathy saw, touched by the exuberance of her love, was magnificent and beautiful.

The Army pilot responded to her enthusiasm and let her sit in the co-pilot seat of the C47. The radio and navigation officers demonstrated their equipment. She could beam and navigate. The pilot let her fly. She was flying! In love, everything was possible. The flight to Denver was over in minutes.

Traveling with them was a newly commissioned Second Lieutenant from Washington, D.C. He had just spent his savings on his uniforms and was depending on this free transportation to get home to his mother in California before going overseas. After landing in Denver, he learned that all flights going west were canceled because of bad weather. With no money for a train ticket, he was stopped.

In Kathy's heart, love for Rocky expanded into love for everyone. She was assured of a flight south to Santa Fe in half an hour, so she loaned him $40. This left her with $4 and her mother's $50 check for any emergency. The stranded kid wrote her a check in payment for future cashing.

Fifteen minutes after he had left, the loud speaker announced, "All south-bound planes are grounded due to bad weather." Kathy took a cab to the train station to buy a ticket with her mother's check.

The train station was crowded. Kathy waited in line at the ticket window. When she confronted the ticket agent, she said, "One ticket, one way, first class, to Santa Fe. When does it leave and arrive? This is my last leave before going overseas."

Kathy expected him to respond to her smile. Instead, he looked bored. Last leaves before going overseas were routine for him. He made out the ticket, "Leaves at 5:17, Track 7. Arrives 12:47. $12.11."

"Thank you." Kathy took out her mother's check and turned it over to sign.

"We don't take checks."

"This is a Collen's check." A Collen's check was always good. Kathy had cashed her father's checks in Grand Central Stations in Chicago and New York, without question, without even identification. She signed the check.

"We don't take checks."

Kathy turned to the MP standing by the window. "Tell him this check is all right."

The MP looked surprised. She realized he couldn't vouch for her check. What could he do? "Check my identification and pass. Tell him they're all right. Call my father. Call the Army. Call whoever you want."

She handed the MP her ID card, complete with picture and fingerprints. He looked them over and told the clerk it was in order.

"We don't take checks." The clerk was bored. "Next."

"If you don't, I can't get home. Why not? Everyone cashed my checks when I wore a fur coat. Is it because I'm in uniform?"

Kathy was shoved out of line. She went to the Travelers Aid, who explained that this was after two o'clock on Friday. The banks were closed until Monday.

The man at the Red Cross Headquarters looked skeptical about her story of giving $40 to a strange Lieutenant. He said merely, "It's Red

Cross policy not to cash checks." She went into store after store. After the stores closed, into hotels and restaurants, asking to cash her check. Most of them flatly refused. Once in a while a sympathetic cashier would look at the check, but when he saw it was for $50 would refuse.

Recognizing for the first time in her life the need for conserving money, she had only a ten-cent glass of milk for supper. She had $3.90 left. There was nothing more to say, nothing to be done. Kathy cried. She didn't want to cry, for her nose and eyes always got red, and she had no handkerchief. People in the crowded lobby were watching, so she retreated to the ladies' powder room.

Several fashionably dressed ladies followed her, concerned and sympathetic. Surely one of them would give her supper or offer a bed. Kathy was without money because she had been generous. Justice demanded that someone be generous to her. No one offered $12 for the ticket. No one offered supper. No one offered a bed. They offered only empathy. When the women had left, Kathy curled up on the couch in the powder room and slept.

Saturday, with flights south still cancelled, she spent the day at the airport. The airfield was an exciting place, and she discovered her uniform was a passport to all parts of it. She ate free sandwiches at the Red Cross Canteen. She talked to mechanics about engines, and to men in the control tower about their work. She felt a kinship with a man in a uniform. While as a civilian, she had easily cashed checks. In a uniform, no civilian trusted her.

A pilot who went by the name of "Tank" offered a ride in his fighter plane. He was putting in flight time, just around the city. She gladly accepted.

"Can't wait to get overseas," he said. "I want a shot at those Germans. Our planes are better, faster, and will put an end to this bloody war. Many of the best German pilots have been killed. They are running out of gasoline, too. Our pilots get hundreds of hours more training than their new pilots as we have plenty of gasoline."

As they approached the aircraft, Kathy asked, "How fast will we go?"

"How fast do you want to go?" Tank responded.

She climbed into the Plexiglas turret with the machine guns. They soared up into the sky. She held her head straight with both hands to not let it jerk. This was far more exhilarating than the lumbering C47 ride.

After the flight, Tank drove her into town. He tried twice with no success to cash her check in stores where he was known. They decided it would be more fun to spend the evening sight-seeing and dancing, with a supper at the Red Cross Canteen. That evening Kathy slept again in the hotel's powder room.

Sunday, it rained, and all flights were canceled. The Red Cross sandwiches, though patriotic and free, grew monotonous. The powder room couch palled. The Red Cross official who refused again to cash her check seemed irritatingly rigid. She wanted to get home and back to Castoria before New Year's Eve.

Monday morning the planes were grounded again. Kathy marched determinedly into the Red Cross office to confront the man in uniform. "I've been in Denver four days just because you won't cash my check. Preposterous! You must help me!"

Solidly entrenched behind his desk, the Red Cross man shrugged his shoulders. "We don't cash checks. There's nothing we can do."

"You'd better think of something. I can't get home. I can't even get back to duty." She had meant to be tough and logical, but her eyes were filling up with tears.

The Red Cross man just sat, looking uncomfortable.

Kathy kept her voice steady. "Do something. Now. Or I'll start screaming and I'll go to the police. At least in jail I can eat. Don't make me. I can. And I will."

The Red Cross man opened a safe, took out some money. "We might give you an emergency loan. You can repay it with your check." He took her check and handed her $50.

Finally, she arrived in Santa Fe, New Mexico for the last two days of her pass. She was welcomed with kisses by her joyous mother. She got a big hug from her typically gruff father. Her smiling sister, with two jumping nieces and one cherubic sleeping baby, surrounded Kathy. It was a homecoming full of warmth and love. It was not a hero's welcome. To her family, she was the same Kathy. After all, her two brothers were in the South Pacific. Her brother-in-law, the children's father, was recovering in a hospital in France.

With kids hopping all over her, there was no serious conversation possible until after the kids were in bed. Her first news was of her new love, of Rocky, of his intelligence, his wit, his wealth, and his charm. Her father and mother listened without comment, for Kathy asked no questions. She had no doubts. As soon as the war was over and she returned from overseas, they would be married. This was a statement, not a question.

Then Kathy spilled out her troubles with Lieutenant Groot. Kathy had failed in her work. Her relations with Lieutenant Groot were beyond salvaging. To gain anything from the experience, she must learn why she had failed. She asked her white-haired father for advice. He was a big, strong man, now retired. He had forged a big business in a growing country, thriving even through the depression. He had served as the CEO of an international dredging firm. The company had drained swamps, irrigated deserts, dug canals and deepened harbors. He certainly knew the elements of success.

"You are intelligent and capable," he said, "hard-working, and honest. In my book you are fine, just fine. If there was trouble, there was something wrong with that hospital administration, not with you. A business that does not take advantage of brains and industry will not survive."

He talked on. "Here in the U.S., we have transformed our factories to support the war effort. Production rapidly shifted from building refrigerators and automobiles to airplanes and tanks. We utilized the ingenuity of Henry Ford's mass production techniques. We have outpaced the Germans. We are winning the war of the factories. After all, it's business that built this country.

"Yet the war is certainly not over. Ever since D-Day, the Allies have been working their way across France and then will be on to Berlin."

He continued. "Earlier this month the Germans initiated a major offense in the Ardennes Forrest in Belgium. Who would expect this, in a thick forest in the middle of winter? Hitler wanted to pierce the center of our front, drive on to the coast of the English Channel, and cut off the Allies' supplies. It worked for him at Dunkirk four years ago, so why not do it again. We were caught completely unprepared.

"They calling it the 'Battle of the Bulge' as the Germans have managed a shift, or a bulge into our front line It's been a fierce fight, and it's just begun. Those Germans will never give up. They should not be underestimated."

Her mother dropped her knitting onto her lap. "I hope in your next assignment you have a more qualified supervisor. Yet in thinking about your situation, I feel sorry for Lieutenant Groot. The poor woman is sick, middle-aged, and without the ability to attract love. She has a job for which she has no training and can't quite handle. She has nothing. You have everything. You have your health, youth, vitality, and love. Your future is full of potential. Her's is dismal."

If she were everything her father and mother believed, Kathy should have done better at Castoria. But her mother was right in feeling sorry for Lieutenant Groot. The woman was maintaining her position not with competence but with pull. If she lost that, she would have nothing.

It was comforting to be so esteemed by her family, but not helpful. To function in the Army, Kathy needed to learn something new. Just exactly what, was uncertain, as was her next location in this war.

Her thoughts returned to Rocky. This, at least, was successful. After her short visit, she flew back to Castoria on a commercial airline. She departed from a sunny climate and a warm family to winter weather and cheerless wooden barracks.

Kathy carried her suitcase to her room. Bosco was there, looking through her drawers. "Good," said Bosco, "You're just in time. Where are your thumbtacks. You had some that you used to tack up paintings."

"Those are gone, but I have more." Kathy's mother had made her a cloth of two dozen pockets, supplied with tiny tools, tacks, wire, anything she might need overseas. "What are you making?"

"Decorations. For the big party." Bosco took the tacks, and bounced out the door. "Come and help. Rocky's looking for a screwdriver."

Kathy hurried after Bosco to see Rocky.

Officers and Red Cross girls were hanging red and silver streamers across the ceiling. Rocky was on a ladder, from which hung wires and a machine for revolving the colored lights. He stood, looking perplexed at the maze. Then he saw Kathy.

He opened his arms, jumped from the ladder. They ran together, and she was in his arms.

"How are you? Honestly, how are you?" Kathy asked

"Better now that you are here. Sitting around with nothing to do is not good. I just pass out. But I never pass out when you're around."

"That doesn't make sense. Tell me…when..."

"I've talked it all out endlessly. Let's talk about the party. A champagne party, the Colonel ordered cases of it. A five-piece orchestra. Formal. You're going to wear a formal."

"I don't have a formal, and regulations…"

"The Colonel has relaxed regulations. Girls will wear dresses."

"This is all I have. You'll have to think I'm beautiful in a uniform."

"You're beautiful, but that uniform's a strait jacket. I'd like to see you in a dress, a soft, swirling dress." His eyes looked her up and down as though re-clothing her. "I bought you a dress."

"Help me get these lights up. Then I'll get you the dress. I like to keep you in suspense. He climbed up the ladder. "You have a screwdriver?"

She gave it to him. They installed revolving colored lights in the corners. Rocky handled the wires and lights like a pro. He switched on the lights. The plates revolved and glowed bright red, yellow, and blue.

Kathy held the ladder on which he stood. "Is there anything you can't do?"

He descended the ladder and winked at Kathy. "You haven't sampled my best talents yet. I have impressive resources. Give us time."

"Time!" She had forgotten time. "We have no time. Just tonight. I leave to go overseas tomorrow."

"What?! Tomorrow?" Rocky jumped as though hit. He turned to the ladder. Slowly, with sad eyes, he turned to look at Kathy.

"I'll be back soon. They don't put dietitians on the front lines." When Kathy put a dime in the juke box, it lit up with lights running up and down. The record dropped into place and the music began, *"I'm in love with you, always. When the things you plan, need a helping hand, that's when I'll be there, always. Always."*

Rocky sat at the game table where they had first met over a game of chess. He dropped his chin onto the edge of his hand, and gazed at Kathy.

"The Germans are retreating; the war will be over soon," she said as she sat down beside him. She didn't want to discuss the Battle of the Bulge now underway or the continued war raging in the South Pacific.

Rocky looked at her with eyes that knew just how long a final hour of war could be. His fingers dug into his neck, as though he could rub out the tensions.

"I'd like to see my new dress," Kathy said.

The sagging left his face, and the twinkle of a smile lifted the corners of his eyes. He took her hand, pulled her up to stand beside him. "Let's eat, drink, and be merry. This will be the best party ever. Merrily, merrily, merrily, merrily, life is but a dream. Wait here. I'll bring you the dress."

Back in the barracks, she tried on the dress. It was a filmy sea-green strapless gown with a white edging of soft ruffles around the neck. It fit her snugly, form-fitting to just below the waist, then spread out in full folds that flowed gracefully when she moved. In this dress, bare-shouldered and bare-armed, Kathy felt light and sexy. This was a dress for romance. She dabbed on her Taboo perfume. She took off her dog tags.

The gold heart-shaped ruby-centered locket gleamed alone around her neck.

When Rocky whistled for her at the side door, she considered grabbing her green coat. She wouldn't need it just to cross the ramp to the club. She floated out to him in this swirling dress.

He reacted visibly. His eyes widened. He raised his bushy eyebrows, and grinned. "Wow!" He rubbed his hands on her arms and over her shoulders. "This is the first time I've seen your shoulders." He put his arms around her. The brass buttons of his uniform pressed cold and hard against her. His hands were warm on her back. He whispered, "With you in this dress, I'll not be responsible tonight."

Kathy, dancing with Rocky, knew she was beautiful, gliding in billowing chiffon. Even the club seemed beautiful. The cracks and splinters were hidden in dark shadows, with the only light coming from Rocky's revolving lamps in glowing colors. The dark polished table tops were shiny. The orchestra was impressive, and the laughter melodious.

They danced as never before. Through the thin, silky dress she could feel the movements of his muscles, the pressures of his arm and hand and leg, and respond to them. They danced as one.

In the intermission they sat at a corner table. "Have you ever tasted champagne?" asked Rocky.

"No. I don't need champagne to feel bubbly and giddy. You do that to me."

He brought champagne. She sipped. It tasted good. She sipped again, and danced again, and felt gay and lightheaded. Suddenly, drinking seemed fun! "I'll have another."

Two drinks and she was hanging onto Rocky, keeping her arms around him even when they were not dancing, kissing him right there in the officers' club. No one paid much attention, for everyone was kissing everyone else. Kathy was surprised at herself, feeling so delighted and free.

Rocky responded with admiring passion that flowed through the touch of his hand on her bare shoulder, from his arm around her, and through his wonderful large brown eyes that watched her flowing dress and sought her eyes.

The look in his eyes grew larger and deeper. "Come out to the car where I can really kiss you." He danced her to the door. "Get your coat. My love will keep you warm, but it's snowing outside. Can you manage, or should I come with you?"

"I'm not that light-headed. Only two drinks." They must have been two potent drinks. She floated in to get her coat.

They walked arm in arm across the snow to the car. It was bitter cold, so Rocky started the car to warm up the heater. As he was working the choke and starter, Kathy put her arms around him.

He turned to her. Pushing her coat from her shoulders, he kissed her neck. "I need you. I love you and need you."

"I'm yours. I belong to you. My love is yours." Kathy said. How inadequate were the words to pledge life-long devotion.

"I want to really make love to you." He put his arms under her coat around her waist and held her tight against him. When he kissed her, excitement flowed. "It's up to you," he said.

He sounded too legal. *It was up to her.* Her bare shoulders were cold. She pulled up her coat, clutching it against her chill. But he was right. It was her decision. Decision? Her light head was not deciding, only feeling. She loved him; he loved her. She would do anything to make him happy.

"You'll be perfectly safe," he said.

"Safe?" He must mean safe from having a baby. She hid her face on his shoulder, his Captain's bars cold against her hot cheek.

Rocky put his hands on her cheeks and raised her head. "You won't get into trouble. I'll protect you." He leaned away from her and pulled a tiny package from his pocket.

He was responsible. He needed her. She responded by giving trusting love.

The next morning Rocky drove Kathy to Camp Kilmer in Trenton, New Jersey. They had talked on the way, but all the talk had been light.

Rocky made their plans, as he had been through embarkation when he left for England. "While you wait to be shipped, you can get a pass out every night. I'll meet you here each night at 8-- until you don't come. You might be here an entire week before you depart. When you don't come, I'll know you'll be sailing the next day."

Rocky drove Kathy to Camp Kilmer's heavily guarded gate. The high fence topped with barbed wire, and the gate flanked by armed soldiers looked grimly formidable compared with the unguarded freedom of Castoria.

The MP on the road by the gate stopped the car. Kathy handed Rocky her mimeographed orders, and he passed them on to the guard.

The guard examined the paper, then scowled at Rocky. "These are your orders?"

Rocky grinned. "I am not Kathryn."

Kathy recognized that those words were not funny. "They're mine."

The guard frowned at Rocky. "Let me see your pass."

Rocky reached for his ID card in his wallet. "I have no pass. Just brought my girl over to replace me at the front."

The guard called to the officer on duty, a young Lieutenant. "The Captain has no pass. He had the nurse's orders, sir."

The Lieutenant scowled with dedication to enforcing regulations. "Violation of security measures. Are you in the habit of showing your orders to everyone interested?" he glared at Kathy. "You nurses can't realize you will be going overseas in a convoy. Thousands of troops are endangered because you pass your orders around like a newspaper."

"No sir. I've not shown them to anyone. I got them only yesterday, and just now handed them to Rocky to pass to the guard. And I'm not a nurse. I'm a dietitian."

"If you divulged no information, Lieutenant, then how did this Captain know where to drive you?"

Rocky leaned an elbow patiently out the open window. "I asked at the hospital headquarters. The WAC knew my interests were purely romantic. Lieutenant Collens' movements were more intriguing than troop movements."

The Lieutenant did not laugh. "Lieutenant Collens, you must walk from here to headquarters to sign in." He gestured to the white building just inside the gate.

Kathy, embarrassed, stepped awkwardly from the car. Rocky, undismayed, laughed, and got out of his car. Ignoring the scowls of the guards, he gave Kathy an enthusiastic hug and kiss that should have convinced them that he did not consider her a military objective. Then he drove past the guard to turn around. When the guards waved their guns to stop him, he grinned and waved back. "See you at eight!" he shouted to Kathy. He drove out through the gate and away in his winged Mercury.

# PART II:
# THE WAR IN FRANCE

# CHAPTER 7

# SHIPPED OVERSEAS

The camp looked much like Camp McCoy in Wisconsin, where her initial Army training had occurred. It was a world of rumbling trucks loaded with soldiers in combat fatigues and helmets, and also scurrying Jeeps. But where at Camp McCoy, uniforms had been like costumes at a play, and marching had been a children's game, here at Camp Kilmer the heavy boots were a necessity in the snow. The orange signs pointing to air raid shelters were no mere stage props. The warning siren amplifiers and the long barreled anti-aircraft guns silhouetted against the dark gray sky proved the steel helmets to be genuine protection from real bombs. At Camp McCoy the men had sung as they rode. Here the men sat silent in the backs of heavy trucks.

Kathy waited in the front hall of the headquarters building for a tall, thin, gangly built Lieutenant to finish signing in at the large book. Along his lower left jaw was a long thin scar. When he stepped aside, she took the pen to sign her own name, rank, serial number and unit. His name was above hers: Harry L. Novotny, 2nd Lieutenant, Quartermaster, 0-5863297, 223rd General Hospital. Since he would be in her hospital, she gave him a second look.

He was looking her up and down with heavy-lidded eyes, appraising her. He stepped behind her to read over her shoulder. "223rd? Going that way, myself. I'll drive you over."

That close to him, she could smell alcohol. Why would he drink so early in the afternoon? Nothing better to do? He picked up her suitcase and held open the front door.

After nine months in the Army, confronted with the same situation as when she had first stepped off the train at Camp McCoy, she still didn't know how to handle it. However, she was no longer as quick to judge him. *People were not as simply good or bad as she had once thought.* She didn't want to refuse friendship to anyone. He was part of her new outfit. There couldn't be much danger in riding in an open Jeep with him, so she climbed in.

Attempting a friendly tone, Kathy shouted "I saw your name on the register, Harry Novotny. Where you from?"

"No one calls me Harry." He held up his large hand with long thin fingers as though to strike anyone who dared. "Call me Hooch. From Arkansas."

The only thing she knew of Arkansas was that it was hillbilly country, and so the conversation dropped.

Hooch drove too fast around the corners as he navigated the streets. Finally, he skidded to a stop in front of the low white wooden building and a sign: HEADQUARTERS 223rd GENERAL HOSPITAL.

Inside was one big room with many men working at large desks. At a corner desk worked an imposing bald-headed man with the eagles of a full Colonel on his shoulders, evidently the commanding officer. A thin-faced Captain, wearing the round metal-rimmed glasses the Army furnished for overseas wear, came to them. Standing straight and broad-shouldered, he glared at Hooch, and said sternly, "Lieutenant Novotny, the Colonel has been looking for you."

Hooch shrugged. He turned to Kathy. "I am a procurement artist. Tell me what you need. I'll see they go with company supplies. See you around." He sauntered to the Colonel's desk and sat on it.

"Thanks for the ride." She smiled, though she was glad to see him leave. His brown eyes felt uncomfortable as though they were undressing her. The Captain's blue eyes were nicer. They looked straight and soberly at her face.

Kathy said, "Do you ask him how he gets supplies?"

His eyes twinkled. "You let Hooch get supplies first, and ask questions afterward. Even then he may not answer. Don't bother asking about the scar. I am Captain Keene. You must be Lieutenant Collens. No, I'm not psychic. It's simply that you're the last girl on our roster to arrive. Sign in here. I'm the official greeter and a fellow officer in the 223rd." He fingered his sanitation corps insignia. The lines crinkled around his eyes when he smiled. His face, with a receding chin and small nose, came alive with his smile.

Kathy picked up and looked at the roster she'd just signed. Hers was the tenth, and evidently the last name. "Only ten girls?" There were two physiotherapists, three dietitians, and five Red Cross girls. "What about nurses?"

"That's right, no nurses. There's an acute shortage. There simply are no more available. The Army has trained ward boys to do nurse's work. Each boy learned the job in three months. Nurses who've struggled three years to learn these jobs believe it can't be done. But we have had no choice." He looked at his watch. "In twenty minutes, Kilmer's chief nurse is meeting you girls in your day room for instructions. You'll have to meet the Colonel later." He handed Kathy her suitcase and pointed towards the next door. "Right there. Barracks 34. So long."

The day room was filled with the nine other girls—or women. One was gray haired. One was Bunts. In the roomful of strangers embarking on a strange voyage, she was very glad to see Bunts. Kathy walked to her to put an embracing arm across her shoulder.

Bunts looked around the room, trying to remember names to make introductions. "Lieutenant Vivienne West from Iowa, meet Lieutenant Kathy Collens."

Vivienne stood up with a toss of her shimmering red hair, a gesture that reminded Kathy of someone. Shorter than Kathy, she must have been about five feet tall. Everything about her was tiny, with delicate features and a small, well-proportioned body.

"We've met before." Vivienne recognized Kathy. "Don't you remember Iowa State? Experimental Cookery classes? You went wild with yeast bread—putting everything in it from chopped mint to dried chipped beef."

"I thought I'd seen that hair before." Kathy envied her red hair. "You've cut it." Vivienne had been energetic and practical, finishing her chem lab work quickly to get out to her waiting fiancé. She had been older than most students, so she must now be over thirty. She had been engaged, yet her name remained as West.

"To cover two years in two sentences, I went to Johns Hopkins for my internship, and I've been in the Army just two months longer than you, which makes me the head dietitian."

"Suits me fine. You're a well-organized administrator, and I like therapeutics better." Kathy spoke sincerely. Certainly, Vivienne was well qualified, compared to Lieutenant Groot.

"I just don't remember names," said Bunts with an indifferent shrug. She looked blankly at the third dietitian, who sat rigidly in a chair, with a pale round face and blond hair pulled back in a tight bun. She was the kind of girl, or woman, for she was about thirty, whose name might be forgotten.

Vivienne rescued her with that charming shake of her red hair. "I've been with these girls since the 223rd was activated at Fort Lewis. Meet dietician Mathilda Stevens from King County in Seattle.

Mathilda stood nervously and shook Kathy's hand with a short, quick jerk. She was taller than either of them, and as thin as Vivienne. While Vivienne's slenderness was energetic and lithe, Mathilda's was brittle and flat-chested. "Glad to know you," she said.

Vivienne continued, "This is Sue, our other physiotherapist. Sweet Sue, we call her." Sue was plain, and a little plump. Her hair hung in loose brown waves. Sue offered a limp handshake. She was Kathy's age. Then Sue smiled cheerfully. She certainly would be pleasant to have around.

Vivienne stood beside an attractive Red Cross woman with shining silver hair. "Mrs. Foster, this is Lieutenant Collens." Mrs. Foster stood erect. Her gray Red Cross uniform was unwrinkled and her gray hair brushed into smooth waves. She held out her hand, the red polish smooth on her long nails, making Kathy conscious of her own chipped polish.

"How do you do?" Mrs. Foster shook her hand, gently and firmly, and she smiled politely. She glanced at her watch. She didn't need to say a word. Her glance reminded all of them it was nearly time for the lecture.

Vivienne nodded her understanding. "First meet the rest of the Red Cross. This is Ada, Betty, Doris, and Virginia. Now, there's just time to run to your room and take off your hat and coat."

Kathy nodded to the four girls. All were the wholesome, typical American type that the Red Cross recruited. All wore gray uniforms with their hair short and loosely curled. Each was a little over 25 years old, the age the Red Cross required before sending a girl overseas.

They returned to the day room just as Kilmer's head nurse rapped for attention. "There is much to be done, and few days in which to do it. The very fact that you are going overseas without waiting for nurses—this demonstrates how urgently you are needed." She shook her head as though to wonder what good a hospital could do without nurses. "We don't tell you exactly how many days for security reasons."

"You will begin as of now using the Army Postal Office APO 78-325. Use it as if you had already sailed. Therefore, the sailing date is not revealed by your change in address.

"Your program will consist of training for ship routine—such things as blackout regulations. And you'll practice embarking on life-boats, use of survival rafts, flares, and distilling sea water. We will have drills to prepare for potential U-Boat detections. There'll be lectures about behavior in foreign lands where you'll be representing the United States. You'll get your papers in order—your wills, allotments, insur-ance, and so on.

"The men are allowed, in addition to things on their lists, one per-sonal item each. The Army didn't want to get involved in an argument as to whether nail polish or lipstick is a necessity or a luxury. I think they like to see their women feminine, but aren't willing to declare it a necessity. You are to take a six-month supply of everything necessary. And they have no idea how much lipstick will last six months. So, they look the other way and leave these matters to me, a woman.

"Nurses are respected. The closer the shooting, the more nurses are respected. But I forget, you're not nurses." She shook her head again, sadly. "Well, medical specialists are appreciated. The men will welcome you. But you would be resented if you demand too much special consideration. After all, they have a war to fight, and can't be stopping to bother with you. The Army will give you the best, warmest quarters to live in. The best is sometimes a tent, so you must have warm sleeping bags. You'll have the best available transportation, but the best is usually the back of a truck, and you'll need warm clothes. The men will carry your footlockers and bedrolls, and carry them willingly. But gallantry would weaken if your luggage were too heavy, so do not fill your footlockers with too many books or bottles."

The head nurse looked at her notes. "Four-hour passes are available each evening, until alerted. Here on the post are complete recreation facilities including movies, officers club, and so on. Available to everyone except Lieutenant Collens. She is restricted to the post as a security precaution. Does anyone want a pass?"

No one did, and she continued. "You'll meet tomorrow with the entire hospital staff at 0800 in the assembly room. If there are no questions, dismissed."

Vivienne walked beside Kathy as they turned into the hall toward their room. "You won't miss a pass. It's more exciting on the post." She left the question unasked.

"I was counting on it, to see my boyfriend, which is why I can't go. No need to be tactful about it," laughed Kathy. "My boyfriend ignores the laws and regulations he doesn't like. He saw no reason why he couldn't drive me right to our headquarters. The guards at the gate disagreed. To them I'm a military secret. So now he's a security risk—and I don't get out."

In their room, Bunts took her guitar from her footlocker and sat on the bed leaning against the wall. "This is the one luxury I'm taking along."

Kathy put her suitcase on her bed to unpack. "What do you hear from Tex?"

Bunts strummed her guitar, dreamily picking out the tune "I'll Be Seeing You." "In his last letter, Tex was in Italy. He said he was eating spaghetti. Maybe just maybe, I'll be seeing him in Italy. Has anyone heard any hints about where we're going? Maybe Italy?"

Vivienne had taken a tiny crochet hook from her purse and began mending a run in a nylon stocking. "If the Army hinted about Italy, we'd go to the South Pacific. I joined the 223rd Hospital at Fort Lewis, near Seattle. I was certain we were headed for the Philippines. That looked good to me because that's where my Stan is. But we went from Seattle to New Jersey." She shook her coppery hair... "Who can understand the military mind?"

"Stan?" asked Kathy. "I thought his name was Bill."

"It was Bill at Iowa State. He wanted to get married when I graduated, and I wanted to finish my dietetic internship. Bill married an Iowa girl. He said he wouldn't wait and he didn't. I met Stan at Hopkins."

Kathy said, "I had hoped we'd go to France because I had two years of French. But if we go to Italy, I'll learn Italian." She turned to Bunts. "One afternoon you had with Tex. How can you be so sure? You should meet him again. Wouldn't it be romantic to meet up with him on the French Riviera? Or maybe go to England. But London's not as romantic as Paris."

Bunts strummed and strummed her guitar. "Who needs glamour? Where was the glamour when you met Rocky in Ohio? You can't call the officers' club at Castoria romantic."

"Depends on what you mean by romantic. There were more lusty romances per square foot there than anywhere in the world."

"Would you care where, if you were near your man?"

Mathilda folded her checklist, carefully matching the corners, and put it in her notebook. "Dreams! Romantic nonsense." She stood tall. "Have you checked your equipment? You lie there and dream while there's work to be done. The Army is for fighting a war."

Sue opened her eyes. "Romantic dreams keep us going. We're better off with our dreams than Mrs. Foster is with her nightmares. She was divorced six months ago."

Vivienne examined her mending. "You'd think with all her psychiatric training, doesn't a psychiatric social worker have a master's degree, she could have salvaged her own marriage."

Kathy pondered. "If the poised Mrs. Foster with all her psychology couldn't keep her marriage, who could? What was love?"

After the morning's training session, Kathy was told to report to Colonel Stone at headquarters. As she approached his desk, she wondered when was the proper moment to salute. The Colonel looked more fatherly than formidable, so she merely waited by his desk for his attention.

The Colonel reached behind his desk. From under it, he took a pair of black four-buckle overshoes, and handed them to Kathy. "A Captain Rockford tried to bring these to you this morning. He was detained for questioning. He could get into trouble for trying to get in without a pass, and of course, the boots were searched. This message was found in the toe."

He handed her a torn scrap of paper. Kathy read the sprawled writing. "Bon Voyage. Love, Rocky."

"They are my boots. I must have left them in his car. Surely, he's not still in the guard house just because of my boots."

"No, he's been sent back to his hospital. The Army is not trusting or romantic as they are too involved in fighting a war." The Colonel watched the snow blowing against the window. "You'd better put on your boots. There's a cold winter ahead."

"Thank you, sir." Kathy saluted him, and left. She stopped at the front door to buckle her overshoes.

After four days of preparation, the staff of two hospitals, the 223rd and her sister hospital, the 222nd, were alerted to board the ship. The girls' foot lockers and bed rolls were loaded onto trucks.

The girls were dressed for war and winter. Each had on long woolen underwear, combat fatigues with liners, a woolen shirt, a trench coat with a liner, both plastic and knit woolen helmet liners, along with the steel helmet itself. Each wore a gas mask on the left hip, a purse on the right and a musette bag on the back. Along with long wool stockings, heavy combat boots and four-buckle overshoes were worn.

Each girl was assigned a number. Kathy was A1, probably because her name came first in the alphabet, and so was first in formation. They marched, or rather, waddled, to waiting trucks in the dark. No lights were allowed. The darkness was to hide them from enemy eyes. "Why bother?" asked Vivienne. "Not even the enemy would give us women a second look in these outfits."

The trucks carried them to waiting trains. Silently, as though to talk would be to tell the Germans secrets, they walked from trucks to the designated train cars. This was it. They were on their way.

The trains were unheated. Windows on the train were broken. Snow blowing in remained un-melted on the wooden seats.

Mrs. Foster looked with disgust at the broken glass. "There's no excuse for that. Not in our civilized United States."

Kathy said nothing, but was not surprised. One didn't go off to war in a heated limousine.

The long wait while the troops boarded the train in the dark was soberly, silently dramatic. Comfortable in her warm Army clothes, Kathy watched helmeted soldiers marching by with duffle bags on their shoulders. Kathy felt that she was part of an unreal haunting movie.

They rode the lightless train to New York, where trucks carried them to a ferry. Waves lapping against the hull were the only sound. The girls quietly boarded first. On the ferry, they stood facing the ocean, bearing the unbroken force of the wind. From the ferry, their ship loomed large in the blackness.

Once at the ship, they began to board. As Kathy led the march with the nine women following, the soldiers whistled and cheered. Since all the girls had done was march, the applause was surprising. She accepted it in terms of what the women stood for. They were ministering angels who would care for soldiers. The spirit was good.

A naval officer guided them across the deck on the ship. He led them down and around a flight of metal stairs, along a corridor, down more stairs, and along more corridors. "Wait here," he said before leaving.

"Wait? What? We just want to get to our cabins. Where do we go?" Vivienne shouted after him. "Hey!" He kept walking.

She turned and asked the girls, "What's his rank?" and got no response.

"Admiral!" she shouted again after the retreating officer as he rounded the corner.

"One minute we're welcomed like angels! And in the next they can't be bothered to show us our rooms."

He was gone. They waited.

"Let's look for our cabins," said Kathy.

"This is a big ship," said Vivienne.

They waited. Mathilda took off her metal helmet, her plastic helmet liner, and then her knit helmet liner. The neat bun of her yellow hair was slipping. She took out her hairpins and put them in again, nervously. "Oh dear," she muttered. "They might not miss us until morning. They might not find us for days."

Vivienne laughed. "The Colonel would send out a search party!"

"We should have never boarded this ship without K-rations," said Kathy.

Vivienne took off her helmet and the liners. Her copper-red hair blazed under the ship's electric light bulbs. "Hey! Let's get noticed!"

"There are three thousand soldiers on this ship," groused Mathilda.

They waited. They huddled together as though one girl cut off alone in the hold of this ship might never find her way to the deck again.

Finally, an MP found them and guided them to their cabin, guarded by another MP.

It was a gray room with double bunks and a narrow metal table. There were hooks on the walls for hanging, and blackout curtains over the portholes. Immediately they started undressing for bed. "Turn out the lights so we can look out," Vivienne said.

With the lights out, they lifted the heavy black curtains, but could see nothing. "Let's go on deck to see out," said Kathy.

Vivienne shook her head. "No. We have finally gotten a bed. We'd better wait until it's light. Besides, I'm not getting lost in that hold again."

"Turn on the light." It was Mathilda's voice. "I'm seasick."

Vivienne flipped on the light. Mathilda hurried into the latrine.

"That is purely psychological," said Mrs. Foster. "There's no motion yet to make her sick."

"You can be certain that it's her stomach that's throwing up," said Vivienne.

"The whole body is affected by subconscious inhibitions and repressions. She's the victim of repressed sex impulses."

"Now that's a practical diagnosis," laughed Vivienne. "Let's invite ten men in here, and then we won't be seasick."

"It's five AM," said Sue. "Maybe we can sleep a couple of hours before it's time to get up."

The sound of engines woke Kathy to a gray dawn. She and Vivienne put on bulky life jackets and found their way up to the deck. The railing was lined with Navy sailors in khaki uniforms.

The New York skyline could be seen in the faint morning light as the ship was pushed by tugs into the harbor. Above them loomed gun stations with their long muzzles reaching to the clouded sky. A shrill whistle blew from a loud speaker. Sailors bundled in pea jackets ran to the gun stations, tore canvas covers from the guns, and waited. Ahead was a convoy of twenty ships that included troop ships, battleships, and destroyers. The tugs left, and their ship went past the Statue of Liberty under its own power to take its place in the convoy.

"Those can shoot," said Vivienne, looking up at the guns and sailors. "I can believe it when they said they wouldn't stop to pick me up if I fell overboard."

"They'd pick up a girl," said Kathy.

"I wouldn't test it."

Four officers from their hospital walked against the wind toward them and exchanged good mornings.

"Good to see all of you again," said Captain Keene, who had initially checked everyone in.

Chaplain Kirkemo was an Irish priest from Boston. He had warm and inviting green eyes, and a playful smile. "You girls all good sailors?"

"Mathilda's a bit seasick. We'll let you know about the others when they wake up." Kathy said.

Major Fellows, a surgeon, with dark eyes and dark hair, leaned on the rail and gazed morosely at the white-capped waves. "The weather is miserable. Cold. Overcast. Dismal."

Captain Keene's blue eyes glistened behind his round steel-rimmed glasses. "Not unusual for January."

Chaplain Kirkemo's face was kind. He had a look of quiet, listening interest. "I suspect this is a more dismal January for Major Fellows here than for most of us. He's closed up three offices of his medical practice to be here. I've left only one."

"You have three offices?" asked Kathy.

"Had three," said Major Fellows. "Now there are none. With such a need for surgeons, I decided it was my patriotic duty to join the war effort. Yet, I've got one young daughter at home, and another on the way."

Vivienne turned to the Special Services Officer. "What do you have to take our minds off the stormy weather?"

"To counteract the loneliness of war for 3,000 men we have a rec room that holds 200 men, equipped with cards, paperback books, and a phonograph. We can dance with you girls. And a ship's newspaper. Would you girls like to be reporters?"

Kathy shook her head. "I couldn't think of a thing to say."

He grinned. "Anything a girl would say on this ship would be news."

"Nonsense," said Vivienne. "Everything a girl does here is watched by hundreds of men, and would be well known before the paper came out."

"You can type?" he pressed on.

"All right. I can type," Kathy responded.

Captain Keene pulled over the flap of his trench coat and buttoned the top of his coat. "I was editor of our school paper, and I can type. I can help."

"On the chance that we might be sailing to France," said the Chaplain, "anyone want to study French with me?"

"Yes," said Kathy. "I brought along a French text. I'd appreciate your help."

"*Moi aussi*, me too." said Captain Keene.

"After our morning training sessions, *bien*?"

"OK. Fine, or good, or '*bien,*' as you say."

Vivienne shook her head. "While on a ship, I'm going to see a ship." She marched off.

At dinner, Vivienne told Kathy one of the Navy officers she had met had invited Vivienne to his cabin to listen to records. She would not go alone, and asked Kathy to come along as a chaperone. The officer would bring a friend. That evening, they listened to records and heard stories of life in the Navy.

The next day, after her French lesson and a newspaper-writing session, Kathy walked alone up to the windy deck. She was dressed in fatigues, field jacket, combat boots and an overstuffed life jacket. Hardly a glamorous outfit, but it was warm. Several sailors were scrubbing decks, their water splashing and blowing. An officer in a gun turret was working with sailors on an anti-aircraft gun. Others were checking lifeboat equipment. Groups of soldiers lounged on the decks, sitting in corners out of the wind.

Vivienne's new friend, the commander, walked along the deck toward Kathy. "See how hard the Navy works, while your Army bums sit around."

Kathy defended the Army. "We'd work if there was anything for us to do."

"Would you work?" he said.

"Sure." She could type. She could supervise cooking.

"OK. Swab the decks."

Kathy opened her mouth to shout an indignant "No," but stopped when she saw the young and friendly faces of the sailors who were scrubbing. She could not say scrubbing was beneath her or too menial. She answered, "All right. Give me a mop."

The sailors grinned with delight to see her pushing a mop.

"I've swabbed decks for years on a boat on Lake Michigan. The deck was smaller, but the idea's the same." She grabbed the mop with vigorous enthusiasm. She swung the mop up into the air. The dirty water splattered across the face of the commander.

He wiped off the drizzle with a white handkerchief. "You win. I'll find something safer for you."

He took Kathy on a tour of the ship. On the bridge, he let her take over the helm. Piloting this huge ship in a crowded convoy of battleships and destroyers was like piloting their little boat, at least for a few minutes. She poured over the charts trying to follow their navigation. In the radio room she watched the amazing green lights on the fabulous new secret radar.

Two bells rang on the ship indicating 1300 Army time. It was time for the staff meeting. Kathy ran down to the recreation room. She found an empty chair at one of the back tables where the well-groomed Mrs. Foster and the steely-eyed Captain Keene were already seated.

Mrs. Foster put her smoothly polished fingers on Kathy's arm. "You know, my dear, that we in the Red Cross are not partial to any service. However, I might suggest the Army does not appreciate that you and Vivienne give so much attention to the Navy. On a ship, the Navy's got an unfair advantage. And certainly, my dear, it is undignified for an Army officer to be scrubbing Navy decks."

"From what I saw," said Captain Keene, "the Army won that round. The Navy got the wrong end of the mop, and all in innocence. The sailors will love our Kathy for that."

Mrs. Foster frowned. "Captain Charles Keene! Don't encourage her!"

"Bosh to dignity," said Kathy. "With a whole ship to look at, you can't expect me to play cribbage all day with the Army. Tell whoever complains that I'm good on a ship. Any ship. I should check up on the Navy once in a while."

Captain Keene put his hand beside Mrs. Foster's on Kathy's arm. "True, and you'll be working with the Army for the duration."

His voice was so nice and his eyes so kind that Kathy decided she was being a little foolish, and she would confine her sisterly attachments to the Army.

Colonel Stone at the front of the room proceeded with instructions for a lifeboat drill. Kathy looked around at the crowd of soldiers. Considering the number of men and the number of lifeboats, she concluded a "raft drill" would be a better title.

After the drill, Kathy stayed on deck with Captain Keene. They watched the waves in silence. Kathy liked the hypnotic surges of blue and green, ever-swelling, ever restless. Around them, floated a multitude of ships.

"Magnificent, isn't it?" His voice was vibrant and strong. "Ships as far as the eye can see. A sight to remember."

"How many ships?" asked Kathy

"This convoy has 39 ships. The ships are assembled in a formation nine columns wide and spans 20 miles long. Escort vessels are equipped with radar, and circle the convoy. They will detect any U-Boats long before they can be dangerous. By sailing in a convoy, ships are protected."

"One U-Boat facing this group wouldn't have a chance," said Kathy.

"That's the idea. When the war began, Germany was determined to stop England's source of supplies, all from the sea. During their "happy times" the German U-Boats sunk thousands of merchant ships with millions of tons of supplies. Then, the Allies developed a system of convoys escorted by warships providing a protective shield. The warships now have radar and sonar and could detect submarines before they had a chance to launch torpedoes. The tables had finally turned. The hunters became the hunted."

Overhead the guns burst out in a volley of noise. The wind blew away the sound of the guns that sounded like loudly popping balloons. The tracer bullets arched over to a target that floated high in the air behind a destroyer.

When the guns were finally quiet, they could hear the splash of the waves again. Captain Keene said, "That is sobering. I'd almost forgotten about war."

"They say it's just target practice," said Kathy. "I'd forgotten about war, too, and was thinking of my boyfriend Rocky. He likes the ocean, and hopefully someday we will sail together on a sailboat, not a warship."

The crossing took seven days. There were stormy days when Kathy stood warm in her hooded rubber raincoat in the bow of the ship enjoying the salt water spray, unless a seaman ordered her below. There were sunny, peaceful days of lounging on the deck studying French, and long evenings of card games and dancing.

The ship stopped off the coast of England. They were told that afternoon to eat a hearty supper. Kathy made two extra sandwiches. Early that evening the ship left for France. Finally, they were aware of their destination.

As they neared France, the coast rose sharp and clear against the moonlit sky. An LST, or Landing Ship Tank, awaited them at the port of Le Havre. With no dock, the LST would bridge the gap between land and sea.

The ten women were the first down the gangplank onto the LST. Then they waited while the others crowded on. It was cold. Bitter cold. Kathy danced in place to stay warm. When Kathy complained that her musette bag was heavy, a Lieutenant lifted her by the bag's straps and briefly hung her on a hook on the side of the barge, to everyone's great amusement.

Vivienne said, "My helmet doesn't fit right."

A soldier standing next to her took it. "I'll adjust the webbing." Looking inside of it he exclaimed, "You have a book in your helmet!" and slammed it back on her head. Then, he took Kathy's helmet, "What do you have in yours?"

"Sandwiches."

He shook his head.

The moon was bright. A quiet breeze rippled the water. The loading operation was eerily soundless except for an occasional hushed order, "Move forward. Cuddle up."

"How many men will be loaded onto this ship?" asked Kathy.

Vivienne responded, "They said this LST can carry up to 20 Sherman tanks. Not sure how many men will be jammed on. They just announced to make room for 100 more."

With the barge finally loaded, an officer on the gangplank gave directions. The ladies were to travel in a truck to a Red Cross chateau, or castle, here in Le Havre. The men would drive the rest of the night to their staging area, Camp Lucky Strike.

Staying here in Le Havre, Kathy determined she had no need for the sandwiches in her helmet. She handed them to the man next to her. "Want sandwiches? Cheese sandwiches?"

"Thank you…thank you very much." She recognized Captain Keene's tenor voice.

The motors of the LST started up with a loud roar. Slowly the barge drove across the water to the shore. The front end lowered to make a broad bridge to the shallow water, allowing passengers to walk onto the shore. The girls were first. Kathy stepped from the LST over the foot-wide strip of water, landing on the dry land. Then she reconsidered, turned around, and hopped back onto the LST. This time, she stepped carefully into the shallow water so she could say she had waded ashore.

Unloaded, the barge left. Minutes later the last of the men drove away in the waiting trucks. The ten women stood alone on the beach with a young Lieutenant from the port in charge.

"Where is our truck?" asked Vivienne.

"That is a good question," said the Lieutenant. After a few minutes he decided, "I'll find out what happened to your truck." He jumped in his Jeep and drove off.

Now the girls stood on the deserted beach, surrounded only by ruins of the heavily bombed area. Not a building was in sight except a tiny lightless shack that looked like an outhouse, about a quarter mile down the beach. There was no sound but the quiet lapping of the waves. Alone in the cold, they waited.

Bunts found flat stones, and threw them skipping across the water.

As Mathilda stood shivering she said, "German snipers might come out of hiding at night here."

Vivienne surveyed the beach. So completely had the harbor area been bombed that not even the stump of a tree or section of a wall was left standing. "They'd have a tough time sneaking up on us. There's not a rock large enough for a Kraut to hide behind."

Mathilda looked at the shack, and shuddered.

"I want a cigarette," said Vivienne. As she crouched low, the others huddled around her to hide the light and maintain the blackout. The light of the match burned dangerously bright.

A loud roar swelled up the beach. Three airplanes flew overhead towards them, dark against the sky.

Vivienne cupped her hand over her glowing cigarette tip. "Can you tell German planes from American planes?"

"No," said Kathy, "But Germans wouldn't waste a bomb on this rubble."

Vivienne glanced at their ship out at sea riding at anchor, and lowered her cigarette into the ocean.

Several men came out from the shack to look at the planes.

"Those must be Allied planes," said Kathy, "or our men wouldn't come out."

"Or those aren't our men." Mathilda's teeth were chattering.

"I'll bet they're Americans, and I'll bet they have a stove," said Kathy.

Seeing the girls on the beach, the men walked toward them. As they approached, their Army uniforms became visible. When the girls were invited into the shack for hot coffee, they did not hesitate. The squat, pot-bellied stove gave a warm heat that toasted their noses, fingers, and toes. Mathilda finally stopped shivering.

"Allow me," said a GI, and poured coffee from a pot setting on the stove top. The lip of his canteen cup was so hot it burned Kathy's lips. While they waited for the cups to cool, the men asked for news of baseball teams. Baseball in January! Bunts knew and answered all their questions. The soldiers asked about their home states. One soldier, an ex-paint salesman from Urbana, became Kathy's special friend just because they were both from Illinois.

It was amazing how warm was the friendship they felt for these unshaven boys who shared their warm stove.

The soldier who seemed to be in charge commented. "The Battle of the Bulge continues just 300 miles from here in the Ardennes Forest. We're working to get supplies from the ships here to the front. Our soldiers were caught unprepared. Coldest weather on record in 40 years. Trench foot, pneumonia, frostbite. Can you imagine? They are wearing summer footwear as no winter uniforms had been issued."

He continued, "It's been a brutal battle, and it's not over. The Germans even sent in their SS. They massacred 84 American prisoner near Malmedy. Just took them out into a field and shot them. At Bastogne, the Germans surrounded our troops, including paratroopers from the 101st Airborne. Tried to starve them out, but they never gave up. Luckily, the weather cleared a bit, just enough for air support to have a go at the Germans and make a badly needed supply drop. General George S. Patton stormed in as well to provide some relief."

The soldier from Illinois said, "There have been significant casualties. Hopefully you can get your hospital functional soon, and closer to the action. It's been one of the bloodiest battles of the war. You are needed."

Vivienne responded. "Hot meals for soldiers are our specialty. But nothing is getting done while we sit here!"

Finally, the Lieutenant returned with his Jeep and a Sergeant with a truck. "Want a moonlit sight-seeing tour of Le Havre before you hit the sack?" asked the Sergeant. Of course, they did.

The Sergeant explained. "Le Havre is one of the largest ports in France, second only to Marseille in southern France. Early in the war, the Germans captured Le Havre. This would be their primary naval base from which they planned to invade England. Most civilians left the area. The Germans fortified the town with pill boxes and artillery batteries, well integrated into the Atlantic Wall along the ocean. The Allies successfully liberated this port just a few months ago—but only after the city had been bombed extensively to weaken the Nazi's stronghold. Despite having almost nothing left but rubble and ash, Le Havre is now one of the Allies' key logistical hubs.

"Several temporary tent cities have been built in France for soldiers awaiting deployment to combat operations. The "Cigarette Camps" are named after cigarettes, including Camp Pall Mall and Camp Philip Morris. Soldiers arriving here will go to Camp Lucky Strike."

The girls rode in the back of the truck. Near the harbor, amidst the rubble, they could see silhouettes of an occasional jagged tree trunk or ragged stone foundations. Further inland, larger segments of buildings remained standing. Kathy saw, amongst shattered buildings, a single wall, with the moon shining through its gaping window. The truck bounced over pitted roads. Finally, they arrived in the residential section that had suffered lesser damage. The truck stopped at a large chateau, square except for an upper corner that had been blown off.

The Sergeant helped the women jump from the back of the truck. He then knocked at the front door. No answer. He banged louder.

A large woman answered the door. Her trench coat with Captain's bars and nurses' insignia had been pulled on over her pajamas. "What do you want at four in the morning?"

"These girls are to be billeted here," said the Sergeant.

"No. Not here. No room. My girls have every cot," barked the nurse.

"My orders are to billet them here," persisted the Sergeant.

The nurse stood squarely in the doorway. "No beds here."

The Lieutenant drove up in his Jeep. "What's the trouble?" He walked up the front steps to look past the nurse's shoulder into the front hall. "Where's the Corporal in charge of these quarters?"

The nurse looked around. The Corporal was not in sight. "Corporal!" she bellowed.

The Corporal came down the stairs into the front hall.

She stamped toward him, evacuating the front door. "What were you doing up there with nurses, young man?"

"Drinking Scotch."

The nurse took a deep breath, but before she could explode, the Lieutenant stepped past her to speak to the Corporal. "Do you have cots for ten girls?"

"No sir, but we do have blankets. They can sleep on the floor."

The girls of the 223rd walked past the nurse, who continued to be in a state of shock, and went upstairs. Stopping only to take off helmets, gas masks, musette bags, purses and boots, the girls rolled up in the blankets on the floor. The moon shone through the large hole in the roof.

In the morning, still dressed in the same combat suits, the girls were driven in a truck to a majestic chateau for breakfast. In the dining room, they ate at an ornately carved cherry table, and sat on scarlet velvet chairs amidst walls of lustrous silk damask. After breakfast they rode in a truck back to the harbor. They were then loaded onto a duck boat for a land-to-water tour around their ship. They waved to friends from the other 222nd hospital who had not yet debarked.

Finally, the women from both the 222nd and the 223rd were gathered together and loaded into two trucks. They drove with a convoy of a dozen truckloads of men through the French countryside.

They had fresh oranges on the ship, and one of the girls had kept her breakfast orange. She sat at the open end, tossing that orange in the air, and catching it. Whenever the trucks stopped, children crowded around the back of the truck to gaze at the gleaming orange. Finally, the girl could stand it no longer, and tossed the orange out to the excited children. Such delight over one orange!

There were no filling stations with public restrooms in France. Twice, the convoy stopped beside vineyards where the men gained privacy simply by turning their backs. But there was not even a clump of bushes for the women, and so they waited.

That evening the trucks stopped in a little village for gas. There was no filling station, just an Army shed full of jerry-cans of gasoline. In the village were three old-world shops that were closed for the night, and a few houses.

Several GIs gathered to help the girls down from the trucks. Kathy and Vivienne jumped into their outstretched arms. Bunts vaulted out on her own. Mrs. Foster, attempting dignity, backed out, cautiously reaching for the two hanging steps. Mathilda came last, peering fearfully at the strange steep houses. The others stayed in the trucks.

"This is the France that we've seen in pictures," said Kathy.

"Picturesque, yes," agreed Mrs. Foster. "Let's see if they have plumbing."

Vivienne led the way, "Kathy, did the good Chaplain Kirkemo include 'asking for a bathroom' in his French lessons? Let's ask at this first house."

An MP escorted the five girls, determined to keep them in sight at all times. Vivienne knocked boldly at the first door.

A thin woman, her head covered with a shawl, opened the door. Kathy explained they were American nurses, simpler to say they were nurses, looking for a bathroom, or "*la salle de bain*." The Frenchwoman shook her head, not understanding.

"Toilette." This might be the key word. Even when Kathy repeated it, the woman looked perplexed. Kathy spelled. Then she understood. Regretfully, she had no toilet.

They hurried to the next house, for they did not want to keep the dozen truckloads of men waiting. But there was no bathroom. Could they please use whatever the French used? The French just looked puzzled and shut the door. Finally, it was suggested that there was a chateau a quarter mile down the road where American officers were billeted. Surely, they would have a bathroom.

The chateau was a large stone building with a wrought iron fence. They knocked at the massive front door. An American officer opened the door and welcomed them with shouts of joy. "American girls! Let's have a party! Get out the champagne!"

"Please," said Vivienne. "We just want to use a bathroom."

The man embraced her. "Call the others! A party! Girls! Call the commanding officer!"

"We have to talk to the commanding officer to use a bathroom?" Vivienne asked.

Other officers ran out to pull the girls into the spacious front hall.

Mrs. Foster raised her voice to be heard above the whooping welcome. "A convoy of trucks is waiting for us to find a bathroom. Will you please show us…"

"No party?!" The Lieutenant was disappointed. Then he added, embarrassed, "We don't have a bathroom."

"We do have a slit trench," offered another. He led them, still escorted by their military policeman, across a field to an open-topped canvas enclosure.

The girls found a single hole, one foot wide by five feet in length. They viewed it with suspicion. It was not easy to get their pants down, encumbered with gas mask, purse, musette bag, long winter underwear, woolen liners, combat pants, trench coat liner and trench coat. Kathy managed as she had been instructed about slit trenches in basic training, and showed others. They helped each other in buttoning back up their pants.

When they left the open-roofed enclosure, the men were doubled up with laughter. *"C'est la guerre,"* the girls shrugged. "That's war. It cannot be helped."

"It's a man's war," said Kathy. "It should be *le guerre*, not *la guerre*."

They hurried to the waiting convoy of trucks only to find the men were just organizing a search party.

They drove on in the dark with no headlights. About midnight the two trucks carrying the girls left the convoy. They turned off the road and through a massive gate with stone towers on either side. They had reached the Castle of Mesnieres. Inside the gate they drove over a moat on a drawbridge and entered an area where they could see the enormous castle. Six slender, pointed towers loomed against the sky in picturesque medieval style. By the light of the moon and two flashlights, the thirty-eight girls crossed a courtyard and entered a tall gothic-arched door in one of the towers.

Château de Mesnières

As they climbed a narrow winding stone staircase, their flashlight beams fell on life-sized suits of armor and axes. When they arrived in the gigantic banquet room, the moonlight dimly showed forty cots in three rows. Two blankets were folded at the foot of each cot.

Vivienne laughed. "Imagine that. The Army has a haunted castle." She tossed her musette bag onto a cot, and brushed back her hair with a flippant gesture.

"Haunted with romance," Kathy said. "Look, there's a raised platform at the end, where the king and queen must have eaten. I want a cot up there." She handed her flashlight to Mathilda. "You can use this to chase ghosts away. I like the dark, to more easily imagine royal banquets."

"Ghosts are repressed sex symbols," Mrs. Foster muttered to Kathy.

"No heat." Vivienne had her hand on a tall thin stove. "The fire is out."

"I found a bathroom!" called Bunts. "One convenience for 36 women."

"Supper is ready. Downstairs," shouted a Sergeant from the door.

Mathilda spread the blanket on her cot. "I'm too nervous to eat. I'll just roll up in these blankets." Mathilda took off her shoes and lay on her cot.

"I'll bring something for you to eat," said Kathy, "if you're awake. It's likely you are tired because you have had nothing to eat."

Taking one flashlight, leaving the other upstairs, they felt their way down the spiral staircase. In another gigantic room, lit by gasoline lamps, a hot supper was waiting. The cooking stoves had warmed the room just a little, but no one took off their trench coat. They unhooked their mess kits from their belts and dished up delicious corned beef hash. They were warmly grateful to these GIs who had stayed up half the night to cook for them.

After supper, they made up their beds. Two blankets would not be enough to keep them warm in the damp, freezing, drafty castle, so they didn't undress. Even with her coat and two blankets, Kathy was miserably cold.

The next morning a French boy came in to build the fires. The stoves smoked so badly they had to open the windows—so they were no warmer.

Mathilda went back to bed after breakfast. Mrs. Foster went hunting for a telephone to call Red Cross headquarters in Paris. The nurses played bridge on their cots or wrote letters. Bunts, Vivienne, and Kathy went for a walk.

In a nearby village, Kathy tried to learn the history of the castle from an old baker. She couldn't understand him so he gave her a book. She read the book with her dictionary. The descendants of Prince Charles, a minor prince, had been forced to sell the castle to King Louis XV in 1766. During the revolution, the land was confiscated, divided, and sold as small lots. No one had bought the castle, so it was given to a monastery who used it for an orphanage. It had continued to be used until the Germans took it over. Now that the Americans had it, it was used as a nurses' staging area.

If the orphans could stand the cold, Kathy felt she should not complain. The building looked unchanged from the fifteenth century. They half expected the suits of armor to start moving and speaking, or a plumed knight gallop across the drawbridge on a horse.

For two weeks they practiced French with the villagers or played bridge. In the evening, officers from their hospital drove in from the nearby Camp Lucky Strike for a visit or to take a hot shower. The bath house with the hot shower was in a small building adjacent to the castle, and required a short walk in the chilling cold. Kathy was never sure which was more enticing to the visiting soldiers, the feminine company or the hot water.

The men brought news of the progress in setting up the hospital. An advance party had scouted Northeastern France, hunting for a suitable place to house the hospital. They found an old French cavalry post located in a small town called Suippes, which was 26 miles east of Reims, and 100 miles from the front. Some of the men had already moved there, temporarily living in tents while buildings were cleaned and repaired.

For this work, some German PWs, or prisoners of war, had been requisitioned. As soon as it was in livable condition, supplies would be shipped in. Then the rest of the hospital staff would move into buildings nearby. Progress was moving, but for now, the girls would have to wait.

At Mesnieres, the weather remained cold and damp. Hours were spent in efforts to fix the stoves. Endless adjustments of damper and drafts and varying amounts and kinds of wood were tried, seeking some combination that would end the smoking. The stoves were never repaired and the room never warmed.

Not once in this time had Kathy been warm, despite wearing long woolen underwear under her pajamas. She even lined her cot with large paper bags. Nothing seemed to help. The only exception was the few minutes in a hot shower. However, by the time she had run back across the courtyard in the freezing cold with wet hair, she was thoroughly chilled again.

The men from Camp Lucky Strike told them they were rationed to one helmet full of coal a day. They spent their days huddled around stoves in their tents. When they came to visit, they declared the castle warm, and the hot showers a downright luxury. On the front lines, in the Battle of the Bulge, American soldiers were literally freezing in their foxholes. And so, it didn't occur to the girls to complain, but simply to shrug, "*C'est la guerre.*"

# CHAPTER 8

# A NEAR-DEATH EXPERIENCE

After three weeks in the castle, most of the girls had coughs and sniffles. Kathy reported to the infirmary, a room in the tower. She received a bottle of cough syrup, which didn't sooth her rasping throat. Upon returning, she crawled into her sleeping bag, rattling the paper sacks lining her cot, hoping the warmth would ease the ache in her back.

Mrs. Foster sat on the next cot polishing her nails. "You know, sleep can be an escape mechanism. Back to the womb you crawl."

Mrs. Foster found a psychological basis for everything. The prevalent colds had an emotional basis. The castle towers and surrounding moat were sex symbols. Everything in Mrs. Foster's world was labeled male or female. Every opening, cup, and keyhole was female. Every bump, bottle, or pencil was male. In her world, no one was rational—just driven.

Kathy considered herself no more than normally frustrated. She was too tired to argue, and her back hurt. "If sleeping, is escaping, it's a better escape than drinking."

Vivienne sat behind Mrs. Foster, knitting socks. "Now, really. It's rational to get in a warm sleeping bag when it's cold. Kathy is rational. I'm rational too."

Mrs. Foster watched Vivienne's knitting needles slipping in and out of loops of yarn, "Did you know that knitting is a form of masturbation?"

Vivienne calmly continued knitting. "You do it your way, and I'll do it mine."

An hour later Kathy woke up and vomited. Her back was now throbbing with much pain, so she returned to the infirmary, and was kept there for the night.

By morning her body was a mass of petechial hemorrhages with red spots of blood seeping under her skin. She was carried down the narrow spiral staircase, slipping and sliding. An ambulance rushed her to an Army hospital in Rouen.

The doctor in the admitting room took one look at her and started shouting orders. She was carried to a single room where isolation was established. Staff used protective gloves and masks.

Within fifteen minutes, two doctors, two nurses and a laboratory technician, all in white gowns, were working on her at the same time. One doctor injected a medicine, another inserted a long needle into her spine for a spinal tap. A nurse set up a bottle of plasma and a rubber tube on a high iron hook. The laboratory technician poked a needle into a vein at her elbow for a blood sample.

The other nurse gave her sulfa tablets to swallow with water—which Kathy immediately threw up—and she held a basin for her. Again, the nurse gave Kathy sulfa tablets and water.

Eventually they all left except for one nurse who sat on a chair at the head of the bed, and a doctor who stood beside her. He gently touched Kathy's leg, lightly because pressure could break more blood vessels and make more red spots. His face was covered by a mask, but his eyes were filled with a tenderness and compassion. He, who had never seen Kathy before this morning, actually cared about her. He spoke in a voice as tender as his eyes. "The pain is bad, isn't it?"

Her back and every joint were racked with pain. Her neck ached, her elbows ached, her shoulders ached. Her hips, knees, and ankles hurt. But that was in her body, which was now somehow separate. The pain, though excruciating, was not important. "Yes, I suppose it is," she answered, smiling.

The doctor pulled the sheet down, and put his fingers on her arm, delicately pinching her skin to test its elasticity. "You're a brave girl."

He must have thought she was smiling bravely. Yet, this was not courage. It was an indifference to pain that was in a separate body. This she could not explain.

She said instead, "The sheets feel clean." How many times had she heard a patient appreciate sheets. Now, she knew their importance. It meant a warm bed and a doctor and nurse to care for her when she couldn't care for herself. "I'm warm." For the first time in weeks, she was finally warm. It was good.

"We gave you the new wonder drug, penicillin. You're lucky. It's available only to the Army overseas. If we were in the states, we wouldn't have penicillin."

She threw up again. The doctor cradled her hot forehead in his cool, strong hand. The nurse cleaned up the mess. Kathy felt apologetic. There was nothing pretty about her now.

Yet the eyes of the doctor and nurse were not disgusted, but even more tenderly caring. The nurse gave her more sulfa pills and more water.

This was a new dimension in humanity. All her life Kathy had believed if she wanted to be liked, she must look pretty, have her hair combed, and her teeth brushed. She must work hard and help others and smile. Now she was none of these. She was helpless. Her hair was a mess, her teeth unbrushed, and she smelled of vomit. And here were two strangers caring for her, not just giving her medicine and clean sheets, but showing deep concern for her.

"What do I have?"

"Don't talk now; save your strength."

She guessed what he would not say. "Is it meningitis?" she asked.

"Penicillin will cure you. Now rest."

Her stomach allowed no rest. The remainder of the day and far into the night raged a battle between the nurse, who was determined to get some sulfa into her, and her stomach, which rejected everything. Kathy, feeling apart from her body, watched the battle almost indifferently.

The doctor stayed beside her, touching her, feeling her skin, taking her pulse and her temperature. He ordered plasma, blood, and medicines. Until another doctor took his place, he didn't go to supper.

By morning Kathy was too weak to pick up a glass of water or lift the edge of her sheet. She was weary and wanted only to sleep. The nurse's voice ordered, "Open your mouth."

Kathy opened her eyes and saw the nurse holding two sulfa pills between her thumb and finger. She closed her eyes.

"Take these pills," the voice gently insisted.

Kathy was too weary to open her mouth and speak. She wanted to be left alone, to sleep.

Her mouth was pulled open by gentle fingers on her chin. The pills and a little water were put in. Kathy swallowed.

Kathy felt the prick of a needle on her arm. She opened her eyes to see she was getting a blood transfusion. Why don't they just let me sleep? I'm tired. She closed her eyes.

Her right side, from her thighs to her shoulder, felt warm—warm as though Rocky was lying in bed beside her. She reached over, making a real effort to lift her weary arm, expecting to feel Rocky's lean body. She found the bed empty. She drooped her arm onto her waist, unable to move it further. Beside her, the bed was empty, yet his presence there was real. Her right side was warmed. This must be the warmth of love. Though they were an ocean apart, their love was real.

Her stomach rebelled again, and it threw up the water and sulfa pills. Again, the nurse was insisting, "Open your mouth." Kathy allowed her lower jaw to be pulled down, and allowed the pills to be dropped into her mouth. She swallowed. But she kept her eyes closed, to shut out the world of pills and vomiting and aching—and to maintain this dream of love, to relish the warmth beside her in the bed.

Days and nights passed with no more recognition than vaguely knowing that her eyes flickered open. It was sometimes light, sometimes dark. Always beside her bed were the doctor and the nurse. Beyond that, her real consciousness was of the love beside her, the warmth against her shoulder.

A cool hand lay gently on her forehead. "She's made it," a man's voice said.

She opened her eyes to see the doctor's eyes glowing triumphantly happy above his gauze mask as he said, "You're going to be all right."

Yes, the pains were gone except for an ache in her back. Her body was at peace with itself. Kathy was slowly coming back to the world.

"Thank you," she tried to say, but her voice was a weak whisper, and the words were inadequate. She wondered, *how does one thank the stranger whose devotion saved your life?*

"We're proud of you. You and penicillin have made medical history. This is the first time that penicillin has been used to treat spinal meningitis. You'll be a bit weak for a few weeks, but you will be all right." He scrubbed his hands and hung up his gown and mask. His face was tired—happy and tired. "I'll be back in an hour or so," he said to the nurse, and left the room.

When she awoke, doctors were standing in the doorway looking at her. Others joined them, looking and whispering to each other. All afternoon, the hospital staff came to the doorway to look and talk, as though not quite believing that she continued to live.

Although she remained in isolation, a ward boy massaged her back. A patient came in wearing his bathrobe. He stood at the foot of her bed and sang all parts to Gilbert and Sullivan's "Patience." Another ward boy came in and rubbed her back. A technician came in holding his tray of tubes and slides, and sang an opera in Italian. A third ward boy gave her a third back rub. Then the doctor hung a sign on the door, "No Visitors," yet the patient and the technician would sing for her, and ward boys rubbed her back.

By the time the two gowns and masks were removed, when the meningitis was no longer contagious, she counted fourteen back rubs a day. The skin on her back was rubbed so raw that they began to use powders and creams. Her contribution to the war effort was to let the Army rub her back.

By now, although she was not sitting up yet, she was strong enough to write. She wrote first to Rocky of how she had been critically sick. She stated she needed no sympathy—especially with all the attention she was receiving as one of only two female patients in the hospital. Not once had she been unhappy, because through it all Rocky's love had been with her. Now she understood the meaning of the idea that nothing mattered as long as she had love.

She wrote to her mother and father. Quite often patients lied in their letters when writing home on the theory that if their parents did not know they were in the hospital, they would worry less. Military policy encouraged not specifying the issue, on the theory that the enemy might find out about epidemics or casualties. But Kathy had never been successful at lying and so she wrote simply that she he had been critically sick. She had received phenomenally good care with the doctor keeping constant vigil for six days. This disproved the criticism that the Army dispensed medicine in a subhuman assembly line fashion. She was now convalescing. Aspects of it were surprisingly fun. Never before had so many people sought her company. Maybe it was because she couldn't talk much and, thus, she had to be a good listener.

When she'd finished her letters and was sealing the envelopes, there was a knock at her open door. She looked up to see Captain Keene. Thrilled to see a familiar face, she attempted to sit up. Her body didn't respond, and immediately she fell back into the bed.

"Mailman here!" he said. "I brought the mail to the girls at Mesnieres. It was just a few miles farther to bring you yours."

"I'm so happy to see you! And you are bringing my mail? Mail! That means a letter from Rocky!" She reached out eagerly. "It was 20 to 40 miles out of your way! I know you need to conserve gas. Thanks."

He handed her several letters. She remembered her manners long enough to offer him a chair before she looked. A letter from her father, two from her mother, and one from the lady next door. That was all. Nothing from Rocky.

Captain Keene sat with one arm dangling over the back of the chair, his long legs crossed. He peered understandingly through his steel-rimmed glasses. "None from your fiancé? Well, most of our mail hasn't come through yet."

Rocky wasn't her fiancé, but it wasn't worth correcting. "None. I'll get a bundle next mail. Will that be next week?"

"We always expect our mail tomorrow. We'll send it as soon as someone comes this direction."

"No rush. My morale is in good shape," Kathy said.

"Good. We were all worried about you, sick and alone." His eyes showed the same concern that had been in the doctor's eyes. It was concern for her. It didn't matter that her hair was straight and her lips pale and that she lay helpless on a bed. "Sick, yes. Alone, no. My problem has been to keep the crowds out."

"Want me to leave?"

"I said the wrong thing again. No! I don't want you to leave. Stay and listen! In this room I will get a private performance of Gounod's "Faust" every day. Is our hospital set up? Are the girls there? Oh no, you said they remained Mesnieres."

"We have gangs of German PWs cleaning and painting the permanent buildings for the patients. They are also putting up Quonset huts for the staff. I'll never understand why they call these huts. With that classic archway design made of 100 percent steel, these buildings will last a lifetime. There is no central heating, but plenty of pot-belly GI stoves. However, the coal ration is skimpy."

"I like those stoves—better than the castle's skinny stoves that made more smoke than heat."

"With that much trouble heating a room, you can imagine the problems of getting my incubator at a constant temperature for my lab samples. It was made for electricity. We converted it to gas, and it's not working. You should hear Fellows describe his operating room. We'll get everything working somehow. That is if we don't starve first."

"No food?"

"Hay. That dehydrated stuff tastes like hay. A man could live longer than he'd care to live. Our cook was a truck driver. Our mess officer an insurance salesman. Our mess Sergeant was a shoe clerk. They try, but the stuff still tastes like hay."

"You need a dietitian who can train them. You need someone skilled at planning meals and supervising preparation."

"We sure do. You have an incentive to get well."

"Why don't you have Vivienne there? And Mathilda?"

Captain Keene shifted his long legs and looked embarrassed. "Well," he said, and rubbed his hand across the top of his butch haircut. "Well, to tell the truth I was supposed to take the girls over in our convoy last week." He scratched his chin. "Well, with all the trouble you had with your convoy finding a latrine, I just didn't know what to do. So, I left the girls at Mesnieres."

Kathy laughed. "Some Army. Can't even conquer a simple problem. I repeat, you need a dietitian. You need Vivienne. You need that quiet Mathilda too—don't underestimate her. She works like a machine; an unstoppable machine. You have two of the best. And they would figure out how to restrict fluids, so no stops needed for latrines."

He laughed, and then looked serious. "Maybe that's not so silly. Restrict fluids before traveling."

"Of course, it would work. Take the girls back with you. Give Vivienne and Mathilda a chance to prove we're worth the nuisance. I know they can set up the mess."

"A decent meal is worth an effort. But it won't be easy. The mess is in a barn."

"A big barn would have lots of room. Get the cows out first, or are we supposed to milk them?"

"Horses. Not cows. It was a cavalry post. They're long gone." He rubbed his knuckles, a thinking gesture. Then, he pounded his fist into his hand, in a "That's it" gesture. "My ambulance has enough room for nine girls. He stood up, grinning. "I'll be on my way. I need to get there in time to tell them…." He opened his hands… "Yet, how do I say it? Promise to drink nothing tonight, you can ride with me tomorrow?" When this struck him as funny, his laughter swelled from deep in his chest.

"There's a place for us women, you'll see. Thanks for the mail."

"Can I tell the Colonel you'll be with us by the time we're ready for patients? Think you can get on your feet that fast?"

"I don't know. I've never been this sick before."

He draped his trench coat over his arm, and turned past the window to leave. "That sunset is worth looking at."

Forgetting that she was not yet allowed to stand up, Kathy attempted to stand on the bed to peer out the window. Instead of stiffening, her knees crumpled, and she tumbled to the edge of the bed.

Captain Keene caught her and kept her from falling out of bed. "Take it slow and steady."

He put an arm under her knees. For a moment she thought he might carry her to the window. Instead, he lifted her to the center of the bed. He gently pulled the sheet and blanket over her.

"The sun sets every night. You won't want to miss it." he said. "Want me to call a nurse?"

"I'm all right, only surprised. I hadn't tried out my muscles. I sort of assumed they'd do what I ordered."

"Easy does it. I'll tell the girls in Mesnieres that you're all right. So long." He left.

Kathy took a small mirror from her musette bag that hung on the metal rungs at the head of her bed. She looked pale and thin with greasy, straggly hair. She rummaged in her bag for lipstick, which brightened her face a little.

A ward boy, a husky Army Sergeant, came into the room. "Back rub?"

Kathy had already had seven back rubs that day, but she answered, "Sure, any time."

He grinned at her. "Lipstick? You must be feeling better."

She turned over on her stomach. "How can I wash my hair without sitting up?"

"I'll push your bed over the sink and wash it for you. Wait while I get the shampoo."

"I wasn't going anywhere."

When he returned, he pushed the foot of the bed against the sink. She crawled to the foot of the bed. On her hands and knees, she hung her head over the sink. He scrubbed her hair, rinsed it, and rubbed it dry with an olive-drab towel.

"If you promise not to tell, I'll try pinning your hair up. If any of the boys see me, they will call me Pierre," said the Sergeant. 'I've never done this. Do you just wind hair around your finger?" Kathy was exhausted, so she gratefully agreed. She lay on her stomach, her face in the pillow, while he combed her hair and, his stubby fingers, surprisingly expert, put her hair up in bobby pins.

The next day she was put to work. Her job was to read and censor the patients' mail. She was surprised to find just how lonely these soldiers were. Some of the letters were from patients she knew to be badly crippled, yet they were casual about their troubles. Some, from patients such as the Corporal who had measles, were too cautious, insisting military regulations would not allow him to tell them the nature of their casualty. Kathy added a note for the Corporal's mother, "I doubt that measles constitutes a military secret, signed, the censor." Some patients had cut large chunks out of their letters. What were they trying to do, make their letter look important, or as though it could have been long but for the censor's scissors? Kathy was tempted to add a note, "Cut by writer, not by censor," but decided it was his privilege to send any letter he chose. One patient enclosed sticks of gum, "One for you, Mom, and the other for the censor. Kathy took the gum, and added her "Thank you" to the end of the letter.

Duplicate letters written to several girls intrigued her. She was tempted to switch them so Mary would get Jean's letter, and vice versa, but didn't. Any soldier in a hospital was entitled to as many letters from as many girls as he could get. She was actually conscientious about her work, doubly so since the fighting remained fierce in the area.

The next day she was allowed to sit up. The next week she moved in a wheelchair to a convalescent ward, which she shared with two other girls.

The atmosphere changed. Now, rather than saving strength, she was pushed into activity. The first day the ward officer ordered her up to the bathroom. She attempted to get up by sitting on the edge of the bed and reaching for the floor with her feet.

"Is this your first time out of bed?" asked Dorothy, the girl in the next bed.

"Yes."

Dorothy shook her head emphatically. "You shouldn't try it alone. You might fall."

Kathy looked around the room. There was no one to help. One girl had a broken leg, she couldn't give support. Dorothy was recovering from virus pneumonia and was not allowed out of bed. "I can walk myself," Kathy said.

She stood. Her knees shook weakly, but they held her up. She shuffled a step. Dorothy got up and walked beside her, steadying her by the elbow.

Dorothy put an arm around her. "I haven't been sick as long as you. It's easier to hold you up than to pick you up off the floor." Dorothy helped her to the bathroom, waited, and helped her back to bed.

Two days later she was ordered to walk to the next building for her meals. She believed she could never walk down and up a full flight of stairs, but she did. After going up and down stairs for breakfast, she was so exhausted that she slept until lunch time. After the exertion of going to lunch, she was too tired to even attempt supper. Instead, she ate part of Dorothy's supper and stayed in bed.

The next day her muscles were as stiff as if she had run a race. Somehow, she managed to climb up and down those long iron steps for both meals. She was certain that she was being pushed faster than she could endure. However, she had no choice if she wanted to eat.

In a week she walked around the block. It was now March. Spring was beginning in Rouen. After a winter of cold and sickness, both her returning strength and the sun were wondrous delights.

Sue, the nurse who had overcome her stomach issues, joined her in short walks through Rouen. The cities' trees were blooming. Narrow cobblestone streets wound around the statue commemorating the burning of Joan of Arc. The cathedral stood majestic as if indestructible. It was the only structure left in an area of rubble. It's soaring spirit had endured the bombing.

The walks were short and delightful, with numerous rests, and always followed by a nap.

Kathy was surprised when the ward officer ordered her back to duty, as she continued to be weak. "Our ambulance will drive you to the Red Cross headquarters in Paris tomorrow. An ambulance from your hospital will pick you up and take you to Suippes," he said. He handed her a 15-hour pass. He didn't ask her how she felt. He left no room for her to object. She packed her musette bag and left in the morning.

# CHAPTER 9

# A HOSPITAL IN A CAVALRY BARN

When they arrived in Paris, the driver said, "Would you like to see the sights before I drop you off at the Red Cross Headquarters?" Kathy was grateful for the offer, and they toured Paris for an hour.

This Paris was not the vibrant city Kathy recalled from her visit when she was 16. The streets were crammed with Army trucks and Jeeps, with no little French cars rushing about and tooting their horns. Women wore clothes that were saggy and gray, lacking the elegance and style Parisians were famous for. Children had burst out of their coats to play in the parks, but were not running or laughing. Stores had minimal activity, with little merchandise shown in the windows.

"It could be worse," the driver said. "Have you heard of the 'Savior of Paris'—General Dietrich Hugo Hermann von Choltitz?"

"Sounds German. How could a German be called 'The Savior of Paris'?"

"When it looked like Paris could be taken back from the Germans, a coalition of French resistance fighters rose up against the German occupation in Paris. German commander General Dietrich von Choltitz had orders from Hitler to destroy the city rather than surrender it. 'Paris must not fall into the hands of the enemy,' Hitler had said, 'except as a field of ruins.' Yet when the French entered the city, Choltitz defied

Hitler's orders. He did not want to go down in history as the one who destroyed one of the world's most glorious cities."

There was, in fact, in this surviving city, a touch of hope. Spring brought sprouting leaves to the linden trees lining the streets. The fountains in the gardens of the Louvre were splashing and sparkling. Fishermen were fishing or just warming themselves in the sunshine, on the bridges of the Seine River. A war-weary world was rousing to new life.

Mrs. Foster and her four Red Cross girls warmly greeted Kathy at the Red Cross Headquarters. However, they had just been informed that their transportation back to the hospital would not be until the next day. Yet Kathy had just a 15-hour pass. She had no authorization to spend the night.

Kathy looked for a place to stay. With no cabs, Kathy walked five blocks to the WAC Leave Center. and then another seven blocks to the French hotel where the nurses were authorized to stay, with no luck. The Red Cross Director was correct; it was impossible to stay in Paris without authorization. It was also forbidden to eat or stay in French hotels.

She dragged herself back to the Red Cross Headquarters, resting at each sidewalk café along the way. She presented her plight to the Red Cross Director, but he still refused permission for her to stay.

Kathy sagged into a chair. "I can't walk any farther." She wasn't pretending. "I'll collapse at your front door. Then you'll have to step over me or carry me to a bed. It'd be easier to give me a cot in Mrs. Foster's room."

Finally, he relented. Kathy, too tired to bother with supper, fell asleep on Mrs. Foster's bed.

They left after breakfast in an ambulance for the town of Suippes, where the hospital was. Kathy was given the privilege of sitting on the cushioned front seat that had a back, while the Red Cross girls sat on the wooden benches in the back.

In the countryside, peasants, cultivating their budding vineyards, wore clothes as dingy as the Parisians—but they did not look as defeated. The lack of gasoline that had paralyzed Paris had not affected those farmers who had horses. Reportedly the Germans had taken food from all, and both Parisian and peasant alike were hungry. Yet out here in the country at least the growing plants promised harvests. Tiny wood-lots assured wood for the fireplaces in their little stucco houses, so the small houses looked warm.

They drove by an area where both the farmhouses and woodlots had been reduced to rubble, although new trees were already making tiny spots of green in the blackened ashes—their growth as inevitable as day after night; sun after rain. Yet it would be decades before they provided plentiful wood for heat, furniture, and new houses. War had stripped the country of more than its civilization. It had destroyed food, heat and shelter, the very foundations of existence.

They passed by an area of brown remains where half a village had been pulverized. A Frenchman, with sagging shoulders that made him look old, though his hair was black, picked up two bricks, and carried them wearily across the road to what looked like another pile of rubble. He glanced at the ambulance, and shuffled back across the road for more bricks. Seemingly, he was accomplishing nothing.

The ambulance drove up a small hill. Beyond it lay the valley of a broad, quiet river. A village of wooden-beamed stone houses was nes-tled in the valley. The cobblestone road widened into a broad stone square in front of a church. Over the town, higher than the steepest roofs in the town, and higher than the trees, rose the church's steeple. The steeple was neither unusual nor ornate, yet it dominated the town.

"This is Suippes," said the driver.

As they continued through the village, they heard a muffled boom. It pounded like a small roll of thunder from a distant storm. Another boom, and another, distant, and barely audible. The booms continued so persistently they demanded attention. Not thunder; but were unmistak-ably the guns Kathy had heard in target practice at Camp McCoy. She figured that it was probably another target practice.

The driver drove them to a group of flat-roofed plastered buildings making up the hospital. The buildings were orderly and clean, sur-rounded by green lawns. On a slope in front of the headquarters building, was a gang of German PWs, guarded by a single GI with a rifle. Four PWs were inlaying a large cross of white stones into a bed of dark stones. Their work was efficient and precise. Two other PWs were spading a border and planting flowers.

The driver opened the ambulance door, and offered to take Kathy's luggage to her quarters while she signed in. Mrs. Foster and the other Red Cross girls led the way, first to headquarters, then to their barracks.

After signing in, Kathy was brought to her room, adjoining and connected with Mrs. Foster's. The room was attractive, with a waxed oak floor and knotty-pine paneled walls. The window overlooked a vineyard and a river flowing through a grove of golden willows.

Hearing of their arrival, Bunts, Sue, and Mathilda came to welcome them. Sue brought bright yellow and purple flowers in a water glass. They gave Kathy a chance to rest before dinner.

That evening, everyone recognized Kathy in the mess. She was greeted with smiles and questions about her health. Colonel Stone left his dinner to talk with her. He put a friendly hand on her shoulder. "How are you?" he asked.

"Fine. Much impressed with this hospital. I'd expected to find run-down smelly old barns."

"We have a hospital of which the United States can be proud. Now, really, how are you?"

"I am quite weak. I couldn't do a twenty-five-mile hike. Thankfully, I'm assured there's no permanent damage."

"Kathy, those guns you hear are not target practice. We're in a battle area. We've stopped the German assault. The Battle of the Bulge is finally over. We are working again to push back the Germans. But they are formidable fighters. The Germans are far from beaten."

The Colonel shook his head sadly. "Casualties have been extremely high. This hospital finally started operating one week ago. Today we have 250 patients; 300 more are due tomorrow. In a week we'll be working at our thousand-bed capacity. We need you. Now. Even if for just two or four hours a day."

Kathy responded. "I'll do whatever I can."

"Report to Captain Wright in the morning for a complete physical before you start work." He stood, smiled, and left.

When Vivienne came off duty after dinner, she brought the mail to Kathy's room. There were letters from her father and mother, written before they had news of her sickness, letters from her sister and brothers, and several friends. Nothing from Rocky. Kathy looked through the envelopes again. Nothing from Rocky.

Kathy was tired. Every muscle was weary. If the doctor proclaimed her healthy in the morning, she would have to, somehow, summon the energy to work. She was needed. She climbed into bed. Tomorrow there would be a letter from Rocky. Or maybe he was sick, so hopelessly sick he didn't want to be a burden to her. Was he fainting more without her? Why did he faint? Maybe she'd get a letter tomorrow. Tonight, she'd sleep.

The examination confirmed her good health, and Kathy began her four-hour day in the barn, now the mess area. The barn was one large room with a cement floor and light green walls. All stalls had been cleared, except one corner stall. Several German PWs and one GI cook were working at field cooking ranges along one wall, with dippers and spoons hanging above them. Along another wall, German PWs were stacking supplies. In front of a third wall, civilian women were loading food into wooden boxes marked with ward numbers. Two doors connected the barn to adjacent small buildings. Through one open door Kathy could see PWs washing pots and pans at deep metal sinks. The other door was padlocked, undoubtedly guarding a supply room.

Vivienne came out of the stall, her red hair looking strikingly red in the green and gray room. "Welcome to our mess. What's the verdict?"

"I'm all right. I will begin with a four-hour day."

"Come into our office and sit down. A nice stall for work-horses." Vivienne tossed her hair as a race horse might toss his mane, and walked with a prance certainly not suited for plowing.

"I'm proud of you," said Kathy, and stood at the entrance to the stall where she could watch the activity. "Everything looks organized, and dinner smells good. That cake looks good enough to eat."

"Enjoy it while you can. We manage, but I'd hardly say anything was controlled. Except maybe the 16 German PWs. They're obedient, and their ranking man Oscar speaks English. Sarge tells Oscar what needs to get done, and Oscar makes sure it gets it done by the PWs."

"No guards?"

"None in here. Every man we could spare has been sent to the infantry, even at the risk of letting a few Germans escape. Why would they want to escape from our mess? Here they are warm and better fed than if they were working a shovel. They're not supposed to be better fed, but they scrape some food from pans they wash, and maybe steal a little. For them, it's a privilege to work here, and they work hard to stay."

Surprised, Kathy asked "They wash cleavers and knives?"

"It's easier to take a chance on one man grabbing a knife and getting away than to keep a close guard on them. Like I say, they like it here. The Germans are no problem to me. They listen to me. They know I am serious.

"Our confusion comes with the women. They don't understand English, and we don't understand their languages. Five women are French, two are Polish, one is Russian, and one is Greek. So, we bless the good Chaplain Kirkemo for insisting on your French lessons."

"I'll bring my dictionary. Only one American cook?"

"Yes, only one American cook. All of the other men were sent to stop the German advance in the Bulge, which was bulging very close to this hospital." Vivienne led the way into their office. The stall was crowded with three desks, in a way that said there was work to be done. "Now, to divide our work. Mathilda is a whiz, an absolute genius with calculating amounts and making lists. She has us organized. If I remember right, you like therapeutics. Think you could handle maybe two hundred patients to determine their unique diets?"

"Yes," Kathy replied with no hesitation.

"And communicate with the natives? Oh yes, I'll warn you now while I'm thinking about it. We use the French 7, with the line through it. Otherwise, when you write 70 pounds of potatoes you get 10. I learned the hard way."

The cook came into their stall. "Lieutenant West, the women are snitching cake and putting it in their sacks."

Vivienne stood and clutched her red hair with her fists. "Our precious cake. That cake is a week's sugar ration! We had only a half piece per patient as it was. All right, Kathy *parlez francais*, speak French, if you please."

Kathy considered her French vocabulary. "I can tell them not to take from *les malades*. And *nous n'avons pas assez de gateau—no du gateau*. What do we do with the cake that they took? It would be terrible to take it to where the German PWs could get it."

"It won't be wasted. We don't have much leftover food, not with Mathilda's expert calculations. What we do have left, we can't keep, as we don't have refrigeration. We put leftovers by the garbage cans for the French to help themselves. There is always a line waiting. That's the plan for the cake."

Kathy talked to the women. First, they looked puzzled. Then, as understanding dawned, they looked a little ashamed. They were a disordered lot, with untidy hair and ragged clothes. Kathy had to remind herself that these women had been through years of war. They weren't working here by choice.

Mathilda came in. Lunch was almost over, so Kathy, Mathilda, and Vivienne began sorting out the food orders for supper. In strolled a tenor singing "Lilly Marlene."

Kathy turned to see who had this romantic voice. He was a good-looking young man, like a movie star, with black wavy hair. He gazed at Kathy, enraptured, with wide-open brown eyes. He spread out his arms as though to embrace her, and dropped to his knees before her. "Vision of loveliness! Fair lady, I love you."

Kathy looked around to see to whom he might be speaking. Kathy was not fair and her hair was dark brown. She was not a vision of loveliness; her nose was too large. She looked back at him. His arms were raised not to Mathilda or to Vivienne, who was beautiful, but to Kathy.

"It is you. You are my one and only love," he said. "Never did I believe in love at first sight. Yet my heart is smitten, and I cannot live without you." He lowered his arms till his hands touched Kathy's knees, then jerked them away as though his touch were too daring, which it was.

Kathy was too amazed to think of anything to say. Vivienne smiled at the show with delight. It was no-nonsense Mathilda who remembered this was a mess office. "Did you come in for something your ward might be needing, Sir Galahad?"

"For something, yes." He answered without taking his enraptured eyes from Kathy's face. "But I can't think messes when I gaze at a dazzling beauty."

Mathilda persisted. "You're from Ward 1. They usually want extra coffee."

"All right." He sighed and stood up. "I'll take them coffee." Then he gazed at Kathy's face. "When I gaze into your eyes, I long for the taste of your raspberry lips."

"What you want is raspberry Jello," said matter-of-fact Mathilda. "You forgot to add the new patients to your diet lists."

"That's it. We need another dozen servings." He obediently followed Mathilda into the kitchen.

In strode a handsome German PW, the picture of Hitler's superman vision. He marched in stiffly, his head high. "Lieutenant, der coal truck ist heer." He spoke in thick accents.

There was no need for him to tell a dietician this. "Rolf, get out of here. Go tell the mess Sergeant," Vivienne curtly issued orders to the PW.

The German smiled at Vivienne as though assured his smile would captivate her. It didn't. He turned this superior smile on Kathy. She resisted the impulse to slap the smile off his arrogant face. Instead, she ignored him by turning her attention to the papers on her desk. He stood beside her, took a photograph from his wallet, and placed in front of her a picture of a large brick house.

"Das ist mein house. Mine father president of the Zeist company." He waited for her to respond to the name. When she continued to look at her papers, he continued. "I am shtorm troopah."

"You're proud of storm troopers?" Vivienne stood, raging to face him. "Proud of killing French and Polish and English? Of killing Russians and Americans? You're proud of that?"

His smile was as assured as ever. "It vas mishtake to fight Americans."

Vivienne's voice was calm disgust. She ordered him: "Go! Now! Leave! Wash pots and pans."

His smile froze resolutely on his face. He put his picture back into his wallet and marched out, holding his head high.

The GI cook, a large no-nonsense man, came to the entrance of the stall. "Is Superman putting on his act again? Should I handle him, Lieutenant?"

"Don't tempt me," said Vivienne.

"Lieutenant, I have a different problem for you." The GI cook carried a large pan of raw liver loaf over to Vivienne, asking, "Shall I throw this out?"

"We can't throw away good meat just because liver isn't popular." replied Vivienne.

"Wormy liver?" He pointed to a fat green worm crawling across the top of the dark red meat. It looped up and stretched out, and looped up and stretched out again.

Kathy pointed up into the rafters. "Maybe the birds dropped the worm." They all looked up to see two birds swooping under the vaulted roof.

"Or some GI cook didn't want to be unpopular so he planted a little green worm," said Vivienne and smiled at the cook.

In a civilian hospital, Kathy would have served liver loaf, confident the patients would at least be polite about disliking it. Army patients here were different. Death was rare in a general hospital like this as the fatally wounded died at the front or in a field hospital. A soldier who had faced the enemy, was wounded and survived, was now removed from danger. Serve them liver, and they would not only refuse it, but would greet her with cat calls.

Throwing away food just because it was unpopular was not to be considered. Vivienne looked almost gratefully at the green worm. "We can't take a chance on infected meat," Vivienne said to the cook. "We'll substitute salmon loaf." To Kathy she said, "You must take and show that worm to Captain Keene and remind him to get rid of these birds."

Kathy found Captain Keen and showed him the worm. "Your cook outsmarted you," he said when saw it. "It's not a liver parasite. Someone planted it."

"Or the birds dropped it."

"They're back?"

"They're building nests in the rafters."

"Let's go take a look. I had no idea I'd be bird watching when I signed up to be a sanitary officer."

He gestured to a bench near the mess. "We have already cleaned out their nests and plugged every hole we could find. We can't put poison on the beams because it might drop into the food. I even considered shooting them."

"I'll bet Superman unplugged the holes. Sabotage!" Kathy said.

They sat on the bench for half an hour. The birds sang and fluttered about. However, none went into the mess.

Finally, Captain Keene stood. "I hate to be defeated by birds. I'll stalk them again this evening. Well, I have to get back to work. But you ought to stay here. The sun would make your cheeks rosy."

"I'm ready for a nap."

The window of the post-office opened, signifying mail call. "I'll get you your mail," Captain Keene offered.

She waited on the sunny bench for him. Surely today she would hear from Rocky. She would get the accumulation of weeks of mail. He would tell her he missed her, had thought of her, and was anxious for her return. He'd be answering her letters about being sick and glad she had recovered. It didn't matter what he'd say. Just something from him, anything, to show he'd remembered her.

Captain Keene brought the mail to her. She could tell from the concerned look on his face that she had nothing from Rocky. She carefully, methodically looked at each envelope. Letters from her mother, her father, her brothers, her sister, her friends and neighbors. Nothing from Rocky.

She managed to say "Thanks" to Captain Keene.

"Is there anything…?" His nice blue eyes showed he wanted to help, but felt helpless.

"No. I'll feel better after a taking a nap."

Kathy returned to her room and laid on her bed. Her blanket was itchy and scratchy, but she was too tired to pull it back to lie on the sheet. She opened her mother's letter that read:

*February 27, 1945*
*Dear Kathryn,*

*Today we received the most welcome letter your Daddy and I have ever received. Your Chaplain wrote us that you were "critically" ill with meningitis—and that everything possible was being done. We were not to try to reach the hospital, and that they would advise us by postcard every 15 days. From the time this letter reached us February 12 until today has been just plain hell. I was never was so scared in my life. I lost 17 pounds, which I admit I should have lost anyway, but not that way. Your Uncle Fred tried his darndest to get more information through some war correspondents he knows. Your Uncle Pidz went to some Army hospital and got all the information he could.*

*Darling, don't ever hold out on us again. I want a promise on that. Get someone who will write us if you cannot. I know you thought we knew nothing about it—but don't think that again. Tell us the situation. I don't believe much in asking for promises from my children, but I do want that. Please, Kathryn.*

*Frank came home on a leave because we were so worried. Bob is in the Admiralty Islands south of the Equator, near New Guinea. Very hot. He says he is moving lumber.*

*Good night, Kathryn. We are profoundly thankful that you are coming out of this alright. Write us short notes often.*

*Much love, Mother.*

Also enclosed was a letter from her father:

*Dear Kate,*

*We received a letter which was relayed from the War Department at Washington saying that you were seriously sick with meningitis. I wired Dr. Penney to find out what this was, so in no time flat, it was common knowledge here in Libertyville. I also called up Dr. Green to find out more. I was really scared after talking to him. About all any of us could do was to ask the Red Cross to try find out details, which they were unable to do. The rest of the scared people in Christian Science, Methodist, Episcopalian, and amateur standing, started praying for your recovery, depending on how they went about doing this.*

*Any way you look at it, we were scared. On receiving your two letters, I wired all these people. We are beginning to rest a little easier, but I am not sure that we are over being scared. I haven't been scared since years ago when you fell out of the car on our way to church, and I took you over to Dr. Penney.*

*Frank is on a shore leave, and came out here to visit us and to rest. With the man shortage, it is not safe for him to wear so much gold—as the women find it so attractive. Ralph was sent to William Beaumont Hospital at El Paso with broken bones and more. He got a thirty-day leave, and Betty managed to get some gasoline, drove down, and brought him here to Sante Fe. He looks well, and I think he is a little heavier than he was.*

*The Navy sent Bob on a nice trip to Australia on a luxury liner, and he had a state room to himself, which represents something or other. He finally was sent to some island north of New Guinea. Think it is the Admiralty Island where the head hunters live, and the gals have lips like a piece of pie. Those dames will slow little Robert down a lot. Mother, for some strange reason, does not like anything about it.*

*I hope that you can write to all, as they prayed for your recovery. Please also contact your sorority in Ames as I believe they printed your obituary.*

*With the publicity that you have had, I am sure they will give you a public reception in Libertyville upon your return. Uncle Fred was in favor of having the "Times" foreign correspondents hunt you down in France. We had much trouble holding him back. You may hear from him.*

*Much love…and be sure to keep breathing,*
*WRE*

Nothing from Rocky.

# CHAPTER 10

## CHERRY PIE

The Colonel's predictions were realized. In a week the hospital was working at its full thousand-bed capacity. After one of the deadliest battles in the war, the Nazis were finally retreating. The Allies were once again on the offense, moving East. By March 1, the Allies had reached the Rhine River. Crossing the Rhine would be the last major geographical barrier on the final assault into Germany. A ferocious river, as wide as two miles in some areas, it served like a moat protecting their homeland.

Attacks, retreats, victories, and defeats—but the progress of the war seemed meaningless in the hospital. As many wounded arrived after victories as after defeats. The hospital settled into a maximum-capacity routine, helping record numbers of wounded.

Kathy's strength increased to match the growing patient load. She did her share of managing three meals a day for a thousand patients, but when supper was over, she could do no more. She was compelled to lay her tired body down and sleep.

With the advent of spring, it was now light when Kathy's alarm rang. She crawled out of bed and lit a match to start the fire in the pot-bellied stove. The day was warm enough, she decided, to pack away her long winter underwear.

At the mess, the PWs and civilian girls were scurrying around, loading the ward boxes. Mathilda and Sarge were standing in front of the pot-bellied stove, sipping hot coffee, watching the activity with a supervisor's eyes. Vivienne was tossing a handful of salt into the pot of oatmeal. She stirred and tasted it. "Fine," she announced, and gave the civilian women lists for dishing it up.

"Good morning," smiled Kathy.

"No," growled Sarge. "Inspection morning."

Kathy stood beside Mathilda with her back to the warm stove. Automatically everyone who came in stood by the stove. "Good morning, Mathilda."

Mathilda frowned over her tin coffee cup. "Good morning. Sarge, I just know Rolf didn't wash the tops of the spices. Sarge, are the spice can lids cleaned?"

Oscar brought Kathy her morning coffee, with canned milk and sugar in it, just as she liked it. She took the cup, remembering not to smile her appreciation to a PW.

"*Vos ist dos, spice can lids?*" Oscar asked Sarge, who was hanging up Kathy's coat on a rack.

"I'll check them." Sarge gestured to Oscar, who followed him out the back door to the storeroom.

"Good morning, Kathy." Vivienne came to stand by the stove. "Mathilda, you fuss too much. No inspector can find any dirt here. Oscar and his PWs keep this the cleanest mess ever. *Das allus bestes mess.*"

Mathilda looked up skeptically at the little brown birds twittering on the rafters.

"Sue says they're nightingales," said Kathy.

Mathilda jerked her head. "It makes no difference. A bird is a bird."

"A message came for you, phoned into headquarters." Vivienne handed Kathy a typed sheet. It read: "Will arrive March 10th to interview you at suggestion of your uncle, Fred Collens, of the "Chicago Tribune." Please prepare statements about your courageous recovery and your noble dedicated service to inspire other girls to volunteer for the war effort. Perhaps describe a routine day." Signed, Mark Skaw, "Times" War Correspondent.

"The boxes are ready to be checked." Vivienne had been watching the civilian girls loading the boxes.

"I'll check them," Kathy said. "A war correspondent is coming to see what we do so he can write an article. Checking boxes is not inspiring. What are you doing this morning that's exciting?"

Mathilda looked suspiciously again at the rafters, and carefully set down her coffee. "Nothing worth writing about. I'll get going on the recipes if Vivienne's decided on a dessert."

"Cherry pie," said Vivienne.

"Oh, no!" Mathilda frowned. "Dan's last crusts were rubber. He's a truck driver, not a cook, and will never make good crusts."

Vivienne smiled, "The crusts will be flaky today. I'll work with him."

Mathilda pulled her shoulders in, she shrunk. "This morning? An inspection?"

Vivienne tossed her red hair back with impatience. "Let Sarge worry about inspections. Stay and bird watch if you want."

There was, so far, nothing exciting for an article. Maybe after breakfast something interesting would happen.

"Attention!" announced the mess Sergeant.

Kathy stood at the entrance to the stall and watched Colonel Stone and Captain Keene enter.

"At ease," said the Colonel.

Kathy and Sarge attended the Colonel and Captain Keene as they walked silently through the kitchen, checking their lists. They were both reasonable, kindly men, and Kathy couldn't imagine why Mathilda seemed so afraid. She followed them and waited confidently for their report.

They stopped beside the door of the attached flat-roofed storeroom. There, leaning against the wall was a ladder. "That should be put away," said the Colonel.

"Put the ladder away," Sarge said to Oscar.

Oscar, who usually obeyed promptly, stood looking down at his feet.

*"Achtung!"* shouted Sarge. "Put it away."

Oscar looked miserable, "Rolf and Sue are there."

The Colonel frowned. Captain Keene frowned. They both turned and walked away without comment.

Kathy returned to the struggle of making special diets to be cooked in five languages. The food was finally being loaded in the ward boxes when Vivienne came in with a plate of cherry pie. "We did it! I knew we could! Sample this."

The cherries were red and sweet and tart. The crusts were golden and crisp and flaky. "You win the cherry pie baking contest with a blue ribbon," said Kathy.

"Today, Dan became a baker." Vivienne sat at her desk and took cards from the file. "That finishes our sugar for the week. Was it worth it?"

"Sure is." Kathy made an entry in her notebook for the article: "Vivienne taught truck-driver Dan to bake cherry pie."

Vivienne looked at her with concern. "The boxes are finished. Why don't you go to lunch now? And take a nap afterwards."

"Thank you. I will." Kathy added to her notebook, "Vivienne cares."

So, Kathy went to the officer's mess. She took a tray and stood in the cafeteria line.

An Army Air Force Captain, with silver wings over his pocket, strode in to stand in line beside her. Any serviceman was welcome to eat in any Army mess. In fact, it was forbidden to eat in any French place. But a pilot here was unusual. If he were a patient, he'd be eating in the patients' mess. As a dietitian, she was part hostess, so she smiled as she handed him a tray. "Welcome to the 223rd. If you're looking for someone, I might be of help."

"No. Not visiting. Ordered here. Emergency flight." He did not smile in the manner she expected. She was used to having soldiers respond to her friendliness.

"You brought in a patient?"

He put a plate on his tray, and looked at it, not at her. "No."

"Emergency landing? Anyone hurt?"

He flushed, "No. If you must know, an emergency cargo of sanitary napkins. And if you ask me, you girls should have stayed home."

"I admit we're a nuisance. But we're necessary. Eating is necessary. It took our training and talents to get this lunch for you."

He speared a slice of Spam and flopped it onto his plate. "Talents on this? We get better than this, and without help from women!"

"Oh sure! The Air Corps. You eat better than the rest of us. You go to Spain for oranges and to Italy for olives. Our patients never had an orange, not once. And you can't blame me for Spam." She turned and walked away. Yet she couldn't fault a man for resenting risking his life for a wartime cargo of sanitary napkins. And if she were any good as a dietitian, she should have a recipe that disguised Spam.

After lunch, she tried mixing Spam with spaghetti sauce. She tried chopping it into scrambled eggs. Spam was still Spam—and the eggs still had that dehydrated straw flavor.

Kathy was suddenly overwhelmingly weary. She returned to her barracks to lie on her bed. She again considered her article. She could not think of anything that would inspire girls to volunteer.

Awakened by the roar of a convoy of ambulances, she sat up to look out the window. Three ambulances drove carefully past the barbed wire and tents of the Displaced Persons camp across the street. Kathy put on her shoes. New patients to see. There would be recipes to change, and food to prepare before supper.

She met Vivienne going into the mess, the census already completed in her hand. "Fifty-six just liberated from concentration camps. Here's where your patients are." She handed her a list: 9 liquid diets, 11 soft, and 30 light diets. These were for men too weak to eat regular diets. "Brace yourself. It's bad." Her red hair was wild and tangled.

"I've seen starved men before."

"I thought I had too." Vivienne's said, with tears in her eyes.

Kathy put her special diet roster in her pocket, and filled a three-gallon aluminum pitcher of eggnog from a GI can. If these patients had been severely starved, they would welcome eggnog. This was the one combination of dehydrated milk and powdered eggs that Kathy had developed that was as good as the real thing. She sprinkled a dash of nutmeg on top, and added sugar for quick energy. She would add to her "Times" article list: "Carried eggnog to newly liberated starved prisoners." That had an inspiring sound.

The first patient she visited lay quietly on his back. He didn't even turn his head when she entered his room. A blood transfusion dripped into a vein that stood out on his fleshless arm as the only substance between skin and bone. The skull-shape of his head showed beneath the pale, translucent skin. His eyes were buried deep in shadowed sockets, his cheeks sunk in hollow jaws. Barely able to breath, he was obviously too weak to eat. Clearly a full glass of eggnog would be too heavy for his emaciated stomach to digest, and the struggle of regurgitation would exhaust him, maybe exhaust the feeble energy that kept him breathing.

She ran back to the mess for cans of orange juice that could be absorbed without taking much energy for digestion. She hurried so this man could begin the tiny sips he could tolerate. His life was saved, though, not by food, but by the blood transfusion. She set two cans of OJ on the table. She lifted the cleaver from its hook on the wall to open the can. She cautiously hit the corner of the cleaver on the can lid. It merely made a dent.

"*Bitte*, I do it," Oscar reached for the cleaver.

"*Nein!* No!" Kathy turned her back to stand between him and the precious juice. She struck the cleaver at the can harder, and again only dented it.

"I help," said Oscar.

"Don't you dare touch that juice! You, you…," she struck again, and this time chopped a hole, "you German!"

She would carry the food to all the starved men—not letting a German PW carry them. Maybe tomorrow she could believe the Germans were ordinary men who wore fatigues just like the GIs wore fatigues, but for now the Germans were monsters.

She returned to the first newly liberated starved patient. She poured a little orange into the spouted cup on the bedside table. If she turned his head and tilted the cup, he wouldn't need even to suck, just swallow.

His eyes were closed, as though even the effort of seeing were too great. She spoke in a quiet voice, not wanting to wake him if he were just resting, but just wanting him to know she was there. "Would you like some juice?" No answer. He might be French: "*Voulez-vous du jus?*" Or German: "*Apfelsine saft?*"

His eyes remained closed. He wasn't breathing. This was the hospital's first death.

Feeding starving men was not the noble gesture she had considered it might be. She felt no nobility, just numbing shock. Until now she had not quite believed the newspaper accounts of German atrocities, and had dismissed them as propaganda. Could man be so cruel? Man was this inhumane? It was a miserable experience.

After the patients' supper, before her own, she carried the evening nourishments to the wards. The shrunken stomachs of these men could hold only small amounts, so they were fed frequently. She made several trips, for she could not let a German touch the food.

On her way out, she passed a six-bed surgical ward. Major Fellows was still working, examining patients. He held up a roll of bandages, with a beckoning gesture to Kathy. He set the roll down on the table of dressing supplies, and turned his attention to the patient before him on the bed.

The patient lay on his back. He held up for Major Fellows's examination two stumps that were cut off six inches from his elbow. The Major cut off the bandages.

Kathy wanted say, "I don't know how." But she did know. She learned more than that at Cook County. She saw how tired Major Fellows looked, and she knew she could put on a few bandages. She looked at the patient, and wanted to run, to turn her eyes from the mutilated arms. Yet she must not show him that his stumps were so grizzly she could not bear to look at him. Her role of nurse was to soothe and cheer him.

"All right," she said, and came to stand beside the doctor next to the bed.

"First sprinkle sulfa on," said Major Fellows, rolling the table of supplies to her. He said to the patient, "They're healing nicely," and went on to the next bed.

Kathy picked up the jar of sulfa that looked like a salt shaker and sprinkled the yellow powder on the puckered red scabs.

"Then a Vaseline dressing," the doctor directed.

She took forceps from a jar of alcohol with one hand and removed the cover from a white enameled jar with her other hand. Using a sterile technique, she took out a pad and dropped it on a stump, covering the puckered red scab.

Gently, she laid folds of gauze over the stub of his arm. Carefully she wrapped the gauze around and secured it with adhesive tape.

What could she say to cheer him? "Sorry you lost your hands"? That didn't sound cheerful. "The war news is good today. Americans are being freed from prisoner-of-war camps?" No, that certainly wouldn't help his lack of hands. "Nice weather, isn't it? Spring is a hopeful time?" No. "Have you ever heard the story about Pat and Mike"? Not that either. Anything cheerful sounded ironic. And it took all her concentration to keep her horror from showing on her face. She certainly couldn't control her voice. So, she didn't say anything.

She pushed the table around to the other side of the bed. She took another Vaseline pad with the forceps and dropped it on the other stump. It was a relief to have the puckered red scab covered.

"It's not so bad, Lieutenant," the patient assured her. "I'm alive. I'm the only fellow in my outfit left alive. You know, I am lucky." He turned his head on his pillow to look straight at her and winked. "Really, I am. I want to be a historian, but every time Mom caught me reading, she made me get up and do something useful. Now she'll have to let me read. See? I am lucky. Now suppose I'd wanted to be a piano player. Or suppose I'd lost my eyes. Now that would have been tough."

Kathy folded the gauze over his stump—and she couldn't agree about his luck. She retreated to her specialty, food. "Have you had your supper?"

He glanced at her insignia. "Oh, You're a dietitian. Say, you baked that cherry pie? Cherry pie! After six weeks of K-rations. Cherry pie! That was manna! That was ambrosia! Is there more of that?"

"If there is, I'll bring it to you."

"Thanks, Lieutenant. Thanks a lot, and say, Lieutenant, you did the best job of bandaging I've had. Yes, indeed, you did a fine job of bandaging. You've made me feel mighty good."

The amazing thing was, he seemed to mean it.

When she bandaged the flesh wound on the next patient's leg, he said, "I'm really lucky, Lieutenant. You know what I mean?"

True courage, nobility, and inspiration were in the patients. Here was the story Kathy would share with the "Time" correspondent.

Finished with the bandaging, and satisfied she had done all she could there, Kathy washed her hands. She wiped them on a paper towel, threw it into the tall waste basket, and stepped toward the door. Crash. She had accidentally bumped into the wastebasket. It tipped and rolled across the floor, spilling its rags and paper. It moved until it clanged into a bed, metal against metal.

She was reluctant to touch hospital trash with her hands, and wondered where the ward broom was kept. The whole ward was watching her, and there she stood not knowing what to do. Ridiculous, not knowing what to do about trash.

Then Major Fellows was there, with a broom and long-handled dustpan. He handed her the dustpan.

While he swept, she set the wastebasket back beside the sink. "I'm so sorry," she said. "My knees weren't working right. Stupid." Was she trying to say her knees had been at fault, not herself?

He swept the last paper into her waiting dustpan. "A bit weak in the knees, eh?" He saw her knees were shaking —and knew the weakness was not from meningitis.

"A bit," she said. After he put the broom back in the closet, they both washed their hands.

"You've got to strengthen your knees, Lieutenant Collens." Major Fellows looked at the paper towel in his hand, and saw it was trembling. He crumbled it and threw it hard into the wastebasket.

Kathy stood beside him just outside the ward door. Even here there was the smell of blood. "Can you tell me how? How have you managed that?" She looked at him. She then wished she hadn't asked because she could see he hadn't.

He took out a packet of cigarettes and a lighter. He looked at his hands, and they didn't tremble. He flicked on the lighter, and the flame was steady. Maybe she had just projected her own tremble to him.

"At home I had strong knees. At home there was a kind of balance, a balance of good against evil. You know: some people died and some were born. There were accidents, but the police, and caution and sense, balanced against them. But this war is huge with nothing balancing against it." His cigarette trembled so he threw it on the floor and stamped on it. His eyes squinted almost closed. "There is no force against it. The good guys and the bad guys are both shooting. So, what's to stop the flow of blood? The river of thick blood gutted with shattered faces and blown-off legs and arms flowing sluggishly. That's my nightmare. The river flows wider and wider. A flood is pushing against me. I can't even stand up. I can't get out. I strengthen my knees or I fall."

He lit the cigarette and blew out the smoke; then looked into her eyes. "You too. You feel the flood of it. Strengthen your knees, Lieutenant Collens."

"How?"

He pulled out his cigarettes and lighter, and now his hands were steady. "We begin," he said, tapping a cigarette against the silver lighter, "by eating a good dinner. Did I hear you talking about cherry pie?"

He had said all he could. "Yes, cherry pie," she said. "Congratulate Vivienne for that. I've another hour's work to do before I can eat," Kathy said.

"I'll see you at the club," he said, cheerfully enough. From the front door, he strode toward the officers' club. She returned to her office.

She had no answers. He didn't seem to have answers. She knew that drinking at the officers' club wasn't going to help. She wouldn't think about that now. For today, she would just keep doing what needed to be done next.

It was dusk when Kathy finished writing the last diet. She leaned back in her chair to soothe her aching back. In the kitchen, the PWs scrubbed the floors. The rush of the evening meal, the clatter of pots and pans, was past. The mess was quiet except for the voices of many languages, each talking to his own kind. As the dusk deepened, rather than lighting a candle, Kathy enjoyed the increasing darkness. In the mess, gasoline lanterns popped as they were lit and then hung, their pendulum swings throwing strange shifting shadows. Oscar brought a lit lantern into Kathy's stall. When he stood on a chair to hang it, his shadow careened crazily around the wall, huge, darkening her half of the room, then shriveling to a small dark patch on the floor. She wanted to thank him for the light, but was determined not to speak to or look at the Germans. Oscar left to go on with his work without pausing for recognition.

Kathy liked the twilight that softened what she saw. She began to shiver, as the lamps provided an ugly yellow glow rather than the silver moonlight, and the shadows were now contorted. She gathered the lists for the cooks for the next day.

Suddenly, from the beam above, a bird's song pierced the room. This was a smooth, sweet melody, not the repeated phrases of birds she knew. All other sounds ceased as Americans, Germans, French, Poles, Greek, and Russians stopped to listen. Nightingales, she once had heard, sometimes sang on moonlit nights. Could this nightingale mistake the lantern for the moon? Certainly, this song was the nightingale's melody of poets. Her spirits were lifted with its dramatic tune. Her body was weary and heavy, yet the nightingale's song soared.

"Is there a Lieutenant Collens here?" a man shouted into the barn. The nightingale's song quieted to chirps, and a tall man in officer's uniform without insignia came into her office. "Lieutenant Collens?" he asked.

"Yes."

"Fred Collen's niece?"

"Yes. You know Uncle Fred? How is he?" This must be the "Times" war correspondent. He could bring her news from home.

The reporter said, "I presume he's as busy as ever. It's been a year since I've seen him, but I had a cable three weeks ago. I'm Mark Skaw, foreign correspondent from the "Times." Fred said to look you up; there'd be a story. I didn't expect to find you working so soon. Bravely working! Got up from your sick bed to help the wounded soldiers. You must be suffering."

"Uncle Fred must have cabled you in journal-ese. That's not quite right. The Army has a new theory; the sooner the patient gets out of bed; the quicker he recovers. They made me get up. I wasn't brave, I was cross. Yet I must admit they were right; I am recovering." Kathy picked up her papers. "Want to see our mess while I take these to the cooks before dinner? Then I'm through for the day. We have 15 German PWs..."

"What?" he interrupted, "Where are the guards?" Mr. Skaw followed her around the kitchen.

"Outside. They are around somewhere. We don't need many."

"You're the only American here? No one to protect you?"

"Usually, the mess Sergeant or the GI cook is here. Sarge will be back in a minute, then we can go to chow."

He pointed to the knife rack. "Butcher knives! Cleavers! The danger! The Germans could grab knives and escape."

"They use knives for slicing bread, cleavers for opening cans. They never have tried to escape that I know. Guess they like to eat."

"I admire your courage. Working right with these monsters. These Nazis are desperate men who will stop at nothing. When I was with the VII Army Corps cleaning up the Breton ports near Normandy after the invasion, I saw four Germans escape…"

Mr. Skaw didn't ask her what she thought of the Germans. Instead, he talked several minutes about the Breton ports. Then, "You have French girls working here. How they hate the Germans."

"I don't think most people hate for long." She thought of Sue's forgiveness of Rolf, but he wasn't interested in Sue and Rolf.

The door opened and in paraded Sir Galahad. He raised one arm in a sweeping knightly salute, and kicked the door shut behind him. He stepped forward three paces, and knelt before Kathy. She graciously put out her hand on Sir Galahad's raised arm.

"Lady Kathryn, star of my sky, the night has been black until this moment that I behold you."

"You want a candle?" asked Kathy.

"Love of my life, let your love flow with the milk of human kindness and lighten my coffee."

"You want a can of milk! Granted. Oscar can give it to you."

"Oscar. I shall accept it only from your fair hand, to touch the can that your hand has touched... ah, sweet ecstasy!"

Kathy brought him a can of milk.

When he had gone, Mr. Skaw wrote in his notebook. "That Corporal said he loves you. He just used the can of milk as an excuse to touch your hand."

"I might agree if he asked me for a date, but he doesn't. He just makes wild speeches. If he sees me at all, it's as a symbol, a projection of an answer to his own needs and dreams. If he saw the real me, he'd be disillusioned—maybe that's why he doesn't ask for a date."

Mr. Skaw wrote on. "The soldiers love you. That scene could inspire girls to volunteer."

"Do you want to know where the real inspiration comes from? From the wounded soldiers."

He scribbled on in his notebook. "You carry on bravely, sing songs, tell cheerful little jokes, give confidence too —telling the patients you'll get them patched up."

"Not quite." Kathy wanted to explain what the patients thought of false cheer, but this was not what Mr. Skaw wanted to hear, and he would not listen.

When Sarge returned, Kathy introduced him to Mr. Skaw. Sarge looked suspiciously at Mr. Skaw, and offered to lock up for Kathy while she took Mr. Skaw to chow.

"Come on," said Kathy to Mr. Skaw. "You can talk to the glamor boys clamoring for girls. See if you think it's romantic."

They walked in the dark, feeling their way along the crunching gravel sidewalks. "How do you find your way?" he asked.

"We're used to blackouts. There's a little light from the moon and stars." There was a sliver of a new moon. "Do you mind waiting just a minute while I change into a Class A uniform? There are usually some of the 82nd Airborne paratroopers around the front door between jumps. Their camp is ten miles away."

"The 82nd Airborne is right here?" Mr. Skaw asked.

"Yes." Kathy responded. "They were moved here to serve in the Battle of the Bulge."

"I just did an article on them. They are some of the finest soldiers in the Army. Tough as nails. Always dropped from the sky into the most dangerous places. On D-Day they parachuted in the dark behind German lines well before the beach landings. In the Battle of the Bulge, paratroopers from both the 82nd and 101st not only helped stop the German offensive, they actually turned them back."

"They certainly have stories to tell." Kathy said "They're cocky, brash, daring. They are the kind of boys who could jump from a plane into German territory, or love a gal and leave her.

"You actually know some of them?"

"A few. Most of the girls have dated them, and sometimes invited them to dinner. They're a generous lot. They give the girls looted German cameras, radios, silver, jewelry, and sometimes an old nylon parachute.

One of the paratroopers flicked on his flashlight. He directed the beam, a yellow path in the blackness, on Kathy, then over to Mr. Skaw, then back to Kathy's face and slowly down to her ankles.

"I like ankles," he boomed in a bass monotone.

"I like hips," sang another, a note higher, turning on his light.

"I like shoulders," sang a third, from behind a third light.

"I like lips," a tenor spotlighted her face.

"We like American girls," the four chorused in harmony, all lights on Kathy.

"Blackout, blackout." Kathy held her arms up, shielding her eyes from the lights. "Everything you do is being witnessed by the press, so behave. Meet Mr. Skaw of the 'Times.'"

The lights gave Mr. Skaw a momentary glance. "No sex appeal," said the tenor, and directed his light back on Kathy.

"How about a date tonight, Lieutenant?"

"Come dance with me," sang the bass, now standing on the hood of a Jeep.

"A fifth of Scotch to kill," sang the tenor, holding up a bottle before her with one hand, slapping Kathy's seat with the other. Another grabbed Kathy's wrist.

"No sir. You can find a French girl more willing than I." She shouldn't have said that, for most French girls were decently and vigilantly chaperoned in their homes and in convents. Only a few untidy wenches hung around camps, willing to drink any soldier's liquor and sleep with him.

"We want an American girl," they harmonized.

"Enough's enough. Tell Mr. Skaw your stories while he waits." She shook her arm loose and ran in the front door, where the men were prevented from following by the MP on duty at the door.

Later, at dinner, Mr. Skaw marveled. "I can see those men love you! Idolize you! They crowd around you like the mobs around a Hollywood queen at a premiere. Just to touch you is a thrill!"

Kathy had never been a movie queen, nor even a campus queen. At first Kathy had been flattered as they didn't beg Mathilda or Sue for dates. The paratroopers were handsome, vigorous men. A month ago, very weak, Kathy had envied these girls who had energy to dance all night. It was tough to stay at home with her book, watching the girls dashing off in jeeps on their exciting dates. Kathy had initially been sympathetic, knowing the next day these men would be jumping behind enemy lines and dangling from a parachute, a defenseless target. She had been truly sad she had not yet recovered the strength to personally give them one last good time.

But in less than a month, the girls had wearied of the fast life of drinking, of dancing turned into wrestling, and kisses dangerously un-inhibited. They were disillusioned with the fast driving that caused mi-nor accidents and threatened major ones. The girls soon preferred quiet evenings at the officers' club with the older married doctors to the riot-ous nights offered, until only Vivienne regularly dated a paratrooper.

Vivienne's favorite date was a Captain Ross. Ross was engaged, and so was Vivienne, but he wanted a good time before giving his life for his country. She was too kind-hearted to deny it to him. Besides, Vivienne had a practical capability that could control any situation with any man.

Even though they could no longer pick up dates, the paratroopers continued to come. They would not consider that any girl would resist them. They sat in their Jeeps or on the grass confident that their virility was the reason these girls had joined the Army or the Red Cross. They were not easily discouraged, and used added inducements of precious Scotch or 1936 champagne. They preferred girls from a hospital, free of disease. By now Kathy had heard their pleas too often, and recognized them not as a tribute to her sparkling personality, but only to her female body. Perhaps she was judging the many by the few, but Kathy was not about to test their intentions.

Mr. Skaw said "What a story! This will inspire girls to join the nurse corps and the WACs and the Red Cross! No girl like an American girl! A life of service adored by the men you serve."

This was not quite what Kathy would have written. It would not be patriotic to say what she thought. She would not want to discourage nurses from joining the Army. The patients certainly did need them.

She introduced Mr. Skaw to the other girls at dinner, suggesting he might learn more from them. Kathy excused herself and went back to her barracks. Finally, she would be able to get some rest.

# CHAPTER 11

# A TOAST WITH THE FRENCH

In her room, Kathy didn't even light a candle. She now had a routine of putting on her pajamas and crawling into bed in the peaceful dark. It was simpler not to see, not to think, but to just get into bed and sleep.

Mrs. Foster brought her candle to the doorway between their rooms. "Are you all, right?"

"Just tired. I can't bounce against life the way I used to."

Mrs. Foster pulled up a chair, and put her polished silver candle holder on the GI stove. Sitting relaxed in her best couch-side manner, she asked, "Anything you want to talk about?"

Kathy shrugged. Her feelings were too mixed up for words. Nothing was as it should be. The world had turned into tangled black shadows.

"Worried about Rocky?"

"I'm always worried about Rocky. He must be sick, terribly sick, or he would have written." Kathy didn't mention the alternative, that Rocky was healthy and didn't care to write.

"I can have him traced and find out where he is, and how he is."

Kathy sat up and held out her arms to hug her. Mrs. Foster did not respond to her warmth, so Kathy dropped her arms. "I'd be grateful."

"Did you do anything you'd like to talk about? Good to get it off your chest." Mrs. Foster seemed to be probing for a confession. She had often suggested that guilt feelings should be talked out.

Kathy wanted to ask what it took to hold a man's love, but, considering Mrs. Foster's recent divorce, decided she might not have the answers. "I'm weary. I'm disillusioned. Life is grim." Then, as if in support of her words, she started to cry, and laid her head down on the pillow.

Mrs. Foster smiled gently at the tears. While she gave Kathy time to cry, she took a bottle of nail polish from her pocket, and brushed dark red onto her long nails. "Of course, you're right," she said when Kathy's cries subsided, "It is not just one incident but our whole environment that shapes our lives, especially the childhood years."

She continued, "Only by talking out the repressions from your childhood can you face them and outgrow them." She held up her hand, spreading her fingers by the candle's flame to examine the red polish. Everything about Mrs. Foster was gray. She had gray hair, gray eyes, and a gray Red Cross suit. Even her voice sounded gray. The only color about her was the artificial red polish. "You should talk about your mother. What was your relationship with her? Why are you escaping reality?"

"There was nothing at home to fear."

"Did she spank you? Were you misunderstood?"

"Of course, she spanked me. I earned some spankings. Was I misunderstood?" Kathy considered the question. "No, my problem was she understood me too well. I could never tell a lie without Mother reading the truth in my face. Am I jealous of my siblings? Yes, I'm jealous of my sister Betty. She has a fine husband, Ralph, and three beautiful children. But I can hardly blame Mother for that."

Mrs. Foster sighed and returned to her room with her candle, leaving Kathy in darkness.

Kathy didn't need to hunt through a happy childhood for problems. Her problems were in the miserable present. Men were shooting men that were strangers to them with whom they had no personal quarrel.

People were starved to death. "Always" ended when the orchestra stopped playing. Rocky must be sick. It could not have ended that easily. Kathy was helpless, and Mrs. Foster blamed her mother!

The next day when all the hospital staff showed a special concern for Kathy, she suspected Mrs. Foster had talked of a rehabilitation campaign. She received offers to go to a movie, or take a hike in the village, yet Kathy declined. She wanted to save her energy for her ward rounds.

At dinner, Chaplain Kirkemo brought his tray over to sit next to Kathy. "How are you?" His concern was genuine.

"Fine, how are you?"

"That is a polite answer." His fine green eyes were direct, and he smiled pleasantly. "Would you like to join our French classes, taught by the charming Mme. Duval?"

"I need classes, certainly. Maybe next week I'll have more energy"

The Chaplain walked her outside to the barracks. He said, "Good night," and shook her hand warmly. He stood as though he had more to say. "How are you?" he asked again.

"Fine."

"I am your priest. You don't need to pretend with me."

*She would remember those words all her life—that there was one to whom she need not pretend to.* "All right, I have problems, but they're not the kind you solve by talking about them."

"Problems are solved by the grace of God, not by our own efforts."

"I'm in church every Sunday." She wanted to say any time God wanted to solve her problems, that was all right by her. Any time He wanted to stop the war; any time was fine. She had prayed, and had heard no answer. She couldn't say Chaplain Kirkemo was wrong. The peace on his face witnessed that he had found the answers. "I'll try, Chaplain. I'll pray."

However, she didn't expect to hear any answers in church. She attended regularly, as a personal loyalty to Chaplain Kirkemo, not to worship a loving Father. He had a non-Episcopalian congregation and needed at least one person to lead the congregation in following the rituals. Kathy sat in the front row in a cold metal Quonset hut. When she stood, the congregation followed. When she knelt, they knelt. Her contribution was small, but they managed to go through the motions. If the church had a message, she didn't understand it. "Peace on earth, good will toward men," and, "Love your neighbor" were ironic in a world intent on killing its neighbor.

"It works, Kathy." The Chaplain's voice had no doubt. "Love works."

"Thank you," she said, and turned in to her barracks.

Mrs. Foster continued her campaign the next afternoon. "There is an all-staff dance at the officers' club tonight. It would be good for you to go."

Kathy had an easy way out. "It would be good for me, I suppose, but since no one has invited me, I'll stay home."

"Everyone is expected to attend. You can come with Mitch and me." She smiled sweetly, but her words were commanding.

Kathy had no choice but to go, or be classified neurotic. She really brushed her Class A uniform because it had not been cleaned in over three months. She polished her sturdy oxfords, rubbed rouge onto her quite-pale cheeks, brightened her mouth with lipstick, and went to the dance.

The building that had been used as an officers' club by the French cavalry was now the admitting room for the hospital. The present officers' club was in a Quonset hut. The corrugated aluminum walls curved up into the ceiling. Draped on the ceiling were gigantic red, yellow, green, and blue parachutes, adding some excitement to the otherwise dull setting. Vivienne had talked Ross into giving her the 'chutes. She had made some PWs hang them.

Standing at the bar were the Colonel, Chaplain Kirkemo, and Captain Keene. Beside them, Mathilda and Hooch Novotny leaned against the counter. Mathilda took dainty sips of her champagne while Hooch gulped his. The drinks were free for the party, and Hooch was taking full advantage. This was worrying Mathilda, and she hovered over him like a mother hen.

Bunts sat at a table with the warrant officer she sometimes dated, drinking coffee. She had come only because this was an all-staff party. Even the Colonel could not make her dance or be interested in any man except her lover-by-letter Tex in Italy. The Sergeant Major and his five-piece GI orchestra played instruments furnished by the Special Services branch of the Army. Ross, dancing cheek-to-cheek with Vivienne, was the only paratrooper in attendance. Several hospital officers danced with Red Cross and civilian French girls. At a corner table, six men played poker. They played poker every night, indifferent to the party, except that now they were drinking champagne on the house instead of their usual beer.

When the Adjutant asked Kathy to dance, she dutifully danced. He was narrow-shouldered and short, so her arm hung loosely around his neck with little support. Hooch asked her for the second dance. His shoulders were broad enough, but he smelled of alcohol and stale tobacco. He danced like a turtle waddling back and forth on wide-spaced hind legs. He rubbed against her as he held her too tight.

Kathy broke loose from him. "That's not dancing."

Hooch pulled in his head protectively, and lowered his thick eyelids, then he turned and left her in the middle of the floor. Kathy returned alone to Mrs. Foster's table. Hooch went back to Mathilda and dragged her by the wrist to dance with him.

Kathy was a wall flower. It was Captain Keene who rescued her. His dancing was jerky, but his shoulders were broad and he didn't hold her too tight while he talked. "I've not yet thanked you for the sandwiches you gave me when we first landed here at Le Havre," he said.

"It was nothing."

"It was surprisingly important. At 0300 on a January morning, on a beach in the back of an open truck, a cheese sandwich given by a sweet little girl was mighty nice. You were an inspiration."

"I'll grant that the cheese sandwich was nice, but not inspiring."

"Inspiration was the Colonel's word for you, not for the sandwich. When you danced on that landing barge, he said to us grumblers: 'If that little girl can dance now, we men should not be complaining. She's an inspiration.' Those were his words."

Kathy laughed. "I remember dancing but I was hardly jitterbugging with joy. I was just keeping warm." Now the music sounded happy, and she could easily follow his dancing. "Well, if you're part of Mrs. Foster's campaign to repair my ego, you're succeeding. I feel a little bit important."

"So now I'm a friend? Then call me Charles."

"All right. Charles."

"Did you notice the light fixtures?"

"No." She looked around the room. The fixtures were shining metal pieces pierced with designs through which the light shone. Some shades were cones reflecting light upward and some were fancy hanging chandeliers. "They're lovely. Where did we get them?" The Army would not have shipped light fixtures overseas.

"The PWs made them from tin cans," Charles said, "They're clever craftsmen."

He was not really interested in lamps. He was watching a civilian girl with long black hair. Most of the men were watching her. She wore a red dress, made of the same bright nylon as the red parachute above them. It fit tightly over her rounded bodice. A full skirt flared out when she twirled, billowing up. "Half the men are laying bets on her," he said.

"Betting what?"

Smiling, he said "Does she or does she not wear panties?"

Kathy watched, intrigued. The skirt swung around her knees. When she twirled round and round, the full length of her shapely legs was exposed. Kathy watched carefully, and waited for the skirt to go higher, but it never did. It tantalized.

"She's one of the paratroopers' girls," said Charles. "Wonder who was brash enough to bring her here? Must be one of the dentists she's with." As he danced, he continued to watch the girl in red.

"You know all the paratroopers' girls?" Kathy asked.

He laughed. "You don't realize what you're asking. The paratroopers kept a house of girls. They actually fed them, furnished and heated the house, and gave them regular medical examinations and treatments. Their girls were, bluntly stated, hygienic whores. When we arrived, and Chaplain Kirkemo found out, he went straight to the 82nd Airborne General. It was quite a battle. The General insisted he was not concerned with morality. To win this war, he was keeping his men healthy. By keeping their own girls, he could keep the venereal disease rate low among his men.

"You can imagine the Chaplain's answer: 'We're fighting this war for human dignity. When we keep a stable full of girls, we're no better than the Germans.' The Chaplain won. He personally chased those girls out. He took me along as a chaperone. That's where I saw that girl."

"Good for him."

"It wasn't that simple. The girls moved out of their house and into the men's barracks. Unless Chaplain Kirkcmo could put a Chaplain under every bed, he was stymied. He just made the beds more crowded, warmer. That's why I'm surprised that girl would dare come here where the Chaplain might recognize her. Though now that I see her, I guess she doesn't care. She's advertising."

The orchestra stopped, and they waited in the middle of the floor. Then the music began again with the orchestra playing a waltz rhythm. The song was "Always." Charles waited a minute, tapping out the beat, and began dancing.

They danced without talking for a minute. Then the Sergeant Major stood up to sing with his orchestra. "I'll be loving you, always. With a heart that's true, always. Always."

Kathy fought off the tears, but they filled her, so she cried. She put her head on Charles's broad shoulder, to hide her red nose and red eyes, until she could no longer control them.

The Sergeant Major sang on. "That's when I'll be there, always. Always."

Kathy sobbed. She could not stop. "I'm sorry," she said. "I'm going to my barracks." With tears overflowing down her cheeks, hoping no one would notice, she hurried out of the Quonset hut.

Charles followed her out. She dismissed him with "Please tell Mrs. Foster and Major Fellows my knees were tired so they won't look for me."

"Are you tired? Or was it that song?"

"Both."

"I'm sorry." He gave her a handkerchief and walked her to her barracks. "Good night, I hope you feel better in the morning."

The next afternoon, Chaplain Kirkemo said he was taking Kathy to French classes, and would not allow her to retreat to her room. The teacher, Mme. Duval, was as charming as he had said. By Hollywood standards, her mouth was too large, but she had an unusually flashing smile that dominated her face and could brighten any room.

After the class, the Chaplain and Charles offered to escort Mme. Duval back to her home, and they invited Kathy along.

On their way, Charles said "Have you heard the news? The American's First Army has successfully crossed the Rhine River near Remagen. When the Germans retreated to Germany, they left a path of scorched earth and destruction behind them. They destroyed all the bridges over the Rhine, to block out the Allies. At Remagen, they tried with demolition, bombs, and artillery, but we were able to stop them. Men scurried over that bridge into Germany. We are now on the highway to Berlin."

Chaplain Kirkemo responded. "In the East, they continue to battle the Germans to get across the Oder River. It's been going on for weeks. They are just 35 miles from Berlin. It's a race to see who can get there first."

"Never underestimate the Germans," said Mme. Duval. "I know. It's possible Hitler may have come to understand losing the global war, but he is now defending his fatherland. The Germans will never surrender."

The Duval home was a large old stone house. It was set in a yard full of flowers and vegetables, in irregular masses rather than in the measured rows of American gardens. A small boy was playing with a man in the back yard, flipping a bucket in the air off a teeter totter.

"*Voila ma famille*," said Mme. Duval. "Would you like to meet them?" She led them into the back yard and made introductions.

"*Bonjour.*" Charles walked toward the boy. "*Qu'est-ce que c'est?*" He stood, hands in his pockets, looking like a big little boy himself. He examined the log, the board, and the bucket, giving the boy time to size him up. Minutes later they were pals, jabbering in French and taking turns jumping and flipping the bucket. The boy took them all to the garage to show his pigs and rabbits.

M. Duval explained, in French, that Kathy could sometimes understand, that the Germans had taken their car. "*N'important,*" for a car was just a machine that was no good without gasoline. Machines and electricity did not have anything to do with the real business of living. Fortunately, the Germans did not take their pigs or rabbits. They had their land, small though it might be, and so they could survive.

Mme. Duval led them into the house. They entered through a chilly formal living room with heavy cherry furniture, furnished over generations, and a cold blue tile stove. They continued into a dining room warmed by a fireplace large enough for roasting a whole pig. M. Duval gathered the papers scattered on the massive round table and stacked them onto the carved chest under the window. He explained that he had been making formulas for dye at their textile mill, where they made yarn like that of the powder-blue suit Mme. Duval was wearing. It was good wool, and he was pleased with it.

M. Duval brought out an unlabeled bottle from his cellar. He took delicate goblets from a corner hunch, and poured the clear red wine.

When they were seated, and the wine passed, M. Duval held up his glass to a newspaper picture of Roosevelt pinned in the wall, framed by two tiny American flags. "*A le President Roosevelt, notre liberateur.*" They lifted their glasses in a toast. Kathy felt that she would be loved by all Frenchmen as long as she wore her American uniform.

When Mme. Duval returned, the Chaplain raised his glass to her. "*A la hostesses charmante,*" he sipped his wine with relish.

"Tell us," said Chaplain Kirkemo, "what is the French woman's secret of charm? You have a distinction our Hollywood beauties lack." He winked at Kathy. "Yes, even an old Chaplain has an eye for beauty."

Mme. Duval graciously accepted the compliment. "I do not say French women are more beautiful than your movie stars. It's just that we have different ideals. Your Hollywood beauticians push all features to look the same. Lipstick is to make a large mouth smaller and a small mouth larger. Powder is to make a big nose average and a small nose average. We French accentuate the differences. That makes distinction. My large mouth makes a better smile." She contemplated Kathy's face. "You have a French distinction. Your face is good. Your brown eyes are beautiful; one can see your heart through your eyes. Your nose is distinguished. We say *Distinguee*. But why do you cover your high forehead with bangs?"

Kathy beamed happily. Her prominent nose *distinguee*! All these years she had not believed her father when he called her nose regal, like the noses in the British royal family. "Thank you. *Merci*," Kathy said.

"I wish we had cakes to serve. Sugar is rare. *C'est la guerre*." Mme. Duval said and shrugged her shoulders.

Charles shrugged his shoulders, repeating her gesture. "We could not eat your food, anyway. You could not have enough food to feed all of us Americans." This was a nice way to express the regulation that concerned questionable sanitation some places. It was, however, permissible to drink French wines.

"Tell us the story of your church," said the Chaplain.

"Ah," said Mme. Duval, "You should not ask a Frenchman about history if you do not have hours to listen." She refilled the wineglasses.

"We have hours," said the Chaplain.

M. Duval poured more wine and talked rapidly of Louis VII and the construction of Notre Dame and of French crusades and wars. The French understood wars. Wars had, after all, been going on in France ever since Caesar first came, saw, and conquered. French and British fought over Aquitaine for four hundred years. M. Duval did not expect the Americans to understand. Americans had never been attacked, not even threatened by war. Even Pearl Harbor was too many thousands of miles away to most Americans to really threaten. Generations of Frenchmen lived and died without knowing a year of peace. Now the situation has changed for Germany, with fighting actually going on in their own country. They are no longer following Hitler's orders, but defending their home.

Here in Suippes they lived with history, and history taught them what was important. The affairs of government were not as important as the affairs of the family. The family went on whether the government was dominated by a Napoleon or a Hitler.

M. Duval had his land and his family, his wife and his children. He made yarn of sheep's wool and raised his cabbages and pigs. These were important. Wars come and wars go. The land endured. Wars kill members of families, and that was sad. But after the war, there were still families.

"Don't you hate the Germans?" Kathy asked because in his talk M. Duval showed no rage.

He answered that the Germans had been stupid to start a war. Hitler had a foolish big head. The Germans were clever and disciplined and strong, but they did not know the meaning of life. They knew progress and they knew science—but they did not understand civilization. Whereas, he had his family and his land.

"*Et la musique. Ton violon*," said Mme. Duval. "Play for us."

M. Duval played his violin, and Kathy loved the French.

"We must be going," Charles spoke abruptly when the music was done. Kathy and the Chaplain rose with him, and put on their coats. The Duvals invited them to return the next evening. Chaplain Kirkemo had another engagement, but Charles and Kathy were delighted to accept.

Hurrying home walking between Charles and the Chaplain through the woodlot, Kathy said, "I like that philosophy. The land and the family are the meaning of life."

Charles snorted. "He underestimates material progress. If he serves wine with his discussions, no one will listen for more than two hours.

Unless, of course, he gets a bathroom. I predict we will flee each night from his charming, idyllic home to rush back to our unromantic American plumbing."

Kathy stood between their rooms to tell Mrs. Foster of her evening at the Duval's. "I'm surprised I'm not exhausted." Kathy said. "They have a beautiful old home and a four-year-old boy. It was good to be with a family again."

Mrs. Foster sat before her table, looking into her little stainless-steel mirror. She pinned her hair into small precise curls. She said, "It must have made Charles homesick for his family. He has a boy almost the same age. His wife's a nice motherly woman. We met them at Fort Lewis."

Well, that ended that. Kathy would not go to the Duval's with Charles, not with a married man.

So, the following evening when Charles called for her, she walked with him a little distance and then stopped under the linden tree where they could talk privately. She wondered how to tactfully break the date, then said bluntly, "I should not go out with you. Mrs. Foster told me you are married."

"I thought you knew. Everyone met my family at Fort Lewis. Oh, no. You didn't join us until later. That needn't keep us from being friends." He nodded, a thoughtful little nod that showed he understood and was considering. His smile was an openly friendly smile and his eyes looked honestly into hers. "There' s no harm in an evening at Duvals. I assure you I won't hurt you."

"I wasn't thinking of me. I love Rocky, and I will marry Rocky. It's that I don't want to hurt your wife or come between you."

"Distance is no danger for us. My love for my wife, and our love for each other is very strong." He paused. "How can I tell you? There is no more danger of anything coming between my wife and me than of your mother ceasing to love you. Now come on; you've earned a few pleasant evenings."

Many pleasant evenings followed. French families welcomed the Americans as liberators. Since Charles and Kathy were among the few who could speak French, they were popular in the village. There were dances in the square in front of the church, and picnics beside the river. There were also occasional trips into Reims, where they walked on cobblestone streets, visited wine caves, and gazed at the sculptures in the magnificent Reims Cathedral.

Kathy was grateful for pleasant evenings. Without them she could not have survived the day's steady stream of wounded patients and the nights of crying into her pillow. Her sorrow for the wounded patients never hardened, and her bewilderment at Rocky's silence increased. It had been four months now without hearing from him. She could only guess at his reasons for not writing.

The rains stopped and the sun shone and suddenly it was April. From the mess door, Kathy could hear the nightingales singing, indoors and out.

Charles walked over, on his way to pick up Kathy for lunch, and stopped to listen. "I thought we had gotten them out."

"They're sitting on eggs in their nests." She put her hands on her hips, barring his way into the mess. "Don't you dare disturb the eggs!"

He was finding it hard to be dutifully hard-boiled about birds who sang so melodiously. "All right! All right! I'll move the whole nest without touching an egg. I'll outsmart them. Are you ready for lunch?"

"Sure." She walked beside him with skipping steps to keep up with his long stride.

He smiled down at her. "You going to the show this afternoon?"

"What show?"

"You haven't been reading the bulletin board!"

"No, I didn't. What show?"

He merely smiled.

"Charles, what show?"

"Curious, aren't you?"

"Are you going to make me walk all the way over to headquarters?"

"You're supposed to do that every day."

"All right. I confess I'm not a good soldier. I'm just a good dietitian. Now will you tell me what show?"

"Two USO girls will perform this afternoon and this evening in the auditorium for the ambulatory patients and staff. Tomorrow they'll go on the wards."

"Let's invite the Duvals. We go there so often; it would be nice to invite them here."

"I've seen the girls. We'd better monitor the show first this afternoon." Charles wouldn't say more. Kathy had to wait for the show to know what he meant.

That evening, two USO girls strolled onto the stage swinging their hips. They wore short tight skirts and spike-heeled sandals. Red kerchiefs held back their blond hair. Their satin blouses were low necked and high-waisted to the point that they could hardly be considered blouses. Their makeup was heavy, with green and blue eye shadow, artificial lashes, and scarlet lipstick. They strummed guitars to the tune of "Over There." Their words didn't quite fit the tune so they added an extra beat with slaps on their guitars and sang: "Roll me over, oh roll me over, roll me over, roll me over and do it again."

Most of the audience hooted and shouted and whistled. Charles and Kathy looked at each other, and shook their heads. They did not invite the Duvals.

By dinner time the report was going around that the Colonel had ordered the girls to clean up the show or leave. He would not allow them on the wards with the show they had presented.

# CHAPTER 12

# PICNICS AND AIRPLANES

"Today is April 14th." Mathilda's eager voice gave significance to the day.

Kathy was walking beside her from their barracks to their supper. "What is special about that? A birthday?"

"Yes. My birthday."

"Well! Happy birthday to you. If I'd known, I could have baked a cake." Mathilda looked at Kathy with a frown, and Kathy corrected herself. "All right, I know. No sugar. I was trying to say I'd like to bake you a cake."

"I'm too old to count candles on cakes. Anyway, I'm getting something even nicer. Hooch is driving us into Reims. Would you and Charles like to come along?"

"I don't know what Charles's plans are, but I'll ask him. Where will you be going? To the Red Cross Canteen?"

"I'd like that, but Hooch wouldn't spend an evening drinking coffee." Mathilda looked uncomfortable. She patted her hair bun, felt a loose hairpin, pulled it out and pushed it neatly in again.

"They have a good orchestra on a Saturday night."

"Hooch is not much of a dancer. You know that, Kathy. I suspect some of the places we go are off limits. But I don't dare ask. Maybe I really don't want to know because I'd go anyway, anywhere with Hooch." She held her head up high and defiant.

Kathy didn't challenge her. "I suspect Hooch knows what he's doing."

Mathilda stopped before the mess door. She took off her hat and put it on again, and straightened her necktie. She never entered the mess or club without first checking her hat and tie. It seemed silly because they were never anything but precisely straight.

Mathilda picked a speck of lint from her sleeve. "I know you think he's a scoundrel. And I know he drinks, and sells cigarettes on the black market, and plays a little poker. But when you know him as well as I do, you know on the outside he's rough but underneath he can be tender."

"He's...," Kathy stopped. She had been going to say that Hooch didn't drink just a little. In fact, she had never seen him sober. He sold more than cigarettes on the black market, and he played more than a little poker. Mrs. Foster called him a compulsive gambler. If Mathilda didn't see this, it was because she didn't want to see. Mathilda was Hooch's girl, and if he satisfied Mathilda, what right had Kathy to object?

"Come with us tonight, so you can understand him as I do," said Mathilda. "He's lonely, and he feels the world is against him. I know how he feels—how it feels to be lonely. If I can stand beside him, show him I love him, good or bad, then he won't be so lonely, and he won't drink so much. Come with us, Kathy."

"OK, if Charles can." It would be all right if Charles went along and drove the Jeep. It might even be fun. The evenings were lengthening, and the air was warm with spring. Hooch could be, in a surprising way, fun.

In the mess they took their chow from the cafeteria line and looked for a place to sit. Hooch stood up in the far corner, waved his arms wildly, and shouted, "Here, Mathilda!" Everyone turned to look. Hooch pulled out a bench for Mathilda and Kathy. They stepped over the bench. Hooch shoved the bench in, knocking their knees out from under them, so they sat down with a bump. "Oops," said Hooch, "These benches are tricky."

"Oh, Hooch," giggled Mathilda. "You're a card." She smiled admiringly at him. "Kathy and Charles are going to Reims with us. Isn't that splendid!"

"Maybe," said Kathy, "if Charles isn't busy."

Charles was carrying his tray from the counter. Hooch stood up, waved and shouted, "Here Charles. Here."

Mathilda beamed happily at Hooch. His thick neck was strong. His shirt was unbuttoned sufficiently to reveal a hairy chest, and he waved his long arms with vigor. She sighed with delight. "I wish I could stand up and shout, just once. I'd be scared."

Hooch slapped Charles's shoulder. "Man, I'm going to show you how to have a good time. I'm going to show you how to live."

Charles nodded mildly to the girls, "Hi Kathy. Hi Mathilda. So, Hooch, old boy, you think I don't know how to have a good time?"

"No, you do not. You're a fuddy dud. You spend your time sitting around talking French with the Frogs. Get alive, man!"

Kathy interrupted him. "They've invited us to Reims to celebrate Mathilda's birthday. Can you go?"

Charles shook his head. "Not tonight. The thermostats on the incubators don't work with this half-power electricity. I've got to keep a check on the temperatures. Maybe some other time."

"Mother-hen Keene incubating his baby germs. Baby-sitting bacteria," Hooch roared. "I told you, man, you don't know how to live!"

Charles nodded. "It's not a matter of my living, but of a patient's living. The doctors can't treat him until I grow a culture and identify the bacteria." He smiled ruefully at Kathy. "I'll admit it's not much fun. Maybe a picnic tomorrow night?"

"Sure," said Kathy

After dinner was finished, Kathy untied the string from the packet of mail she had just picked up to censor, as usual, at dinnertime. She then took out the first letter from an unsealed envelope.

Charles frowned with his eyebrows and smiled at the corners of his mouth. "Don't you ever read the bulletin board?"

"Now what have I missed?"

"We don't censor mail at meal time anymore. When we brought the mail here, the enlisted men watched us reading and talking and laughing, and assumed we were talking and laughing over their letters, even though we were usually laughing at Hooch."

"That figures. Do I take the mail to the privacy of my room?" she asked as she retied the packet.

"We can censor the mail at the club after dinner."

After supper, they carried their dishes to a table by the door. Here they scraped their meal scraps into the labeled cans, one for meat, another for potatoes, and so on. The scraps were then set out by the garbage. Since the French sifted through everything for edible food, it was determined to be more sanitary to have food sorted rather than scattered. The starving French, carrying sacks, lined up at the garbage cans to get the scraps. Disease-contaminated garbage was burned.

Kathy, Mathilda, and Charles dutifully sorted their scraps. Hooch left his tray with scraps unsorted. Mathilda took his plate and scraped it for him.

At a table in the club, Mathilda, Kathy, and Charles censored conscientiously. Hooch did not even glance at the letters. He did not even remove them from their envelopes, but just sealed and initialed them. "That's good enough," he snapped at Mathilda. He stuffed the rest of her letters into envelopes and initialed them. "This censoring's damned foolishness. There are no military secrets here." Hooch heartily slapped Charles's shoulder, "Go hatch your germs." He pulled Mathilda to walk away.

Mathilda called over her shoulder, "We'll have that picnic tomorrow. Good-night." And they were gone.

Charles put down his letters. "He's a worthless rascal, yet he makes it seem so exciting. And me so stodgy. Have you ever found a military secret in your censoring?"

"Nothing important. Have you ever been in an 'off-limits bistro'?"

"I've been in some pretty shabby places. They're more dirty than fun. In those places, I can't stop counting bacteria long enough to relax." He opened another letter. "What are you doing tonight?"

"As long as you have to work, I'll wash my hair." She opened a letter, and they methodically finished their censoring.

She had washed her hair and was drying it with an olive-drab towel when she heard Charles's whistle. She put on her wrap-round seersucker uniform, the quickest to get into, and tied a square of parachute nylon around her damp hair. She ran down to meet him.

"The bacteria can incubate without me for an hour. Want to go for a walk?"

"My hair's wet. I'm not in uniform." She had no cap, no insignia, no makeup, and no shoes.

"We'll stay out of public places. It's too nice to stay inside, anyway."

They walked along the damp path behind the hospital into the woodlot. Barefoot, she could feel the smooth, cold stones and the soft mud. She wiped her toes on velvet moss. The smooth glossy leaves of the lilacs caught the moonlight. All smells were washed away, save the sweetness of lilac and mimosa.

Charles spoke reverently. "God created the world, and it was good."

Above them, a nightingale burst into a song, a soaring melody. They looked up, hunting for the bird, standing side by side, his arm warm around her shoulder. The bird remained hidden in the branches. The branches curved in silhouette against the golden moon. The silvered violet clumps of lilacs, immersed in the fresh warm spring air, were a sight to hold their eyes upward.

Charles's arm tightened around Kathy. She looked from the moon to his face looking down at hers. He put his other arm around her, pulled her toward him, and kissed her forehead, gently.

She stood for a minute feeling the kiss as a part of the warm spring. Her nylon kerchief slipped off and her hair fell onto her forehead and cheek. Charles touched her hair with his fingers, pushed it back from her cheek.

A kiss. A kiss, Rocky. Rocky. A kiss was for Rocky, and she wanted Rocky. Kathy cried, she put her head on Charles's shoulder, and sobbed. He gave her his handkerchief, and she soaked it with tears. She wept until her tears were gone. The sobs ended with a trembling sigh, and she rested her weary head on Charles's shoulder.

Charles held her with both arms. "Didn't you want me to kiss you?"

"Yes, I did." She shivered. "It was a lovely kiss."

"Cold?" He unbuttoned his blouse and wrapped it around them both, the warmth of him warming her. There they stood, listening to the nightingale.

Finally, he said, "I hate to break the spell with a naughty word like bacteria, but I see the lights are out, so I must get back and start the gas burners."

The next afternoon in their office, Mathilda asked Vivienne, "Would you take my turn at locking up tonight? So, I can go on a picnic with Kathy and Hooch and Charles? I know it is my turn…"

The mess Sergeant was sitting on Vivienne's desk. "I'm not staying late so you can go on a picnic. If you think I'll do your stinking work while you and your stinking Lieutenant…"

"I wasn't asking you, Sarge," Mathilda jerked out the words. "I was asking Lieutenant West.

Kathy was amazed. Mild Sarge and timid Mathilda flaring at each other!

Vivienne put her hand on Sarge's arm. "Something's been bothering you. You've been barking all day. Hangover? Heard you were on a binge last night."

Sarge relaxed under her touch. "You know what's bothering me."

"Yes. We know." It had been a month since he'd heard from his wife, and a gnawing worry had been growing in him. The mail was all fouled up, and this was probably merely a mix-up of mail, but Sarge was upset.

Kathy could think of nothing to say or do to help him. It would be useless to complain at the post office. Kathy sat in helpless silence.

Vivienne tried to be encouraging. "No mail has come for anyone in three days. You can't blame your wife for snafued mail."

"Three stinking days? I've had no mail for a month—31 stinking days. Can I blame that on the stinking war?"

Vivienne persisted in being cheerful. "How'd you like to go to a movie with me tonight, Sarge? And take your mind off your troubles."

Mathilda raised her hands to her mouth in shock. "You wouldn't dare!"

Vivienne flipped back her red hair defiantly. "There's nothing to dare. I go to the movies with whomever I please."

Kathy wished she had thought of so nice a way to help. Easily Vivienne showed the Sarges and the paratroopers that she liked them. She cared for them with an inner strength that controlled any situation, yet put men at ease. She was right; Kathy had never heard anyone object to a girl's dating an enlisted man. The separation of women officers from enlisted men seemed more from having separate mess and clubs than from regulations. The girls were willing to date the enlisted men, but few even asked. That was what made Vivienne's invitation to Sarge so nice. She had broken this barrier so easily.

Vivienne patted her hair into place. "Then it is settled? Sarge and I lock up, and we will go to the show afterward. You two go on your picnic."

Mathilda pulled out her pad of paper. "What shall we take?"

Kathy considered. "Sandwiches. Peanut butter? Tuna or cheese?"

"Hooch hates peanut butter. Maybe cheese. We don't have apples or oranges. No cake, no fruit. Not much of a picnic."

"Raisins. Dried fruit bars. A canteen of coffee. Wish we had Cokes."

"Hooch would drink whiskey anyway."

Vivienne opened her drawer and took out four wax-covered boxes. "K-rations with lemonade. Perfect for picnics."

It was later than they intended when they finally finished their work and left. Hooch and Mathilda walked ahead, carrying their lunch basket, and Hooch swinging his inevitable bottle.

Charles, with a basket of lunch and a bottle of red wine, walked behind with Kathy. "How did we get into this?"

"It was Mathilda's birthday, and maybe if we're nice to Hooch we can help him," answered Kathy.

"Hooch Novotny has been Hooch Novotny since he was ten years old, maybe since he was six. A nice picnic isn't going to change him one bit. Does Mathilda really think she can reform him?"

"She's trying. Nothing ventured, nothing gained. But I don't think it matters to her whether she reforms him or not. She'd do anything for him, just as he is."

"Something ventured, something lost. Well, it's her life."

They walked along the river past white-blossomed pear trees, red-budded apple trees, and pink cherry trees. An old stone farmhouse was set peacefully among masses of honeysuckles and lilacs. Kathy took a deep breath. "It smells heavenly."

Mathilda and Hooch stood by the stone wall, waiting for them. Mathilda commented disapprovingly. "Full of weeds. They should cultivate."

"That's part of the charm," said Kathy.

Hooch spit into the dirt on the path. "It stinks." He jerked his head to the wooden sway-roofed barn that looked ready to collapse. They looked beyond the stone wall to a pigsty of sickly pigs that did indeed stink.

Charles sat on the wall, settling there as though he would become part of the scene. "They are a real problem. This farmer doesn't get his work done. He doesn't get cultivating done. He doesn't clean the place. He's not really an old man, but he acts old and tired, and defeated. I hear he lost two sons fighting the Germans."

Hooch pulled his head in, retreating into his shell. "He's no problem of ours," he coldly replied.

Charles shook his head. "But he is. Those pigs are diseased, and the drainage is from here toward the hospital. They could contaminate our wells. And now that the weather is warming, flies breed here and fly in our windows. We have no screens. We might get some made soon. The pig's sickness can spread."

"Can't we help the poor man?" asked Kathy.

"We tried, but it's tricky. We ran into international relations. I offered to run tests on the pigs to make a diagnosis. He insisted he could take care of his own pigs. I offered to send a gang of PWs over to scrub the barn and clean the pigsty. I thought maybe he'd accept German help as a kind of retribution. Instead, he was insulted that I thought his barn was dirty. Maybe I should have offered the PWs to help him cultivate, but his weeds won't hurt us. His pigs really might."

"We can take care of ourselves," said Hooch. "Waste of time to help him. I never had any help, and I managed. I've managed for myself since I was six, when my mother ran off. No father gave me no college education or set me up in business. My old man kicked me out when I was eleven. I worked for what I have, I never asked for help, and no one ever gave me nothing, so why should I give any?"

Charles stood straight before him. "I was left an orphan, too. No one gave me a college education. I worked for it."

Hooch took Mathilda's arm and pulled her onto the path. "Come on. Let's get out of this rotten place."

Charles took a last searching look at the pigs. "I still think we must help that farmer. Someday I'll get a better look at them."

They followed Mathilda and Hooch to a tangled thicket of grapevines where a bird sang an uplifting melodious song. Kathy stopped, holding her hand up for everyone to be quiet and listen. "A nightingale," she whispered.

"A mockingbird." Hooch picked up a stone and threw it into the thicket. A small, reddish-brown, white-throated bird flew out and away.

"Nightingale," said Kathy.

Hooch pulled Mathilda on along the path, while Kathy and Charles remained in the vineyard, waiting for the bird to sing again.

Kathy broke the dead wood from a grape vine. "These vines need pruning. My mother would be sad to see such neglect."

Charles took a jack-knife from his pocket, pruned away the weaker shoots. "A vine can't bear grapes if you let it waste its strength in unproductive branches. This vine should be a lesson to Hooch. He shoots off in the wrong directions, unkept and undisciplined. He needs trimming. He's strong, intelligent, energetic. He could be productive. Actually, he must be brilliant. After all, he loses $500 a week at poker, yet no one can prove any black-marketeering."

"Sounds stupid to me. If he loses, why keep on playing?"

"He is sharp, but not reasonable." Charles worked with his knife, until a trunk emerged from the thicket, twisted and gnarled, with two strong green shoots. "I'd like to prune more, but the farmer would probably accuse me of wrecking his vines." He folded his knife and put it in his pocket. "Vines make a good analogy. Mathilda is like a vine that has had all the shoots removed. She is completely enclosed in a trunk of fear. But vines were made to grow. Buds will pop out in unexpected places and grow into productive shoots."

They followed the path along the river to where Mathilda was trying to unwrap the K-rations. Hooch was hampering her by putting his arms around her waist and pulling her down onto the sandy beach. "Oh, Hooch," she giggled, "Don't you want to eat?"

"K-rations? Hell no," he said.

"A cheese sandwich? I made you a good sharp-cheese sandwich." She reached for the basket. "Pickles or olives? What do you want?"

"Whiskey." He tilted his bottle and put it to his mouth. He sucked it lovingly, then tossed the empty bottle away.

Mathilda picked up the bottle and put it in her basket. She unwrapped a K-ration package. "Have a fruit bar?" She held it out for him.

He grabbed her wrist and the dried fruit bar fell into the sand. He pulled her to him. He held her with one arm, and with the other hand pulled hairpins from her tight, neat bun, tossing the pins onto the sand behind him.

"Hooch, don't! Hooch! Stop! My pins! My hair! Her long, shining hair cascaded over her shoulders, across her cheek and down her back. Hooch glanced at the last pin, and tossed it into the river.

Mathilda broke loose from him. She crawled on her hands and knees, feeling in the sand with her fingers for her lost hairpins. Hooch laughed, and pinched her bottom. Mathilda sat on the sand to offer no temptation to pinching. Her pale cheeks were flushed, her golden hair was silken and flowing around her face. She reached her arms up to brush back her hair. Mathilda, the dull, brittle Mathilda, was a glowing woman.

"Now you've done it, Hooch Novotny." Mathilda was trying to sound cross, but happiness glowed in her eyes. You've lost my hairpins. I have no more. I can't put up my hair up."

"Good."

"But Army regulations say..."

Hooch made a face. "That" he said as he snapped his fingers, "to an Army regulation. You're a woman, not an Army."

Mathilda looked up and saw Kathy standing with Charles, watching. "What can I do?"

"Didn't you bring a six months' supply of hairpins?"

"I never lose hairpins. Those would have lasted two years."

"I'll see Mrs. Duval. Certainly, here in France, the land of fashion, there are hairpins."

They ate. The K-rations were good, and the red wine mellow. The river and Mathilda's long hair reflected the shimmering red and yellow of the sunset. Arm in arm, Hooch and Mathilda walked away into a grove of golden willows. Charles and Kathy waited, listening to the babbling of the spring-swollen river. When it grew late, and Mathilda and Hooch didn't return, they started for home without them.

They stopped again by the stone wall beside the lilacs and honeysuckle. The air, so fragrant, so charged with spring, and so filled with the nightingale's song, that it was almost palpable, subtly pushing Kathy to Charles, and Charles to Kathy. They stood peacefully together, his lips touching her soft hair. His arms were around her, savoring the air, the fragrance, and the melody.

In the west where the sun had set, they heard a sound like buzzing bees getting louder and louder. They felt it before they saw it. It was the distant roar of airplanes that flew nightly, delivering bombs and destruction. They flew in a tight, strict formation, black against the silver sky. They zoomed towards them unswerving, then over above them.

Fifty, a hundred, then a thousand. Soon the entire sky was filled, from one horizon to the other. More planes flew than seemingly could have existed in the entire world, as if gushing forth from an underworld.

The air vibrated, shattering spring, the perfume, and the nightingale. Kathy cried, unheard, under the overpowering thunder of the planes. Warm tears soaked Charles' shirt until he felt their wetness and gave her his handkerchief. Finally, the last plane had flown over the eastern horizon, and the sky went silent, except for the quiet babble of the river.

"They are going to Germany," Charles said.

"More killing. More devastation. When will this bombing end? If the war is nearly over, why can't they meet up in Switzerland and come up with a truce?"

"No, the Allies will not stop bombing." Charles said. "The Allies are clearly winning the war now. It's only a matter of time before the Russians take Berlin. Several German cities have been hammered incessantly and reduced to rubble. The Germans have been beat, but they refuse to put out white sheets and surrender. With their reign of terror, the millions of Jews massacred, their concentration camps, and so many of our soldiers lost—no, the Allies will not stop the bombing.

Silently they walked back to their base.

Kathy lay awake on her tear-soaked pillow a long time. She gave up trying to sleep, and lit a candle to read one of the books she had from the Red Cross library. She picked up the collection of poems, hoping for songs of flowers and love. She found a half-remembered poem by Edna

St. Vincent Millay: "To what purpose, April, do you return again? It is not enough that yearly down this hill, April, comes, like an idiot, babbling and strewing flowers."

Kathy blew out the candle and returned to her bed. Beauty is not enough. She must find something that *was enough.*

When she closed her eyes to sleep, the darkness closed in around her. She saw swarms of planes hovering above, shadows of Germans who shot off hands, and paratroopers clawing at her door. Reality was huge and incomprehensive. She wanted something to take hold of, something useful, a way to grapple with this reality. She lay awake, feeling inept and hopeless.

She couldn't even find out if her true love was dead or alive, true or false. Where was Rocky?

# CHAPTER 13

# A PARIS INQUIRY

The following day after supper, she saw Major Sam, the psychiatrist, sitting alone on a davenport reading his mail. Kathy felt like a younger sister in the hospital's family to be free to join in any after-dinner gathering.

When she approached, he looked up and said, "How are you, Kathy? Sit down."

"Fine," she said, and laughed. "No, that's a joke. I do have a problem."

He laughed, not unkindly. "The world is convulsed, and you...you have a problem. Seems you have all the confidence that a psychiatrist can straighten everything out. That's great. Can I get you a creme de menthe? This is special." Without waiting for her answer, he went to the bar and brought back a small glass of green liquor. "Try it. Sip it. Tiny sips."

She took a mouthful and made a wry face.

"You took too much. Tiny sips. Just a little bit at a time." He tasted his own drink, and beamed in satisfaction. "Now, what is your problem? I didn't mean to laugh at you. And I'm not completely defeated. Once in a while there's a problem I can handle."

"I don't understand what happened to Rocky. It's been almost four months now with no letters."

"That sounds definite. I would guess he's not going to write. What's the problem?"

"Why doesn't he write? He had fainting spells. He didn't faint in action, but only in inaction. He never fainted when I was with him."

"There is a reason for all behavior."

"Neither doctors nor psychiatrists could find a reason. His wife had left him while he was overseas. Then I had to leave him to go overseas. Could he be fainting away without me?" She continued, "If he's not sick, then why is he not responding? All I do is cry."

"You're lucky you can cry. That's healthy."

"To weep at a dance? To cry at a kiss?"

"Cry at a kiss? Oh. You do have a problem. You want to know what happened to Rocky? The solution is obvious. Ask him. Call him from Paris. Done. Wish all conflicts could be so rationally resolved."

"Oh, that is a good idea. Thank you. I'll do just that. Charles is driving to Paris this week. There is a conference about how to clean up the water supply without calling the French 'dirty.' Now there's a problem."

Two days later Kathy and Charles left for Paris. In the late afternoon they drove from the open countryside into a small village and then into a wooded area. "The Bois de Vincennes. We're just outside Paris," explained Charles. "Somewhere in here is a castle by the Duval's crusader friend, Louis VII. Louis liked to hunt deer and rabbits here, and fish."

Charles stopped the Jeep by a drive lined with poplar trees that led to a crumbling stone castle, and looked in his guidebook. "That flat-topped tower is part of Louis' keep. Louis changed the concept of justice. He fined a nobleman for hanging three boys who shot his rabbits with arrows in these woods. Unheard of in those days when a nobleman could do as he pleased to a common man. Justice was one thing for the people and quite another for aristocracy. You see, we have made progress in something besides the science of war."

"The heck we have. Now justice is one thing for pure Germans and another for Jews," said Kathy.

They reached Paris, emerging suddenly from the woods into a narrow street of four-story buildings with overhanging second stories. Charles said, "They kept Paris contained inside walls. Walls were built to keep the enemies out of the city. Not like New York where the country gradually changes into a city."

New York. In the morning she'd call Rocky in New York. She'd hear his voice, talk to him. What could she say?

Charles drove on. "This is the Place de la Nation, and that's a statue by Dalou."

Kathy glanced at the statue of a man on a ball hitting lions with a stick. It meant nothing to Kathy. She had no idea who Dalou was and didn't care. Rocky would say "Hello," and Kathy would say, "This is Kathy. I'm calling from Paris," and then he would say...well what would he say?

Charles looked at his map. "We leave here and go on to the Place de la Bastille. You will recognize it by a tall column. Bastille; if you picture the Bastille with your emotions, you see misery and tragedy. If you study it with your mind, it was not as bad as Dickens made it seem. At first it wasn't a prison at all, but a sturdy fortress. Some of the prisoners were wealthy, important men, and were treated decently enough."

Kathy wasn't paying much attention. She wouldn't have much time on the phone, just a few minutes, so she decided she would ask Rocky right away. "Are you alright?" That's what she wanted to know.

They drove through the dreary Faubourg St. Antoine, the breeding place of poverty, ugliness, and revolution. Next, they moved on to the more luxurious, colonnaded Rue de Rivoli, past the straight Tour St. Jacques.

Then the Jeep stopped. Charles wrapped his long arms around the steering wheel. "Here is the finest view Paris offers. From la Place du Carrousel. Beside us is the Louvre with the greatest variety of history of any building in the world. Look, Kathy."

Kathy roused herself to pay attention. This, was, after all, Paris, and she should look at the Louvre. "It seems steady and...enduring, unruffled."

"The outside doesn't show the turbulence of the inside. It was begun by the Philippe who followed our Louis VII with just four towers and a central keep, a prison. Next, Charles V added the French National Library. Later, Louis XV had his fabulous parties with fantastic orgies of food and drink and lust—while Paris starved. Then the Louvre became a quiet museum, full of statues and paintings. Now they've been taken out and buried to save them from bombings, so the Louvre is empty."

Charles started the Jeep and drove over to park in front of the Arc du Carrousel. "This, Napoleon built to his own glory, then decided it was too small and had the more colossal Arc de Triomphe built." He leaned over his wheel and gazed along the tree-lined Champs Elysée to where the Arc de Triomphe towered high against the sunset-colored sky. "Twice it was an *Arc d'Humilité*; when the English armies marched through it after Waterloo, and then the conquering Germans in 1871. Twice again it was an Arc de Triomphe when the Allies marched through it in 1919 and now again in 1945."

Triumph and humility. For centuries they alternated. Tomorrow's call to Rocky, would it be love triumphant, or Kathy humiliated? He might say goodbye—a final goodbye would be better than not knowing.

Charles drove on and stopped on the spacious Place de la Concorde. "In the eighteenth century this statue of Louis riding a charger surrounded by four virtues was designed. It took twenty-one years to build that statue. By then Louis was the 'Generally Hated,' and the king's horse seemed to be trampling the virtues." Charles leaned forward to look into Kathy's face. "Kathy, do you know what I am trying to say?"

"You certainly know your history."

"I wouldn't have come to Paris without reading a few books first. But that's not what I mean." He spread out his arms to include the ghosts that were alive in the dusky shadows. "This history lights the present, learn from it. You want to believe a man is good so you put him on a pedestal and surround him with virtues. Then you find him less-than-perfect and see him as surrounded by vices. When you think with your emotions, you see all good or all bad."

He continued, "Don't you feel the dimensions of history, the waves of good and bad mixed with good and evil, of hope and disillusion, that are in all men? When the French hopefully saw the good in a hero they erected a statue of him, and then, disillusioned, they guillotined him. That's what happens when passions rule. Far better to use your mind, to understand a man, to see him as some good and some evil, to know him for what he is."

"When Mathilda looks at Hooch, she sees only the good, and doesn't look at the bad, doesn't want to. Is that what you mean?" Kathy added.

"Exactly."

"And I put a well-beloved Rocky on a white charger and surrounded him with virtues. I can't decide whether he's upheld by virtues, trampling them, or surrounded by vices. Since he's human, it is probably both."

"In varying degrees. I doubt that you really know Rocky at all."

"Oh, I do. I spent every afternoon and evening with him for three months. He's intelligent and clever. He's a phenomenal dancer. He can tango like fury and waltz like a dream. He gave me six Christmas presents. He's exciting and I love him."

"Does he like children?"

"There were no children around the hospital."

"Is he honest? Could you trust him?" She opened her mouth to declare an indignant yes, then she stopped and said, "I don't know."

"Could he have a temper about a badly ironed shirt? Or a poorly cooked meal?"

"I would never iron a shirt badly or cook a meal poorly."

"There would be days when you're not at your best."

"I don't care. I love him and he loves me...I hope."

"If you knew him, really understood him, you would know why he didn't write. You would not need to call. That's what I've been trying to tell you. Like the Louvre, the outside doesn't tell much. It looks serene, but houses turbulence. We have always shown what we wanted to show, seen what we wanted to see, believed what we want to believe. That's humanity."

"And when I meet an attractive man I should give him a battery of tests, and then fall in love with a set of statistics?"

"I guess I don't know," sighed Charles. He turned the Jeep and drove along an avenue of sidewalk cafes and into an area of fashionable and expensive hotels and restaurants. Here the Parisians' clothes looked less shabby and gray, but did look worn. Here the elegance of the hotels looked out of place among the tired people and Army uniforms.

They dined at white damask-covered tables served by white-jacketed waiters at the Hotel Normandie. This most luxurious hotel had been taken over as a leave center by the Army. "It's ridiculous to be eating in so much luxury in the middle of a war," said Charles. He carefully cut his meat which had been dipped in a batter and French fried to make a crisp crust. He tasted it and laughed. "Under that crust, we're still at war. Taste it."

Kathy tasted it and smiled. "Spam, it's still better than anything we've managed. The sauce helps. I have to find out how the chef did that." So, Kathy took Charles back into the kitchen and gathered recipes. The chefs were delighted to give their secrets to the heroes in American hospitals and welcomed them as American liberators.

"Freshen your lipstick, and we'll go to the opera," said Charles. He glanced at his watch. "You have fifteen minutes."

"Fifteen minutes to get ready to go the Parisians Opera House in Paris, one of the most famous buildings in Paris. I ought to at least polish my buttons."

With no more preparation than a fresh coat of lipstick, Kathy walked beside Charles up the grand curves of the famous double horse-shoe staircase at the Opera House. They walked under the magnificent marble carvings and gold chandeliers. Elegantly dressed ladies smiled admiringly at Charles. Tuxedoed gentlemen smiled pleasantly at Kathy.

They both wore their uniforms with pride, as the best-dressed opera-goers there.

The program was a ballet, the *Swan Lake*, and a pantomime, *Le Coq d'Or*. They shifted from the golden splendor of the Opera House to impressionistic scenery of the Swan Lake. When the music stopped, the lights went up.

The woman who sat next to Kathy tried to explain it to her, and laughed with delight at Kathy's outlandish French accent.

"Don't laugh at that accent," said Kathy: "It has made me more French friends than a proper accent ever could."

The woman's husband invited Kathy and Charles to their apartment. "Come with us" he said. The sleeves on his jacket were frayed. Her severely simple black dress was worn looking; yet had a quality that commanded respect.

His wife said "Tonight, we have much to offer. We have good bread and aged cheese, and we have... fresh eggs."

"We do?" Her husband was impressed. "How did you get eggs?" he said.

"You know very well how I got them. I cycled into the country to the farm."

"We will be happy to come with you," said Charles.

Their apartment was simple and elegant. Walls of bookshelves were lined with worn leather-bound books. A dozen lively men and women talked energetically about government. With the French now liberated from the Germans, a new form of government somehow had to be made. Left and right, Catholic and non-Catholic, de Gaullists and anti-de Gaullists, were struggling to cooperate. Kathy and Charles were not expected to say anything. They were respected enough simply by being American officers who understood some French.

At the moment when the arguments became almost violently heated, the hostess brought out bottles of wine, a loaf of bread, cheese, and a plate of deviled eggs. The guests gathered around. Each took a cheese sandwich and a glass of wine.

"Notice," Charles said to Kathy, "that there is one-half egg per person, if you and I do not eat any." To their hostess he said, "We will be pleased to drink a glass of your wine, but we cannot eat your food. Army regulations."

"How long has it been since you've tasted a fresh egg?"

"*Pas important*. Not important. We have enough food." Charles said.

She halved each piece of egg. "I am not ashamed at how little we have to offer. I would be ashamed only if we had too much while others have nothing."

Kathy was delighted to eat a quarter of an egg. The yolk softened smoothly on her tongue, with an unbelievable texture.

That evening Kathy stayed at the nurses' leave center. After breakfast, Charles took her to the Army communications headquarters. He made arrangements to meet her again at the Normandie for dinner, and left.

Kathy approached the MP on guard at the front door. He saluted her. She returned the salute. "Where can I place a call to New York?"

He looked surprised and directed her to a back room on the second floor. She went up the stairs, showing her ID card and saluting her way through roomfuls of soldiers.

She finally reached someone with a higher rank, a First Lieutenant, who saluted her. Though, as a Second Lieutenant she should have saluted him. In his eyes, this established her as unmilitary. He had an armful of papers that he seemed in a hurry to take somewhere. He stood, waiting, unwilling to give her more than a moment's attention.

"I must call New York to a Captain Roger Rockford."

He glanced impatiently at the door. "The telephone is for military use. Only high priority calls."

"My call is important."

"It had better be. We're fighting a war! Who authorized your call?"

"Major Sam Rand."

"Who is Major Rand?"

He would scoff if she answered "psychiatrist." Instead, she said "I haven't heard from my fiancé in four months."

He gasped. His eyebrows arched. His arm went up in a helpless fury. "This is a military headquarters, not a lonely-hearts club. We are fighting a war! Go to the Red Cross. See your Chaplain. But do not bother me!" He continued to mutter in disbelief as he turned and rushed out the door.

Kathy's love was of world-wide inconsequence.

She ran down the stairs and out of the building, not taking any time to answer salutes. She headed towards the bridge facing the water. No one would be able to see the tears and red nose that she would have when she cried. But her eyes were dry. She didn't cry at all.

She leaned on the stone wall of the bridge across the Seine. She could see the Ile de la Cite, with Notre Dame Cathedral and the Palais de Justice. Notre Dame had been built in the 12th century. Certainly, Notre Dame could see events "under the aspect of eternity" of which Charles spoke. Would anyone care about Rocky's love eight centuries from now?

Here Mary Queen of Scots had married the Dauphin. Here Marie Antoinette came to offer thanks for the birth of a son who never became king. Here Josephine was crowned empress with Napoleon, and was then divorced by him. Here Eugénie married another Napoleon, and was exiled for long, dreary years.

From the towers of Notre Dame, grotesque gargoyles grinned down on Kathy. France, land of romance and love, hah! Were all the women of France tragic figures? Was there no lasting love?

She gazed at the sturdy square towers of Notre Dame and the graceful supporting buttress. The up-flowing lines of the cathedral showed strength and beauty. To look at it was to know enduring beauty, to be assured of lasting goodness.

Kathy went inside the cathedral, and lifted up her eyes to the ceiling. She saw the magnificence of the altar, the height of the arches, and the richness of the stained-glass windows. She knelt quietly in a pew. She watched beams of colored light change as the sun rose high at noon.

The world was created good and beautiful—and man willing, could again become good and beautiful.

She went from the church toward her leave center along an avenue of art shops. Remembering she should buy two wedding presents for girlfriends at home, she stopped in a shop. A girl about her own age, the daughter of the owner, waited on her. Kathy was treated not as a customer but as an American heroine who had liberated France. Kathy had long ago abandoned the role of heroine, but allowed it to help her make friends. She invited Kathy to her home for lunch. Kathy promised herself that the next time she was in Paris she would refund the food, and lunched with the family. All afternoon they walked, seeing Paris as an artist saw it. Kathy forgot her heartbreak until she met Charles for supper and he asked about her call to New York.

After dinner they rode in a horse-drawn carriage on cobblestone streets to the Tuileries Gardens. Fountains splashed along the Champs Elysee. New York seemed far away. Couples, GIs and French girls, strolled arm in arm, and kissed in doorways and on park benches. Paris in April was romantic, and Charles put his arm around Kathy.

They sat on an iron bench on the edge of the Place de la Concorde. "Here we have the Luxor Obelisk. It's Paris's oldest monument and the oldest thing I've ever seen," said Charles. "Rameses II erected that in Egypt in 1250 BC—twenty-one centuries ago. As a gift to France, it was moved here in 1833."

"I don't know who Rameses II was, and I can't imagine twenty-one centuries." She didn't care about Rameses, and she didn't think Charles cared either.

He pulled her toward him, and her head fit nicely on his shoulder. His fingers brushed her hair, while he talked of Rameses. "He was the Pharaoh whose daughter rescued Moses from the bulrushes. Twenty-one centuries..." His mouth was on her hair, and his words were muffled. His hand on her chin, he tilted her head back, and kissed her lips.

The kiss upset Kathy. The strong and contradictory feelings of the day could only be resolved in tears. She cried, and felt herself stupid for crying. Charles was patient with her weeping. He just patted her shoulder until she was calm.

Then he spoke quietly. "Right now, this seems sad. Right now, this is sad. But in time, in time it won't seem so bad. It fades away. You will start again."

Kathy raised her head to protest, but Charles pushed it gently back onto his shoulder, saying, "I know what I'm saying. I've lived through real tragedies. When I was in eighth grade, when our family was gathered round the table for Sunday dinner, my father slumped forward in his chair, his head on his plate, dead. A heart attack.

"My mother never recovered. She died two months later, which I still feel sad about. But I managed, with my older brother taking care of me. Maybe I depended on him too much, but he was all I had. I had to work my way through college. But it was a good life, with just my brother and me.

"Then when I was a sophomore, my brother died. I was alone."

Charles continued, "I rebelled against these three deaths. First with a passionate fury, and then later with a determination to fight death. I would be a doctor. I was a promising student and was given a scholarship to medical school. It was a start at picking up the pieces.

"Then when I was a senior, I married. I was lonely, and wanted a family. We were happy, for a while. Then we had a baby girl. I refused the school scholarship, and instead worked as bacteriologist to support my family. I didn't mind giving up medical school because I loved my wife and our daughter. The day the baby was eight months old, I came home from the lab to find a note on the kitchen table. My wife had left me, and taken our daughter to her mother. She said she just didn't like married life. She's still a career woman, never remarried."

Charles paused, rubbing Kathy's hair. "Yes, I've known real tragedy. I've lost my family, rebuilt a life, lost my career, and lost another family. In time I recovered again and rebuilt another life. I married again. This time I had better judgment. I know the love between my wife and me will never fail. We have a little boy, three years old. Then came the war. Monday, I had a letter that my boy is sick—and here I am in France, helpless."

They sat on an iron bench on the Place de la Concorde in front of the obelisk that was the oldest thing they'd ever seen. Kathy searched for words to help him, to comfort him, and could find none. She sat in silence wondering what to do, and then she knew what to do. She put her arms around his neck, pulled his face down to hers, and kissed him. Man and woman were made to stand together against the loneliness and insecurity of this world.

Back in their own mess the next evening, eating from plastic trays on wooden tables, Kathy looked at the men and women with new sympathy. Yesterday she had been preoccupied with her own anguish. Today she knew they were all struggling against the same loneliness and insecurity. Each girl was away from everything familiar to her. They were in a foreign land where the streets were cobblestone and the language strange. Their clothes were impressive uniforms, yet were not enjoyable like dresses or skirts and sweaters. Even their underwear was olive drab.

It was as though they had all left their homes for an evening at a theater, and were partaking in a play about war. Or as though their real selves were sitting at home in a warm, comfortable living room on overstuffed furniture, reading a book. They knew that when the war ended, and the book was closed, they would look around and find themselves back on the same furniture in the same living room.

They all lived like this. There was no continuity between their old familiar life and this strange life. The essence of the story was the finding of someone to stand beside you against the war-torn world. Then, to continue to stay at each other's side to withstand the horrors of the war.

Luxor Obelisk, Paris

# CHAPTER 14

# THE PARATROOPERS' JUMPING-OFF DANCE

Kathy was dressing for dinner when Vivienne came in. Her versatile golden-red hair was swirled back and pinned up. Kathy knew she was going out to something unusually elegant. Kathy envied Vivienne's hair; that golden-red shone brightly against her olive drab uniform. Vivienne was able to have a touch of glamor any time she brushed out her hair. Kathy's brown hair would brush only one way and added no color to her attire. Kathy took lipstick from her drawer. A bright smile was the best she could do.

"Kathy, this is a special dance. The paratroopers call it a jumping-off dance. It's a kind of a combined bon voyage and final feast for condemned men. Ross's Major wants a date. Would you go with us?"

"You've seen me at those parties, Vivienne. I'm not much good. I don't like to drink, and that's always a battle. I still get too tired when I stay out late. I just don't belong."

Vivienne picked up a bottle of Kathy's perfume, dabbed it behind Kathy's ears—just as though Kathy had said "Yes" and Vivienne was helping her get ready. "We'll have to be back early because they leave for the airfield sometime after midnight. Ross will drive. You know how careful he is, so you can have no objections. You don't need to drink, just dance."

Kathy shrugged indifferently. "I can't see that dancing is much help."

"There will be cocktails before dinner in the General's chateau. It's a palace, really. Have you seen it?" Vivienne dabbed perfume on Kathy's wrists.

"No. I've never dated a General."

Vivienne took Kathy's coat from her closet. "You're missing something. You'll get an idea of how Louis XV must have lived. Or, Kathy, was it Louis XVI?"

"Both. OK." It seemed she should do something special to get ready. A year ago, she would have spent several days in Chicago, buying a dress, gloves, hat and shoes, and having her hair styled and nails manicured. Now, she didn't even own nail polish. She had on a clean shirt. She put on the coat Vivienne held for her. "I'm ready."

Ross and a huge Major waited beside the Jeep parked by the front door. Ross smiled at the sight of Vivienne. The Major gave Kathy a quick glance up and down, and he grinned at her. He was a tall, handsome blond man, and Kathy returned his smile.

Ross reached for Vivienne's hand, and holding it, made the introduction. "Major Forand, meet Lieutenant Collens."

"Ross," said Vivienne, "You may be an officer and then a gentleman, but we are ladies first and then officers. Please make the introduction in the correct order. Lieutenant Kathy Collens, meet Major Fred Forand."

Kathy and the Major sat in the back seat, and he behaved like a gentleman the whole ten miles.

Major Forand led Kathy into the entrance to the General's grandiose chateau. Here was a mosaic floor with intricate star patterns and larger-than-life white marble statues. Major Forand snapped his fingers, and a Private took their coats. The reception room where cocktails were being served was plush with oriental rugs, enormous tapestry drapes, and red leather furniture. Massive tables had legs carved as lion claws clutching gold balls.

There was none of an atmosphere of "condemned men" at this party. A hundred officers and French women in formals were talking in groups and helping themselves to a fantastic array of bottles. A few of the women wore long formals, yet most wore waltz-length gowns. The theory was that the shorter dresses saved scarce materials. Jewelry sparkled from ears, necks, and wrists.

Their hair! The French ladies' hair was fantastic, piled high in ornate swirls. Their makeup skillfully applied, with shades of green and blue around their eyes, making their faces fascinating works of art. Kathy had been to fashionable parties, even to debuts, but never had she seen so much flair and color. The fashion in Chicago had been tempered with conservative simplicity. Here fashion was daring, flamboyant, and brilliant.

Kathy would have felt plain and wholesome, except that she and Vivienne were immediately surrounded by men. Evidently her military uniform was more attractive to jump-bound paratroopers than satin and chiffon formals.

Major Forand took her arm and forcefully guided her to the table of variously colored bottles and assorted delicate goblets. "What will you have?"

Kathy trusted no paratrooper further than she could jump, and intended to maintain her senses. Among paratroopers she was living dangerously, and she must remain sober. However, Major Forand was so big and strong, so much in command, that she decided it would be simpler to hold a glass of wine than to argue. She took a glass with a flaring wide top. "I'll take that." She pointed to a bottle. "It's a pretty sparkling red."

"Not that." He took her glass and set it down on the table. "Not that glass, and not that wine. You never drink a good wine from a wide glass. The rim should come together at the top to concentrate the scent. And you don't want _Neac Mediocer_!" He picked up another bottle, uncorked it, and held it under his nose to savor the scent. With his huge bull chest and large brown eyes, he looked like Ferdinand the Bull, the silly cartoon character, sniffing flowers.

"Try this. *Château Ausone, 1929.*" He held the bottle under her nose. It smelled like any wine. He looked at her, expecting some comment. She sniffed again, but could distinguish nothing different. "I'm afraid I don't have a delicate nose, Ferdinand."

"Forand's the name. That is from St. Emilion," he explained as though that should mean something to her.

"Oh," said Kathy. "Then don't waste it on me. I'll just carry this pretty red *Neac* around, Ferdinand. I don't intend to taste it anyway."

"Forand. You could refuse a *Château Ausone, 1929?* Well! Actually, you are right; a table wine's not right before dinner. An Apertif... which? Dubonnet? Vermouth? Sherry? Here is one you could never refuse: Montilla." He picked up a small bottle and held it up her for to admire. "We flew this in from Cordova for this dinner."

"Cordova? The Cordova in Spain? For a bottle of sherry?"

"That's not just sherry. That's Montilla. Diversionary tactics confused the Germans to see paratroopers in Cordova." His chest swelled with pride, and he looked more than ever like a bull.

"How far?" she asked.

"Southern Spain. That's 500 miles across France and another 500 miles across Spain. Nothing's too good for the 82nd Airborne!"

The man was not to be trusted. If he were telling the truth, he had flown 2,000 miles for sherry, using scarce gasoline. If he was a liar, he was making a preposterous effort to impress her. Either way, he was a man who expected to get what he wanted. So, while Kathy now felt capable of handling most men simply by staying out of dark corners, she was up against an unusually dominant man. "No thank you. I'll take the *Neac*. My loyalty to France wouldn't let me drink a Spanish wine."

Ferdinand poured her a glass of Montilla wine.

"You can lead a horse to water, but..." Kathy carried the glass around with her, but didn't drink it.

When dinner was announced, they took their coats and walked into the next room. The dining area was a gigantic wood-paneled room with a feast spread across enormous tables. Some 200 officers and French women were helping themselves to dinner. GIs served the food. Evidently PWs didn't have the freedom here, where there were military secrets, that they had in the 223rd General Hospital.

Something smelled delicious. Kathy considered the smell. It was…unbelievable. There was no doubt. It was steak. Steaks frying! She followed the scent to the field ranges set up behind the serving tables. A Corporal was frying fresh steaks!

"How do you want your steak, Lieutenant?" asked the Corporal.

"That's the first fresh meat I've seen in four months! Where did you get it?" asked Kathy.

Major Forand raised his bushy eyebrows and said, casually, as though they ate steaks every day, "Nothing's impossible for the paratroopers. Medium? Well-done? Rare?"

"Medium." Kathy told the Corporal.

"While it's cooking, help yourself." Major Forand swept his arm in a grand gesture over the table.

Dishes of peas and beans, far greener than the canned and dehydrated vegetables the quartermaster gave their hospital. Oranges! Bright gleaming golden orange oranges! Kathy couldn't resist them. She took an orange. Without waiting for a plate or to sit properly at a table, she dug her thumbnail into the thick peel, and broke off a piece. From the rind came the tangy, pungent smell of oranges. She took a plate, set the orange in the middle, arranging the peelings around the edges, and opened the sections. No rose opening its petals was ever so beautiful. She separated a section, and bit off a tiny piece. It was cool, juicy, and sweet. When she popped the whole section into her mouth, she felt gluttonous.

She ate another section, then hesitated, suspicious. "Ferdinand, where did you get these?"

"Forand! Italy." Again, he had that off-hand, casual tone, cock-sure of himself. "Nothing's too good for…"

"Yes, I know. Nothing's too good for the Airborne." Since there was no way she could take it back to the starving Italians, she might as well enjoy it. The Major's self-importance was almost ridiculous, and yet it required an inordinate conceit to jump behind German lines and start shooting. Also, in this time of uncertainty, in her own confusion, it was good to be with a man so confident, even if his confidence was self-centered.

So, Kathy enjoyed the steak, peas, beans, and oranges, a little surprised at how extremely delicious they were. This was food to be served the gods on Mount Olympus, which Ferdinand appropriated as his "just desserts."

After dinner, the GI orchestra started. The Major and Kathy began the dance. For a few measures they waltzed and swooped alone. It was almost like dancing with Rocky again.

Crowds of men swarmed after them to cut in on the Major. He evaded them, but not for long. Never had Kathy been so popular, so sought after. While she was at school, she managed to attract a partner for most of the dances, but men weren't competing for her. She'd never been at a place where cocky men so lopsidedly outnumbered the women. There was not an unhappy face in the room, with everyone smiling or laughing.

Except sometimes Major Forand frowned. He grew fighting mad when he couldn't complete even one dance with Kathy. He grabbed her back from a competitor, danced her toward the door, refusing to let others cut in. "Come on," he said in a voice that wasn't asking, but commanding, "Up to my room where we can dance without those wolves cutting in. I have a phonograph and Glenn Miller records." He didn't wait for her to walk voluntarily, but forcefully pushed her with his arm around her waist.

Kathy tried twirling out of his arm. "Should I be insulted or flattered, Ferdinand?"

His arm held her tenaciously. "Forand!" he growled. "Come on. What's the harm in a dance?"

"Not a thing. Let's stay here and dance."

His face was confidently determined, his arm persistently pushed her toward the door. "We'll dance upstairs."

"Ferdinand, I'm suspicious of bedrooms."

When he pushed, Kathy turned to face him. She said, "Now don't go ruining a nice evening. It was so delightful. Lower your horns and attack the Germans, not me."

"I will dance with you, alone, where no one can cut in."

"No," she said firmly. "Just plain no."

They returned to the dance floor, but the Major did not give up. Why? What was he? He was far more than just an animal. Last week he had brilliantly planned and executed strategies that killed multitudes of Germans, earning a Silver Star. Was he just looking for simple pleasure? Or was this a display of his animal instincts struggling for survival, knowing tonight he might die, with no descendants? Could a woman ever understand a man's reasons? Whatever it was, he had Kathy's sympathies—but not her cooperation.

It was a relief when Ross and Vivienne brought Kathy her coat and announced, "It's eleven-thirty. Ready to leave?"

Vivienne put her overseas cap on at a jaunty angle. "Better hurry," she said to Kathy. "They're to be at the air-field at 0100."

Ross scowled. She was divulging a military secret, but Vivienne just laughed. "Every woman here knows that the only thing that could stop your party at eleven-thirty would be a jump at one. Why else?"

Ross looked stern. "Training rules." Kathy hurried. She dashed across the room to the serving table, grabbed two oranges, and hid them in her coat pockets.

On the way back, Vivienne sat sideways in the front seat, and kept a watchful eye on Major Forand and Kathy in the back seat. The Major was a gentleman again. He and Ross talked of the coming jump. The campaign to clutch Kathy was forgotten, and the campaign against the Nazis resumed.

When Kathy and Vivienne got out of the Jeep, they entered the hospital's headquarters to sign in. After the Airborne luxury, their own office looked shabby. Charles Keene and Dick Castle, the engineer, were sitting around a plain wooden table on plain straight chairs. They were drinking coffee with Major Fellows, who was the OD, Officer on Duty. They all stood as Vivienne and Kathy entered.

"Have a chair," offered Charles, pulling out GI chairs for Kathy and Vivienne. "Have a good time?"

"The kind of evening girls dream about. A hundred men wanting to dance with me!" Kathy replied. "And I didn't like it. The General's chateau is like a princess' fairy tale palace. Wines flown in from Spain! Steaks! Fresh steaks! And you won't believe this…" She took the two oranges from her pockets and placed them reverently in the center of the table. "Oranges!"

They all sat around the table, gazing admiringly at the oranges. "Well," said Dick. "We can offer you coffee. Anyone for coffee with canned milk and no sugar?" He lifted the sooty five-gallon pot from the stove. With his strong hand tipping the heavy pot, he poured steaming coffee into aluminum cups for Kathy and Vivienne.

Charles picked up an orange, held it up in wonderment. "Beautiful. I never saw before how beautiful an orange could be." He rolled the orange back and forth on the table, catching it delicately with his long fingers. "Know what we had for dinner? Dehydrated potatoes, canned meat balls, dehydrated carrots, and canned peaches. Now why would the quartermaster give oranges to paratroopers and not to patients?"

"The quartermaster didn't. They flew 2,000 miles to Italy for oranges," said Kathy.

Major Fellows twirled the other orange on his fingertips, balancing it dexterously with his slender fingers. "That makes oranges more precious than rubies. I'm jealous. I'm jealous over an orange!"

"Help yourself," offered Kathy. The three men just looked at them, so Kathy repeated, "Go ahead. We've had ours." The two girls started peeling them. The men nibbled at the peelings. "There's vitamin C in the peelings too. Speaking of vitamin C, when you miss breakfast, Charles Keene, you miss your orange juice. It's the only source of vitamin C we have. Either you get up for breakfast, or stop in our mess and I'll give you some juice."

Charles's smile was surprisingly tender and grateful for the mere offer of a glass of juice. "Thanks. I'll come."

Major Fellows slapped the table. "No one noticed that I don't eat breakfast."

So, it wasn't the glass of juice, it was the caring that brought gratitude to Charles's face. *Caring was no little thing.* Kathy couldn't stop the shooting. She couldn't reform the world, not even one man. She wouldn't give the Major his baby, nor feed the starving French nor replace shot-off hands. Yet she could care. She could peel an orange. She divided the orange sections among the men.

Vivienne divided the other orange. "There must be a hundred men who don't cat breakfast. No wonder there's an epidemic of colds. We'll serve citrus juice at lunch for those who missed." She picked up her cup, but the metal was hot and she hastily set it down. "I don't like metal cups. Tonight, we drank from china cups, and coffee tasted like coffee, not like aluminum."

"What's the General's palace like?" asked Major Fellows.

"Plush," answered Vivienne. "Like a movie about Louis XV. There must have been a dozen mirrors, big fancy things with carved frames."

"Oranges!" Major Fellows sucked juice from a section. "Steaks! When was the last time we had steaks?"

"It isn't fair." Dick stood up to set the coffee pot back on the stove with a clang. "What have paratroopers done to deserve oranges and mirrors?"

Vivienne rose, indignant. Tiny Vivienne, barely five feet tall, 100 pounds, shouted up at big Dick, over six feet tall and 250 pounds. She shook her head of glistening copper hair. "Right now, they're getting into planes. By dawn they'll be surrounded by Nazis, and most of them will likely be wounded or killed. Can you begrudge them a last meal of steaks and oranges?"

Major Fellows stood, as tall as Dick. "Would you give oranges to a man who might get wounded, or to a man who is wounded?"

"That's not the question," said Dick. "We three are big men, as brawny as any paratrooper. I consider our brains are more valuable. Who should have oranges, brain or brawn? Is shooting men more valuable, even in war, than keeping equipment working?"

Charles nodded his agreement. "How about Doc? Paratroopers shoot men apart. Doc sews them back together. Which men get newspaper headlines? Which men should get the oranges?"

"The poor man who was shot apart and sewed together," said Kathy.

"The man who has the plane," said Vivienne, raising her voice. "Paratroopers can get them. We cannot. Our patients deserve the best food we can get, and that's what we give them. It doesn't help the patients for us to get mad at paratroopers."

"They might have better food," said Kathy, changing the subject, "but we have a nicer commanding officer."

"The General's all right," said Vivienne, sitting down again. "You just don't like Generals because of the one at Riley." She touched her cup, and finding it cooler, sipped her coffee.

"What happened at Riley?" asked Charles. Now they were all sitting around the table.

"I went to Riley after basic training. I hadn't yet learned to look at a man's shoulders for his rank. A white-haired old man came into the mess and sat alone in a corner. He looked so unhappy. Old men always had liked me, so I sat beside him. I hadn't said two sentences before I knew that he wanted to be alone. He acted indifferent, so I left him alone. The next day I was called into the offices of four head nurses and head dietitians, and told that a Second Lieutenant does not speak to a General unless the General speaks to her. He must have told them, as we were the only ones in the mess. So now I save my cheer for lower ranks. Generals get no sympathy from me."

"Was the Airborne General like that?"

"I don't know—I didn't speak to him. He didn't speak to me first," said Kathy.

Vivienne knew him. "He's a good General. You wouldn't expect an Airborne General to be as nice as the commanding officer of a hospital. I do resent it that our Colonel lives in a little room with old GI furniture, while their General has a whole chateau of fancy furniture and carpets. I wouldn't mind having a mirror. It's a shame to waste a dozen mirrors on one man. Mirrors are for women."

"A dozen mirrors. Could the old geezer be that vain?" asked Charles. "If we had five, one for each pair of girls, seven would remain."

Dick rubbed his chin. "Are you sure they're jumping?"

"Certain," said Vivienne.

"Everyone goes?" asked Dick.

"A jump is a unanimous effort. The place is deserted. No guarded gate. No wall."

When Dick stood, he smiled and looked directly over at Charles, catching his eye. He jerked his thumb towards the street and said "Let's go! Our truck is outside, full of gas."

Charles stood. "I'll get Sam and Toby from the club."

"Time for me to be going on my OD rounds," said Major Fellows. He stood, looking at his watch. What he wouldn't see wouldn't concern him.

"Come along, girls. You can pick out a table and chair for Colonel Stone. You've got the joint cased." Dick held Vivienne's coat for her. "Show us to those mirrors."

It would be a satisfaction to rob the rich of their oranges and distribute them among the poor.

The four men and two girls drove slowly, finding their way by the dim light of the half-moon. An Army truck driving without headlights would attract no attention. This was the standard way to travel at night. They drove in the open gates and through the paratroopers' camp, peering in the shadows. Satisfied that the camp was deserted, they drove around the General's chateau. They drove up to the back door, and waited. No one came out.

Vivienne led them with a flashlight into the hall of mirrors, while Kathy and Charles searched the kitchen for oranges. Finding no oranges, they went on into the big hall. Vivienne selected an overstuffed leather chair and a massive cherry table for the Colonel. Dick stared at a white marble nude sculpture, then draped it with a tablecloth.

While the men carried five mirrors out to the truck, Kathy decided on the red and gold drapes, and stood in her stocking feet on a table to unhook them. The men carried out rolled rugs, chairs and tables, working faster and faster as they felt the danger. When they heard a car backfire, they grabbed final armfuls and scrammed. Dick had a German clock and radio. Charles had German binoculars and a telescope. Vivienne had a pillow and gold brocade bedspread. Kathy had a silver teapot and tray. They clambered into the truck, and drove slowly away. Not until then did it occur to Kathy that a paratrooper might have shot first and asked questions later.

They watched the road behind them, relaxing as no one followed. By the time they reached the hospital, they were singing. The men unloaded the girls' things at their quarters. Shouting ahead they carried the loot into their rooms.

"Let's have a party," said Kathy. "I can serve you tea in a silver teapot." The other girls, wearing their pajamas, brought their metal cups and rounded up cookies and candy sent in boxes from home. The ten girls and four men sat in Kathy's room. Charles poured coal from a coal bucket onto the fire. Kathy put an old aluminum pan of water on to heat.

"How can you hang drapes without a curtain rod?" asked Vivienne.

"Nail them up. I have tacks and a hammer." Kathy took out her the tiny stainless-steel hammer from the many-pocketed cloth hanging on the wall.

Mrs. Foster, sitting on the bed, ran her hand across the drapes spread over her lap, fingering the satin green leaves, the soft red petals, and the rough gold background. "You can't put tacks through this. It's far too precious. You must hang them properly."

"I want to hang them now. I want bright colors, something cheerful to look at." Kathy held a drape up at the window.

"I could get a pipe, or a wire," offered Dick.

Full of fear, Mathilda lifted the corner of a black-out curtain to look outside, as though she expected a paratrooper. "Not in the window," she said. "You can't hang it in the window. The paratroopers would see it."

Vivienne had washed the teapot and now she put tea leaves in it. Kathy poured the hot water into the pot. When she had waited three minutes, she poured it. The tea was pale. The heavy silver pot had cooled the water.

"We should have heated the pot with hot water first," said Vivienne.

"We didn't have that much hot water. Just one pan. I'll put the silver teapot on the stove to heat."

Mrs. Foster took it off. "You'll melt the silver! You can't put a silver teapot on a hot stove."

Kathy poured the tea into the battered old pan on the stove. In a few minutes it was hot and strong, and the aroma filled the room. They relished the tea.

"It tastes the same whether it was poured from silver or aluminum," Charles said. "Perfect with cookies."

The stolen silver teapot was worthless.

Kathy stood in front of the mirror that leaned against the wall. "Maybe I can't use the drapes, or the teapot, but I can use my mirror." The image was far clearer than her stainless-steel mirror, yet had an ugly brown tint. "Hmm. Maybe not. I don't like to see myself tinted a dreary brown."

Mrs. Foster neatly folded the drapes, placed them in the center of the bed, and crossed the room to admire the mirror. She traced the gilt carved design with her red polished nails. This mirror belonged to Mrs. Foster. She saw people as tinted brown and covered with a thin veneer of civilization.

"Would you like the mirror?" Kathy asked Mrs. Foster.

"It's beautiful."

"It's yours."

"Does your conscience bother you? Is that why you want to get rid of it?" asked Mrs. Foster.

"No. It's not the mirror that I want. I would like to give it to you."

"You stole a truckload of furniture, and your conscience doesn't bother you?"

Kathy considered. "No, not a twinge. It ought to, but all I feel is that it was fun. It was stupid, and we might have been shot. I can't even use the things we took."

Charles stood beside her and looked at her seriously. "My conscience is calm, too. What has happened to it? Dick, do you feel guilty? Sam? Toby?"

Sam stood and shook his head. "That's what happens in war. Our consciences learn different standards." He shrugged, "*C'est la guerre.*"

"I search for something more enduring than that," said Kathy, wondering if she would someday recover from this loss of morality. Kathy had lost her trust in her own integrity.

Then, because it was almost three, the party was over.

When Charles came into the mess for his orange juice the next morning, his coat was soaking wet. "*I'l pleut*, It's raining," he said. He went to the stove, but it was cold because the wet wood made only smoldering fires.

Kathy poured orange juice from a can for him. She said "You would think the Airborne could have predicted this weather and stayed home. Or maybe they can hide better on cold and rainy days when intelligent Germans stay inside."

"They're not on a picnic. War doesn't wait for weather," Charles responded.

"Poor guys. Vivienne's worried about Ross. I'll bet Major Ferdinand's in a warm, dry cottage surrounded by *frauleins*."

A week later, Kathy sat in her comfortable red leather chair, her feet propped up on her warm stove, reading her book, *Magic Mountain*—hoping for magic for the consumptive characters.

Vivienne ran in through her open door. "Look out the window."

The paratroopers were carrying their rugs and furniture out from the men's quarters. "They hunted through all the infantry divisions and artillery camps in the area. They didn't suspect our mild, non-belligerent doctors. Then when they'd looked everywhere else, they came here, and there they are. At least they didn't find all the pieces to take back."

"Have you seen Ross?"

"Yes. See. There he is—all in one piece. Thank God."

Kathy looked out the window. She noticed Ross now had oak leaves on his uniform. "I see he's been promoted. He's now a Major. I'll congratulate him," said Kathy.

"Don't. It was a battlefield promotion. Those are Major Forand's oak leaves. That evening when they went out, Major Forand was shot down immediately. They were waiting for him. He didn't have a chance."

# CHAPTER 15
## STATUS UPDATE

It rained steadily for a full week, making nasty weather for the infantry guys in fox holes. It was unseasonably cold, near-freezing outside, and not much warmer inside. Kathy and Vivienne worked at their desks with their coats on because the mess was without heat. The coal supply was low, and what there was, was pulverized and wet. Oscar would have managed to get the fires going someway, but he had the flu and had stayed inside his tent. A cold tent in the PW stockade would be a miserable place to have flu.

Sarge would have made a fire, but Sarge was sick too. His Quonset hut was dryer, but not much warmer than a PW tent.

With so many sick, it was all they could do to get three meals to the patients. No one had time to fuss with fires.

Kathy had just returned from her ward rounds. At least on the wards she had been warm. Now she was checking the next day's food orders. This was usually Mathilda's job, but Mathilda had the flu. "I hope I didn't add wrong again. I'm just not as accurate as Mathilda."

"No one is as accurate as Mathilda. Don't worry so much. Your mistakes weren't fatal." Vivienne was writing requisitions for cleaning supplies, which was usually Sarge's work.

Kathy's mistakes actually had been bad. She had ordered too little food for two wards. By the time the wards had discovered their shortage, and sent for more, all leftover food had been eaten by the civilian women and the PWs. Either Sarge or Oscar would have made sure all wards were sufficiently fed before handing out leftovers. Kathy or Vivienne should have noticed, but they didn't.

To finish feeding the wards, Kathy had made Superman open cans of stew with a cleaver. He put the stew into the big square pan on top of a field range to heat. When they went to dish it up, they found it was cold. The range had run out of gasoline. Sarge would have checked the tanks. They lit another range and finally got hot food out, but so late the schedule was disrupted—all because of the cold.

For the next day's order, Kathy checked and re-checked her figures, and hoped for no more mistakes. She carried the lists into the mess.

After a cold week, everyone in the mess was irritable. A Russian and a Polish woman were screeching at each other, in Russian. Kathy was too tired to tackle their problem, and just let them screech. Two Germans growled guttural noises at each other, shaking fists. With Oscar gone, Superman was the only PW who spoke any English. Kathy would not give Superman the satisfaction to intervene. With the work finally done, they could all go to their own stockades to fight. All five feet one inch of Kathy had had enough. She stood and faced them, the nine women and the fifteen Germans, and ordered "Go home. Shoo. *Allez! Gehen-sie. Vamoose!*"

They all put on their ragged, damp coats and left. They left so meekly; their collars turned up so futilely against the steady rain that Kathy felt sorry. They had no place to go but their sodden tents. While the mess was cold, it was dry and warmer than the tents.

She and Vivienne put on their four-buckle overshoes and pulled their hoods over their heads. Neither the Germans nor the civilian women had boots. Kathy took a hot bowl of soup for Mathilda, covered it with a plate, and waited outside the door while Vivienne locked up.

"We should take soup to Sarge and Oscar," said Kathy.

Vivienne looked at Kathy and laughed. Kathy knew she was right. Two girls just didn't carry soup into a Quonset hut of 25 men, or into a PW stockade.

From the road by their barracks, they could see the two compounds, one side was for PWs and the other for the Displaced Persons, each fenced off behind barbed wire. The ground in the PW stockade was mud. Their tents, heavy with water, sagged. Their fatigues hung shapeless and dripping on a clothesline. The PWs, shuffling through the rain, were as droopy as their tents.

In the DP enclosure, the ground was also mud. A line of Frenchmen stood behind the mess waiting for garbage. Everything was gray or brown. Nowhere, not in the sky, the tents, the clothes or the faces, was there even a speck of vibrant color. Germans, Poles and French—all were dreary and miserable.

In her room, Kathy hung her trench coat on the back of the wooden chair to drip. She opened the door of the brown stove, and lit the paper and wood set there by the Polish girl that took care of their quarters. She sat in her leather chair, her feet propped on the warming stove, and watched the gold and red flames grow. The fire radiated warmth to her face and her hands. The red glow of the fire changed the dull leather furniture colors to warmer tones. The fire was cheerful, alive, and fascinating. What a simple, primitive yet gigantic pleasure a fire was.

For the first time that day, Kathy was warm. All around her were peoples who did not have the warmth or the glow of any fire. The Allies were winning the war, and all Kathy could see was an expanding number of PWs and DPs in wet tents, and a longer line of hungry Frenchmen standing in the rain. She felt sorrier for them now, in April, than she had in January. Now she had seen them, knew some of them, and each shivering body was a person.

It shouldn't be so cold in April. Those who had endured a bitter winter had the right to the relief of a warm spring. Cold, miserable cold. Cold made suffering. It made people sick. It froze the food. It starved the people.

Kathy put more wood into the stove. She should leave the fire to change from her damp woolen slacks, which smelled like wet wool, to a Class A uniform for dinner. Instead, she sat and absorbed the heat.

Mrs. Foster rapped on her open door, came in and stood by Kathy. "Last month you wanted the Red Cross to trace Rocky?"

Kathy held her breath. "Yes."

"The report arrived today." Mrs. Foster sat on the bed and watched Kathy. "Roger Rockford was discharged from the Army in January, 1945. He is practicing law in New York, and living with his wife and two children at Apartment 227, 5721 59th Street, New York City."

A drop of resin burst into red flame and was gone. Kathy let her breath out, and breathed again. "Thank you. That was what I needed to know."

Mrs. Foster carefully looked at Kathy, and left.

Kathy sat on her red leather chair and gazed unblinking at the fire. Rocky was living with his wife and two children. She had not divorced him. She was, after all, the woman with whom he should be living. This was the answer, the right answer, the only answer. Kathy was relieved. She no longer owed any loyalty to Rocky. She was free.

Had he lied to her? Perhaps, but whether he had lied or honestly believed his wife was divorcing him, Kathy had been wrong. Kathy had been the "other woman." She'd clung to the image of love. Had she married him, could she have faced Rocky's wife and said, "Sorry I took your husband, the father of your children, but you must understand, I was lonely."

She had believed Rocky, and had believed in his decency. She had not known that a married man could toy with love. That's what he had done—or had he? He'd known she was going overseas. He could play with a toy until she left. Yes, Kathy had been wrong. Though she had thought she was helping him, she had known he was married. *She had thought what she wanted to think.*

Her mistake was in believing him. Not all men were good, and not all men were to be trusted. Maybe no man was to be trusted. She'd be more careful about whom she trusted again. It hurt too much to be wrong.

What had Rocky offered that was important? Rocky was a good dancer. Could he and she dance down this street past French, Poles and Germans in the cold rain and mud and say, "Watch us dance! Watch my rhythm! Dance! Forget the cold and hunger. We'll make you happy! Dance!" Could she ever go back to living with two big cars and a yacht, knowing people shivered in tents? Could she ever admire the sparkle of a ruby, remembering the Frenchmen waiting to search through the garbage? Rocky's wit, his dancing, his ruby, were of no value. He had shown her no sympathy in her problems with Lieutenant Groot. He had not helped her to grow or learn in any way, except dancing. They had danced away from problems, escaped from everything real in a big car, with hot music and warm kisses.

The fire glowed. The fire was real. Fire drove away cold. Rocky had taught her something. She knew now what was useless: big cars and yachts, and rubies and dancing, and cleverness without humanity, and lust without responsible love.

Now she knew that two things, at least these two, were necessary for survival. Fire and food. Those Germans and French and Poles and Russians and Greeks who had no fire or food would die. She had fire and food. She would survive.

# CHAPTER 16

# VE DAY IN THE CEMETERY

On May 7, 1945, Kathy was monotonously checking the food boxes against her ward lists while PWs waited in line by the open door to carry them to the wards. Box 9, four gallons of salmon casserole, check. With her eyes on the boxes and lists, she was vaguely aware of someone behind her. She turned to see Charles, just standing, his hands in his pockets, watching, his affection showing on his face.

"Hi," he said. "Time to drill for the parade. Though someone should have told the mayor of Suippes that the 223rd can't march."

"*Gehen sie*." Kathy gestured to a pair of PWs to carry out box 9. "What parade?"

"You still don't read the bulletin board? The war could be over, and you wouldn't know it."

Kathy said, "I could read it and still not know. I read every word about the Russians surrounding Berlin and hoisting their flag. Hitler is dead, the Third Reich is crumbling, yet fighting continues. There has been no official surrender, just a lot of rumors. I guess I will believe the war is over when patients quit coming in heavy with German lead."

"This time it is official."

"Can it really be?

"Yes. Donitz accepted Eisenhower's demands. General Jodl, acting on behalf of the German government, signed the surrender in Reims this morning at 2:41 a.m."

"Hooray! Finally! That means today is Victory in Europe Day! The long-awaited VE Day! Let's parade!"

"Tomorrow, we parade. VE Day is officially May 8. The Mayor of Suippes has planned a celebration dance in the village square tonight. Will you come with me? And a parade through town tomorrow. Speeches in the cemetery by the mayor and our Colonel."

"The cemetery?"

"The cemetery. So, we drill now. Bad as we are, we're the only Army near Suippes, so we parade. If you hurry, I'll wait for you." He looked at her with an affection that had no suggestion of hurrying for drill. Kathy was delighted.

Two PWs moved to pick up box 10. Reluctantly Kathy turned from the wondrous way Charles was looking at her, and held up her hand to stop the PWs. "*Eine minute*," she said to Charles, "All right, soon as I've checked these."

She looked at her list. Five gallons salmon casserole, box 10. She looked into box 10. Was it five or six gallons? She looked back at her list, and forgot which box. Charles was a disturbance beside her. He didn't touch her, yet her whole consciousness felt him.

The PWs stood waiting to carry the food to the patients. She tried again. She looked methodically into box 10 at three gallons of salmon casserole. She lifted the lid of the black metal container. It didn't smell like salmon. It smelled like stewed apricots. Charles waited, leaning against the doorframe with his fond smile, enjoying watching her bend over the boxes.

She couldn't think with Charles nearby. "Sorry, Charles. You'll have to wait outside. You distract me."

His smile widened with delight. His eyes, blue and round, looked straight into hers. "Do you feel that way too?" Kathy gazed at this face, moved by the sight of a man unmasked, a heart revealed. They stood, looking at each other for uncounted moments.

Two PWs reached for box 10. Kathy stopped them with the gesture that was their command. "Charles, I have to check these darned boxes. Go on. Outside. Just a minute. Please?"

He went out the door. Kathy returned to her boxes, and though she looked dutifully into each one, she didn't know what she saw. She could think only of the stirring emotions around her heart. She motioned the PWs to take the boxes away, unchecked, and went outside to join Charles.

Her hand was secure inside his warm, strong hand. They walked, Kathy skipping to keep up with his long strides, to the field behind the officers' club. This was the area where rehabilitation patients did calisthenics to make them fit for battle. Today, the doctors and staff would practice a victory march.

Their marching practice was so confusing that staff started laughing. No one cared. The war was over in Europe, and they were jubilant. The sun gleamed on polished brass buttons. Shined shoes stepped on dry ground, not mud. They sang marching songs with voices loud and strong, and it didn't matter which foot was left or right.

They had canned ham for dinner, which Kathy decorated with pineapple and slivers of canned apricots glazed with a mixture of syrup and jelly-like agar from the laboratory. They splurged all their sugar and shortening on a cake. It was unfrosted as there never was enough sugar for both cake and frosting. Red, white, and blue paper flags on the cake gave it a triumphant flair.

Even the weather celebrated with a fresh warmth. That evening as Kathy and Charles approached the dance in the square with others from the hospital, they heard an accordion, drum, and violin playing the bouncy music of "Beer Barrel Polka." Electric lights were strung across the square. They were just bare light bulbs, but they were the first lights they had seen in the village. The blackout was finally over!

Although there were no young Frenchmen in Suippes, the older ones danced with the glee of youth. The surplus of American men made up the deficit. The women were attractive, the dancing energetic, and the wine abundant. French danced with Americans; no one was a foreigner. Kathy danced with M. Duval, who considered Kathy's dancing excellent and her accent hilarious. She danced with a schoolteacher who wanted to teach her to correctly pronounce her French R's, but settled for teaching her a polka. Everyone talked and laughed. It didn't matter that most of them could not understand each other. The joy was complete.

At the end of the dance, they played and sang the "Star-Spangled Banner." This was sung by the French as a salute to the liberators, with the enthusiasm of a grateful liberated country.

"*Regardez, voyez-vous aux clartes de l'aurore...L'etandard etoile...a.*" The French knew and sang the words all the way through.

Then they played and sang "La Marseillaise," the national anthem of France, the most patriotic, spirited and stirring of national anthems. "*Allons enfants de la Patrie...*" The Americans didn't know those words well until they sang the chorus: "*Aux armes, citoyens. Formez vos bataillons. Marchons, marchons...,*" when everyone's shouting was rousing.

As Charles and Kathy walked home through the woods, they could hear from a distance a man singing "*Aux armes, Citoyens...*" Under an old linden tree, Charles kissed Kathy, and she kissed him. They did not speak of the feelings they had seen and half-admitted that afternoon. This was not a passion to be bound by words, but to be communicated by look and tingling touch.

Kathy was too thrilled to sleep that night. She sat on her footlocker by her window, hugging her pillow. She watched gathering clouds scurry past the moon until a late-night rain chilled her spirit and sent her to bed. The sound of the rain on the roof lulled her to sleep.

They assembled the next morning in front of the headquarters building to begin the parade in a drizzling rain. Their hooded olive-drab raincoats had no brass buttons, and their overshoes were brown with mud. A skeleton staff was left for the patients, and everyone else lined up in pairs. While Vivienne was the ranking officer among the girls,

Bunts was a better drill Sergeant, so Bunts stood beside the nine-girl platoon at the end of the column.

The Colonel shouted, "Left, face," forgetting to bring them first to attention. Major Sam, the first platoon leader, hollered, "Left face," on time. Major Fellows barked his orders a second later, and Bunts didn't repeat them at all, so they didn't all turn at once, and not even in the same direction.

Again, the Colonel shouted, "Forward, March." A third of the column started forward, a third waited for the platoon leaders to repeat the command, and the last third continued turning left or right. Yes, the war was over in Europe—and the parade began in good spirits if not in good order.

When they marched by the PW camp, Kathy purposely walked unmilitary out of step on the muddy gravel road. When they walked past the DP camp, where the refugees stood hopefully by the fence to watch, the columns straightened and they walked in step, in a show of order to assure the homeless that the war was now over, and they would soon again have homes and food.

They marched into the village unhindered by traffic, as it would be a long time before gasoline would be available. Their feet slid down the humped cobblestones into crevices, and it was impossible to march with rhythm. A scattering of Frenchmen lined the streets cheering as they waved damp French and American flags. While Kathy had not made an impressive contribution toward winning the war, she was on the winning team, and enjoyed being cheered.

When the girls' platoon reached the square in front of the church, two blocks from the cemetery, the men ahead stopped, though there were no orders to halt. The girls also halted. Bunts walked ahead to see what had happened. She reported back: "The cemetery is full. There is no room for us." Of course, there wouldn't be room with most of the villagers assembled there.

They stood waiting, hearing nothing but the rain dropping on the hoods of their rubber raincoats. Then the Mayor and Colonel made their speeches, unheard in the distant cemetery. Mrs. Foster kept the Red Cross girls standing at attention as befitting the formal ceremony. Sue and Mathilda shifted wearily from stone to stone, seeking a comfortable place to stand. Bunts, Vivienne, and Kathy paced impatiently back and forth as befitting the fiasco.

From the road to the east, they heard the sound of heavy motors. They turned to watch. A convoy of ambulances roared into the village, past the waiting parades, and turned onto the road to the hospital. A couple of doctors, followed by Vivienne and Kathy, left the parade formation to wave an ambulance to a stop. All the ambulances behind it slowed and stopped. The driver impatiently lowered his window.

Major Fellows put his hand on the green window sill as though to hold the ambulance there. "How many?"

"250." The driver closed his window against the rain, and started, slowly, gently, driving on.

Major Fellows stepped back to let the other ambulances roll by. He gestured to the men standing ready in parade formation in the square, "Come on."

They turned from the victory celebration to follow the ambulances full of the victorious soldiers to the hospital.

# PART III
# POST WAR IN FRANCE

# CHAPTER 17

# WAITING FOR ORDERS

The war was over in Europe, yet the war persisted in the South Pacific. Redeployment plans were drafted for the soldiers. Some would be needed to stay and occupy in Europe, others would be transferred to the Pacific theater, and some would be sent home.

The War Department announced the point system. There were 85 points as the minimum for immediate discharge for men, and 44 points for WACs. One point was given for each month in the army, plus an additional point for each month overseas. Five points were given for each child under 18, and wounded men and liberated PWs would have priority to return to the U.S.

Plans were made for the 223rd Hospital to go to the South Pacific, as just a few staff had enough points for discharge. The preparation was mostly talk, for the Army moved slowly, especially in moving to the other side of the world. In the Pacific, the Allies were island hopping, making their way to Japan, utilizing a great portion of available ships and transport vehicles. It had taken years to get American soldiers and equipment into Europe; it would take several months to move them out.

The hospital kept its full patient load. Life continued at much the same tempo as before. The shooting war was over but the war against starvation, disease, and degeneration continued. Venereal disease increased as war casualties decreased. The hospital also serviced the ever-growing Displaced Persons camps, with their diseases of debilitation and filth.

The doctors gave daily lectures on tropical diseases of the South Pacific to prepare the hospital staff. Their conclusions were usually that prevention was essential. Treatments were only partially effective. Prevention was Charles's field, as sanitation officer, and so he began a series of lectures.

Kathy, Vivienne, and Bunts had gone to their barracks after lunch for their notebooks, and were now walking to the Quonset hut for Charles's lecture.

Vivienne pulled a V-mail letter from her notebook. "Got a letter from Stan today, full of helpful hints for the South Pacific. Bring rayon underwear; it doesn't mildew as fast as cotton. He seems to think we can just go out and buy clothes. He's expecting me on every ship."

"What an optimist!" hooted Bunts. "I've been on the same continent as Tex for six months now. Have I seen him? I have not. And the ETO has not spread out across an ocean like the CBI," she said, referring to the European Theater of Operations and the China Burma India theaters of war.

They smiled and waved at hollow-eyed patients sitting on benches in the sun. These patients were displaced peoples from Russia, Italy, Belgium—all of Europe.

"Bunts, what happened to the leave you planned with Tex?" asked Kathy. "I thought the Colonel said you could go to the Riviera, or wherever you wanted."

"He did. It's Tex's CO that's stopping us. Everyone in his company wants a leave for the Riviera, or Paris. He has to wait his turn. If our hospital goes to China before he gets a leave approval, then...," she stopped to scoop up a handful of gravel... "If we go to China, I'll...I'll desert." Bunts threw the gravel underhand. It splattered against a tree trunk. "If we took a leave in Italy, we could get married. Just a few days is all I ask before they send us to different islands in the South Pacific." She scooped up another handful of gravel, and let it fall harmlessly to the ground. "Of course, I won't do any of that. I'll go meekly with the rest of you, as one of the herd."

Vivienne folded her letter and shoved it between the pages of her notebook. "There's plenty of time. We haven't started discharging patients. That takes a month. You'll find a way. If I can just get into the same part of the world with Stan, I'll find a way. Though it's been so long since I've seen him, I wonder if I'd even recognize him. Two years! His pictures even look different now."

Kathy counted the months off on her fingers. "Give us to the end of June here to discharge patients and pack. In July we will be in a staging area. By August we will be on a ship to the South Seas. By fall we'll be wearing bathing suits under a palm tree. We won't be cold in a castle again next winter." They turned onto the walk to the Quonset hut.

"You're a sun-worshipper," said Vivienne.

"A cold hater. I'll spend the winter on a sandy beach soaking up the sun."

They went into the hut, and sat among the officers. Charles was a serious, almost stiff lecturer. His talk about preparation for the Pacific would have been considered dry a month ago. Now, however, the mosquito was a familiar enemy, known to carry both malaria and yellow fever. Their interest was sharp, as their lives now depended on learning how to avoid them.

As Charles talked, Kathy's vision of herself in a bathing suit wearing flower leis on a tropical isle changed. Now she thought of herself sweating in the humid heat, wearing long sleeves, and covered with smelly insect repellant and mosquito netting.

Charles talked of prevalent diarrhea and fungi penetrating the skin of bare feet. Kathy added heavy GI boots to her vision. He also spoke of premature aging in the tropics, with nurses aging four years in one.

Vivienne leaned toward Kathy and whispered, "Think I'll wait for Stan in the States. I'm 35 now. I can't afford to lose those years."

Kathy whispered back, "France is looking better by the minute."

After the lecture, Kathy and Vivienne waited behind to compliment Charles, who had been reluctant to face an audience of medical professionals. "You managed to make *wuchereria bancrofti* sound horrifying," said Vivienne.

"The worms sound more deadly than the Japanese," said Kathy.

"They certainly can be, if infected." Charles held the door open for them to walk out. "If I can finish early this afternoon, Kathy, I have a Jeep. We can drive out to dinner at the transient Army mess on the Chalons-sur-Marne Road."

"I've heard that's charming. I can make the ward rounds now, but..."

"Go ahead," offered Vivienne. "I'll check the supper diets if you can just visit wards 9 and 10. I've been avoiding them. Not that they deserve any attention."

"I have no special diets there. Why me?"

"Hadn't you noticed? They're all venereal disease patients. They constantly complain about the food, and their talk is nasty. I just can't be nice to them. You still act as though every patient were a hero, and deserving the best we can give. Please just walk through 9 and 10, so they can't say they never saw a dietitian. But don't treat them like heroes."

"Sure. I'll just walk through."

Charles walked Kathy to the wards, on his way to the lab. Near the door of Ward 1, a man on crutches approached the ramp. He stepped cautiously with short steps, and carefully placed his crutches—evidently out for his first walk. Charles held his forearm to steady him.

Kathy stepped ahead to open the door for him. She smiled assurance. "Feel good to get out?"

The patient said, "Sure does," to Kathy, and, "Thanks," to Charles, and concentrated again on learning to walk with crutches.

She didn't follow the patient in right away; she needed a few seconds to brace herself. "It's getting harder instead of easier. You'd think I'd get used to suffering, but now I stop for four deep breaths before I enter a ward. I used to be able to go in with only two."

"Don't harden. You might lose that something that makes patients love you." Charles' smile said he understood what she was saying. "Well, come to my lab when you're through. It'll do you good to get away."

However, Kathy didn't go in. "It's the sunken cheeks and dull eyes that get me down. Broken bones heal. But when you sprinkle sulfa powder on a refugee's ulcerated arm, and send him back to a filthy camp without decent food, you're not curing him. You're just...you're just... It seems so useless, Charles, so hopeless."

He put a reassuring hand on her shoulder. "You know it's not useless, nor hopeless. The war is over. Things will get better fast."

"The war is over, and things are worse," Kathy responded.

"It takes time. Give her time, and France will struggle onto her feet again." Charles looked across the street at the DP camp, at the misery of which Kathy spoke. "I'm not really disagreeing with you. Let's go see something healthy. Run your rounds. We can leave as soon as you're ready."

They arrived at the village inn an hour before dinner, with time to walk the quaintly crooked streets. A cat that slept on the sunny stone steps of a medieval church opened a sleepy eye when Kathy petted him while Charles opened the heavy copper door.

The church was empty and hollow. The stained-glass windows were gone, leaving deep gaping holes in the thick stone walls. The pews were absent, leaving the church desolate. Even the late afternoon sunlight that poured in was a cold white. From the shadows behind the altar, they heard scraping and shuffling sounds. Walking a little closer, they saw an old Frenchman pushing a stepladder against the wall. He bent down, and picked up from the dust a huge round stained-glass window, so large he could barely hold it. Balancing it precariously on one arm, he slowly climbed up the ladder.

"Must be one of the priceless windows they buried during the war," whispered Kathy. At the top of the ladder, the old Frenchman cautiously lifted the window up toward the empty round hole above him. It slipped. He grabbed. He missed. The precious stained glass fell to the floor.

Slowly, painfully, the old man descended the rickety ladder. He shuffled to the window, picked it up, and contemplated the now-empty spaces in the lead tracing. He leaned the leaded window against the wall. He picked up broken pieces of colored glass and stuck them into the lead tracing, with no cement or putty. He put the window under his arm and again ascended the old ladder. This time he placed the window in the hole, and this time it stayed as though it had never been any other place.

The sun shone through the stained glass, and the light in the church changed from a cool white to brilliant reds and yellows, and glowing oranges and purples. They waited, silent in the now-living church, while the old Frenchman climbed down his ladder and shuffled out. "It's as I said," said Charles, "Give the French time and they'll recover. You think they're broken, and they revive more dazzlingly than ever."

Kathy looked where the window had fallen, and picked up some slivers of broken glass. Held up to the light, they were as brilliant as the window. Guessing that the old man would not look in the dust for them, she put them in an envelope in her purse.

A jovial proprietor met them at the open door of the inn. He led them into a dining room with shiny copper pans hanging on the walls and yellow flowers in vases on polished tables. They listened to the proprietor's tales of the heroic French underground. Away from the smells of blood and antiseptics, the food, the same dehydrated food furnished to the Army, tasted better. Charles left four cigarettes as tips. The proprietor was wildly enthusiastic over his generosity as the usual tip was a single cigarette.

After dinner they climbed a spiral staircase in a crumbling castle to the top of a tower. Below them spread the peaceful green hills of vineyards. Above them floated clouds rosy with the sunset glow. Kathy sat on the low wall, on a large flat stone warm from the sun's stored heat. Charles sat beside her, his shoulder touching hers, his hand warm over her hand. The moon rose huge and orange from behind the hills.

He put his arm around her. She could feel his quickened heartbeat and his tight breathing. She received his warm kisses, at first in passive wonder at the miracle of the mounting feeling she had inspired. Then, without decision, without willing or wishing, she felt a response deep within herself. Her response, her arms around his neck pulling him to her, was ardent, yet as natural and as easily evolved as nature had intended.

It was Charles who ended the kiss. Putting his warm hands on her cheeks, he held her head, and moved it back to look at her. His face was nice, with a tender smile. His voice was quiet and gentle. "We'd better be getting back."

Arm in arm, they cautiously felt their way down the now-darkened winding stairs, and drove home.

They returned to the door of the women's quarters at the same time as Mrs. Foster and Major Fellows. Charles gave Kathy an embarrassed kiss, said a quick good night to all, and left.

Mrs. Foster followed Kathy into her room. She stopped in the doorway joining their rooms, watching Kathy take off her olive-drab blouse, while unbuttoning her own gray jacket. "Charles looked frustrated."

Kathy tossed her blouse onto the chair, and untied her necktie. "Yes, he must be."

"And you are frustrated and inhibited."

Kathy considered. "Yes," she admitted. She sat on her leather chair. "I expect to be inhibited until I marry."

"Charles loves you, you know."

Kathy hesitated. This was touchy. "He's never said that."

"Whether he's said so or not, he does. And you love him."

Kathy bent over to untie her shoes, and tossed them beside her bed. She had no answer.

Mrs. Foster stepped into her closet to hang up her uniform. She emerged in her pajamas, her corset in her hand, opened her bureau drawer, and carefully folded her corset into it. "You love him, so why do you frustrate him? Inhibitions and repressions cause turmoil in the subconscious mind." Mrs. Foster, looking at her image in the gilt-framed mirror, brushed her gray hair.

Frigid and rigid Mrs. Foster, with a divorce she never mentioned, what must be her turmoil? If compulsive neatness characterized her inhibitions, maybe she knew well the turmoil of repression. Mrs. Foster was winding her hair tightly around curlers. "Free yourself. You're damaging Charles and yourself. Don't you love him enough to have relations with him?"

"Charles is a moral, religious man. He's never tried..."

"When in this society it was all right to take a truckload of furniture you wanted, you took it without a twinge from your conscience. If you'd been brought up in another society, with no restrictions on sex, you'd feel free to sleep with Charles. Sex drives are dominant. Don't reject them. Rejected, they cause neuroses. Fulfill yourself. Fulfill Charles. Live! Fear rigidity and sterility, not sex."

"I'll be fulfilled when I have six babies," Kathy said, but she continued to wonder. Certainly, she had experienced turmoil. She had felt the torments of loneliness and the misery of failure. She knew of a desperation that grasped at anything that could to ease the pain. Charles's love had dispelled her loneliness and inadequacy.

Kathy finished undressing, and regarded her body with pride. She didn't encase her own curves in a corset. She did not fear her body. She put on her flannel pajamas, so as not to shock Mrs. Foster, the Freudian Foster who hid in a closet. "According to your theory, our patients on the venereal disease wards should be the happiest and best adjusted. And a prostitute would be an ideal woman."

"That is not what I said." Her usually unruffled voice rose to an irritated pitch. "There are other factors..."

"That's exactly what I mean. There are other factors. All around us loneliness and insecurity are coupled with free sex. Our humanity is in reverence for life." Even as she said it, Kathy knew that in war there was little reverence for life.

Kathy knew Mrs. Foster was right—and she was grateful that Charles filled their time so full of activity that control was possible.

They worked long days. They drove a Jeep into Paris about once a week, visiting the family that owned the art gallery. Most evenings were spent with the Duvals or other local villagers. Always the French were friendly, and always the visits were interesting.

# CHAPTER 18

# A BABY IS BORN

Now the summer sun burned hot. Ward 8 was sleepy as Kathy made her rounds. Patients were complaining. It was about 1330, when she should have been resting in her room in the barracks, which was cooler, but she was listening to patients. A young Frenchwoman was mopping the floor. It seemed she was spending more time changing the water than she was mopping.

A patient with his right arm in a cast called from his bed, "Hey, Lieutenant! Write a letter for me!" His tone implied it was a command, not a request.

Kathy was tempted to walk past his bed, ignoring him. She did write letters dictated by war casualties with broken arms, but this man had been driving drunk and crashed.

"To my mother." He added, in a manner he was certain she would comply.

By writing his letter, she wouldn't have time to complete her visits to Wards 9 and 10. She might as well agree cheerfully, as his wrist was broken. "Sure. Where's your paper?" She took her pen from her pocket and sat on the foot of his bed.

She noticed that Charles had come into the ward. She looked up to watch his long easy stride, to look at the face that was so comfortable and kind. She was fond of his face. At one time she had wished his chin were stronger, but now she liked it as it was.

The Frenchwoman took her bucket into the latrine for more water. A patient ran out, clutching a towel around himself.

He stood before Charles, dripping water. "I refuse to take another bath until you put a lock on that door."

"You'll get mighty dirty. Hospitals never have locks on bathroom doors. If a patient should faint in the tub, we'd like to be able to get him out."

"That woman keeps getting water."

"So?"

"She gets it from my tub." She stands there while the bucket fills. Six times. I'm counting. She's not that interested in clean water." Charles smiled, and his face became handsome. He glanced at his watch, and talked across the room to Kathy. "Can't you ever be on time? It's four minutes to two."

"Oh no! Thanks!" She tossed the patient's letter onto his bed. "You finish it."

"Sure. I'm left-handed, anyway."

Kathy ran all the way out and over to her room. Everyone was aware that at two o'clock the water was turned on for fifteen minutes. That was all that was allowed. Kathy could save one helmet-full for washing her face and brushing her teeth at night. The water supply in the Reims area had been drained. Thousands of redeployed troops living in miles and miles of green tents had crowded into the area, during one of the dustiest droughts in years.

She grabbed her helmet, clothes, towel, and shampoo. She dashed out to the shower, an open room with five sprays hanging from pipes across the wall.

The other girls were following their usual procedure. They arrived early to soap themselves before the water was turned on. When the water was on, they put clothes to soak in a helmet full of soapy water. Next, they rinsed themselves, then rinsed their clothes, and then finally collected fresh water in their helmets. Kathy arrived at eight minutes after two. She undressed in one minute and dropped her underwear into her helmet. By ten after she was sudsing her hair in the shower, with five minutes left over for rinsing.

Suddenly, the shower stopped. No more water. She wrung out the soapy water from the underwear in her helmet. Soap suds dribbled down from her hair to her neck and back. In the 100-degree heat, they dried quickly and sticky on her skin.

She surveyed the roomful of dressing women. Not daring to ask for such a precious a gift she hoped someone might offer a cup of rinse water, Mathilda had turned her back to the room to dress—so she wouldn't see Kathy's predicament. Mrs. Foster had stepped from the shower into a robe made of two Army towels, under which she was dressing. Others had long since given up any effort for privacy, and were dressing at the benches along the wall.

Vivienne poured a cupful of her water over Kathy's hair.

"One day you'll learn to read the bulletin board. The new regulation is only ten minutes of water."

Kathy brushed her still soapy, gummy hair and shaped a wave with her fingers. She dressed to go back on duty.

When she stepped out the front doors she looked out at the Prisoners of War and Displaced Persons camps across the street. She turned her irritation to gratitude for the few minutes she did have with a shower. The DPs and PWs lived in windowless tents and had no soap and no showers. These men, women and children also had no refuge from the sun until late in the afternoon.

A pregnant woman wearing a dusty Army shirt that strained across her unbelievably huge abdomen waddled across the street toward Kathy, who stared at the woman's shape. She had seen pregnant women in camouflaged maternity smocks, but never one that swelled so obviously. No maternity smocks were furnished by the Army for the DPs. Realizing she was staring, Kathy shifted her eyes down to the woman's edema-swollen ankles, and up to her sweat-streaked, strained face. The woman came directly to Kathy, asking something in Polish. Not understanding, Kathy managed a smile and shrugged her shoulders.

The woman clutched Kathy's arm, speaking loudly, urgently. Suddenly she stopped speaking. Her face contorted with pain. Kathy understood. Thinking Kathy was a nurse, she was asking her to deliver her baby.

Kathy had watched deliveries at Cook County, but this hardly qualified her as a midwife. She'd take the woman to the hospital. But where in the hospital? Their Army hospital had no delivery room. The admitting room? This was no time for a routine admission. The operating room had at least a table, anesthesia, scissors and thread, blood and oxygen. Kathy led the woman, who clung to her and followed with confidence that Kathy could take care of everything, to the ante-room beside the operating room. She handed the woman a hospital gown. She told her to put it on while she went for a doctor, hoping she would somehow understand.

She found Major Fellows on a ward. "A Polish woman's delivering a baby in the scrub room."

He looked startled. "A baby?" He looked questioningly at a ward boy, then at Kathy, evidently deciding on Kathy. "You come with me." To the ward boy he said, "Find another doctor to help us. Get someone from the lab to take blood samples." The ward boy started toward the door. Major Fellows shouted after him, "And find someone who speaks Polish." He and Kathy hurried to the scrub room. They heard the shrieks before they reached the door. The Polish woman lay writhing on the floor, screaming with a shrill, piercing sound. She quieted when they helped her onto the operating table. Major Fellows told Kathy to undress her. He talked to the Polish woman in a calm, commanding voice while he scrubbed his hands, but with the return of pain she screamed hysterically.

With a gush of blood-streaked water, and a screech that displayed the torment of a woman outraged by man and war, the woman delivered a baby.

"It's all over," the doctor shouted over her screams. "It's a boy!" The woman did not hear—and could not have understood had she heard.

He held the baby by his heels. The infant's first newborn cry was drowned out by his mother's shrieks. The Major held the baby for the woman to see. She turned her head away. She screamed till her voice was hoarse from the howling. Still, she screamed, with shrieks that rose high and penetrating while she gasped for breath and started again.

The Major handed Kathy the baby, wet and splotched with blood. He was warm and alive in her arms. His eyes stared wide open and unfocused, yet wise. His first sounds he heard were screams, yet his trusting eyes found the sense of light good. His lungs expanded and breathed life-giving air. He kicked his tiny legs, testing his new freedom. Kathy cradled the naked baby in her arms, telling him that she would take care of him.

Suddenly the room was crowded with people. Charles was there at the foot of the operating table. She knew his broad back and the tilt of his head. He stood beside the Major, showing him a small square bottle, and the Major nodded and handed him cord blood samples. Major Sam, on the other side of Major Fellows, was helping attend the mother. A Sergeant was at the head of the table, talking in Polish to the woman, and her screeches quieted to sobs.

Charles turned to look at the baby, and then at Kathy. Their eyes met. He tenderly looked at the baby again. He unscrewed the cap from his bottle, and squeezed the rubber end to fill the dropper with silver nitrate. Cupping his hand against the side of the baby's face, he squeezed out drops to bathe the baby's eyes, washing out the dreaded diplococcus that could cause blindness.

The Major asked the Sergeant, "Can you get her name and the father's name?"

The Sergeant shook his head, "She doesn't know who the father is."

"What nationality? Where was she nine months ago, and who was occupying that area?"

"She says American and she says she was here, but we weren't here nine months ago."

"Tell her that."

When he talked to her, the woman cried hopelessly, and turned her face away. "She doesn't know what nationality."

Major Fellows spoke to Kathy, "Wash his face so he'll look pretty for his mother."

Kathy looked at the bottles on the shelves for oil, and saw none. She reached for sterile cotton, then realized she hadn't washed her hands. Charles opened a sterile sheet pack, and put the folded sheet on the instrument table that was beside the operating table. Kathy lay the baby there, where the mother could see him as she would turn her head. She hurriedly scrubbed her hands. Then with clean hands, soft cotton and sterile water, she gently washed the baby. Cleaned of the gore of birth, the tiny rosy face was petal soft and smooth, a face to appeal to the maternal love of any woman, if she would just look.

Kathy tore a strip from a sheet, and wrapped him in it. She held him up, all pink and white, in front of his mother. "Your baby."

The mother turned the back of her head toward the baby, and did not look back. "*Nicht milch.*" Her voice was a hoarse whisper. "*Nicht milch.*" Among her other words, this "*nicht milch*" was repeated. The Sergeant repeated to the watching group. "She has no milk. She cannot keep her baby because she cannot feed him. She cannot look at him. No milk."

"We can give her canned milk," said Kathy.

Again, when the Sergeant talked to the woman, she turned from her baby.

Major Fellows looked at Kathy holding the newborn babe. He looked at her knees to see if they were trembling. His eyes were sad, and they said that not even birth balances against the bloody flood when the baby comes into the world this baby was meeting.

Then he spoke to the Sergeant, his eyes were controlled again. "Put mother and child in the recovery room." He washed his hands, and when the blooded water had gone down the drain, he spoke to Major Sam. "In four years as an Army surgeon, I've forgotten an infant's formula. Can you remember?"

"Don't look at me. I've been in psychiatry for eight years."

They both looked at Kathy. She responded, "I brought my nutrition and diet book. I can manage the canned milk and sugar and water, but what do we do for bottles and nipples?"

Charles unhooked an empty plasma bottle from its stand. With a scalpel from the instrument tray, he cut the black rubber tube two inches from the rubber stopper. "You can clamp the tube so the milk dribbles out. It will do until we can get nipples. That might be some time yet as I doubt that the quartermaster stocks rubber nipples."

"Surgical pads for diapers?" suggested Major Fellows.

"We can sew clothes from our flannel pajamas," offered Kathy.

"Major," said the Sergeant, "I have four kids. I know about bottles. Could I take care of the baby? Looks like the mother won't name him. Until she does, while he's here, he's Uncle Sam's baby. I'll just call him Sammy. I've got four kids, back in Indiana. I could take care of him."

"All right."

Kathy clung to Sammy, not wanting to give him away. The Major had handed him to her—so Sammy was hers. She looked over at the men's faces. She saw in them the same feelings, maybe even stronger, for they were all fathers, fathers whose children were a thousand miles away. Major Fellows had never seen his own new baby. She surrendered Sammy to the Sergeant.

The Sergeant and doctors took the mother and child out. Two ward boys stripped the sheets from the operating table and left. Kathy and Charles were left alone in the operating room looking for empty plasma bottles.

Charles filled a bottle with water, adjusted the clamp on the tube. "That's about the right flow for a baby."

Kathy handed him more stoppers and tubes for cutting. They faced each other across the instrument table.

Charles cut the tubes with a scalpel. "You wanted to keep the baby, didn't you?"

"Are my maternal instincts so obvious?"

He nodded. "Yes. All mixed up with shock at a mother who has no maternal instincts."

"She must have some." Kathy's yearning for the baby who had touched her arms for only minutes was so strong she could not believe the woman who had carried him for nine months could feel less. "When she's rested, when she touches his smooth skin, she'll love him."

Charles shook his head sadly. His own first wife had given their child up to her mother, so he knew a mother's love could shrivel. He must have pondered the denial of mother's love for years, and but had no words to explain it.

Kathy assembled the bottles on a tray. "I'll bring her some milk. Maybe when she sees milk, ready to drink, she'll believe and keep her baby."

"First make the formula." Charles collected the tubes and stoppers on the tray beside the bottles.

He reached across the table, over the bottles, to hold Kathy's hand. "For your own good..." He dropped her hand, put his own hand over his mouth as though he didn't want to say what he was going to say. His eyes were grave and sober. He was feeling his words deeply. "For your own good, I... I won't go with you anymore. You must date only single men."

His blue eyes sought hers, pleading for understanding. "Nurses, overseas, get so they prefer married men. They've learned to get along with women in order to make life tolerable at home. The corners of his lips twitched up in a smile, but his eyes were sad.

Kathy nodded. She understood and she agreed. She wanted to say...What? Instead, she said "I'll boil these bottles and calculate a formula. How much would you guess Sammy weighs? Calculations are based on weight."

"Hard to tell without scales." His eyes were questioning her reaction.

"Your guess would be better than mine. You've had two babies."

"Five, maybe six pounds."

Kathy, who usually met life's crises with tears, was surprised that she could talk so casually of formulas when Charles had just decided to leave her. He was, however, right. Since she wanted babies, she'd have to find another love. She loved Charles. This love was not a consuming, possessive love, but a positive, creative love. He had strengthened her. He had taught her that she was capable of earning the love of a good man. Now she must resume her search, with the assurance that having found a man to love once, she could find another. She felt no sadness toward Charles, just gratitude. She hoped her smile showed her acceptance and gratitude.

Charles put his tubes of blood samples on the tray with the plasma bottles and carried them to the mess. Kathy ran in ahead to announce to Mathilda and Vivienne, "Have you heard? The Army just delivered a baby!"

"A baby?" they chorused.

"A baby! A Polish Displaced Woman just walked in, and delivered a baby. It's a boy! Sammy. All pink and cuddly."

Vivienne raised her hands up and jumped with joy. "A baby! Where is he?"

"In the recovery room."

"The mother?"

"She's all right. She's in the recovery room too." Mathilda sat straight and quiet on her chair. Her face was stony white. "Where is the father?"

"She doesn't know anything about him."

Charles came in with the bottles. "Want these on your desk?" He set the tray down, and took from it the tubes of cord blood. "If there's nothing more, I've got work to do." He turned to leave, then turned back to look again at Mathilda. "Are you alright?"

"Me?" Her hands fluttered up to her bun, and she pushed at hairpins. "Me? Yes. I'm..." She took out the hairpins, and stuffed them in, distractedly. "It's hot."

"Yes. It is hot. Well…" He looked at Mathilda again, concerned, "It must be a hundred." He looked at Kathy, wondering, hoping. "So long," he said, and left.

Mathilda's face, usually flushed in the heat of the day, was pale. Her eyes darted from the door to the ceiling to the floor. Her fingers darted from hairpin to hairpin, in turmoil.

While the others left to see Sammy, Kathy sought to ease Mathilda's discomfort. "You'll forget the heat when you see the baby, Mathilda. You'll love him. He's tiny. Maybe six pounds. Maybe less. I'll make his formula and I'll feed him. You can too. He's in the recovery room. Mathilda, don't you want to see him?"

Mathilda burst into wailing tears. There was no predicting her reactions these days. Kathy tried to reassure her. "The baby's all right, Mathilda. So's the mother. The mother's afraid now. She wouldn't or couldn't tell us who the father is." That was not the cheerful note Kathy had intended. "She is afraid because she has no milk to feed him. But when we give her milk, she'll…"

Mathilda moaned, a deep, forlorn sound. She doubled over in misery with her head cradled in her hands. This was worse than her usual sobs.

Kathy knelt before her, to talk into her face. "What is the matter?"

"Hooch is going to China. I'm going home," Mathilda sobbed. "I'll never see him again."

Kathy could sympathize with this. "I know how you feel."

"No, you don't. I love him." She flung her arms around Kathy's shoulders and clung to her. "I was a dried-up, shriveled-up old maid. Hooch made a woman of me. He's going to China and I'm going to the States. I'll never see him again." She put her head on Kathy's shoulder and sobbed in wretched desperation.

Kathy patted her thin back, a useless gesture but the best she could manage. "He hasn't gone yet. Maybe the Colonel can get your orders changed to go with us. We need you. Remember how many mistakes we made when you were sick?"

Mathilda clung to Kathy, weighing heavily on her shoulders. "I have to go home. I'm pregnant."

No wonder poor Mathilda had reacted so desperately to the news of the fatherless baby. With or without a husband, Mathilda would have a baby. She had had no one to love and to love her. A baby, even a fatherless baby, was better than no one. Where was the sin? She had been, as she said, a dried-up, shriveled-up old maid, and Hooch had made a woman of her. Kathy could almost envy her.

Mathilda found no comfort in her condition. "I can't. I can't keep him. The baby, I can't raise him myself. And I can't give him up." She clutched Kathy in panic.

Kathy could think of no helpful words, could only pat her shoulder, which was really no solution at all.

This was no movie. This was not a book that could be closed. Reality had shattered into the make-believe. There was a past and a future. Kathy did not know how to meet it.

The mess was suffocatingly hot. Mathilda's tears soaked through Kathy's shirt, mixing with sweat and unrinsed shampoo. There was no water for a soothing cool bath. Silly, the problem was not of getting a bath but of getting a husband for Mathilda. What to do? Her mind could grasp no idea, not even a wild idea, for a solution, so she thought of the heat.

Mathilda might at least find relief from the heat in her room, which was cooler than the steaming mess. "If you want to lie down in your room until supper, I'll take over here for you. I'll stop by and we can go to supper together."

"Thanks. I do feel sick," Mathilda sobbed. She sighed and rose painfully to go. Wiping her reddened eyes with an olive-drab handkerchief, she passed Vivienne at the door.

Vivienne looked puzzled, concerned. "Mathilda's getting hysterical," she said when Mathilda had walked out of hearing range. "Every little thing upsets her. I'll have to talk to Major Sam about her."

"It's not a little thing. Mathilda is pregnant."

"Oh, my aching back!" Vivienne clutched handfuls of her copper hair. "Of course. I should have guessed. Well, I don't need Major Sam to tell me what Mathilda needs. Hooch is going to have to marry her."

"From the way Mathilda's acting, my guess is that he won't."

"He will. I can... The Colonel would never let him escape. Major Sam can be persuasive. I can find a shotgun somewhere." Her face brightened from determined outrage to confidence. "Our baby! Even Hooch's hard heart will soften when he sees Sammy. Our fatherless, motherless baby."

"Motherless? She didn't die!?"

"No. She walked out. Just left, without a word. We don't know where." Vivienne stood silent, considering the next words, the next action.

"Well," said Kathy.

"Well," said Vivienne.

"The formula."

"First the formula. We dig an inch at a time into a mountain." Vivienne said.

"We have the bottles." Kathy took the diet book from her desk drawer. "And I can calculate the formula." She turned the pages to find the directions. "110cc of milk for each kilogram of body weight. How many pounds in a kilogram? I've forgotten."

Vivienne did not answer. She leaned against the wall, staring at two flies buzzing against the window pane. From the kitchen she heard male guttural German voices, and female giggles.

Vivienne sighed and said "Mathilda pregnant. Mousy, rigid, and scared Mathilda will marry her first love."

Kathy calculated changing pounds into kilograms, a nice simple problem with a single right answer. An inch at a time into a mountain.

Vivienne recovered, and together they boiled bottles using forceps from the operating room for handling them. They made the formula in the huge GI kettles. They kept everything covered from the nightingales that were nesting in the rafters.

After supper the girls and officers gathered as usual in the officers' club. Tonight, some of the girls cut out and sewed tiny clothes for Sammy. Mrs. Foster sat with Major Fellows; Vivienne sat with Dick; Bunts sat with Warren; and Betty with Toby. Each with his own. Charles stood at the bar, drinking. Kathy sat at a table, alone, sewing. When anyone came into the room, Kathy looked up, smiling hopefully. Each man smiled back cheerfully, and passed on. No one sat with her.

They had no sewing patterns, and guessed at the size and shape of Sammy's nightgowns. Kathy considered the pajama pants laid out on her table. She could cut off the end of a leg, fixing a hole for the head and two holes for the arms. She cut raggedly, and she stitched unevenly. The thread tangled. She jerked it, and broke it. She attempted to poke the thread at the needle eye, and missed. She couldn't even thread a needle.

Charles poured another drink from a flat bottle, not wine. He, who never drank more than a sociable glass of wine, was drinking too much. Other girls were dancing, but no one asked Kathy to dance. She'd rather dance than sew. Vivienne held up a finished gown, neat and nicely made. All the girls but Kathy could sew. Everyone had a love, everyone was dancing, everyone but Kathy.

Kathy could stand it no longer. She carried her flannel scraps to Vivienne's table. "Use this if you want. I'll make Sammy's formulas. I'll change his diapers. I cannot sew, not even for Sammy. I'm going to bed."

As Kathy walked by the bar to the front door, Charles deliberately turned his back, leaning on the bar, looking at his glass. His head hung forward so sadly, his shoulders sloped so drearily that Kathy wanted to touch him, to cheer him, and to ease her loneliness. She paused. He gazed steadily at his glass. Kathy walked outside.

It was not going to be easy for her, or for him. He was right. He did belong to his family. She must find her own man, but...but.... She walked slowly toward her barracks, reluctant to leave the cool air for her hot room. She lingered under a linden tree, finding solace in the shapes of restless leaves black against the star-studded sky. The stars remained in the heavens. A baby had changed her world, yet the stars shone on.

She heard steps behind her on the gravel walk. It was Charles, following her. She moved back against the tree, wanting Charles to see her, to talk to her, to kiss her—and then, hoping he would pass on.

He came to her. Her arms stretched out as they met. He hugged her and kissed her, not gently but fiercely, so her lips hurt against her teeth. He held her tight with a violent strength. "I love you," he said through lips so pressed against hers that she could not be sure that was what he said.

Suddenly his strength ebbed; he slumped against her. "I love you," he said, clearly. He sank to his knees, his arms around her waist.

Strong Charles was helpless before her. He was hers for the taking. Whatever she wanted, whatever she asked, she could have. It was not good to see a strong man made weak.

She stood before him and raised his face. "Oh Charles. What have I done to you? You gave me strength. You lifted me up when I was defeated. And what have I done for you?" She held his head high between her hands. She could not have it bent low.

They knelt, knees touching. "You saved me." His voice was strong. "Without you I would have been drinking and gambling as per the norm. With you...we had good times."

Kathy dropped her hands to her knees. He was now holding his own head high. She wanted to lean her head on his shoulder. Instead, they rose on their feet and stood apart. Charles walked beside Kathy to her quarters, and said good night without touching her again.

# CHAPTER 19

# A LATE NIGHT IN REIMS

Kathy could not face another evening in the officers' club, and so the next day after supper, she returned to her quarters. Increasingly large groups of young men were clustered around their front door, competing to pick up a date. The men were now mostly infantry officers, for the paratroopers were reassigned to Germany for occupation duty.

One man, handsome and young—they all were handsome and young—left the group and approached Kathy. "Hi, I'm Peter Smith. I'd like to take you to see Bob Hope in Reims tonight. I have a Jeep. We'll dance at the Red Cross afterward. Please, my first date in three years?" He spoke quickly, not giving her time to say no until he'd made his full plea.

"Three years?"

His smile was appealing. "It seems that long."

"All right. I'll go. Drive me to headquarters to sign out."

Charles, as Officer of the Day, was sitting in headquarters, his long legs up on a desk. "I'm going to Reims to see Bob Hope," she explained, pleased to show she could get along without him. She signed the big book.

"With whom?" He put his feet down, stood up, took two steps to the window and looked out.

"Lieutenant Peter Smith." That was all she knew about him, only his name. She shouldn't go with a stranger, yet she didn't know how to get out of it. If Charles would ask her to stay...

He just stood at the window, hands in his pockets. "Be careful." He would not keep her from making her own way.

"Sure," she said, and left.

In the Jeep, determined to have a good time, she babbled cheerfully to the lieutenant. "Bob Hope is just what I need—laughs. Remember his road movies, when he and Bing Crosby..."

He drove slowly through the village, and Kathy was relieved that he was a careful driver. Her relief, however, was short-lived. He turned off the cobblestone road lined with the charming houses onto the black-top road and into the dusty, drab tent city. He opened a cognac bottle and drank. He drove with one hand on the wheel and the other on his bottle.

By the time they reached Reims, the crowd waiting for the show was so large that the theater was already filled, and the doors were now closed. Peter Smith and Kathy went to the Red Cross Canteen to dance. Peter poured cognac into his glass under the table. Peter was a good dancer. Kathy hoped for a tolerable evening, if he didn't get too drunk to drive.

"Kathy! Kathy Collens!" From among the dancers, a gray-haired WAC ran across the floor to hug Kathy. It was Mac the WAC, the stiff, stern schoolteacher charge nurse she had known at the hospital in Ohio, shouting and hugging with joy. Kathy returned the hug, happy to see her.

"We heard you were dead," said Mac, looking directly at Kathy. "Killed in action. Just now, I thought you were a ghost."

"Gross exaggeration. We don't get that kind of action in a mess. I was sick, that was all. Mac, I'd like you to meet Lieutenant Peter Smith. Peter, Lieutenant McClain. Everyone calls her Mac the WAC."

Mac pointed to her shoulder. "Captain McClain now. My promotion party's tomorrow afternoon. Can you come?"

"Captain! Congratulations. I'll try to get there. Can I help? Maybe bring some refreshments?"

Peter stood and pulled out a chair for Captain McClain. She thanked him politely, sat down, and turned her smile on Kathy. "I'm so glad you're alive."

"So am I. How's Rocky? I heard he was discharged."

Captain McClain shook her head sadly. "He drooped after you left, Kathy. His fainting spells increased. He'd be sitting looking at his dinner and keel over. He'd recover quickly enough, and then keel over again. No one ever figured out why. We finally discharged him."

"Have you heard of him since?"

"No. That's all we know. Haven't you heard from him?"

"The whole thing was a mistake, and I'm forgetting him. I'd just like to think he was all right before I forgot him. Where are you stationed?"

"At SHAEF headquarters, the Supreme Headquarters Allied Expeditionary Force here in Reims. We work under General Eisenhower. We are in what they call the 'Little Red Schoolhouse.' My promotion party will be at my quarters. I'm at a chateau just two blocks west from here, 29 Rue des Gobelins, named for a president."

"The house is numbered?"

"I guess it's not. It has a high brick wall, a huge wrought iron gate, and a large crest in a circle over it. Most of the chateaus on that street have that. The pillars by the front door are unusual. They're deeply carved. You can recognize the house by them."

"I'll find it. Should I bring sandwiches?"

"I have a few cookies from home. Yes, we would enjoy sandwiches. How is Bunts?"

"Endurably the same. She never changes. How's Lieutenant Groot? And Bosco, Boltz, and Kincaid?"

"When I left, the same. I'll tell you all the news tomorrow." While they talked, Peter drank. Captain McClain noticed this, and rose to leave. "I'm neglecting my Colonel." She stood straight and looked sternly, again a schoolteacher, at Peter. "You'd better be getting back while you are able to drive." She smiled at Kathy. "See you tomorrow."

Kathy decided to bribe Peter into leaving. "You can finish your drinking at our well-stocked officers' club."

To her surprise, he made no objection. "Happy to leave this place," he said. He really was good-natured and obliging, and Kathy felt a little guilty that she'd left him out of her talk with Captain McClain. He led her out to the Jeep, and held the door open for her.

She sat in the open Jeep, admiring the square. The mighty towers of the Reims Cathedral, silver on one side, black on the shaded side, reached high into the starry sky. In the magic of the moonlight, the carved figures could have been alive.

Peter jumped into the Jeep to sit, not behind the wheel, but close beside Kathy. He put his arm around her with a kind of grabbing reach. "The night was made for love."

"We're going back to Suippes," Kathy said.

"Just a kiss in the dark," he pulled his arm tight around her.

"I don't pass out kisses like bonbons. Take me back."

He leaned against her, determined to kiss. Kathy shifted away, he persisted, with a relentless hardness.

Kathy opened the Jeep door, and walked away from the Jeep, and then had to decide where she could go. She headed to the Red Cross Canteen, hoping to find someone from her hospital. She recognized no one there. Captain McClain must have left.

She could walk the two blocks to Mac the WAC's chateau, yet unsure if such a walk were safe. Maybe she could spend the night there or call to her hospital for transportation.

She found the Rue des Gobelins. It appeared a black cave in the wall of four-storied buildings that edged the square. Their overhanging upper stories almost met over the narrow street. With a glance back at the open square, and the Jeeps careening crazily around it, she entered the shadowy street.

In the middle of the block, a GI stranger stepped out of the darkness of a doorway. "Hi, Lieutenant."

This was no place to talk with strangers. She walked faster.

"I'm lonely," he said, walking beside her. He could easily walk as fast as she could.

"That's the way it goes. It's a lonely world."

He put an arm around Kathy's waist. "Come with me, and I won't be lonely."

She put her hand on his arm and firmly moved it away. "Sorry, buddy. Go play with someone else. Not me."

He stopped. She walked on when another GI came toward her. He stopped before her, and reached toward her. "I like American girls."

He didn't even say hello first. She stepped aside. "You like us because we're so decent and moral. You know you can't pick up nice girls on dark streets."

He didn't follow her.

She walked on alone, a little worried, but not afraid. Steps behind her clumped closer. She glanced behind, which was a mistake as the soldier behind her considered this look an encouragement. "Hi Toots. What's cooking?"

"Not a thing."

His hand reached for her, patting her waist. "Nice curves," he said.

"Run along, like a good boy." She shooed him away with the backs of her hands as she would a pesky dog.

"I like your curves," he said, standing back, not reaching for her again.

"Bribe some girl with cigarettes. I don't smoke." She walked on ahead of him.

In the two blocks, six soldiers propositioned Kathy. She was beyond being shocked by soldiers. This was the behavior she now expected of them. She could laugh at them, and ward them off as casually and as firmly as they approached her.

Yet she was relieved to reach Captain McClain's quarters. She was glad to leave the Rue des Gobelins through a wrought iron gate and felt safer behind a brick wall. A welcoming light shone above the front door of the grandiose chateau.

Although no one answered the doorbell, Kathy was reluctant to stand outside alone. Without even stopping to admire the deep carving on the pillars that flanked the steps, she pushed open the massive door. She entered and walked through elegant rooms of silk and velvet, calling, "Captain McClain?"

No one answered. What would she say, if at the wrong house, to the duke or count that might own it?

She returned to the front hall to look for uniforms in a closet. No closet in the front hall. She started up the curved staircase when the front door opened. She turned to see who came in. Was she in the right house? Luckily, it was Captain McClain.

"Well, hello," said Mac. "You're full of surprises this evening."

"Am I glad to see you! I don't think my date intended to take me straight home, so I walked over here." Kathy leaned over the bannisters. "Sanctuary!"

"You walked here? You walked down the Rue des Gobelins alone? And got here unmolested?" Captain McClain put her key in the lock on the front door, but it wouldn't go in.

"Some GIs had a few propositions. Nothing I couldn't handle."

Captain McClain turned the key over and tried to insert it into the lock. "You must have quite a method for handling men. I didn't believe there is such a thing. No young girl should be out alone at night."

"Not exactly a method. Just a firm 'No.' To slap his face or run would...would be rejecting him, and he'd have to try harder—and then there'd be trouble."

The key finally turned. Mac tested the door. It was securely locked. "How did you get in? Wasn't this locked?"

"I just walked in. It must have been unlocked. I must admit I was glad. It was a bit uncomfortable outside."

"You're welcome to stay, if you like."

"May I call the 223rd? They ought to be told where I am."

"You can call from the library." Mac led the way across the hall to a bookshelf-lined room. A phone was on a corner desk. "We're on the SHAEF switchboard. Roger, the operator is a capable boy from Indiana. He lived about 100 miles from my hometown, so that made us old friends. He'll get the lines straightened out if anyone can. I'll fix tea while you're calling."

Just like Captain McClain. An evening of warding off six—add Peter Smith to that—seven soldiers, and Captain McClain fixes tea.

Kathy asked Roger to get headquarters at the 223rd General Hospital in Suippes. She waited and listened. He talked to Paris, who got him a line to Brussels. He started again. This time Paris got him a line to Berlin. After half an hour, Roger said, "Captain, I go off duty in five minutes. I have a truck here. Want me to drive out and deliver the message?"

Indeed, he was a nice boy. Kathy said, "I wanted to tell my outfit that I had no way to get home, and was staying with Captain McClain. That's a long trip for you, but if they didn't know where I was..."

"I'll be glad to drive you there, ma'am. Captain McClain can vouch for my driving."

"That's chivalry beyond the call of duty. I'd certainly appreciate it."

When Roger drove Kathy back to her hospital headquarters, she gratefully thanked him and jumped from the truck.

Through the open front door, she could see Charles shaking the telephone. His face was tight with worry. She wanted to run into his strong, safe arms. Instead, she stood in the doorway, waiting until he saw her.

He dropped the phone and stared at her, very worried. Only after he had checked her face, her arms, and her legs did his face relax into a smile. "You're alright?"

"Of course."

"Don't ever do that again."

Her resolution melted, and she was in his arms.

He held her out to inspect her again. "Are you sure you are all right? Your Peter Smith was brought in with compound fractures. A fractured arm and a fractured collar bone. Drunk driving. Lucky to be alive. He didn't know where you were. We were just getting out a search party. You little fool. Don't do that again."

Kathy laughed. It wasn't funny, but she laughed anyway. With a whole Army to choose from, she couldn't find a decent date.

Right now, Charles's arms felt wonderful. She would have to leave them to search for others. She would worry about that search tomorrow. At this moment, she needed Charles's strength.

Charles checked his watch, ending the moment. "It's three a.m. I've not yet made the OD rounds."

"I'll walk with you," offered Kathy.

"No. I'll take you to your door. You get yourself tucked safely into bed."

# CHAPTER 20
# THE ANGEL'S SMILE

The electricity was off again, so Kathy undressed by candlelight. Usually, she liked the soft candlelight, but tonight the flickering shadows were alive and mocking. "Men are evil," whispered the shadows. She blew out the candle to stop the shadows.

Standing at her window, she looked at the moonlight glimmering on the river, now polluted with the sickness of pigs. The moon cast shadows of war, beside the tents of the Displaced Persons and on the Prisoner of War camp, of men defeated. The black leaves of the linden tree waved back and forth, going nowhere.

The shadows persisted. "You sought to help the world. What happened to you? You seek to change the world? Ha! One Lieutenant Groot can stop you."

She had no answers, yet believed there must be an answer, somewhere. "Right will triumph, it will, it will."

Kathy jumped from the window onto her bed, past the blackest shadow under the bed. She stuck her head under the pillow, without relief. She had to find an answer, to shut out the terrors.

She had no way to face this miserable war. No way at all. She'd tried to hate the Germans, but that didn't strengthen the starved. She'd been shocked by the wounded. She was angered by those with venereal disease. She'd found a refuge in Charles's loving arms, yet this was no solution. She had no answers.

In the morning the sun had dispersed the shadows. She set aside the problem of facing life, and resumed the simpler tasks of feeding a thousand patients three meals a day, and making sandwiches for Captain McClain's promotion party. She had arranged to ride into Reims with an infantry Major who was a patient. She had made her ward rounds and had written the special diets. Her last job was to tell Mathilda about a diabetic's diet.

Kathy took the diabetic's diet list from her desk and handed it to Mathilda. "He comes through the cafeteria line and chooses his own food. You check his tray by this list."

"Don't you write his diet for him?"

"No. I've taught him to calculate his own."

Mathilda's lips tightened into a narrow, straight line. "That's not the way it is done. The dietitian writes the diets, not the patient. He doesn't know enough." Mathilda looked to Vivienne for support, but Vivienne sat at her own desk with her back turned.

Arguments with Mathilda had flared easily lately. Kathy would have dropped the issue with a less-important patient. "He's learning. Please, Mathilda. He has to do it himself. He won't go home because he is afraid to inflict his special diet onto his family. It's taken me weeks to convince him he can choose foods from a cafeteria line, and I've shown him how to get the right amounts. He's beginning to realize he needn't be a burden to his family. Please don't undo all my efforts."

Mathilda stood, caught her rayon stocking on a splinter of the chair, and began to cry. "If you want that fancy service given to the patients, you'd better stay and give it yourself. I won't." Head high, not stopping to inspect the damage to her stocking, she walked out.

Kathy looked sadly after her. "That must mean Hooch won't marry her yet."

Vivienne swung around in her chair to face Kathy. "Not yet. That's why I didn't want to side with you against her. She has enough against her. I'll take care of your diabetic."

"I could go another day, but I don't want to miss Captain McClain's party—and the ride with Major Powers. There's something about him I'd like to know better," Kathy said.

"Go ahead. You did my work yesterday." Vivienne took the diet from Kathy's hand. "Why hasn't Major Powers gone home? He became well before VE day. We never keep amputees two months."

Kathy slung her purse across her shoulder. "Thanks. Major Powers says he won't go home. He says his place is here with his outfit. Every day his driver picks him up and takes him to his men. They are in the paratroopers' old camp. Two legs or one, he's still his company's commander." She looked out the window for his Jeep. "Today he's going to SHAEF headquarters, to the Little Red Schoolhouse, to fight for his command at General Eisenhower's office. That's also where Captain McClain is stationed, so I'm riding along. We'll have dinner with his company, so don't expect me till late."

"Remember to salute the brass. We get out of practice here."

Outside, a Jeep drove up. With another "thank you" to Vivienne, Kathy hurried out.

"Hi," she said to the driver, a Sergeant who opened the Jeep. The Major moved his short aluminum crutches to make room on the seat beside him.

"Hi," said Kathy. "Any news? Are you going?"

"To Reims? Yes." He spoke with a rich vigorous voice that rose from deep in his strong chest.

"No, I meant to China." She should not have mentioned China, but the words were out before she considered them.

The Major was not bothered. His smile stayed relaxed. "That will be decided today. I've a new weapon." He held up a fat manila envelope. "My men petitioned to keep me, unanimously. The brass can't ignore this. My men know what I can do."

After arriving in Reims, the Major told the driver, "Park in the parking lot beside the cathedral."

"I can drive you right to the schoolhouse, sir." The driver spoke with fond respect. The Major was a man his troops would admire. He was a fighting man, a tough-whiskered man, so powerful it was impossible to think of him as handicapped, even with a single leg.

The Major accepted no concessions. "No. Stop at the cathedral. Do me good to walk a few blocks. We leave at 1500. All right by you, Lieutenant? And you, Sarge?"

When they stopped, the Sergeant opened the door. When Kathy stepped out, Sarge offered her a gentleman's steadying hand. When the Major hopped out, he steadied himself on the Jeep while the Sergeant stood at attention. Major Powers dismissed him with, "See you here at 1500."

The Major swung his crutches with long steps over the cobblestones. Without bothering to look down, he set the crutch tips on the stones, letting them slip securely into the crevices as he shifted his weight onto them. His foot was large enough to bridge the cracks, and so he hobbled with remarkable sureness over the uneven stones. "I want to look at my angel."

"Your angel? On the cathedral?" Kathy hurried to keep up with his long stride. Her heel slid into a crevice and turned her ankle. She hopped quickly to regain her balance.

"The Angel of the Smile. *L'Ange au Sourire* the French call her. How could you look at the cathedral without seeing her smile?"

Angel of the Smile, Reims Cathedral

"I've looked at the cathedral many times—without seeing any particular smile."

"She stands over the center door. Just looking at her makes me feel good. Funny, if you'd told me six months ago that I would walk blocks out of my way to look at a cathedral, I'd have snorted. One church was like another. You've seen one; you've seen them all. That's what I would have said. Now each has personality."

He was right. At first, cathedrals had been buildings of stone carvings. With increasing familiarity, they took on individuality. Notre Dame in Paris was sturdy and enduring. Here, Reims Cathedral was delicate and soaring. Notre Dame's towers were squat and flat-topped. Reims' towers raised to the heavens with slender spires. Notre Dame said God created the earth and the earth was good. Reims' complex and upward sweeping arches said something else, something spiritual.

Reims Cathedral took on different faces as the lights of the day changed. In the daylight, the stones were light and porous. At sunset the stones changed to a rose color. In the evening the cathedral loomed as a massive shape with the towers reaching for the stars. Most tourists just cast the angel a brief glance, yet one had to study her, to know her as living.

The Major stopped in front of the welcoming church entrance. Three brass doors were deeply recessed under row upon row of statues of angels and saints. He leaned on his aluminum crutches, looking up at the Angel of the Smile. "There she is." He pointed with his crutch tip up to the stone carved angel.

She was larger than human size. She stood near the central door, on a pedestal under carved gothic arches. One huge wing was spread high behind her right shoulder. The other wing broken off. If she had she two wings as powerful as the one, she could surely have flown. One arm was raised in benediction, so that all who passed beneath were blessed. The other arm had been shattered at the elbow. For eight centuries she had stood, unharmed by spears or arrows. Not until the twentieth century, when man created weapons of war that reached higher than man, did man break off her wing and shatter her arm. But her smile endured.

Her head was tilted forward and a little to one side, so she smiled down at everyone who passed through the doors of the cathedral or stood before it. What words describe the warmth of her smile? Kind, benevolent, encouraging. Loving. Love, that was her smile.

"Know that smile. You have to look up to see it." The Major hobbled forward on his aluminum crutches to stand directly in front of the angel's gaze. "She has lost a wing and an arm. Still, she smiles. All I have lost is a leg." He did not look down at his stump that had been blasted off at the knee, but up at the angel. "I, too, can smile." It was then Kathy knew God's gift of love. She received the peace that passes all understanding.

After Captain McClain's promotion party, before meeting the Major at 1500, Kathy stopped at a wood carver's shop beside the cathedral to buy a two-foot statue of *L'Ange au Sourire*—"The Angel of the Smile."

Kathy waited for the Major at a sidewalk cafe on the edge of the square facing the cathedral. She pondered the Major and the angel. She took pencil and paper from her purse and wrote a poem, "God's Gift of Love."

All Kathy had lost was her pride. Kathy could not understand nor judge; this was not her obligation. Kathy could not reform; this was not her obligation. The world was what it had always been and would be. Her obligation was simply to love. This she could do. And...she could smile.

In love and with love and by love she could live—with love for the struggling people in it. By God's gift of love, she could live!

Kathy had dinner with the Major's company. She was in the same chateau where she had eaten steaks and oranges with the paratroopers. This time there were no oranges, only the same canned and dehydrated foods the hospital received. There was little drinking. The only music was the men's singing. This was the Major's farewell to his men, as he was not approved to continue on as their commander. The singing was tinged with sadness. Here was a dignified esprit de corps worth infinitely more than steaks and oranges. Here was respect for women, or at least for Kathy, the only woman present. Dinner was a pleasure.

Kathy's only regret was that the Major, who could maintain this dignity in war, would leave the next day. He was going home to the States. He had taught her the source of his strength—the angel's smile, the love of God. He had given her the way to face war. Kathy at least knew the direction in which to grow.

The Major disliked lingering farewells. After dinner, he said a gruff goodbye to his men; then at the hospital, an abrupt goodbye to Kathy.

# CHAPTER 21

# WEDDING BELLS

Kathy returned to her quarters and contemplated her finished poem about the Angel of the Smile. It said so much, but said it so inadequately. She hoped it would somehow convey the love of the angel's smile.

Mathilda knocked at her door and danced in. "We're going to be married. We're going to be married! Saturday."

Kathy hugged her. "Wonderful! Saturday! Just four days."

"In four days, I'll be Mrs. Hooch Novotny." She whirled around the chair.

"Mrs. Novotny."

Mathilda stopped at Mrs. Foster's room to tell her too, but she was not there. She went in, stopping in front of the gilded mirror. "The wedding will be simple; our Chaplain, our chapel..." Her hands fluttered from her hair to her skirt. "My hair. How do I fix my hair? A dress. Is there time to make a wedding dress? I can't have an olive- drab wedding—I won't have an olive-drab wedding. Olive drab uniform. Olive drab underwear."

"In this land of fashion, we can find a dressmaker. But, where could we get material?" asked Kathy. The quartermaster and PX wouldn't stock wedding dress material. The 82$^{nd}$ Airborne and their white nylon parachutes had flown off to Germany. "The dress doesn't make the wedding. You need only a Chaplain, a bride and a groom. Or should I hunt in Paris for material?"

"Flowers. I must carry flowers. Can you make a bouquet? A bridal bouquet? I want a pretty wedding." She turned before the mirror. Handsome as her uniform was, it was not a bridal gown.

"Yes," said Kathy. "I can get flowers."

"No. There aren't any flowers." Mathilda ran from the mirror back into Kathy's room and flopped dejectedly onto her olive-drab bed. "The flowers have all dried up. No wedding dresses. No flowers. I'll be an olive drab bride."

"Mme. Duval has white roses. And maybe some pink ones for your maid of honor."

"Her roses are all dried up, too."

"No. They are beautiful. She watered them with dishwater."

"The soap would kill roses."

"She had no soap. Her roses are fresh and beautiful."

"Will you be my maid of honor?"

"I'll be delighted to be your maid of honor, Mathilda."

Vivienne came shouting down the hall. "We're moving out. We're moving on. Next week. South Pacific, here we come."

Saturday was as hot as the rest of July had been, yet no one questioned that Mathilda's wedding would be conducted in full dress uniform. Mathilda, with flushed, perspiring face, twisted her necktie and patted her hair straight. "I wish, I wish there was at least one thing dressed up for my wedding. Same shirt, same skirt that I wore yesterday."

"You'll have one new thing, a wedding ring." Kathy brushed Mathilda's woolen jacket. It didn't need brushing, but Mathilda wanted someone to fuss over her.

Mathilda straightened her collar. "You should be able to tell the bride from the bridesmaids. How can you when we're all dressed in olive drab?"

Vivienne gave her a reassuring smile. "You look different. Your eyes sparkle. Your cheeks are flushed rosy. You're a beautiful blushing bride. The rest of us are all slightly green with envy, wishing we were getting a wedding ring." She glanced at her watch. "Ready?"

Kathy took the bouquet of white roses that she had bound together with adhesive tape, wiped the drips on an olive-drab towel, and handed them to Mathilda.

She glowed happily. "Perfect. Kathy, they're beautiful. I'm a bride."

Kathy took her pink roses, and they walked from their barracks to the chapel in a Quonset hut.

Hooch waited at the front of the church, with Chaplain Kirkemo on one side and the Colonel as best man on the other. He looked uncomfortable, with perspiration dripping on his chin, but he managed a fond smile for Mathilda.

The organ played the wedding march. Kathy, as maid of honor, walked down the aisle. Hooch watched her, and she lowered her eyes to look at the pink roses quivering in her hands. Hooch should be watching only Mathilda. What kind of life was ahead for her, always wondering, never certain of Hooch's love? She would want him to conform, but he would seek escape. Hooch would in fact escape right after the honeymoon, off with another unit to China, while Mathilda would return to the States. However, even if he never returned to her, she had a child to love, a better life than the empty one she had lived.

Kathy looked up again, and Hooch was smiling at Mathilda. She loved him. Mathilda's love would reach him. With love, anything was possible. Hooch would be a good husband. At a wedding, you anticipated a good marriage. At a wedding you thought of the miracles of love.

Kathy passed Charles. His sober eyes were eloquent. This, he was thinking, is what you want.

The Chaplain spoke. "Harry Laurence Novotny, wilt thou have this woman to be thy wedded wife, to live together after God's ordinance in the holy estate of matrimony? Wilt thou love her, comfort her, honor and keep her in sickness and in health; and forsaking all others, keep thee only unto her, so long as ye both shall live?"

"Love him, comfort him, honor and keep him..." No, Kathy would not catch a man, nor trap him, nor find a father-figure to hold a shotgun on her groom. She would find first a man who wanted to love, comfort and honor and keep her—and she him—who wanted the responsibilities of children. Mathilda's wedding was fine for Mathilda, yet Kathy wanted more.

At the officers' club, Hooch and Mathilda together cut the wedding cake. The Colonel proposed a toast in champagne. Then the bride and groom drove off in a Jeep to Paris for their honeymoon.

When they had left, Charles took off his uniform blouse and necktie. "The wedding's over. Back to the war."

Kathy wrapped a piece of cake in a napkin, to have to dream on. "Don't you have something flattering to say about the cake? It had frosting! I made the figurines of mashed dehydrated potatoes. Fortunately, no one tasted them."

"What dreams will you get on mashed potatoes—dehydrated mashed potatoes, that is? Think you're clever, don't you? That's all right, you are. The cake was superb." Charles grinned down at her, proud of her. "I say, back to the war. I'm leaving tomorrow."

"We leave the day after tomorrow, don't we? Or have I missed something on the bulletin board again?"

"I'm not going with you. I've been transferred to England. You know we must...you understand this is best?"

Kathy took a deep breath and nodded in mute agreement. He must have requested the transfer.

He put his strong hand gently on her shoulder. "I leave for Paris in the morning. Can you come with me, to Paris...our last day?"

Kathy could almost look forward to saying goodbye in Paris, tomorrow. Tomorrow could always be a pleasant day, but today was harder to face.

Today she had to say goodbye to baby Sammy. Plans kept changing. Today he was being sent off to an over-crowded, under-fed orphanage. She had a PW put a case of canned milk into the Jeep that would carry Sammy away. One case of milk, twenty-four cans. Sammy, at the age of one month, would know the pain of hunger. Sooner, if the milk were shared with other children. What difference would it make to send two cases of milk?

She had to hold Sammy one last time. He looked at her, with his helpless, trusting look. "You know I would keep you if I could," she told him. "I must first finish the war. Fight the Japanese to make the world free for you."

When she returned to the mess, three PWs came forward to greet her, their hands behind their backs. "We had few tools," Oscar said. His round face was pleasant and intelligent. Where were the Germans who had fought in the war, the ones that starved Sammy? Oscar smiled. "Only a hammer, a saw, and a file. We made these for you."

Rolf brought a book rack from behind his back. It was made of a polished dark wood, a shelf along which two carved book ends slid into a grooved slot. He handed it to her. A second PW gave her a cigarette case made of hammered aluminum cut from a German plane that had crashed in a neighboring field. Inside the hinge was a spring, wound from the same aluminum, that flipped the lid open. On the lid was etched a fine dog, with deep strokes making his eyes and nose, and delicate strokes making his fur.

Oscar gave her a box made of the hard brown sheets of plastic used for electrical insulation. The corners and hinges were filed and hammered from brass shell casings into three-dimensioned curved flowers and leaves. It was an exquisite box. These men, to whom Kathy had scarcely spoken, had transformed scraps into beautiful presents for her. There was certainly something good.

That evening, Kathy and Charles said goodbye to the Duvals, thanking them for all they'd done, and promised to return. The next morning, they rode to Paris in the back of a supply truck.

They jumped from the truck and stood by the Red Cross's sidewalk cafe-canteen. "The day is before us in Paris. Where do you want to go? Visit your artist friends? The Louvre? Tonight, the Folies or the Opera? Or just sit on a bench in the Gardens?"

"The Louvre. Mrs. Foster said they had unburied and replaced the sculptures that were returned from Hitler and Goering's collections. She didn't think much of them. She has no use for modern art."

"That sounds like her. Under each person she sees murky murderous aggression and insatiable lusts."

"She just talks that way. She acts differently."

"She has a preoccupation with the uncontrolled, destructive id." He took her hand. "Well, on to beauty. At least it will be cool in the Louvre."

Inside the ancient palace, where a brilliant Matisse painting hung on Lescot's sixteenth century wall, all centuries blended. Here, life was displayed as under the aspect of eternity.

As they looked at statues, workmen brought in a Bourdelle bronze statue that Kathy recognized. "Hercules drawing his bow against the Stymphalian birds. My mother had a replica of this and told me the mythical story. I used to believe it, that Hercules actually did shoot the huge birds with cruel beaks and sharp talons. He saved the villagers from being devoured. The statue looks so strong and realistic. Hercules balances so smoothly against the rocks and with the rocks. I can almost believe it again."

They watched another statue being set on its pedestal. It was a Picasso, a large white confusion of masses and gyrations and empty spaces that bore no relation to anything recognizable. "There's one I find hard to believe," said Charles.

Kathy walked around it. "That's the kind of art that takes time to know. It's heavy, and yet light. It falls apart and is unified. Try to make sense of that. That's how I see life. Two years ago, I would have preferred a nice romantic sensible statue. Now that seems too simple."

They laughed and wandered through the ancient palace where they lost the sense of tomorrow and yesterday in the eternal beauty before them.

Finally, they returned to the entrance where reproductions were sold. Charles, stopping to look in the glass- topped display counter, said, "I want to give you something. Not just something to remember me by, but something that will keep telling you what I would if I could." He grinned at her. "It should tell you to go right on seeing everyone as good and lovable. Go on seeing a beautiful day when it's raining. What can I give you that will say that?"

"I don't need anything. I'll not forget. Anyway, nothing says that much."

"I am going to give you something." He leaned over the costume jewelry display. "How about that bird?"

He held the bird in the palm of his strong hand. It was a golden pin, smooth and plain except for a blue enameled eye. Its beauty was in her graceful lines and in the spirited tilt of her head.

"A nightingale?" asked Kathy.

"She might be. I had thought of her as an Egyptian falcon that perched on a royal shoulder, a symbol of courage."

"I don't need courage." She had felt or seen the worst this life had to offer, and still believed life was good. "I don't have enough sense to be afraid."

"All right. She's a nightingale, a nightingale who sings at night when other birds have tucked their heads under their wings."

"OK. I'll take your nightingale. I'll hold my head high when I think of you."

Charles ran his long slender fingers over the bird with a delicate touch. He had a doctor's hands, sensitive to textures. She wanted to give him faith in himself, and hope that he could finish medical school. She picked up a pair of cuff links, a triangle imposed on a rectangle. "That is a standing star. Think of it as an ancient Egyptian symbol of faith, faith in your future. You can and you will finish medical school. You know so much already. You won't have to study as much as others."

"Not enough money."

"A part-time job, plus the GI bill, would be plenty."

"I'm too old; it would take four years."

"How old will you be in four years if you go to medical school?"

"Thirty-four."

"How old will you be in four years if you don't go?"

They left the Louvre and walked along the Rue de la Paix to a sidewalk cafe. Something sharply reminded Kathy of Rocky. It was the red-and-white checkered tablecloths, and the glass vase with a single yellow rose on each table.

Charles pulled out a chair for her, and ordered a goblet of red wine. In her memories, Rocky had sat opposite Kathy at a little table like this one. Rocky had held the wine, and when Kathy hadn't understood, he had put his hand on his throat, and his eyes had been appealing. Kathy put her hand on her neck, and rubbed it just as Rocky had done, digging with her fingers.

"Don't do that," said Charles.

"Don't do what?"

"Don't hold your fingers on your carotid arteries. You'll cut off the circulation to your head and faint."

"What did you say? Charles! You're brilliant! One hundred and one doctors and two hundred and two psychiatrists couldn't diagnose Rocky's fainting! He's not sick! He's not neurotic! I knew it. He's healthy!"

"Hold on. I have a suspicious mind. Do you think he knew he was knocking himself out to get out of the Army?"

"Of course not. I'll write and tell him. Maybe that will atone for trying to take him from his wife. I can give him back his health—you gave him back his health."

The sunlight was brilliant on the yellow rose. The war was over in Paris. Charles had finally resolved to go back to school when the war was over in the South Pacific. The day was good with dinner at the Normandie and an evening at the opera. There were happy endings.

At midnight when Charles took Kathy to the Army truck that was driving back to Suippes, there were no tears. Only a feeling that what they had had was fine, and that what was ahead would be fine.

"I don't like sending you back alone in a truckload of men," said Charles.

"Men are…just men. They no longer shock or frighten me. You'll like England. And maybe I'll see you on a tropic island. Who knows?"

They kissed a gentle goodbye. Kathy had one last thing to say. "Thank you. You picked me up when I was down—you've lifted up my head. Thank you."

Kathy climbed into the truck to sit near the open back. As they drove away, she leaned out and waved. This was goodbye to Charles, to Paris, and to their quiet hospital.

Tomorrow she would leave with her hospital for the port of Marseille in southern France. From there, they would sail off to serve in the CBI, somewhere in the Pacific.

She wasn't afraid. She could look forward to the trip.

# CHAPTER 22

# SUNNY SOUTHERN FRANCE

Two weeks later, the 223rd Hospital was no closer to Marseille. On August 6, 1945, an atomic bomb was dropped on the city of Hiroshima. Three days later another bomb was dropped on Japan, this time in Nagasaki. An ultimatum was given that more bombs would be dropped unless there was an unconditional surrender from Japan.

Even the certainty of Japan's defeat did not change the Army's plans for the 223rd. They boarded trains the next day for Marseille, and then would go on to the Pacific. For three days they ate K-rations and watched the slow-moving scenery. With the huge doors of the train slid open, they had a splendid view of France. They stopped often. At each stop they asked, "Is it VJ Day yet? Is the war over? Did Japan sign an armistice?" No one seemed to know exactly when, but sometime during that trip, the war did end.

After nearly six years, the war was finally over. President Harry Truman broadcasted an announcement of Japan's surrender. A formal event was planned for September 2, 1945.

Confusion reigned in the Army in Marseille. Men with both high and low "going-home" points were shifting in and out of units, with ships sailing to Pacific or the States. No one seemed to know who was going where. The 223$^{rd}$ would have to wait in southern France while the Army revised plans.

While adjusting to victory, life for the nurses was relatively peaceful. They had their own large private swimming pool in the villa where they stayed. The Jantzen Company gave them bathing suits—the first feminine, bright-colored civilian clothes the girls had while serving.

While most of the nurses were content to sun-bathe, Kathy explored Marseille. She walked up the steep winding road to the celebrated Notre Dame de la Garde, the highest peak of the old city. Surmounted on top of the basilica was a 30-foot golden statue of the Virgin Mary. From there she could see both a panoramic view of Marseille and the blue Mediterranean. She walked along La Canebière to the old harbor. She was fascinated by the old fishing boats and nets full of strange-colored fish, and the Arabs and Africans in exotic clothes. She watched a tank ship, similar to ones that carried oil in the United States, unloading wine through a hose.

She waved happily at a French family hoisting the sails on a sloop. They waved back, and in a few minutes, when they discovered she spoke French, invited her on board. The father, on vacation, took his wife and two children sailing every day. They came over to the pier to pick up Kathy.

A Lieutenant, sitting on the pier said to another Lieutenant sitting beside him. "Look at that. How does she do it? She just walks down and gets invited to sail. We've been trying for months." The Frenchman asked Kathy what they said, and when she interpreted, invited them along too.

"My friend, Brad Green," the taller Lieutenant made the introductions. "I'm Clinton Johnson, at your service." He saluted. "Please tell your French friends I'm a mess officer. If they like, I can bring K-rations for lunch, or anything else."

The French had no idea what K-rations were, and were puzzled at the waxed boxes Clinton brought from his Jeep.

Kathy hoisted the jib, to show she was a sailor. They cast off, the wind caught the sails, and they slid silently away. They crossed the harbor on three tacks. This gave the Americans a close look at boats and docks, some ruined by war, while they passed out into the open sea. The wind, unhindered by hills and buildings, blew strong across the water. Clear water splashed the decks.

Once safely away from other boats, the Frenchman gave Kathy the helm. He pointed ahead to their destination. They were headed to an island, the Château d'If, where the Count de Monte Cristo had been kept prisoner. Kathy had forgotten the feel of the helm. She alternately spilled the wind from the sails or caught the full force of the wind. Gradually she learned her boat and was able to hold the course. The sun sparkled on the spray, making miniature rainbows. The sea rushed by, the wind sang in the stays and halyards, and Kathy worked with them both. She melded her strength and wits with the sloop, the wind and the water, and soared ahead. Apply natural laws of force and angles, harness the elements, and reach your destination. Kathy was back in a world she understood.

She sailed daily with the French family and Clinton Johnson without getting involved in their lives. While she remained indifferent to the people, her interest in the sloop grew. She learned how quickly the sloop could come about, how to trim her sails in a light wind or a strong wind, how she would behave in a squall. Over it all was the joy of the feel of the helm. When she pushed or pulled, she kept the sloop in harmony with wind and water.

People, human beings, could no longer bewilder nor scare her. She could love them, feel compassion for their troubles, without participating in their lives. She could now work effectively, harmoniously with people as she could with the sloop.

Kathy sailed every day, yet she could not get any of the other girls in her hospital unit to go with her. She made friends in the Marseille art colony. She became a close friend of a Florentine girl when Kathy gave her a pair of nylons. Yet the more friends she made among the French, the more isolated she felt from the American girls, who still preferred sunbathing.

The dark and narrow streets of Marseille were truly dangerous— and were off limits. There was an abundance of the more dangerous type of American soldiers in Marseille. The Army's policy did not allow any man with a venereal disease on board a ship. Instead, they were transferred through hospitals into units remaining in port, giving them increasingly high rates The VD rate for soldiers was said to be 334 percent. The average man in that unit had contracted VD three-and-a-third times. But Kathy was not afraid of these men. Instead, she pitied their loneliness, and their pathetic struggle to find peace.

When Bunts offered to go sailing with Kathy, Kathy was delighted to have an American companion. From their villa, they rode in the back of the Army truck that routinely drove to Marseille and back twice daily. Next, they walked in the stifling heat from the Red Cross Canteen over to the old harbor. A cool breeze came across the water. They wore bathing suits under their uniforms.

Just as they arrived, the sailboat was sliding away from the pier. Her sails were well filled with a speeding wind. Kathy shouted and waved and ran along the harbor road trying to catch the sailor's attention. Two white-helmeted MPs in a Jeep rushed to Kathy and screeched to a stop. "Need help, Lieutenant?" asked the driver.

Kathy was apologetic. "I was just trying to catch that sailboat to ride with them, but we are minutes too late. It's not important." Yet it was important. She wanted to take Bunts out on the cool water, away from the hot smell of fish. She wanted to give her the joys of sailing, and thus earn her friendship. Then maybe Kathy wouldn't be exploring Marseille alone, but have Bunts as a companion.

"Hop in." An MP opened the Jeep door for them. "We'll catch them."

Kathy and Bunts climbed into the Jeep. The MPs raced down the narrow, crooked road, honking the horn loud and long. Everyone in the harbor looked except the friends on the boat. Finally, those on the boat saw them and brought the sloop into the wind to wait.

A fisherman in a rowboat offered to ferry them out, so Kathy took off her shirt and skirt and shoes. Bunts took off her shoes. They climbed across the huge jagged rocks at the shore to the rowboat. Kathy gave him a package of cigarettes for the ride, which he accepted as bountiful.

It was a delightful day for showing off the pleasures of sailing. The breeze was good, the water blue, the sun dazzling. Kathy pointed out the gilded Virgin giving her blessings over the city and ships, the old forts at the harbor's entrance, and the crumbling castle on the Château d'If.

Bunts showed no enthusiasm. Kathy laughed, determined to show her a good time. "The ride with the MPs was ridiculous. They must have thought we were two nurses with an emergency!" She dangled her bare feet over the port side to splash in the cool water.

Bunts wiped her feet with her olive-drab handkerchief and put on her sturdy shoes. "How can you laugh? I was so embarrassed. It's bad enough to be always conspicuous, always the only girls in American uniforms. It's worse to be ridiculous too. Running and waving. Racing with the horn blowing. Barefoot. Sliding on those rocks, with everyone watching!"

"When in France do as the French… They don't mind being different..." As soon as Kathy said it, she regretted it. Bunts had been too deeply embarrassed to speak lightly. A gloom settled over the boat that even the bright sun and sparkling water couldn't disperse.

Now she realized that the other girls might not want to speak French in such a funny way as she did. Every time Kathy spoke, the French laughed at her accent. Kathy was used to this, could even value it as an ice-breaker as long as they understood her. Yet others might be unwilling to go through the stages of nonsensical-sounding speech to learn a proper accent.

None of the American girls went sailing with Kathy again. Kathy had more sympathy with their sunbathing. It took a certain indifference to appearing ridiculous, and lot of courage just to walk along the street in Marseille. To Kathy it had been the Arabs in their long robes, the Turks in red fezzes who had looked different. Now she realized, with surprise, that to them, it was she who was conspicuous.

She began to think she could never achieve a harmonious, effective relationship with these girls, only with the sloop. At the end of their day,

Kathy and Bunts rode the trucks back and walked over to the nurses' villa.

The hallway leading to the room they shared with fifteen other girls of the 223rd Hospital was covered with open bedrolls, which the girls were packing.

"Where are we going?" Kathy asked Vivienne who was spreading a uniform over the blankets of her bedroll.

"You know where we are going. We're going to the South Pacific," Vivienne responded.

Bunts, ever the ball player, took her olive-drab underwear and threw it the length of the hall, with it landing on her bedroll. "You're saying that just because you want to see Stan. Stan is in the Pacific. I say things have changed. I say we're going home."

Vivienne walked along the edges of the bedrolls to the door of the room. "Wishful thinking, because your Tex is home. You have a higher number than we do. You saw Tex for three full days. Wasn't that enough?" Her smile laughed at what she said. "Now I have it figured out scientifically. We can predict where we're going by how many points our men have. Right after VJ day when we thought we were going to China, all the high-point men were taken out, replaced with low pointers. The high-point men were going home."

"So, with the high-point men, we go home." Bunts picked up an armful of shoes.

"That was three days ago." Vivienne folded her shirts. "They've changed again to low-point men. That means we will go to the South Pacific."

Mrs. Foster and Betty came from the room in their full Red Cross gray dress uniforms, hats and gloves, carrying small suitcases. "We are all ready to go. We have our orders. We are off to Germany. We will be part of the Army of occupation stationed in Germany, aiding in rebuilding the country. Maybe you will end up there with us. Write and let us know." Mrs. Foster shook Vivienne's hand, and then Kathy's. "So long."

"I hate to have you leave us, Mrs. Foster. You've been a good friend. I'm grateful...," said Kathy.

"I said so long, not goodbye. Maybe I'll see you next week. There's a shortage of dietitians in Germany. If not, then we'll have a reunion some day in the States."

Kathy shook Betty's hand. "We'll miss you. Write. Let us know where you are."

When they'd gone, Kathy dragged her bedroll from under her bed and spread it in the empty space by Mrs. Foster's bed. "That leaves just three of the ten girls who started with the 223rd." Mrs. Foster was going to Germany because Germany would be a new country, and she had no one to go home to. The other three Red Cross girls had left for the states to take up life where they had left. Sue had been transferred out, but where?

"Have you heard from Sue?" Kathy asked Vivienne and Bunts.

"Yes," said Vivienne. "I saw her yesterday. She's been assigned to three hospitals in five days, but hasn't left the staging area yet. She's confused. I told her that it could get worse. One nurse was assigned to four hospitals in three hours."

Kathy knelt on her bedroll, arranging the blankets. "Say, why did Mrs. Foster think we might go to Germany? Didn't our orders name a ship?"

"We haven't seen the orders. We just know the 222nd Hospital's ship sailed today. So, the 223rd will sail tomorrow."

Kathy stood up. "No. They did not sail today. I just passed them. There weren't loading. They were actually unloading their trucks and moving back into their barracks. Some had even marched onto the ship, and then had to march back again."

Vivienne threw her shoes into her footlocker. "That does it. I'm going to headquarters. Now. I'll find out what's happening."

She returned waving typed orders. "Bunts, you are going home. You have enough points! Lucky you! Kathy and I are going to the only place in the world no one guessed. We are going to the place that no one wanted. We go back to Mourmelon for more waiting until reassigned.

I'm no closer to Stan in the South Pacific. At least, Kathy, you and I will still be together.

"Just outside of Reims. Again." She continued. "Miserable Mourmelon. Right back in the middle of the tent cities. The ETO now has a chief dietitian in Versailles. That's new. When she discovered two dietitians were about to sail away, she phoned our headquarters to yank us out. This is the first time any brass ever noticed us, and they send us back to Mourmelon. She wants us here in Europe. Specifically, she plans to send us on to Germany. Maybe now that they've noticed us, they'll promote us to First Lieutenants."

"Mourmelon. That's tough," sympathized Bunts. "I feel for you. But I'm happy to go home."

Bunts sat beside the clothes piled on her bed, picked up her guitar, and slowly, sadly, sang, "I'll be Seeing You," a forlorn hope.

Vivienne knelt by her footlocker, neatly arranging the shoes in it. "Bunts, you don't want to spend three days on a train getting back to Paris. Since our orders were phoned in, I can cut our own stencils. I'll authorize air transportation. Bunts, I just might slip your name in under ours."

The next morning, the three of them said goodbye to the Colonel and executive officer, all that were left of the original 223rd General Hospital. The family of men and women who had lived and worked together with dedication and harmony had now scattered around the world. Gone also was the esprit de corps, and the romance. Gone was the war, and the need to work together to win.

# CHAPTER 23

# WAR CRIMES

With musette bags on their backs, the three girls flew by Army plane to Paris. In an open Jeep, they drove on to the dismal tent cities of the redeployment area of Mourmelon.

"It's cold," said Kathy, hugging her coat collar around her neck.

"In late September, what did you expect in northern France?" Vivienne was always logical.

"We flew into winter so suddenly, I'm not ready for it," said Kathy.

Neither was France ready for winter. A cold wind blew the shriveled brown leaves from the trees. Beside some homes were small piles of twigs as the large wood had been burned last winter.

Upon arrival in Mourmelon, they realized their footlockers had not followed them from Marseille. Bunts and Kathy arranged for a driver to take them the next day to Reims to search for the footlockers. Bunts would leave from there and go on to Le Havre and on to the States.

Before they left for Germany, Kathy wanted to visit the Duvals. She got a driver to take her to Suippes in a steel-roofed ambulance to take some presents. Kathy had never given the Duvals anything more enduring than a bar of soap. When Kathy's mother had sent turquoise and silver Indian jewelry, Kathy used that as an excuse for a visit.

They parked before the Duval's house at about 2100, after dark. The old stone house had no lights on. Evidently no one was home. They were about to drive on, when Kathy noticed a thin sliver of light from a back window. She went to the door to knock. A shutter on a peep-hole slid open, then the door opened. M. and Mme. Duval greeted her, "*Entrez. Entrez. Comment allez-vous? Parlons Francais.*"

Never before had Mme. Duval asked to speak in French. Even though her husband did not speak English, she had wanted to practice English. Now she preferred French. Why were the black-out curtains up? Why the reserved welcome?

Mme. Duval led her into the cool, formal living room rather than the warm dining room where they had so often spent their evenings. "Sorry I cannot offer you wine. Our wine is rationed."

"*Ca ne fait rien,*" said Kathy. "No matter. I must be getting back soon anyway. My driver is waiting."

"Do you know why we don't have wine?" asked M. Duval. "Because your American soldiers take it. Do you know why we have black-out curtains up? So, you Yankees won't know we are home. If they see we are home, they bang on the door till we open it. They push in, shouting, 'We liberated you; you owe it all to us. Now pay us. Give us your wine and give us your women.' If we do not give them what they ask, they fight. Do you know no woman is safe in the street after dark? Reims and Nancy and six villages that I know have asked to be placed off limits to American soldiers. The Yankees should go home."

"They want to go home." Kathy said. "They're going as fast as they can. It took years to get them over here. It will take a long time to get them home. I know the idleness breeds mischief. For some it's much worse."

Kathy handed M. Duval her basket of small packages wrapped in red tissue paper. "I brought you presents, made by the Santa Fe Indians. This is to show you our appreciation of your hospitality. The thunderbird design is an Indian symbol of good luck. That, I wish to you."

"*Pardonnez moi.*" M. Duval brought forward a chair for Kathy. "Sit down. We forget. The Americans are our friends. We are grateful to you. We do forget—that if there are 50,000 men crowded in miserable tent cities around Suippes, and 5 percent of them come to the village looking for excitement—that's 2,500 men. We know the 5 percent make an impression that the 95 percent who sit quietly in tents cannot change."

"It is more complex than that," Mme. Duval spoke now in English. "We believed that after the liberation, the war would be over, and we would live in peace and comfort. We do not live in comfort nor in peace. We are divided against each other. Catholics are divided against non-Catholics, de Gaullists against Communists, men of the resistance against collaborators. Ninety percent of the Frenchmen were collaborators at the beginning of the occupation, and 90 percent were in the resistance at the end. Yet we cannot even agree as to who was which. So, we do not have an organized government. We still have no gasoline. We are still hungry. If the American Army would leave, we could recover. Yet we still need American aid. That is hard on a Frenchman's pride. So let us sit in our dining room like the friends that we are. Let us have a glass of wine"

"It is true," said M. Duval, continuing in French, "that the GIs are not well-disciplined."

"That is true. For that we are sorry," said Kathy. He was being polite. Kathy had heard there was an average of four violent deaths a night during the last month in the little town of Reims alone—with a civilian population of around 100,000. Not just some nights, every night, four violent deaths. American and French deaths, both.

Kathy decided not to attempt a discussion of blame. "I really cannot stay. My driver is waiting. Perhaps I can stop for a visit on my way back from Germany. Good luck, and au revoir."

The next day, Bunts and Kathy went to Reims in search of the footlockers. At the train's transportation headquarters, the Sergeant told them, "Come back tomorrow. The plane they were on will be back by then."

Kathy hitched her musette bag onto her shoulder, and turned to walk toward the leave center. Bunts dropped her musette bag beside a bench and sat down to wait.

"He said to come back tomorrow," said Kathy. "Let's check in at the leave center."

"Nope. I'm leaving." Bunts strummed her guitar, her old refrain, "I'll Be Seeing You."

"You want to go without your footlocker?"

"Yup. I don't care if I never see it again." She strummed and hummed, "In all the old familiar places..."

"You lose a footlocker of clothes and you don't care? Winter's coming. You will need that lovely long woolen underwear. Doesn't anything bother you?"

Bunts smiled her quiet, passive smile. "I will be with Tex soon. I'm getting married. I do not intend to be wearing olive drab underwear."

Bunts had endured the war without any scars. She was seemingly untouched. She survived with a strong steadiness that did not get disturbed. The war was over. She would now resume her life as though nothing had happened.

"I'm glad to have known you," said Kathy. "I'll see you sometime. Should I wait with you for your train to Le Havre?"

"I don't mind waiting by myself. A few minutes, a few days...it's been years waiting now. Good-bye, and good luck to you." She dreamily strummed her guitar as Kathy walked away and waved goodbye.

Kathy left her musette bag at the leave center, and walked over to the SHAEF Headquarters. Captain McClain always had interesting news. Captain McClain was not in her office. Walking down the hallway, Kathy stopped at an open door marked "WAR CRIMES INVESTIGATING TEAM." There would be something interesting in that room.

The room was an old-fashioned, dark-wood-trimmed schoolroom. The children's desks had been replaced with consul's tables and a judge advocate's bench. Behind the tables sat uniformed officers and testifying civilians stood in front. A brown-haired captain waved his horn-rimmed glasses toward Kathy, inviting her in. He offered her a chair beside his table.

She listened all afternoon to testimony about the oats and cattle the Germans had taken. When court recessed, Kathy turned to the consul. "Thank you for inviting me in."

"You are welcome to listen. This office is working to prepare for the war crimes trials that will be held in Nuremburg, Germany."

"Thank you. Today I learned something. I had thought France's starvation was because men were fighting instead of plowing. Does this mean babies starved because the Germans took the food?"

"There were many complicated reasons for starvation. We're trying to estimate how much to blame on a by-product of war, poor distribution—and how much to the grabbing Germans. Crop production was reduced about 10 percent. That itself couldn't cause the extreme starvation. The Nazis took two thirds of the production of Belgium and Holland. We're estimating now what they took from France. So far, we've traced over eight million tons of French oats that went into Germany, and we're not done.

"They must have known that the Belgians, the Dutch, and French would die if they took the food."

"Of course. And Poles and Czechs and Slavs would die. The Nazis wanted them to die. Kill off the inferior races and populate the world with the Master Race. When starvation didn't kill them fast enough, the Nazis shot them. When shooting them wasn't fast enough, they built extermination camps. At Auschwitz alone they could efficiently kill 6,000 a day, mostly Jews. If you can believe their bragging, they exterminated three or four million, which was a more certain way of getting rid of people than starvation. Some camps used gas and others killed by shooting. They killed them so fast that getting rid of the bodies became a problem. They couldn't cremate more than 6,000 bodies a day so their murdering was limited to 6,000 a day."

"Why? Why? How could they hate so much to do such a thing?"

"If you believe that only blue-eyed blond Germans are worth living, you kill off black-haired dark-eyed people so they won't contaminate the stock. If you do keep a few black-haired people as slaves, you sterilize them so they can't reproduce." His eyes looked at her dark eyes. "You'd have been exterminated."

"I saw the patients from Dachau. I sort of thought, I wanted to think, they just ran out of food, and I didn't try too hard to find a more sinister reason."

"Starvation was planned from the beginning. Read Hitler's *Mein Kampf*. The Nazis were radically evil," he said.

"During war all men are driven to evil. Even our wonderful American GIs are doing some rotten things," Kathy said.

"You resist believing that depth of their evil. Who can comprehend four million exterminations?" He took off his horned-rim glasses and rubbed his eyes. Then he pointed his glasses at Kathy. "I can show you the difference between the Nazis systematic evil and rotten things the American GIs did. After dinner, we'll go to an M.P. station. I'll show you."

Kathy forgot that she had determined never again to go out with man who was a stranger. This man was interesting, though, and she had lost her appetite for dinner.

The MP station looked much like a Chicago precinct station, but a little cleaner. A Sergeant was behind a high desk, a wooden railing dividing the room from battered wooden benches for waiting. Kathy and the consul sat on a bench and watched and listened. MPs brought in American soldiers. French civilians came in with complaints—charges of disorderly conduct, drunken brawls, knife fights, drunken shooting, accidents, robbery and rape.

Kathy said to the consul, "I never thought the Germans could have been worse than this."

"If this were a German court," said the consul, "the civilian who complained would be put in jail, and the Nazi soldier would go free. The whole idea was that every non-German existed only as slave to the Germans. Therefore, the Germans could commit no legal wrong against an occupied country. They frowned on German intercourse with non-German races. This was not because of any respect for the women but because they didn't want to breed impure stock.

"Anything they wanted, they took. Anything. No one could complain and live. They took 137 freight car loads of art treasures."

"And I thought art had been buried so bombings wouldn't shatter it," Kathy said.

"Some was. The point is that the Germans were masters, and we were to be slaves. Our investigations get nastier and nastier. We nice Americans can't believe the depth of their evil even when we see the German records. They proudly recorded their mastery over inferior scum."

He took off his glasses, looked directly at Kathy and said, "There's one compensation. This war was worth fighting. Certainly, Hitler had to be stopped—stopped with guns, not words."

"Was there a time that words, that reason..." Kathy said.

"Perhaps. The shocking thought now is that if any group in Germany, or the French or British or Americans, had stood staunchly against Hitler in the beginning, he could have been stopped. People in Germany believed Hitler's promises, and were blind to the evils he imposed. This is original sin personified. Each person selfishly seeing only what he wanted, and blindly ignoring the greater evil, to his own eventual destruction."

The consul had exposed the radical evil of the Nazis. Kathy faced it, reluctantly, unable to find excuses or reason for it.

# CHAPTER 24

# WAITING FOR ORDERS

When Kathy returned to her room, Vivienne was packing. "Brace yourself. You and I are not going to Germany. We've been transferred to the 191st, across town, but we will remain here in Mourmelon."

"Oh no! Here in the heart of the tent cities, where a hundred thousand red-blooded American men are waiting to embrace us. What more could a girl want?"

"I'd settle for one man." Vivienne showed Kathy a green bottle of Mumm champagne. "I've bought that one man of mine his Christmas present, so he won't forget me."

They drove through Mourmelon, which was actually a pleasant old village. It was the tent cities around it that were lonely and desolate, empty of everything but tents.

The 191st General Hospital was a cluster of clean, well-kept permanent buildings. When Vivienne and Kathy signed in at headquarters, the Adjutant phoned the mess officer to announce their arrival.

Seconds later the mess officer banged open the front door and held out his arms with a welcome that made Mourmelon seem less bleak. The stripes on his arm indicated three years of overseas service, yet he grinned like a rookie for whom the trip was a lark. "I'm Captain Kemp. Pretty girls like you may call me D.B. And you are?"

"This is Lieutenant Collens, and I'm Lieutenant West."

"You have first names?"

"Kathy and Vivienne. We are the two remaining dieticians of the 223rd."

D.B. put a friendly arm around their shoulders and led them toward the front door. "Glad to have you here. We've been without a dietitian for two weeks. I'll show you around."

"How did you manage your special diets?" asked Kathy.

"Simple. We sent them to the 179th. Here we have four good cooks and a capable Oscar leads a dozen well- trained German PWs. No problems at all."

"Sounds like our Oscar. If you inherited the PWs from the 223rd, we'll take credit for training them," said Vivienne.

"If that's a sample of your work, we are glad to have you." He dropped his arm from Kathy's shoulder to open the door, and led Vivienne outside. Kathy followed. He gestured to the right, where patients in maroon bathrobes were standing in lunch line outside. "The patients' mess and hospital buildings are there. Our census is down to 350."

He turned to the left, to quaint old two-story stone buildings. "Your quarters. The small building is your shower, the PX, clubs, and assembly. Way down at the end is the post office."

D.B. opened the ambulance door. They got in and were driven to one of the narrow two-storied barracks buildings. D.B. patted the green glass bottle that Vivienne carried in her lap. "Celebrating your arrival at our happy hospital? May I help you two celebrate, tonight?"

"Yes, but not with this bottle. This is my Christmas present to my fiancé in the South Pacific."

"Let me tell you how to send it. Take it to the cast room. I'll show you where it is. First, have a plaster cast put on it. Next, pack it in a box of sawdust. Then send it. Not even the Navy can break that."

"Thanks. I'll do that." The girls picked up their musette bags and climbed down from the ambulance. D.B. opened the rear door, pulled out a footlocker and hoisted it onto his broad back with an amazing strength and grace. Kathy considered getting help for the other footlocker and two bedrolls. A wave of the hand, or more subtly, tugging helplessly at a bedroll strap could bring men running, but she decided that D.B. was enjoying his demonstration of strength. She and Vivienne followed him through the front door into the living room.

The living room was like an ordinary small-town living room. Here was an overstuffed davenport, a wing-back chair, a desk, and bookshelves with books, a floral-patterned rug, and a blue tiled stove. The furniture was dingy gray and worn, more comfortable than elegant.

D.B. trotted up the stairs and turned left into a bedroom. "This will be your room." He set the footlocker on the floor. He stood, hands on his hips, not panting, and pleased with himself. He winked and bounded down the stairs for another footlocker. In the desolate world of waiting tent cities, where even the young men drooped, his vitality was a delight. He made Kathy want to slide down the bannisters.

D.B. introduced them to other officers at lunch, and afterwards in the patient mess to the men and civilians. All faces were strange—friendly, but strange. The only familiar faces were Oscar's and the PWs'. Oscar smiled a warm welcome, but the conversation ended there. The Germans were still prisoners of a horrible war that was not that easily forgotten. Oscar spoke to his men who returned to cleaning field ranges, and scrubbing tables.

"Your office." D.B. led Vivienne with an arm around her shoulder. The gesture was that of a man who was strong and sure of himself toward a small helpless girl—or that of a conceited wolf who thought every girl ached for his embrace. D.B. had not yet noticed that although Vivienne was tiny, she was far from helpless. If he were conceited, D.B. had the good looks, his regular features merited some conceit.

Their office contained a potbellied stove, three desks and four wooden chairs. D.B. pointed to the bulletin board. "There are the menus for supper and breakfast. Tomorrow the patients' mess is yours." He held out his arms in a gesture of generosity. "Our census doesn't change much. Nothing to do right now, so you two might as well take the afternoon off to unpack and get that bottle mailed to the South Pacific."

Vivienne was already looking through the drawers, noting the absence of files. She shook her head emphatically so her red hair tossed back and forth, saying, "If you don't mind, I will first make an inventory." She looked over at Kathy.

"I know. I know. Off to the wards to inventory patients, I go." Kathy said and pointed her finger towards the door.

"There just might be an ulcer, or post-operative..." Vivienne said.

D.B. patted Vivienne's shoulder as though she were a child. "Nothing the nurses can't handle," he said.

With a toss of her red hair, Vivienne spun around, out from under his arm to face him. "Not even the best nurse can if we don't send the right foods."

"OK. Work this afternoon," D.B. gave in with good humor. "But first let me help you get that champagne off to your fiancé, or it won't arrive before Christmas. First things first."

"I didn't mean to be critical." Vivienne smiled the smile that could always soothe a man. "You're obviously doing a fine job. The lunch was delicious. Everything's clean, and each man knows his work, but there are some things that need a specialist, a dietitian—me." She spoke with so much charm that she might have been admiring D.B.'s manly muscles. She put her hand on his strong arm. "You're absolutely right about Stan's present. I'd love to have you show me to the cast room."

Captain Kemp led her out, still believing he was the captain, the man and the master.

Kathy headed for the wards. D.B. was right about most of the diets. These patients were victims of venereal disease, knife wounds or drunken driving. They didn't need therapeutic diets. She found some hepatitis patients for whom the only treatment was a special diet, yet they got the same menu the other patients. She visited them, read their charts, and returned to the mess. Vivienne was not there. Since the special diets could not be written until Vivienne had written the regular menus, Kathy returned to her room to unpack.

She walked alone along the sidewalk. She opened the front door that led into the living room, furnished as for a family but there was no family there to greet her. She went up the stairs to undertake the chore of unpacking—to put her things away again in strange closets, to begin again the hopeless task of finding a place for herself in a strange world.

They'd never done much toward making their barracks home-like, but then they'd never had a living room with furniture of their own. Cheerful, colored curtains and matching bedspreads would look happier than olive drab blankets.

Vivienne lay on her bed, on her side, her legs pulled up under her chin. Kathy spoke to her, "Maybe we could fix up this room. I've heard we can buy material in the PX in Paris…"

Vivienne was crying. The tears streamed across the bridge of her delicate nose and dropped onto the olive drab blanket. "Are you all, right?" asked Kathy. Vivienne obviously was not all right, but she didn't answer.

"Want to be left alone?" Kathy asked.

"No. I'm just shocked."

"I didn't think there was anything left that could shock you."

Vivienne just lay there. She looked so lonely and cold curled on the bed that Kathy was moved to cover her with a blanket. "If I can help..."

Vivienne said nothing.

Kathy opened her footlocker. It reeked of spilled perfume. The bottle must have broken, spilling out that precious liquid. It was revolting. She searched carefully for broken glass.

"Whoof," said Vivienne.

"I'll open a window."

"It stinks worse outside," said Vivienne sitting up, cross-legged on the bed, pulling the blanket over her shoulders. "They put the champagne in a cast and in a wooden box. I mailed it at the post office. In three months, Stan can drink a toast..." she stopped.

Kathy lifted out her olive-drab long underwear. The perfume smell reeked stronger.

"I came out the post office door. I saw, straight ahead, across the street—I saw on the bulldozed dirt field—I saw ..." Vivienne glared at her diamond engagement ring.

Kathy unfolded a damp towel, and exposed the bottle, not broken, just cracked. She looked for a non-existent wastebasket. She sat on the floor beside her footlocker, gazing at the empty perfume bottle, waiting for Vivienne to say what she saw.

"There were a lot of soldiers in the field, maybe a hundred." Vivienne pulled the blanket tight across her chest. "They stood in a ring—they were watching a naked man and a naked woman on the ground. They were..." She fumbled in her pocket for her olive-drab handkerchief and wiped her eyes. "Well, they weren't playing tiddle-dywinks. I didn't stop to watch." She blew her nose. "Should I have reported them?"

Kathy lifted two bars of soap and a tube of toothpaste from her footlocker. The label read, "Don't let romance fade because of bad breath." She tossed them into the dresser drawer behind her.

"What should I have done?"

Kathy had no answer. She pondered, then resumed unpacking a jar of deodorant. She read on the side of the jar: "Don't smell like an animal." A small safety razor in a package had a label: "Don't grow animal hair. Be smooth." Under the creams and lotions, the thin smears of civilization, man was animal. Even with a shaved chin and natural smells removed, man was less-than-human in this war.

She tossed the deodorant and razor into the drawer.

Lifting out a combat suit, she uncovered the wooden statue of the Angel of the Smile, her wings supported by a rolled woolen sweater. She elevated the angel above her head, so as to look up at her smile, and think of God's love. She set her on top of the dresser, turning her so her smile beamed onto Vivienne. "God's love endures."

Vivienne rolled sideways to lie again all curled up, covered in the olive-drab blanket. "I've been waiting four years for an ideal of love that never existed."

"If your love for Stan survived for four years, it could survive in Stan for you, too."

"Stan is a man."

Kathy could not disagree. She could not find a single helpful word. Finally, she offered, "I'll write tomorrow's menus for you."

"Why? At this hospital these patients were either drunken or promiscuous or they wouldn't be here. When the men were coming in from the battlefields, our men were heroes. Even those that got shot because their heads were up when they were supposed to be down were heroes. Now all men are bums! Men!" But even as she spoke, Vivienne was getting up, rinsing her face, putting on lipstick, and brushing her red hair.

In the patients' mess, Vivienne wrote the menu, and Kathy wrote the special diets. When the food was ready on the ambulatory patients' cafeteria counter, they checked it. After the patients were fed, Vivienne said, "You might as well go on to your own supper. I'll stay to check inventories with D.B."

"That gives me time to shower. I feel dirty." Kathy put on her coat, started toward the door, then turned back. "Where is the shower?"

"In that little building two buildings north of our barracks." Vivienne seemed to have recovered. She was in control, and knew the right answers. Kathy left her.

Scrubbed and wearing a clean shirt and a uniform that continued to stink of spilled perfume, Kathy picked up her dinner at the counter in the officers' mess. The food was good and hot, served on china plates, not tin mess kits. There were white-clothed tables with chairs, not benches. A group of nurses sat on one side of the room. Kathy considered joining them. They had reacted to the degeneracy of this redeployment area by retreating into their own group. If they let her join them, even though she was not a nurse, Kathy would spend the evening at a movie or playing bridge.

On the other side were groups of men, all strangers, talking and laughing as they ate. Kathy would have liked to sit with them. Although she distrusted men, and had given up all hope of finding a normal love in this abnormal life, but she did find them interesting. While life was horrifying and dangerous, it was exciting and fascinating, and Kathy was not ready to withdraw.

Since it would be too forward to sit with a strange man, she walked towards the nurses. Then she recognized Major Fellows, whom she had not seen since he left the 223rd at Marseille. He smiled at her, and stood up to pull out the chair beside him, a clear invitation. She had not known him well in Suippes, but now, surrounded by strangers, he seemed a close friend.

She put her tray on his table, and facing him, shook his hand warmly. "I'm so glad to see you."

"G-G-Glad to see you, K-K-K..." He stopped. He tried again, "K-K-K-K." His face was stripped of composure. She could see through his unveiled eyes an emptiness, edged by fear. His big man's body masked a small, scared, lonely boy. He was hollow, vacant. The power inside him that had made him a skilled surgeon, a strong man, had been torn out. He was like the shells of crashed airplanes that dotted the fields of France, from which the insides, the engines and instruments, had been torn. Empty, useless shells that had once roared in the skies.

However, the Major stammered on. Kathy interrupted him to give him time to recover. "Vivienne West is here with me. Bunts is home by now, and we expect a wedding announcement from her any day. Hooch married Mathilda. Chaplain Kirkemo wrote me from Le Havre. He's building a memorial chapel in a cave there. Mrs. Foster is in Germany..." Kathy went on. "Heard from her last week. She likes Munich." She could think of nothing more interesting to say. While Major Fellows pushed in her chair, she sat down.

"How are you?" he asked when she was seated. The words came out easily, and his face had regained composure. It was more comfortable to look at the mask than to look inside into his emptiness.

"I'm fine. I like this spell of Indian Summer," Kathy replied. Weather was a safe subject. "Nice hospital here. We have hot water, living rooms—all the comforts of home." She hadn't intended to mention home. She picked up her fork and ate her canned hamburger.

"They say we'll be g-g-g..." He stopped again.

Kathy took another bite of meat.

He tried again. "G-g-going to Germany next week. Latest rumor." The mask slipped from his face, and Kathy saw into the desolate inside. He needed not food, nor clothes, nor shelter, nor water, nor toothpaste nor deodorants. He needed love. How could Kathy help him? His hand lay twitching on the clean white tablecloth. Could she put her hand on his? What would that mean?

He saw her looking at his hand and controlled it to pick up a fork and spear his canned peaches. "I'm all right. Not much surgery here. Elective surgery gets sent to the States. How about a g-g-g... How about bridge after supper? At the c-c-club?"

At a bridge table in the club, he introduced her to two Captains. While Kathy shuffled the cards, Major Fellows went to the bar for two drinks. He drank till he couldn't keep his cards straight. Kathy ignored her drink, though she wondered if it might be easier to watch a brilliant surgeon fall apart if she drank till her own eyes were hazed. When she knew there was nothing she could do to help him, she walked back to her barracks.

She opened the front door and entered the living room, warmed and lighted by a bright fire. Sitting before the fire, his long legs stretched out in front of the wing-backed chair, sat D.B. Vivienne was curled up on his lap, her head relaxed on his shoulder. Without lifting her head, she said, drowsily, "Hi."

D.B. echoed, "Hi." He looked big and virile. She looked tiny and dependent.

Kathy said, "Hi. Major Fellows is here. Played bridge with him."

Vivienne said, "How is he?"

Kathy said, "I'll tell you later." She wanted to sit by the warm fire, to have someone to talk to, but she was interrupting them. She went upstairs.

The door to the other bedroom upstairs was closed, and from behind it came muffled giggles, a woman's and a man's. Every giggle, a gasp and sigh, every thump that came through the wall was tight with meaning. Kathy quickly got into bed and covered her head with a pillow.

When she woke the next morning, the room next door was quiet, and Vivienne had already gone. Kathy found her in their office with D.B.

Vivienne put on her trench coat. "Everything's in order. Just make the usual rounds and checks. I'm driving over to the supply depot with D.B."

D.B. grinned down at Vivienne, then scooped her up in his arms and carried her to the door. Vivienne giggled, and waved goodbye from the height of his shoulder.

The day loomed long and lonely for Kathy. She had breakfast with several nurses, made her ward rounds, and returned to her office to write the diets. The phone was ringing; she answered it. A man's voice spoke. "This is Major Oden. We'll be transferring out all patients after lunch. They won't need dinner."

Kathy found the mess Sergeant standing by a field range, and told him. He told Oscar, who with the other PWs started returning cans to the supply room.

Kathy returned to her office. She started to throw the food lists and recipes and diets into the wastebasket, then decided to keep them on her desk. The phone rang again. "Major Oden again. Our hospital is now a staging area for nurses—250 will arrive at 1300. You'll mess them for lunch in the patients' mess. Another 500 will arrive for dinner."

They went to the supply room to see what could be prepared for lunch in a hurry. She wrote the recipes for lunch and gave them to Oscar and the cooks. She then turned her attention to supper. Did they have enough field ranges to cook for 750? Enough dishes? Enough food? The phone rang again. "Major Oden again. The patients will not leave until after dinner." The original 350 patients plus 750 nurses—that's 1100 for dinner. She began her lists again: field ranges, pans...

A blonde Captain came into the office. "Lieutenant Collens? I'm told Captain Kemp is out-of-town, so it's up to you. Which of these girls do you want?"

"We're getting 750 nurses. I really don't want any more."

"I'm Captain Hill, personnel officer," he explained. "There's a new program of aid for displaced people and refugees, which means we are hiring a dozen girls. You get four in this mess. Thought I'd give you first choice. They're out in the mess."

"Those that speak French or English. I don't know much German or Polish," said Kathy. "Could I interview them later? I have to dispatch a supply truck right away..."

"There's one Polish girl you should look at, though she can't speak French or English, she does speak German. One glance and you'll know what I mean. She's different," said the Captain. "I've interviewed the others. I'll choose for you if you're rushed."

He led her into the mess, where the patients were now standing in line for their lunch. The group of girls and women he had brought in were wiggling for the patients and the GI cooks who were serving. Their hair was straggled, their clothes too tight and dirty, and they giggled when the GIs pinched them. They were the kind of girls you'd expect to find wanting to work in an Army camp.

One girl stood quietly apart from the others, standing erect, her head high. Without makeup, her skin glowed rosy and smooth. Her short, softly curled brown hair was shining clean. She wore a shapeless dull brown skirt, and worn brown shoes with no stockings. Her short-sleeved pale blue sweater hung loosely, neither hiding her well-developed figure nor advertising it. She carried herself with dignity, with her shoulders squared, not thrusting herself forward as the other girls were doing. When she saw Kathy, she looked straight at her, neither submissive nor arrogant, but with a look of equality. Kathy, wearing sturdy, polished shoes, nylon stockings and a pressed uniform bright with brass buttons, felt shabby beside the quiet dignity of this girl.

This girl smiled in a friendly way to the GIs who spoke to her. She managed to discourage familiarity without being aloof, with the dignity of her smile, and the way she held her head. These men, who considered any civilian girl in the mess fair game, stood back and looked at this girl with respect.

"She is different. I'll take her," said Kathy.

"Her name is Krystyne Winiauski."

"Krystyne. OK. I'll take the three French girls, too. Have they all had their medical examinations?"

"Of course."

"I can use them right now, with 750 nurses dropping in for supper." Kathy chose three girls. "*Nous avons de travail pour vous. Venez.*" To Krystyne she held out her, hand, palm upward, to invite her to come along. She had them wash their hands, and put on aprons and hair nets to serve the patients, while the regular workers started preparing lunch.

Kathy told the three newly hired French girls to clear the tables after the patients had eaten, and set the tables for the arriving nurses. They giggled and flirted with the men more than they worked, and they didn't know where to set the silver. Krystyne, without being told, saw what needed to be done, and did it.

When Vivienne and D.B. returned at 1800, the mess was completely rearranged. Five field ranges had been added with four new helpers, and dinner was prepared for 1100 people. However, dinner was served to just 150 patients. The expected nurses didn't arrive until the next day, and 200 patients had been transferred out.

Immediately, they made adjustments to being a staging area. They learned to not actually prepare the food until people in fact arrived. This necessitated an efficient readiness and a rush of last-minute work. In both, Krystyne showed capable foresight. Kathy and Krystyne worked well together and became friends. Vivienne continued to spend her time with DB.

Today was going to be one of those days. They had a 6 a.m. breakfast for 87 nurses and for 124 patients that were being sent to Le Havre. Then they prepared meals for another hospital that was closing, involving 600 men and 387 nurses. Now they waited.

A GI cook came into the mess where Kathy and others were working. He opened the stove door and threw in a shovel of coal dust. "Got new pictures from my wife today. Want to see, Lieutenant? There's my boy. Some boy, huh? There's my girl. She was a month old when I left. And here's my wife."

Kathy's admiration of the pictures was automatic, and sincere. All the GIs that had families had beautiful children and beautiful wives.

Kathy returned the pictures, with the proper appreciations, and held her cold-stiffened fingers over the stove.

"Some of those men who left for home this morning had only 41 points," said the cook. "I got 46 points. So how come they went home and I remain here?"

"Write your congressman," said the mess Sergeant.

"How many points you got, Lieutenant?"

Kathy responded, "26."

The cook shook his head. "Just 26? That means Germany. If you'd get married, you'd have... you'd have 38 points. Then you could go home too."

Kathy returned to her typewriter. She had been typing letters to search for a new job for Krystyne. Now she wrote to the head dietitian at Versailles. This hospital, as a staging area, could be closed any day now. When she finished, she looked around the mess for Krystyne.

Kathy watched Krystyne stacking trays and dishes on the counter with Oscar. Oscar was speaking German, a language Krystyne understood. Krystyne was not only laughing, she was laughing with Oscar, a German. It was a little surprising, considering what the Germans had done to Poland. Krystyne had shown neither bitterness nor hatred toward the Germans. Kathy did not interrupt. This was the first time she had seen Krystyne talking easily to anyone.

Krystyne came into the office with a pleasant "Now we learn?" This was Krystyne. She had worn the same blue sweater and brown skirt every day. She might be alone and friendless, poor and without hope for a job, yet still she walked in with dignity to say, "Now we learn?" Kathy had asked Krystyne to teach her German while they waited, paying her with warm underwear, stockings, and cigarettes which Krystyne could exchange.

They went into the kitchen, where Kathy gestured to a pot of coffee and a pan of hot chocolate. Since she suspected it was the only food Krystyne had there, she offered it often. *"Haben sie Kaffee mit Zucker und Milch? Oder Schokolade heiss?"*

Krystyne would not let her ignore the gender. She corrected, *"Der Kaffee, der Zucker, die Milch und die Schokolade heiss.* I like the hot chocolate*, danke."*

They carried their cups into Kathy's office and sat at her desk. With sketches and gestures, and occasional use of a dictionary, Krystyne told Kathy her story.

She drew a three-story house with twenty windows on the front. She drew four people next to the house and pointed to each one. *"Meine Mutter."* She was stout, and smiled pleasantly. *"Mein Vater."* He was tall with a straight, strong mouth. *"Mein bruder, ein student."* He carried a book, was as tall as his father, but slender. "Krystyne." She was a little girl with long curls tied back with a big ribbon.

Krystyne had been fifteen in 1939 when the Germans invaded Poland. Her father, a Major in the Polish Army, was shot. *"Mein Vater tot."* The tone of Krystyne's voice made "tot" sound very dead. Her brother had escaped to England, joined the Royal Air Force, was shot down and killed. *"Mein Bruder tot."* Krystyne and her mother were taken into work camps in Germany. She saw her mother die of hunger and exhaustion. *"Mein Mutter tot."* This was 1939, the year Kathy started college, joined a sorority, and was a cheerleader at basketball games.

Kathy learned that during the war, Krystyne had lived in German work camps. At the age of 21, she was released from the camp when the Allies swept across Germany. She had tried to return to her hometown, but the entire town was rubble. She returned to France and started working in the United States Army's mess for Kathy.

That afternoon they studied together until it was time for supper, after which Krystyne went home. She never stayed after dark.

Kathy took a hot shower, but was chilled walking in the freezing night back to her barracks. The living room was almost warm, but the bedroom upstairs was cold. She dressed quickly, shivering, and hurried off to the officers' mess.

She stood in line behind a slender, narrow-shouldered doctor who was called Dewey, which might have been either his first or last name.

He handed her a tray. "How are you this miserable day?"

"Cold." She put silverware on her tray.

"They say there's a shortage of coal in the ETO," Dewey said, taking a slice of bread and a spoonful of canned butter.

"I can believe that." She helped herself to dehydrated carrots.

Dewey looked at the platter of corned beef. After consideration, he passed it by. "They say we can convert the stoves to oil."

Lieutenant Lee, the Special Services Officer, stepped in line behind Kathy. "That won't help. They say there's a worse shortage of oil. Not that it makes any difference to me. I heard of an MP going home with 36 points. I have 38. Soon, I'll be basking in that good old Kentucky sunshine with my wife handing me mint juleps."

"Got a job in mind?" asked Dewey.

"No. All I know is that I don't want my old one. Might go back to school." He turned to speak to Kathy. "Speaking of school, your correspondence courses came, Kathy. You thinking of being a radio repairman? Not that I'd blame you. It must be discouraging to be a dietitian with canned and dehydrated foods."

"First, I'll study the psychology courses. When I give up on understanding people, I'll repair radios. It would be easy to fix broken wires. Give me something to do these cold winter evenings."

"You could spend the winter at Biarritz," said Lee.

"Where is that?" She poured coffee into their cups.

"On the Bay of Biscay in southern France. Near Spain, on the Atlantic Ocean. It was the royalty's playground of Europe. It truly is, though maybe the Riviera's more fashionable now. It's warm and sunny."

"Just how do I manage to get there?" She poured canned milk into her coffee.

"The Army has set up a university for redeploying troops. You'd be eligible, since we're not functioning as a hospital. They've taken some teachers from our troops in the ETO, and they've also imported excellent professors, the best."

"I'll apply, in triplicate." Kathy responded. The choice was between waiting in Mourmelon for a transfer to Germany, and studying in Biarritz in sunny southern France.

Kathy returned to her room early that evening, still thinking about Biarritz. Coming in sometime in the middle of the night, Vivienne woke her. "D.B. asked me to marry him."

The news penetrated Kathy's sleepy mind slowly. "Oh?"

"I worried about that." Vivienne took off her tie and unbuttoned her top shirt button.

"About what?" Kathy replied.

"About our ages. I told him I was ten years older than he. He said that didn't matter." She looked at the skin on her temples in the mirror.

"Oh. I wasn't thinking of that." Kathy wasn't thinking at all, just struggling to wake up.

Vivienne opened a jar of cold cream and smeared some on her face, neck, and elbows. "Stan? We didn't forget Stan." She massaged her neck. "We didn't decide easily. I ought to see Stan first, but that would mean months of waiting. We've decided that we should both break our engagements. You knew D.B. had a girl in the states? We feel badly about that. But don't we have a right to some happiness after all these miserable years? I'll write Stan in the morning." She massaged her face, vigorously, almost furiously. "I'm going to grab what happiness I can get. Here. Now."

That didn't seem like a good basis for marriage, but it was as good a basis as Mathilda had. It was better than anything Kathy had found. Kathy sat up in bed, wide awake now, but not capable of thinking with wisdom. "When will you be married?"

"As soon as we can. Maybe I'd better write now. A 'Dear John' letter is kinder than a wedding announcement. Or is it?"

By the end of November, after three weeks of effort, Kathy found a job for Krystyne in an American hospital in Metz. The job would begin the first of January, which was encouraging.

Vivienne was not married yet, which was discouraging. D.B. would not agree to a specific wedding date. He left for the States with the promise of a wedding date set sometime after Vivienne's return.

# CHAPTER 25

# CHRISTMAS EVE AT THE CATHEDRAL

The prospect of waiting, just waiting, in a world of troops in tent cities, was dismal. Vivienne escaped with a ten-day leave in Switzerland. While she was gone, their hospital was reopened, several hundred patients were admitted, and then discharged. The hospital was closed as a hospital, and continued as a nurses' staging area. By the time Vivienne returned, Kathy was ready for a vacation.

At the leave center, Kathy looked at a wall map showing the tours of Switzerland, where Vivienne had gone. Kathy hoped to find a refuge from degeneration. She chose an isolated spot in the Alps, Davos Platz, after first checking to be certain there would be at least one other girl on the tour.

A modern, heated train carried them across Switzerland into the Alps. They traveled past picturesque mountain villages and snow-covered mountains, powerfully serene. The dozen men and two girls in the car forgot to feel sorry for themselves. They forgot about counting points or going home and just watched the majestic scenery.

They arrived at a snow-capped station at twilight. Prancing horses with harness bells jingling merrily pulled sleighs up to meet the train. These horses actually pranced. In France, the horses had been tired.

There was more to this merry music than just the bells. There was also joyous laughter coming from children. Children were running, sliding, and throwing snowballs. All were rosy-cheeked and bright-eyed, dressed in warm snow suits with caps and scarves and boots. Children were laughing! This was the first children's laughter Kathy had heard in a year. These children wore warm clothes! The children of France shivered and did not laugh.

They glided on to their hotel, past homes with stacks of huge logs, promising warm fires. Store-front windows displayed piles of oranges. Oranges!

There were no bombed-out buildings, no holes in the streets, no convoys of GI trucks. It wasn't fair. It wasn't fair for Switzerland to have so much, and France so little. Maybe the Swiss had been right to stay out of the war. Who could say? Certainly, now they could share their food and clothing with those who had done their killing for them.

The leave was as glamorous as a movie version of an Army nurse's life. The movie would include visiting hospitals in the mornings, skiing in the afternoons, and dancing late into the night with men from Spain, France, and Italy. Then, finally, sinking into a soft mattress to sleep under enormous feather comforters in their luxury hotel.

On their last evening, they returned just in time to dress for a cocktail party that their guide considered to be a privilege. A wealthy family had invited Kathy and some of the higher-ranking officers to a party. The family said they had escaped from Germany at the beginning of the war, thus establishing themselves as anti-Nazi, and waited out the war comfortably in a Swiss chateau.

A butler opened the front door, and ushered them into the plush-carpeted living room. Her hostess, Frau something whose name Kathy couldn't remember, greeted them wearing a ballet-length, off-the shoulder gown. Kathy was introduced as an honored guest, as she was the only girl in uniform. Kathy was shown to a pink satin bedroom, and then back to the living room to meet the local celebrities.

On the banquet table were trays of elaborate sandwiches, and Kathy recognized only the olive rings. There were platters of many sausages and exotic seafoods, of which she recognized only the shrimp. There were pretzels and nuts, crackers, and a variety of cheeses. There was the grandest display of bottles Kathy had ever seen—tall and short, round and flat, green, red and amber, liquors and wines, sparkling and clear.

The hostess presented her table with pride, an assurance that this bounteous wealth would impress Kathy, that belied her words, "We haven't much to offer—the war, you know."

"The war, I know," said Kathy.

"We suffer from shortages. You have no idea how we have suffered. We're proud to share with you what we have."

Kathy was impressed, though not as the hostess intended. She resented this lush extravagance. Kathy's distaste must have shown through her face, for her hostess increased her efforts to impress, "We have everything you could possibly want. Name your choice, and it's yours."

"Anything I want? Milk."

"Milk?"

"Milk."

The hostess gasped. "In all the years I've given parties, the best parties, the most fashionable parties, no one ever asked for milk instead of a decent drink."

"Well, if it's asking too much, you needn't bother. It has been a year since I've tasted fresh milk. You did say anything I wanted. All right, I'll take a red wine. I don't want to deprive children of milk."

"We have plenty of milk. No one here is deprived. Milk! I never!" She led the way into the kitchen, took a quart of milk from the refrigerator and poured it into a cut-glass goblet. She had a refrigerator! A modern, white-enamel refrigerator. This was not living as the suffering refugee she claimed to be. A refrigerator! What right had this woman to a refrigerator when France was starving.

"I went to a party in Paris where there was a half an egg...," Kathy began.

The hostess did not want to listen about Paris. She hurried back to the living room, determined to impress Kathy. She showed her pictures in a family album of the palace that had been their home in Germany, with hints of royal blood, and of horses, and swimming pools. She hurried past one page, but not before Kathy got a glimpse of the husband and son in Nazi uniforms. If this hostess and her daughters had left Germany when the war began, Kathy was guessing the war began for them when the Germans started losing.

Kathy was ready to return to Mourmelon. She could never again tolerate wasteful abundance while the Sammys and Krystynes shivered and starved.

Upon return, Mourmelon looked more bomb-crippled and gray than ever in contrast to the wealth of Switzerland. Vivienne was touchy. Kathy knew she was worried about the hurt she had inflicted on Stan, and also that she had not heard from D.B. Krystyne's future looked bleak. Although another job was lined up for her, it would last only as long as the Americans stayed in France, which was just months, not years.

Then suddenly it was two days before Christmas. The new mess officer had brought in a fir tree that touched the ceiling in the mess. German PWs had cut up tin cans and made gold and silver bells and balls and hung them on the tree. French girls made scarlet decorations from the red paper in which apples were packed, and strings of popcorn. Sugar saved from two weeks' rations was used to make cookies. GIs had made cookie cutters from tin cans in star and Christmas tree shapes.

Krystyne built a large paper mâché creche. Oscar had set up a platform built of rough-bark pine branches. Krystyne had knelt on the floor. She had surrounded herself with torn strips of newspapers, with all the miserable news of murder, freezing, and starvation. She dipped the news into wheat flour and water. She put the strips across wire frameworks of father, mother, and infant. Under her hands, they took shape. She molded them into a solid, tangible holy family.

Kathy and Krystyne surveyed the gray figures, beautifully shaped. "I have no paints," said Krystyne.

"Nor I. Hospitals don't. Oh, wait! Yes, we do!" replied Kathy.

Krystyne yellowed the straw in the manger with yellow Atabrin. Mary and Joseph wore mercurochrome red and gentian violet robes.

Their hair was iodine brown. The infant Jesus was made flesh-colored with the miracle drug sulfadiazine. Their eyes were a brilliant methylene blue.

Krystyne had taken the evils of her life, had transformed them with nourishment and medicines that eased suffering, and had created beauty.

The afternoon before Christmas they gave a party for the local orphans. They showed movie cartoons, understood in any language, and gave the children apples and fancy cookies and PX candies. The children watched seriously, silently. They each ate one cookie and one candy, and stuffed the rest in their pockets. Even at their young age they knew that they had to save for the morrow, where there would be no more goodies. The party, intended to make the orphans merry, could not rouse any shouts of joy or laughter in these weary children. This was not enough, not nearly enough.

On Christmas Eve they gave a dinner for everyone who worked in the mess. There were French, Polish, Russians, Germans, and Americans. White sheets were spread as tablecloths. Kathy placed the most beautiful of decorations—food—down the center of the table in between pine branches. Together they enjoyed eating red apples and oranges, brown walnuts and pecans, pumpkin pies and mince pies, and round bowls of shimmering cranberry sauce and strawberry preserves.

All food was placed on the table so that all could eat together, and no one had to serve. Fresh turkey had been flown in from the States for the Christmas feast. There were bowls of mashed potatoes and brown gravy, peaches, cherries and pineapple, candied carrots and sweet potatoes, and fresh hot rolls with butter and raspberry jam.

Each said his own grace in his own language, or simply bowed his or her head. Kathy sat across the table from Krystyne. They ate and talked, and it didn't matter whether the words were understood or not, the good will flowed in happy communication. Kathy could say to a Russian, "This turkey is good," and the Russian could nod an enthusiastic "*Da,*" with some other words that clearly said, "Yes, this is good."

In minutes everyone had learned to say "Merry Christmas" in every language, and all the accents were good ones.

Near the end of the meal, while a few were enjoying eating their pie, someone began singing Christmas carols. Singing "Deck the Halls with Boughs of Holly" the words were mixed, but the tune was the same for all, and the "fa la la, la la's" were universal. In "Oh Little Town of Bethlehem," the language differences were forgotten and the vowels blended together in glorious harmony. The war was ended, in peace they blended in friendship and good will.

The singing of "Silent Night, Holy Night," with the long, smoothly flowing harmonized vowels—"si-il, nt night, ho-oly night"—was inspired. "A-all is calm, a-all is bright." This was Christmas.

Kathy looked across the table to share this beauty with Krystyne. Krystyne's eyes were shimmering blue. The tears over-flowed down her cheeks to drip onto her shabby blue sweater. The song was suddenly irony. What was calm, what was bright for Krystyne?

Krystyne should not return to her room alone among people whose language she could not speak. Kathy planned to go into Reims to the midnight mass at the Cathedral. The Chaplain had ordered an Army truck to make the trip. Kathy spoke to Krystyne in German, inviting her to come along and spend the night with Kathy.

Two Red Cross girls and twenty GIs went along with Kathy and Krystyne. The ride in the canvas-topped truck was cold. Inside, the Cathedral seemed even colder, sitting among cold stones. The stained-glass windows had been so brilliant when the light of the day shone through. In the dark night, the windows were a dull gray framed in leaden black. A harsh light glared from bare electric light bulbs hung by long black wires from the vaulted roof, deepening the shadows in the walls damaged with bullet holes.

There were no evergreens, no poinsettias, no banks of warm candles along the walls. The Cathedral seemed a pile of cold stones and statues. The candles on the altar were feeble under the glaring light bulbs. When the choir sang, their music was overwhelmed by the shuffling of people, their sneezes, sniffles, and coughs. The bishop's magnificent gold-and-purple embroidered robes, and the red-robed acolytes swinging a smoking incense burner, seemed out of place.

Suddenly, the electricity went off. The electric light bulbs faded. The organ music dwindled to silence. In the darkness, the candles on the altar glowed warmly and brightly. The silver cross above the altar seemed to float, gleaming in the darkness. The congregation caught its breath in the wonder of the light in the darkness. The shuffling and coughing stopped. Now, only the music of glorious singing filled the church.

Flashlights were silently switched on. Their beams followed fluted columns up till they blended into the heavens above. Beams of light picked out statues that seemed to rise out of the darkness. Apostles and saints soared in light.

Kathy remembered the words heard in Episcopalian services all her life, "...therefore with Angels and Archangels, and with all the company of heaven.... Glory be to thee, O Lord Most High."

The bishop was escorted up the circular stairway to the pulpit by acolytes carrying candles. They left him in darkness alone in the pulpit. He began to speak, and his voice seemed to come not from this world, but out of the darkness above. His deep voice rolled out over the unseen congregation.

"The war is ended. We can again know peace on earth. Good will toward men makes peace on earth. Peace doesn't just happen; it is made. Now is the time in which we are to live and to act. Do you know what forces we could unleash in so many areas with the love and service of our fellow man?

"There are some 500 people here tonight. What an impact we could have. We could change history. We could make history.

"We can do it. This is our hope. This is our joy. This is the Christmas hope and the Christmas joy—because, after all, what we are celebrating tonight is the way God changed history with just one man."

The choir sang the jubilant "Handel's Messiah." Krystyne and Kathy joined the French singing the universal "Alleluia." The echoes of music faded, and the congregation knelt for the final benediction. "The peace of God, which passeth all understanding, keep your hearts and minds in the knowledge and love of God, and of his Son Jesus Christ our Lord; and the blessing of God Almighty, the Father, the Son and the Holy Ghost, be amongst you and remain with you always. Amen."

Krystyne stayed on her knees a few minutes in silence.

She turned to Kathy, kneeling beside her, and spoke in a quiet, serious voice. "After my mother died...in the work camp...after they killed my mother, I hated. I knew I too would die. I could not endure. A nine-year-old boy had been in that hungry camp three years. He said to me, "Pray. Forgive. Live." I prayed. I forgave. I lived."

The congregation brought their flickering flashlights beams down from the vaulted ceilings and statues to the floor, to light their way out. The two Red Cross girls left the cathedral through the center door, passing under the benediction of *L'Ange au Sourire*, The Angel of the Smile. They smiled back at the angel. Her snow cap sparkled in moonlight. Ridges of snow heightened the folds of her robe. Her wings, edged in snow, were luminous. The stars shone so brightly in the sky over the cathedral that Kathy could imagine a star in the east gleaming above the rest. Krystyne stood under the angel, her head tilted at the same angle, smiling the same smile.

The men in the truck offered helping hands to lift the girls in. Two men stood to offer them seats, one seat on each bench on opposite sides of the truck. Sitting closely together, they warmed each other, and the atmosphere was not so chilling.

From the open back of the truck, the charming village houses and rolling hills were peacefully covered with white snow. Bomb-shattered rubble was hidden under mounds of soft snow. Rows of round tents, covered with snow, blended in with the hills. The moonlight sparkled on the snow on tents, hills and houses alike. The heavens were starred and the earth was white, except where the Army truck left two black lines on the road.

The Private on Krystyne's left put his hand on Krystyne's wrist. She moved her arm away. He put his hand on her knee. She lifted it off. A chill wind blew through the truck.

The Corporal on Krystyne's right said, "Promenade?"

Krystyne sat silent.

He put his hand on her knee. "Promenade? *Amour amour? Couchez-vous?*"

She pushed away his hand.

So, this was why the "gentlemen" had offered them seats on opposite sides of the truck, to get Krystyne away from Kathy's protection. Kathy would put them straight. "Now don't get the wrong idea about Krystyne. She's a lady."

The Corporal answered by putting his arm around Krystyne's waist. He spoke in GI German. His meaning was clear. Krystyne sat straight and still.

Kathy spoke sternly. "I said she is a lady. She's my friend. Leave her alone." The Corporal removed his arm.

The Private put his hand on Krystyne's thigh. "*Couchez-vous?*" He laughed. Two other men joined in, and in a polyglot of languages invited Krystyne into bed with them. Krystyne did not answer. She did not move, even to push away their hands. The wind, now bitter cold, swirled under the canvas. The wind blew fiercely against the round tents, whirling away the clean snow, leaving black cones shivering in the cold.

Over the roar of wind and engine, Kathy shouted at the men. "Didn't the sermon mean anything to you? Have you no good will? You can make peace on earth, you can..."

The Corporal laughed. "Couldn't understand a word. He didn't speak my language."

It was after 2 a.m. when the truck stopped at their hospital. The lights were out here too. The area was deserted, except for a solitary barking dog. The two girls, clutching their collars against the wind, hurried off to their quarters. All the men started in the opposite direction, except the Corporal and the Private, who followed the two girls.

"Come with me," said the Corporal. "I have Scotch."

"Come with me," said the Private. "I'll warm you without Scotch."

The girls turned their faces away from the men, away from the wind.

"Come. *Couchez*," said the Corporal. He grabbed Krystyne's wrist.

Krystyne took a step away. The Corporal pulled her wrist, stopping her. She tried to jerk it away while he held it tight. He pulled her a step toward him. Her feet slid on the snow trampled by his big brown boots.

Kathy grabbed Krystyne's other hand and pulled her back. They tugged her back and forth between them, Together, Kathy and Krystyne could not free her wrist from his clutch. Women needed a force stronger than brute strength against men. Kathy assumed a command. "Let go! That is an order, Corporal."

He let go. Kathy pulled Krystyne into their barracks and into the safety of the living room. She lit a candle.

Krystyne was shivering. Kathy opened the doors of the tiled stove. The fire was low, but alive. When she added fresh wood, the bark caught fire and lit the room. They stood in front of the stove to warm their frozen fingers and toes.

"It is not good to have a baby without a husband," said Krystyne. "My friend in Paris had a baby, no husband." She cradled an imaginary baby in her arms and shook her head. "It was not good."

"Krystyne, come to my home." Kathy reached out to hold her hands. "Come to America and be part of my family. My father has money." She took some francs from her purse because she hadn't learned the German word for money. "A lot of money. He could buy you clothes and send you to the university. You would not be cold or hungry again. You would be safe." Krystyne looked thoughtfully at the money. She sat down on the wing-backed chair, and with her worn shoes, propped her feet up by the fire.

"My father can buy you shoes. He has enough money to care for many families. This is his pleasure. He would take care of you."

Krystyne did not answer.

Money itself was not enough. Kathy stuffed it back into her purse. She had more to give. "I want you. I want you in my family." But Kathy was not yet going home.

"My mother would love you. It's easy for my mother to love. She would be delighted to have you."

Krystyne gazed into the fire a long time before she spoke. "You do not need me."

"We do." Kathy looked up words in her pocket dictionary. "We need your character, your spirit." She knelt beside Krystyne.

Krystyne faced Kathy, with her calm, dignified look that respected herself as it respected Kathy. "I will stay." Everything Kathy offered, clothes, college, everything that money could buy was, not rejected, but passed by as unimportant.

"You cannot stay here, to freeze and starve in rubble, and to be prey to wolves," Kathy said.

"My country needs me. My people need me. I have work to do. I will stay."

Krystyne could and would help rebuild a country and a civilization. It wasn't the impossible task for her that it seemed to Kathy. She believed in the Christmas hope that she could make and change history.

After the disasters of war, these people, the Krystynes and the Oscars, would regroup themselves to make a new country. Kathy had a feeling, not rational because the Germans remained enemies and the Russians allies, that Krystyne might marry Oscar and live with him in Germany rather than return to Russian-occupied Poland. If anyone could build a civilization destroyed by war, they could.

They tip-toed up the creaking stairs, trying not to wake anyone. Vivienne turned over in her bed as they came in. "I'm awake," she said. "I couldn't sleep. Hi, Krystyne. Nice service?"

"*Ja*," said Krystyne. "It was good."

Vivienne sat up in her bed. "Your orders to Biarritz came, Kathy. You leave January second."

The mimeographed sheet was pinned to Kathy's pillow.

She unpinned it. "Good. Did you get your orders too?" Vivienne now had enough points to be sent home. She expected her orders any day, to get home and marry D.B.

"Yes. I got my orders." She sounded sad, and instead of dancing, sat sullenly and pulled the blanket up around her shoulders.

"Congratulations! Oh, happy day! Now you can go home."

"I'm not going home. I'll go back to New York City; to Columbia University to study for a Ph.D."

"You… You're not…"

"No, I'm not." Vivienne took an engraved white card out from under her pillow. "D.B. married his first fiancé, and sent me the announcement."

Kathy searched for suitable words. Finding none, she busied herself taking two pairs of blue-and-white striped flannel pajamas from a drawer. She handed one pair to Krystyne. She unfolded a cot, and found a sleeping bag. "Vivienne, go home and talk to Stan. Maybe he might understand."

"No. I can't undo what I did to him. I'll find another career."

Of the three girls who slept in that room that Christmas Eve, Krystyne, who had had the fewest advantages and the most suffering, was the only one whose future had a clear and meaningful purpose.

On Christmas morning, Kathy woke up coughing, with a fever and a backache, the same symptoms with which meningitis had begun. She was put in the infirmary, which they had to open just for her, taking a nurse, a ward boy, and a doctor away from their Christmas holidays. It was not meningitis, only a mild bronchitis. Kathy was convinced that she could no longer survive cold. The freezing ride in the truck, the cold in the cathedral, and the windy ride back had made her sick. She could survive only if she went south to Biarritz.

In the afternoon, Krystyne came in to say goodbye. She was on her way to her new job in the hospital in Metz. Krystyne stood at the foot of Kathy's bed. The snow had melted into little drops of water on her worn coat. Krystyne said, "Thank you."

Kathy said, "Thank you." Krystyne said "Goodbye," and Kathy said, "Goodbye." That was all they said, and those words included a sadness at parting, and hopes for good will in the future. When Krystyne left, Kathy was lonely.

Vivienne came in to say goodbye. Her red hair curled up around the edges of her overseas cap, she looked as strong and capable as ever; perhaps even more in control of herself. "I have your home address," she said. "I'll write you when I find an apartment in New York. Look me up when you get there. I'll be registered with the New York Dietetic Association. My name won't change." Warm, sensitive, giving—a woman born to be a wife and mother, yet she would live alone. This was a tragedy, a tragedy caused by war.

Vivienne was left alone. Kathy was left alone again.

She shivered under Army blankets, and dreamed of warm Biarritz. This hospital was closed so there was nothing to do. She might as well spend January and February in the sunshine of southern France. She could go to school and study the problems of man. She looked over the courses offered. She would take psychology to understand how the Germans had allowed the war to happen, and why armies behaved as they did. She would take music appreciation to hear the controlled precision and order of a symphony. For the two days she stayed in bed while her throat healed, she dreamed of sunshine.

On the 28th of December, the Adjutant called her into his office. "Orders for you," he said, handing her the mimeographed sheet.

"I already have my Biarritz orders," she said. "Vivienne gave them to me three days ago."

"These superseded those. You don't go to Biarritz. You go to the 158th General Hospital. It's on the other side of Mourmelon."

"Here in Mourmelon? No. I won't go," said Kathy.

The Adjutant shrugged. "Don't argue with me. I don't write them, I just pass them on."

Kathy went. She arrived at the 158th in a blizzard on New Year's Eve. When she saw the snow blowing through the cracks in the walls of her barracks, she dreaded the winter. Everyone in the mess was a stranger. A Colonel announced a general invitation to all to attend a New Year's Eve party. Kathy decided instead to sulk in a warm bed.

Two hours later, a man shouting in the front hall of the nurses' quarters brought all the girls to their doors. Evidently most of the nurses had decided to forgo the party. The Colonel stood in the front hall, saying, "We want all you girls to come to the party. Come and give us a happy party. Major Barrett will call for you in one half hour."

The girls obediently brushed their hair and powdered their noses, and left with Major Barrett for the officers' club.

There was a great deal of action at the party, with free-flowing wine and dancing, but no real gaiety. Kathy danced with strangers, and didn't like the dancing. She drank a glass of champagne to uplift her spirits, yet was sad. She drank another glass of champagne, and danced. She drank yet another glass of champagne, and started crying. She didn't want a party. She wanted to be in the comforts of a home. Major Barrett took her back to the nurses' quarters.

The wind howling down her chimney awoke her early on the morning of New Year's Day. Her footlocker and bedroll were not yet unpacked. She put on the clothes she had worn the night before, and put her toothbrush and soap back into her musette bag. She hurried to the motor pool, ordered a Jeep, and had it loaded with her luggage. She went to the Sergeant Major on duty, told him, not asking, that she had orders for Biarritz and was leaving. She signed out and left Mourmelon. It would be several hours, perhaps even a day, before any officers came on duty and discovered she had gone.

At the Reims train station, two engines shuttled back and forth, puffing and belching black soot that settled on piles of grimy snow. The grinding roar made her shiver. She knew her chills were unreasonable as the noise should be encouraging signs that transportation was beginning to roll again.

She entered the Reims station, and checked on the time for the Paris train. With a few minutes to spare, she approached the phone booth to call Captain McClain to tell her she was leaving. A GI and a French girl were in the booth. While waiting for them to finish their call, she slipped off her musette bag, resting it on the floor. They were not using the telephone. There were... They couldn't be! They were. In a phone booth! Could that be love?

She slapped her musette bag over her shoulder and rushed out to meet the train leaving for Paris. She was able to board before it finally roared away. She had no real hope that she was running to anything good. War had disintegrated all character. There were no good men. She could at least run from wind and snow to warm sunshine. That was all.

# PART IV:
# BIARRITZ AND CAMP HOME RUN

# CHAPTER 26

# WHERE HAVE WE MET?

Kathy had deliberately disobeyed orders. Only when she was safely out of Reims did she allow herself to think of possible consequences. She had, in fact, deserted her post. At each station she half expected an MP to board the train and pull her off. Upon arriving in Paris, she predicted an entire platoon of MPs would be waiting. Surprisingly, no one questioned her orders to Biarritz.

That evening in Paris, she slept in the still-unheated leave center. Early in the morning she went to the Gare d'Austerlitz, the large rail station in southeastern Paris.

On the platform, among the crowds of soldiers, was one girl in a nurse's uniform. She was listening to and laughing with two Captains. One was telling a story, interrupting himself with his own laughter. The girl was tall, large-boned and square-jawed. She looked about Kathy's age, though with her brown hair brushed softly back into a bun, she looked more matronly.

The girl seemed delicate beside the huge talking Captain. He towered over her, broad and muscular, a handy man for carrying footlockers and bedrolls in this station without porters. The other Captain, shorter, leaner, stood quietly beside them, listening. Kathy estimated his broad shoulders would be just the right height for her to lean her head on. But then, *she had no intentions of leaning on any man again.*

Kathy approached them. She waited for the Captain to finish his story before introducing herself to the nurse. She wanted to travel with another girl if she could. She saw, on closer look at her insignia, that the girl wore the caduceus of a dietitian. The Captain stopped talking when he saw Kathy, and looked embarrassed. The lean Captain had a stern, tight and controlled look between his eyebrows.

Kathy spoke to them, "I didn't mean to interrupt you. I just wanted to ask if this is where we take the Biarritz train, and to say hello to another dietitian."

The girl shouted, "Glad to see you!" She put a muscular arm around Kathy in a welcoming hug. "Yes. We're waiting for the Biarritz train, here. Are you going to the Biarritz University?"

"Yes," Kathy replied.

"Ride with us, please. I'm Frieda Norton." She kept her arm across Kathy's shoulder as she introduced the men. "This is Mike Mulligan. Mike is the Army version of an Irish policeman," as she nodded to the husky man. Then as she nodded to the leaner man, "and Jim Duncan. We've all just arrived from England."

"How do you do. I'm Kathy Collens."

Frieda put her other arm around big Mike. "Go on, Mike. Finish your story."

Mike said, "Naw. There's a lady present."

Frieda said to Kathy, "You don't mind a good story, do you?" Pointing out Kathy's two overseas stripes to Mike, she said, "She's been in the Army long enough to be one of the boys. Go on."

Mike hunched his shoulders. Since he was obviously reluctant to finish his evidently off-color story, Kathy rescued him. "I am in the Army, but I am not one of the boys," she smiled gratefully at Mike. "I consider it a compliment that you don't want to finish your story in front of me."

"Aw, come off it," drawled Frieda. "No swearing? No four-letter Anglo-Saxon words? You tell the boys, 'Speak pretty!?'"

"No, I don't say anything to stop them. Yet only once have I ever heard foul language. Once a cook didn't know I had returned to the mess, and I overheard him. He was so embarrassed that he apologized. Then he followed me into my office and apologized again."

Captain Jim was looking at her with curiosity. Well, let him think she was prissy. Kathy pondered this situation. Seems there was something about her that compelled some men to watch their language. Yet something else about her that encouraged them to proposition her. She understood neither.

Jim had tilted his head to one side, and was looking at her with friendly gray eyes. The thinking lines between his eyes deepened. "This isn't just an old line," he said. "Where have I met you before?" He smiled like a little boy wanting to be understood. "You look familiar."

"That is an old line." Kathy looked at his face, the fine, straight nose, the deeply cleft chin. Certainly, an interesting face, one to be remembered. There was something, perhaps. "Were you a patient in Suippes or Mourmelon?"

"No." Jim wore Air Corps insignia. "I've been in England the last three years. Been there?"

"No, I've spent this last year in France."

"My home was Hastings-on-Hudson in New York. Ever lived there?"

"No, my home was in Illinois." She wanted now to have known him before, to find something in common, to have a friend in this world of strangers.

Jim asked, "I studied chemistry at Pratt Institute at New York University night school. Were you…?"

"No, sorry."

"I was studying at Iowa State when the war began."

"Yes," Kathy said. "Yes. I was at Iowa State too! Were you in a play, or on the yearbook staff? Or at a fraternity exchange?"

"No. I worked my way through school. I had neither time nor money for fraternities or plays. You might have seen me in a chemistry lab. I assisted there."

Jim was interrupted by the roaring arrival of the train. "How about your luggage?" he shouted.

"Right there." She pointed to it piled on the platform.

"We'll load it for you." Mike easily swung her footlocker into the baggage compartment. Jim as easily lifted her bedroll and the other luggage.

"Thank you. You're so strong," Kathy told them both admiringly.

"You know what that means, don't you," Jim said to Mike. "She's talking us into carrying footlockers from now on."

"You're sweet to offer," Kathy laughed. "I could never manage by myself."

Frieda snorted, "By yourself, my eye! You've got the whole Army to carry things for you!"

"That's all right," said Kathy. "I have a working arrangement with the Army. I can't carry footlockers, and the Army can't cook. So, we help each other out."

"OK. We expect dinner from you first thing at Biarritz," said Jim. "Now let's get on the train. I don't like last minute rushes."

Frieda climbed independently up the train steps. Mike followed. Jim, standing behind Kathy, put his hand under her elbow. She jerked her elbow free. She didn't want any pilot pawing her, and then wondered if he just might be simply helping her up the first high train step. Mike reached down to her with a helping hand, and she accepted. Frieda could be one of the boys if she wanted. Kathy found it more fun to be a girl—or did she?

Two double seats faced each other in the compartment, and these four would cozily fill it. The train started slowly, giving last-minute passengers time to jump on. While they rode through the dreary industrial sections of Paris, they unharnessed their musette bags and took off their overcoats. In general, military personnel wore the latest fashion in uniforms, the new waist-length Eisenhower blouses.

"Your blouse looks British," said Frieda to Jim.

"It is. I traded with a Royal Air Force Major. I like the British weaves, rougher, more rugged." He took off his jacket to pass around for the girls to inspect. His shoulders did not come off with his jacket but remained amazingly broad, giving him, with his slender hips, a movie star physique.

Mike tossed part of the bags and coats onto the baggage rack. Jim reached up to rearrange them in compact order, to make room for all. The sight of his muscles moving under the shirt that stretched tight across his lean back, not padded with a layer of fat, appealed to her dietitian's heart. She rejected the impulse to offer him a K-Ration. Too bad a man with such interesting muscles was a pilot. Pilots were as able to aggressively *love 'em and leave 'em* as were the paratroopers.

Kathy returned his blouse, which he tossed upon the baggage rack. She said, "You're overestimating the heating system on French trains. I love the French, but they don't know how to get this compartment warm."

"This is warm, compared with the damp chill of England." Jim sat by the window in his shirt sleeves. "My Scottish blood scorns a jacket when the sun is shining." And sure enough, the sun was shining. The sky was blue, and in the suburbs south of Paris, the grass was green.

Mike settled beside Jim, on the seat facing the girls. "You are dietitians. Where do we eat lunch?"

"You never know till you see it," answered Kathy.

"Sometimes the train stops to take on water for the engine while we passengers eat in transient messes. Or it might not. If not, I have a musette bag full of K-rations, and a canteen of water. I might give you the dinner you earned before we reach Biarritz."

Jim took a stick of wood and a jack knife from his pocket. "What's in a K-Ration?"

"You've never had one? And you have been in the Army how long?"

"I wouldn't ask if I had."

"That Air Corps! While the poor infantry slept in the mud and ate K-rations, you Air Corps had fresh oranges and steaks. You even lived in heated buildings."

Jim nodded an agreeable grin. "With a batman, to light the fire and serve hot tea before we even got out of bed. With riotously drunk nights in London where girls swarmed Piccadilly Square, eager to please American pilots. I'll not judge men who've been flying a fighter plane through enemy ack-ack, hour after hour in the cockpit, returning with pants wet from fear." He opened his knife, and cautiously tested the edge with his thumb.

"You in England were never invaded. You never met the Germans face to face. The war was in France," said Kathy.

"That's right. We never met the Germans in England. Why?" With two deft, strong strokes of his knife, Jim cut a deep V in his stick. "Because we fought them off. We stopped them. We didn't give up like Petain did here in France. Because we had Churchill—and blood, toil, tears and sweat. Good thing the British are stubborn."

"Plenty of Frenchmen fought…," started Kathy.

"Let's play bridge," said Frieda.

They played bridge without further quarrels. Between games, Jim carved beads. He carved with efficiency, knowing exactly where to cut to make each bead with the fewest cuts. He carved with determination, as though these wooden beads had an importance. He stopped to eat their K-ration lunches. He paused to look out the window, not missing a bit of the scenery. He didn't stop carving until he had thirty beads strung on three strings.

In the late afternoon, the train entered the port city of Bordeaux, and stopped for a two-hour wait. Jim folded his knife, and put it and his strings of beads into his pocket. He put on his British jacket, while the girls put on their overcoats. All adjusted their caps and stepped off the train.

"Shall we walk," asked Jim, "to see what we can see?"

Kathy was determined not to like a man who was a pilot. But the air was full of the sweet smells of spring, and she did want to walk. "I would like to see the harbor."

Frieda unbuttoned her coat. It was warmer in the sunshine than it was on the train. "I would like to see the shops."

Jim said, "All right. Mike, you and Frieda see the town. We'll cover the waterfront. When we meet, we'll exchange descriptions."

Kathy wondered if this could be a ruse to get her alone with him, but even a pilot was harmless in the bright sunshine, as long as she stayed out of darkened bedrooms and phone booths. It was sad that he was a pilot. His back was strong, his expression controlled, and his eyes kind. Maybe he was, in spite of being a pilot, a good man, *if there was such a thing as a good man.*

They crossed the river on the ancient Stone Bridge, with its 17 arches, offering a beautiful view of the docks and harbor. They stopped at a sidewalk cafe under a tree at the end of the Place des Quinconces, France's largest public square.

"Would you like to sit here?" asked Jim. "I know the best drink."

The best drink. He was no different than other pilots, thought Kathy. Get a girl alone, give her a few drinks, and then.... She should never have let her hopes rise that perhaps this man was different.

They sat with elbows leaning on a yellow-and-orange tiled table, looking over to the monumental lighthouse and the harbor. A small green vase held violets and a daffodil. The sun was warm on her neck.

Jim ordered the drink from the waiter by pointing to something on the menu.

"How many cigarettes are good for tipping here in France?" Jim asked.

"Two cigarettes are a generous tip. You can get twice as much for cigarettes in Switzerland as in France," she said.

"Switzerland's a better market?"

"France, as you can see, is just beginning to recover. Switzerland was not as badly hurt. They made money from war by selling supplies to both sides. I was told by the smart boys to hold out for high prices for my raincoat and boots. Soldiers sold everything they could spare."

Jim took out his knife, to whittle on a stick. "You got better prices in Switzerland than here in France?"

"Not me." Kathy shook her head. "Rather than sell to the Swiss, I'd give to the French. I don't want black market money." She considered a minute. Actually, I don't know any prices. That might just be rumor."

"You're judging the Swiss, on the assumption that each person had control over what his government did, over how the war was fought. Some individuals were trapped."

"You think it was right for the Swiss to sell supplies to both sides?" she asked.

"I didn't say that. I just can't say what was right or wrong for each person under his unique situation. Should the Swiss have joined the slaughter instead of staying neutral?"

The waiter brought the drinks. The red wine scattered rosy rings of sunlight across the table top. Kathy tapped her glass with her finger, and watched the lights ripple.

Jim sipped his drink. "It's good." He smiled at Kathy; a smile deceivingly innocent for a pilot who was asking a girl to drink. "Drink away. When in France do as the French!"

Kathy decided to argue instead of drinking. "The French drink wine, but rarely get drunk. They know when to stop."

Jim smiled. "The French like to drink. You can't deny that. Their morals are, shall we say, easier than the British and Americans."

"I have no illusions left about American morality, or anyone else's during war," said Kathy. "War disintegrates all men's character. The British were no exception. I read in the "Stars and Stripes" about an Army Sergeant that got a mother and her two daughters all pregnant within a short time period. Now there was a man that was a man! Big Joke!"

Jim sipped his drink. "Aren't you going to taste yours? I said it was good."

She sipped her drink. It was sweet and tart. It was...she sipped again to be sure. It was grape juice! Unbelievable! He was not enticing her with wine, but with plain fruit juice!

He emptied his glass. "Yeah. That was not funny. Tragic, really. Some of the pilots were.... Well, I won't judge. I don't know what I would have done if I'd been a pilot and lived in that strain and learned to be proficient at killing. The Army chose and developed good fighters for pilots. This shattered part of their morality. War tore out the sixth commandment, thou shall not kill. Then a little tugging ripped out the seventh and eighth commandments, thou shall not commit adultery and thou shalt not steal. Then the whole was weakened and gone."

"Weren't you a pilot?"

"No.

"I was part of the headquarters staff for the 4th Fighter Group of the 8th Air Force in Debden, England. That's where I traded the jacket."

"What was your job?"

"Because I had been a chemist before I joined the Army, I was a Training Officer for Chemical Warfare Services. Fortunately, there was no chemical warfare. Therefore, I also worked as an Adjutant and a Transportation Officer while in Debden."

Kathy drank her sweet fruit juice. Jim continued, "Don't judge the British by one man. I learned to know and love the British. I got into London some weekends, and saw the sights. I dated girls, mighty nice British girls, a nurse, and even a young duchess. After I'd seen London, I spent weekends in the rest of the country, visiting Land's End, Wales. I picnicked with a Scottish General and his daughter. I visited my aunts and uncles and grandparents in Scotland. Good sturdy clan, the Duncans." He tilted his chair back, and surveyed the gray-sailed boats and fishing skiffs on the blue water. The British are like any other people. There are some good and some bad. I'd rather say they're all struggling along as best they can. He winked, and stood up. "You might say that of the French, too, I suppose. Let's walk."

They walked to a park covered by lush grass, and trees with new leaves bursting out in buds. Little children were shedding their worn overcoats to play in the sun. They stopped to watch the children. The children stopped playing to peek sideways at them.

Jim held up a finger, saying, "Now watch this." With the wink of happy conspiracy, he led Kathy to an area facing the bench where the mothers sat, where the children clustered.

He whistled a cheerful folk tune. When every child was looking at him, he took from his pocket a cellophane bag of brightly colored hard candy. He held up the bag, making noise by rattling the cellophane. The bashful children remained on the grass.

Jim made a funny face at a little girl. She giggled. He stuck out his tongue at a little boy. He giggled. Jim tore open the sack, took out a single candy twisted in an individual rapper. He swung it tantalizingly before them. The children inched toward him. When he rattled the paper again, he was surrounded by kids.

"Sing for it," he said. The children stood silently eyeing the candy.

"*Chante pour les bonbons,*" translated Kathy.

"No need for that," said Jim. "Funny faces, candy and music are universal. He sang, his tenor voice swelling out to them. "Sing a song of sweetness, a pocketful of rye."

One little brave girl repeated, "Sing, song, sweetness."

He rewarded her with a smile, and a bow, and a piece of candy.

"Encore? Sing a song of sweetness." His head nodded to the rhythm of his song. Half the children repeated after him, phrase by phrase, his meaningless yet meaningful sounds. He tossed out handfuls of candy. He carefully handed pieces to those who bashfully stood on the edges of the scramble.

With delight, he winked at Kathy. "Children are the same the world over. If we can teach that to all children, the world will live in peace and harmony."

He cut four short sticks and tied them into a rectangular frame. He took his string of wooden beads from his pocket. The children watched him tie them across the frame. Three rows of ten beads made an abacus. "*Comptez*...count," he said.

The children looked puzzled.

He counted the beads, one by one, "*Un, deux, trois*...." One older boy smiled and understood. Jim handed the abacus to him.

They returned to the train and resumed their journey, with Mike now riding beside Frieda, and Jim beside Kathy. Jim began carving another set of beads.

They watched the landscape change from the rolling green vineyards of France to the rugged foothills of the Pyrenees Mountains. They emerged from the train into the ancient town of Biarritz. Mike and Jim loaded their luggage onto trucks that carried them along winding streets for a quick moonlit tour.

Biarritz lay on a narrow strip of flat land beside a large white sand beach. The beach curved around on the Bay of Biscay from the lighthouse that topped a rocky peninsula to an arched bridge that reached out to a rock island. Buildings perched on hillside ledges well behind the beach.

"No shattered buildings. No signs of war here." Kathy marveled at the unspoiled magnificence of the villas.

"No industry to destroy," said Jim. "Just a beautiful beach and elegant houses. This place was plush society, the destination for European royalty. It was the playground of Empress Eugénie. '*Coût d'argent*'. Doesn't that mean 'coast of money?'"

"Coast of silver," Kathy said. "Because the waves are always foam-capped with silver. Yes, this was the playground of the wealthy. Now France no longer has wealth, and no longer plays in luxury. So, this is now a place for ideas."

They drove along the town's quaint crooked streets. In the window of the Bon Marche department store was an Army-stenciled sign: "Enlisted Men's Recreation Center." Kathy said "I guess they may as well rent the building to the Army. There's nothing in France to sell."

They drove by a huge white modern building with large gold block letters spelling "Casino." Below this, was a smaller Army-stenciled black lettered sign that said, "Library, Biarritz American University." GIs were unloading containers of books from an Army truck parked at the front door. Jim said, "I'll bet that Casino never saw a book before.

For that matter, I'll bet that Army truck never did either. There *is* hope for better ideas ahead."

Their truck then stopped before the most imposing of villas, ornate with wrought-iron balconies and a many-windowed tower. The black-on-white Army sign hung over the coat of arms on the front door, "Headquarters, Biarritz American University." Inside a Lieutenant assigned them quarters.

Then they drove through a wrought iron gate displaying an elaborate Victorian coat of arms. They continued up to Empress Eugénie's Palace, now the Hotel du Palais. The truck circled round a courtyard and backed up under the domed canopy at the front door. They jumped down off the truck and walked around to the side of the seven-story building, marveling at its size and magnificence.

Empress Eugénie's Palace, now Hôtel du Palais, Biarritz

Kathy said "I was told that after Napoleon III married Eugénie in 1853 he built this lavish palace for her on the beach—in the shape of an "E" for Eugénie. As the most fashionable woman in France, Empress Eugénie turned this area into an international center of luxury. It became an aristocratic gathering place."

"It figures," said Jim. "Just what I'd expect of a French palace. About this time of night, a gallant knight should climb out a fourth-story window, run along that iron balcony, slide down those columns, dash along the stone balcony around the second floor, and pop into the room of his mistress. What red-blooded Frenchman could resist the set-up?"

Mike and Jim carried the girls' baggage up to their second-floor room, and set them on the deep-piled maroon carpet. Kathy pulled open the golden damask drapes and opened the French windows to step out onto the balcony. Jim, Frieda, and Mike followed to lean on the chiseled stone railing and watch the waves splashing over craggy rocks. The lighthouse beam circled around under the stars and moon.

Kathy deeply breathed in the spring-scented air, a blend of lilac and sea-salt. She opened her arms wide, "It's a lovely world."

Jim sat on the stone rail, half facing her and half watching the light-house beam sweeping round under the moon and stars. "Will you like living in a palace?"

"Certainly. I'm even more thrilled by the air and the ocean. In the spring, my brothers and I would always build a raft and dream of reaching the ocean. Now I smell the lilacs of home, and I've actually reached the ocean."

Mike clapped his hand on Jim's shoulder. "Come on, let's get our gear up and get to chow."

While the men carried their things up to their fourth-floor room, the girls washed their faces. Then they all went down for dinner. The dining room jutted out over the beach in a semi-circle of picture windows. They sat at a white-clothed table and watched as the rising wind blew the waves higher and higher. The waiters served crisp-crusted fish with a tartar sauce. The mashed potatoes were fluffier than anything Kathy had achieved with dehydrated potatoes. The green beans were in a sauce of onions and mushrooms that smothered the dehydrated processing.

"Can you cook like this?" Mike asked Frieda.

"Well, maybe if I had the mushrooms...," Frieda responded. "Well, if you must know, no."

Kathy shook her head. "I'm going to learn. French cooks always give me their secrets."

Dessert was an apple-filled flaky crust. "I'll bet," said Kathy to Frieda, "this is plain old GI rations—flour and shortening and dehydrated apples. I was always proud of our pies."

The ocean spray was now splattering against the window in magnificent patterns, repeatedly lit by the lighthouse beam.

Jim watched. "The tide is coming in. The waves will be pounding against the windows soon."

As they drank their after-dinner coffee, the waves broke against the window with a fascinating force. There was an excitement in watching from behind the window, with two men and a girl who were already Kathy's friends. Sitting in the Empress Eugénie's palace was a world away from the drunken misery of Mourmelon. It was with reluctance that they left to return to their rooms.

The next morning Kathy woke to the cheerful music of an organ grinder. She quickly dressed, and ran out on the balcony. The ocean waves were now gently rolling in, swirling silver around the rocks and onto the beach. Across the bay was the rugged Spanish coastline. Below, in the sunshine, stood the organ-grinder wearing a black beret, and his monkey wearing a red pillbox hat. The sweet scent came, not from lilacs as she had thought, but from a cluster of pink-flowered camelia bushes below her balcony.

Kathy and Frieda signed up for classes, and located them on the map of their classrooms. Twenty-two villas were taken over by the Army for the university. They were told the rules. Restrictions of rank were removed. Enlisted men could date officers. Wearing of hats and neckties was no longer mandatory. On campus, Kathy recognized Dutch, Polish, English, Spanish, and Canadian uniforms.

Kathy and Frieda walked to their class building. On their way, they met an old woman selling violets. They bought a bunch, and delighted in the bright purple against their olive-drab uniforms. They walked to a sidewalk café where GIs, with berets on their heads and violets in their buttonholes, drank Cokes at tables piled high with books.

An infantry Sergeant stood up, and invited them to have a Coke with him and his buddies. "And maybe you can explain this," he said. He pointed to a book on comparative religions. "We're trying to understand the Hindu concept of time. It's the first time in three years I've tried to think." He hit his head with the heel of his hand. "It ain't easy," he grinned. "and if I expect to become a minister, there'll be some changes made." The Sergeant had three battle stars on his ETO ribbon.

That evening, Kathy and Frieda met Mike and Jim in the dining room for dinner. Mike greeted Frieda warmly, "There's a concert tonight; a piano concerto and a violin something. Or would you rather go to the officers' club?"

"Both," said Frieda, "The concert, and then the club afterward. Jim and Kathy, will you make it a double date?"

"OK, Kathy?"

"Sure."

They played ping pong after dinner until time for the concert. First Jim and Mike took off their blouses and played in their shirt sleeves. Somehow those long-sleeved cotton shirts almost sensuously revealed their muscles. Mike, with bulging muscles and huge strength, slammed at the ping pong ball, which then overshot the table, or with slow reflexes missed the ball. Jim was alert and quick, played with his head as well as his muscle. He moved with unbelievable precision, placing the ball where he intended it to go. He lured Mike farther and farther away from the table with long, strong hits, and then dropped the ball just over the net.

Then they played doubles. Mike and Frieda played together, Frieda on the left, Mike on her right. Jim told Kathy how to play as a team:

"You play close, get the short balls. "I'll be behind you, for the long ones." Kathy was not a good player, but that didn't matter, for Jim was behind her and hit the balls that she missed. There was never a word about those she bungled.

"You play very well," said Kathy.

"I've played a lot of both tennis and ping pong, ever since I was a kid. Actually, I was asked to represent Army in some of the Army – Navy tennis games in England. We even played at Wimbledon, although several courts had been badly bombed. With so many top American tennis players serving in the Armed Forces, there were some grueling matches."

"Well, that certainly is an interesting way to make a contribution to the war effort." said Kathy.

Jim smiled. "It was an honor. I learned a lot from playing sports. If I practiced and worked and worked, I could get better and better until I became a champion—champion in the state of New York. Then I tackled organic chemistry the same way. I learned it cold. I knew everything about the preparation of pentoses that there was to know. And I helped develop a new method and published a paper about it. Now I'll work at education the same way. I'll work and work, and I'll learn to teach. I'll teach children—in them is our hope for a better world."

*Here was a man with worthy plans for after the war, Kathy thought.* At the concert Mike held Frieda's hand. Jim sat absorbed in the music, and his hands scratched his chin or pulled his ear, but did not venture near Kathy. It was a pleasure to date a man who didn't make passes.

Afterward they danced at the Chambre d'Amour, the officers' club. The orchestra was good, but Jim was not much of a dancer. He knew two steps, one for waltzes, and one for fox trots. He was more interested in talking than dancing.

Jim lacked something. He was poised, and yet a little controlled. Kathy suddenly understood. He was not married. He would gain ease with women when he married. "I'll bet you're not married," she said.

"Of course not," said he. "Do you think I'd be dating you if I were?"

"It's been my experience that marriage doesn't stop men from dating."

"I would have told you. I have rather envied those men that had someone to go home to, someone to take care of, but I'm not married." He stopped dancing and scratched his ear. "Shall we have a Coke? I'm not much of a dancer."

"You could be, if you worked at it like ping pong. You have a nice sense of rhythm." Kathy knew there were more important qualities than dancing ability. "Yes. A Coke would be nice."

They walked along the beach toward the Empress Eugénie's palace. The waves swirled foaming silver around the jutting rocks, and the lighthouse beam swung around.

Jim kept his hands in his pockets and whistled a theme from Rachmaninoff's violin concerto. He was a good man.

Classes began the next day. In social psychology class, Kathy was the only girl. The professor asked Kathy to serve on a series of radio programs about marriage. Kathy protested that she was in no way qualified. He answered that she was better qualified than anyone to give the woman's point of view. He said marriage was of great interest among the soldiers. Finally, she agreed.

In the afternoon class, "Problems of World Peace," there were two civilian French girls. Kathy introduced herself. When the professor walked in, Kathy recognized his face from having seen his picture in a textbook. He was Thomas Mathan, one of the great sociological-political thinkers of the age.

After class, the French girls in the class invited Kathy to their home that evening. At dinner, she invited Jim to go along.

Jim frowned, with that tight, controlled look across his forehead. "I'd like to go but I must study."

"You can read books anytime. When again will you have a chance to visit these people?"

"Tomorrow morning our education class visits a French school. I must study French education tonight. We have students from every state in the union and from all over Europe. I must be prepared."

"Oh," said Kathy.

"Kathy, you don't understand what education means." He leaned on the table, and looked earnestly at Kathy. He stopped to think of the right words. "I hope that we can teach people to understand each other. Through education we can end the stupidity of war and bring dignity back to our earth. Those aren't just words. And they're not easy ideas."

"Yes, of course."

"Unless you need someone to accompany you so you don't have to go out alone at night?"

Kathy wished she had a purpose important enough to demand her dedication. "I feel safe here. I haven't seen one drunk man, nor one fight." She laughed. "Anyway, as one of twenty girls among 4,000 men, I'll find someone else to go with me"

"Will I see you at breakfast? Please tell me about it then."

In the first month in Biarritz, while Kathy dated many men, it was with Jim that she liked to begin the day. They met early for breakfast. "Anything interesting happen to you yesterday?" he would ask as he held the chair for her.

"Of course. This is Biarritz." Yesterday morning had begun like the others. "First, I wake up, and my room is full of magnolias that the French girls bring me every morning. Yesterday a Major walked with me to class. He read a poem composed for me. Do you want to hear it?"

"Not particularly."

"Then in our afternoon psych class, four boys took turns proposing marriage. I'm getting to be an authority. Counting yesterday's proposal, that makes fifteen. But I can't really count them, as they didn't really mean it."

Jim sat in a relaxed way, drinking his coffee, listening with a slightly amused smile. "Are you getting conceited?"

"I could use a little conceit. If I could believe the Major wrote poems to *me*, or those four GIs..."

Jim winked, "They weren't serenading *me*."

"They don't know me. Maybe they're dreaming what they dream in their loneliness. But it is fun."

The waiter brought a plate of scrambled eggs, bacon, toast, and a glass of orange juice. Jim picked up his fork, said an interested, "Go on," and ate as she talked.

The waiter brought a pot of coffee to refill their cups. Jim put two spoons of sugar in his and stirred. "How was your evening?"

"Last night I was determined to study. I refused eight dates—and then weakened. The Lieutenant from Cincinnati and I took sixth place in the jitterbug contest. Am I proud or embarrassed at winning a jitterbug prize?"

He grinned, "Surely, you must be proud of it."

"There are more important things. What did you do yesterday?" Kathy asked.

"Our prof and the French principal discussed the French system of turning out an elite intelligentsia as contrasted to our more mass-directed education. A teacher can work with students like an artist does. What stimulates the gifted child bewilders the slow learner. And the gifted child is unique. One can be verbal, another analytical."

Kathy's purpose was even more modest than his. She wanted to be a wife and mother; a wife supporting a man in his purpose, a mother cuddling his six babies. But one could not talk about this over here in this war.

"This is Saturday," said Jim. "No classes. Want to go on the Chaplain's tour into Spain?"

With box lunches and a copper pan of pastries a cook had given Kathy, they climbed into the open-topped back of the Chaplain's truck and sat on pews taken from the chapel.

The truck meandered through mountain country, past shepherds tending their flocks, into a Basque village. The truck stopped at the Spanish border barricade, made of crossed logs. GIs jumped from the truck and vaulted the logs. The single Spanish border guard held up his arms to stop them. Just when he stopped two GIs, two others swarmed across. After accepting gifts of two packages of cigarettes, he turned his back. He protested again when they took pictures. Jim took movies of the guard trying to make them put away their cameras as he was shouting in Spanish. Again, he was quieted with two packages of cigarettes. What was one lone guard against 20 irrepressible GIs—and the potent bribes of cigarettes?

They walked into Spain just far enough to say they had visited Spain, bought a pair of coiled-rope shoes, and returned, much to the Spanish guard's relief.

As they headed back toward Biarritz, they stopped beside a babbling brook to eat lunch. Jim looked up the stream to a waterfall. "Let's see where that begins."

Jim stood up against the snowcapped mountains. "Life is a struggle." He spoke facing the trees and the mountains. "Fight! Fight! Fight! Once I fought only in sports, just to win. Now I've learned that the fight is in all of life. Especially in the Army, where you can't choose your environment."

He spoke up to the mountains. "Hurray for the mountains that are strong and immovable."

He spoke to the blue sky. "It matters not how straight the gate, how charged with punishments the scroll, I am the master of my fate, I am the captain of my soul."

Kathy wanted to touch this man that spoke to the sky.

Jim turned to Kathy with an apologetic smile. "I was carried away."

"You carried me along with you." Kathy leaned against the gnarled bent pine. "After living through a war, do you continue to believe you are master of your fate?"

A stern frown deepened between his eyes. "I must believe that." He stepped back onto the path. "That was "Invictus." Would you like to hear some Tennyson? "Ulysses" is a good walking poem."

Kathy would have liked to hold this man's hand down the rocky path, but he walked behind her.

"Sometime, when I've finished school I might go—maybe to China, maybe South America, to teach.

"Sounds good. Today anything is possible." Kathy returned to the tree where she had left her copper pan, took a spoon from her purse and scooped the soft black earth into the pan. "Today I shall plant a dish garden, and it will bloom."

"Better to foresee the problems and be prepared. For me that means years of school: a year for my master's degree, two years of teaching before I begin my Doctorate, if I do begin, and then two years for that."

Kathy dug up a tiny mimosa plant, whose sensitive leaves curled at her touch, and put it into the soft earth. She transplanted a budding cactus. She covered the dirt with soft green moss and a few pretty pebbles. "I've been without roots too long. I look forward to going home to my family, for a while, anyway."

The Chaplain honked the truck's horn. They walked down the hill, climbed into the truck, and drove back to Biarritz. As Kathy sat beside Jim, her shoulder was warm where his shoulder touched her. If he had put his arm around her, she would have been warmer, but he didn't.

As they entered the revolving front door of the Palais, they passed a Sergeant with a chest full of decorations and an armful of books. He followed and came into the lobby after them. "Kathy?" he asked.

"Yes?" She looked at him, his medium height, black hair and dark eyes without recognizing him.

"You don't remember me? Cook County Hospital in Chicago? The dishwashers?" he said.

Kathy then recognized him. He was one of the Japanese American dishwashers taken from the internment camp in Kansas to wash dishes at Cook County. There had been six of them; industrious, pleasant boys. They were given loyalty clearance by the FBI and brought to Chicago to fill jobs that were deserted for war-production jobs. Kathy had been glad to see these boys. It was far easier to manage a kitchen with someone to put dishes into the dishwashing machine. The cooks and other workers were horrendously indignant towards them. They had refused to work in the same kitchen with the "Japanese," and complained to their unions. They scowled with suspicion at the six boys, although what they might suspect them of in a charity hospital wasn't specified.

Kathy felt a twinge of conscience. She had not shown her friendliness or gratitude by more than an occasional smile for fear of alienating the cooks and helpers. As a new student dietitian, her control over them was shaky anyway, so she had not offered to help the six boys. Once in a while one of these boys had waited outside the hospital door for her, offering to walk her across the street and down the block to the nurses' residence. This small favor she could not refuse, even though everyone else on the street looked at them with hatred. At the door of the nurses' residence, she had quickly dismissed them with a smile. A smile was all she had given this boy whose chest now displayed battle stars, a purple heart, and a citation for bravery.

"Yes, I remember you. Jim Duncan, I want you to meet a friend from Chicago and California. Your name was…, I…, I never could remember names."

"Harada. Fred Harada. May I talk to you a minute?"

"Certainly." She glanced at Jim, who looked agreeably friendly as he shook Fred's hand. "Have a cup of coffee with us."

They sat in the dining room by one of the big picture windows against which the wind blew salt spray. "I have just a minute," said the Sergeant. "I wanted to thank you for your smile." He spoke first to Kathy, then turned to explain to Jim. "My father and my grandfather were farmers in California. We were good Americans. After Pearl Harbor, they put all of us of Japanese descent behind barbed wire." Fred, who had looked Asian as a dishwasher, now, in the uniform of the United States Army, looked like a typical GI. Speaking in a solidly American voice, he said, "There were bitter factions in the camp. Maybe half decided if Americans treated us so badly, they deserved no loyalty. When we six came to Chicago, there was not one American who could smile at us."

"That must have been quite a shock. From a home on a green California farm, to a Kansas camp, to washing dishes in the slums of Chicago." Jim already saw his picture more vividly than Kathy had thought of it.

The waiter brought coffee. Kathy sipped it, not knowing what to say about the unfriendly Americans.

The Sergeant put his fingers on the edge of his cup, but did not drink. "We wanted to be loyal to America, but what had we to be loyal to? Why fight for people who scorned us and hated us? We had done nothing but raise oranges. They feared us, and we were just kids. If only one person would treat us as Americans...," he looked seriously at Kathy. "You did that, Kathy. You smiled. In a scowling world, you smiled."

"It...," Kathy almost said it was nothing, but obviously it was something to Fred. She continued listening.

"Your smile reassured us. When you left County for the Army, we joined the Army too."

"It was easy to smile at you. You were nice boys."

"No one else saw us that way. No one."

"Where are the others?"

"In Italy, waiting to go home to our farms in California. Well, thank you from the six of us. Please excuse me, but I must get going." Fred gravely shook their hands, picked up his books and left.

Kathy watched the rising waves, pondering what Fred had said. "There must have been more to their patriotism than my smile."

Jim reached across the table to put his warm hand on Kathy's. "Now do you believe in the power of love?"

"But it was just a simple smile. Then, I believed everyone was good. Everyone. I didn't know men could be cruel. I was a monkey in a tree smiling happily at everyone."

"Would your smile have worked if it had been forced or dutiful? Or tinged with pity? If you were being condescendingly kind to the Japanese?"

"Maybe I'm not just an idiot running down a hill scattering flowers!" She wanted to hug Jim for finding something good in her. Being too puritanical to hug him outright, she said, "Makes me want to dance. Come on. Let's dance."

They danced at the 'Chambre d'Amour.' Jim danced his same two steps, yet it didn't matter. His strong arm was around her and his lean body close against hers. She could rest her head on his broad shoulder, her forehead snuggled under the rough scratch of his chin.

The third dance, the orchestra broke into the strains of "I'll be loving you, always, with a heart that's true, always." This was the song that made Kathy cry. Her nose would get red, her eyes bloodshot, and her lips would blubber. Better to run out into the dark than to have Jim see her bleary-eyed. Maybe in the dark Jim would put an arm around her and comfort her.

She ran out into the wind, onto the soft sand. The waves rolled toward her, crashed into the rugged rocks, and receded. There were no tears, just sand and wind and waves and the circling lighthouse light. Beside her stood Jim who put an arm across her shoulder. "Why did you run?"

"For a year now, I've cried every time I heard that song. Tonight, I'm free of it. No more tears."

They stood facing the ocean. He stood behind her and wrapped his arms around her. Her head tilted back resting against his shoulder. His arms were strong, and they shut out the world. Here was peace, a peace she had never known. Passion too, for she felt warmth from the length of his body standing close behind her.

They stood watching the ocean until the rising tide and wind splashed spray around them. He took his arms from around her, and they retreated. To entice his arm around her again, Kathy ran. In exultation at freedom from tears, she ran. She ran with the leaps of a dancer, jumping freely in the dark.

Suddenly she crashed into a high wall. She fell back, dazed. By the returning beam from the lighthouse, she saw a concrete wall six-foot high and two-feet thick.

Jim was kneeling beside her. "Are you alright?"

"What did I hit?"

"You ran into a German blockhouse. This was part of the German's Atlantic Wall, part of their coastal defenses. Yesterday you were walking along the trench, jumping from the walls onto the sand. You must have seen it"

"I saw it without seeing it." She stood, brushing sand from her bruised knees. "That's the story of my life. Dance believing in a beautiful world—and then crash into a cement wall." Well, no more of that. She was a grown-up. His shoulders were broad enough to hold her weary head. Nonsense! Romantic nonsense! He was a man who would forget her tomorrow. She had almost forgotten the world was full of evil.

If he would put his arm around her again, she would twirl out from under it. He didn't. He stuck his hands in his pockets and whistled a melancholy tune as they walked back to their separate rooms.

Frieda greeted her with indignation. "You know what those boys are doing? All five of Jim and Mike's roommates are making five-dollar bets on which gets his girl first, whether Jim gets you or Mike gets me. They have a chart. It begins with meeting, dating, holding hands, kissing..., you know the rest."

"The one that makes his girl first wins five dollars?"

"No. Jim is not betting. Neither is Mike. The five roommates are."

"Like betting on a horse race, with us as the horses."

"Calm down and I'll explain..."

"We're not even the prize, just the horses!"

"Let me finish..."

"I'm not a horse. I've got a soul."

"Listen," called Frieda, but Kathy had already heard too much and turned away.

"Will you listen to me?" cried Frieda

"Sure." Kathy took off her blouse and went into the closet.

"Jim told Mike... Kathy! Stop! Come out of there! You can't hear me in that closet."

Kathy came out of the closet, and sat on the bed.

Frieda sat up. "Jim told Mike that he wouldn't play with you. He said that you were the kind of girl with whom he could get serious, and he's not ready. He has to finish school first. That's why he won't hold your hand."

Through the open French doors came the roar of the ocean. The waves rolled and rolled, and finally soothed Kathy into sleep.

The next day Jim announced, "The sun and drum are against me. I can't study today. Want to go to Bayonne?"

Together Kathy and Jim took the train to the ancient walled city of Bayonne. Here, for centuries monks had made their meditations. They walked under the vine-covered arches of the cloisters and along the crooked cobblestone streets to the cathedral.

They returned to the Red Cross canteen in Biarritz to talk over coffee and doughnuts. Here the long-haired violinist played romantic music by their table, delighted to have found lovers for whom to play.

They walked along the beach. Jim held Kathy's hand in his warm, strong hand. They walked to the wrought-iron bridge that arched across to the Isle of the Virgin. "Want to go over? We'll get splashed," said Jim.

"I like salt spray. Let's run through it." They ran over the bridge, and along the stone wall that spiraled the island.

Jim licked his chin. "Salty. No wonder no trees or flowers grow here."

"Except the gulls. Tougher than we humans."

"No tougher than my grandfather and grandmother. They built a house on a rock almost this barren in Scotland. They fished the sea, and raised a good family. We humans are tough too, at least the Scottish are. Good God-fearing people we are." He put an arm around her, and held her head on his shoulder. Under that arm, against his shoulder, was shelter from the wind. "Kathy, you like this rock and the waves, don't you?"

"Yes, it was primitive." No, what was the word she wanted?

That didn't say what she meant, but Jim understood. "It's like a man's soul, strong, enduring. Thrust up alone in a restless sea, the lonely soul stands."

"Have you felt your soul within you?" Kathy asked.

"I believe I have. It's like this rock with most of it under water. I just get glimpses of what emerges."

"Do you believe I have a soul?"

"If I have one, you must too," he said. "Occasional glimpses of something in you. I think I've seen yours. That's why I can love you." He put his other arm around her. The circle of his arms shut out the surges of the sea. From within his arms, she could watch the waves, but they could not reach her. Here was a peace beyond any feeling she had known.

His cheek was beside her cheek, his mouth at her ear. "You're a good girl. That might not sound like much, but in our family that is the highest praise. You're a good girl."

"That's too simple. I'd like to be a woman of mystery."

"You're not. You're easy to understand. That's why I can say you're a good girl."

He must be seeing past the parts of her that made foolish mistakes, said the wrong things, or acted silly. Never had anyone seen so deeply inside her. She didn't know how he could. Was this the magic of love?

She felt his strength and goodness. He had a purpose in which she would like to share. Let him have the magnificent purpose, let her be his wife and bear his children. She snuggled closer.

Jim tilted her chin up and kissed her. That kiss, the gentlest of kisses, stirred her passions, gently and deeply. Passion and peace, these he gave.

"I love you," he said. "But..., well you know I'm going to be a teacher. That means two years before I get my master's degree. Then two years teaching before I start my doctorate. If I do, that means another two years."

"Sounds like a good plan."

"Then, when I'm through school, I still won't earn much money. Before I marry, I..., I want to give my wife a house, furniture, a car. On a teacher's salary, that would take more years. That's ten years before I can marry."

Was this why he withheld a part of him? "No, Jim, I don't agree. You're assuming a wife is a burden that must be supported in style."

"You were brought up in wealth. It's the manner to which you were accustomed..."

"I was brought up in wealth, so I know exactly what money can buy, how important it is—and how unimportant. Money to buy food, warm clothes, and shelter—that much is essential. I'd settle for a double sleeping bag and a good GI potbelly stove. But man's nature would be to climb out of the sleeping bag and run lusting after another woman."

"Not me. I've envied the man that had a wife and children to go home to. My marriage would last. Even if I should stop loving my wife, my wife would never know. I could never hurt her." Jim took one arm away and shoved his cap to the back of his head.

He kissed her again, his lips marvelously soft in a man so lean and firm. "I thought when I told you this, you would walk away. I do love you. I want to marry you. Yet I can't ask you."

"Don't ask. I've had a dozen proposals. Not one was sincere."

"I am sincere."

"Maybe one would be sincere where life isn't so desperate as in this war, where woman is not so rare."

"You're bitter. I dated lots of girls in England. I know what I want."

"Well, bluntly, you're a man. A man can love a girl and leave her."

"Love is more than that, and you know it."

"Sometimes I believe it." Here under the moonlight, she could almost believe it. "In two weeks, we'll be leaving Biarritz, but for where?"

Jim said, "I'm going back to New York, then maybe back to Iowa State."

"That's a long way from New Mexico where my family is. Maybe I will see you there. Maybe back in the States I can learn to trust a man again. So many pieces of my heart have been broken that I'm hoarding what's left."

That was all they had to say. They sat silently watching the tide rise. The waves rose higher, driving them off the rock. They walked back down the chiseled ledge. The waves surged restlessly against the black rock, throwing up silver spray.

Still, they met for breakfast, and lunch and dinner, too. Still, they played with orphans, and walked and talked on the moonlit beach. Still, they danced under the potted palm tree, and still the violinist at the Red Cross canteen played love songs to them. Still, Jim declared his love. Still there was profound peace in Jim's arms, and strength on his shoulder and passion in his kiss. *Yet their love had no hope.*

The last day of school, Kathy was assigned as officer in charge of a company of ten WACs to escort to Paris, then on to Le Havre. Kathy and Frieda were getting ready to leave in the morning, when someone knocked at the door.

Kathy looked out to greet Jim and Mike. Mike turned to Frieda, "Are you ready?"

"Almost."

Frieda tightened her necktie. "We'll see you there." She put on her blouse and left with Mike.

"Wear your Eisenhower jacket. You look good in that," said Jim.

Kathy packed her last uniform, checked the emptied drawers, and with Jim's help, rolled up her bedroll. "There. I'm ready."

Jim stood before the desk and looked at the copper dish with the Pyrennes plants. "What will you do with your garden?"

She stroked the delicate, sensitive leaves of mimosa, leaf by leaf, and watched the leaves curl up at her touch. "I feel like these plants. Pull me up by my roots once more and I'll shrivel."

"I'll throw them out for you." Jim carried the copper pan onto the balcony and tossed the uprooted plants and dirt over the railing.

Kathy followed him and watched the waves below lap gently on the shore. The lighthouse beam poured silver over the water. "Let's not dance. Let's walk along the beach."

Jim set the copper dish on the carved stone railing. "I brought you a present. It's not an engagement ring." He took from his pocket a silver ring, and put it in her hand. His hand was warm where it touched hers.

Kathy took the ring to the light pouring through the open French door to look closer. On the ring was a small square of silver on which a map of France was etched. Within the map was a tiny circle for Paris and a slender line indicating the Seine River that went on to Le Havre. There was the Rhone that flowed to the Mediterranean. Tiny mountains were etched for the Alps and Pyrennes. A deeply etched star illustrated Bordeaux.

Jim pointed to the star, "I had the jeweler make a mark where we met."

"A friendship ring?"

"Something more than that. But not an engagement ring."

She slipped it onto the third finger of her right hand. "I'll treasure it."

His arms were around her waist, and there was both that peace and that thrill she always felt in his arms. "Let's walk."

They walked and they kissed. Although the stars sparkled brightly and the camelias were sweet-scented, and the waves whispered, there was no hope in their kisses.

"Let's dance," said Kathy. So, they danced. "I'm tired," said Kathy. She meant she was lonely and empty, and tired was a good word, too.

"You'll be leaving early in the morning," said Jim. His voice was sad and lonely.

They returned to the Palais. Jim kissed her softly, sadly. "Good night. Goodbye."

"Good night."

When Jim was gone, Kathy went into her room alone.

She was leaving in the morning. He would leave soon after, and Biarritz would be a memory. She would never see him again. His ring would be added to her collection of Rhys's returned watch, Rocky's locket, and Charles's nightingale pin. *C'est la guerre.*

In the morning she waved goodbye to Jim and Mike and Frieda and the Empress Eugénie's palace from the back of a two-ton truck that drove her and her company of WACs to the train station.

They arrived safely in Paris, where the WACs scattered in all directions. This didn't disturb Kathy at all. She was now sophisticated and capable of handling such minor crises. The only place they could stay was in the WAC leave center. She arranged with the WAC Captain for her company to stay two nights, and to pick them up on the second morning. They could have one last two-day visit in Paris before returning to the States.

Kathy was now a different girl from the weak, tired girl who had come to Paris a year ago after her hospital stay in Rouen. Paris had changed, too. It had been gray and weary then. Then when she had been in Paris, she had tried to call Rocky. Here she had said goodbye to Charles. She had returned to cold Paris from sunny Marseilles, and had fled to Paris from miserable Mourmelon. Her life kept returning to Paris.

This was a new city. Spring had returned. The chestnut trees along the Champs d'Elysees were in bloom. People were wearing bright, new clothes. No longer did she see the worn, gray clothes of the war. Gasoline had returned. Little taxicabs honked and rushed about. No longer were Army trucks and Jeeps the only vehicles.

Now a sophisticated Kathy had two days in gay Paree. She had friends to call: artists, chefs, and doctors. She knew her way around the Army and the city. She could manage the WACs, the French, and any man in any situation.

She called her friends, and she handled the men. And it was nothing. Her life was empty. She had built around her a capability that protected her heart from hurt—and it was protecting emptiness. *The wall that protected her heart from hurt kept out hurt, but it also kept out the meanings of life, kept out love.*

# CHAPTER 27

## HEADING HOME

A truck carried the WACs and Kathy back to Le Havre. They drove by piles of rubble. They passed by Frenchmen still tediously picking out bricks, one at a time, just as they had 14 months ago. Remnants of shipwrecks in the shallow water still stood, with barren metal rising from the dark water. Clanging bells marked sunken ships.

They finally arrived at Camp Home Run, just outside of Le Havre. Kathy turned the WACs over to an officer. Kathy went on to her own staging area. At the headquarters hut, she signed in and talked with the harried WAC Captain in charge.

"This is the Army," complained the WAC, "250 women officers sit idle in Quonset huts, while I struggle to house, feed, process and get you all on board a ship to go home."

Kathy offered to help her, which was gratefully accepted. She would supervise and serve as interpreter for the French civilian workers in the area. Kathy would begin the next day.

Kathy asked if Chaplain Kirkemo was here in Le Havre. His last letter had been sent from Camp Home Run. The WAC said he was, and directed her to the Chaplain's hut. She also pointed out the Quonset huts for female officers on top of a high ridge.

Kathy dumped her gear on a lower bunk in her quarters in the end hut, and walked outside. She stood on the edge of the bluff overlooking the harbor. The sky was gray, not blue. The land was black and brown, not green. Trees that should have bloomed were blackened stumps. A few ships threaded their way through a channel marked by buoys, past submerged ships, some with tilted smokestacks.

This was depressing. She wanted a friend. She slid down the rocky bluff to the beach that would lead to the Chaplain's office. On the sand, amidst the wreckage and dead fish, were tarnished brass ammunition shells. She kicked over a snail shell, a pink shell in a gray world, and watched a pink hermit crab run for cover. She found a red rectangular stone that she rubbed between her fingers, revealing a carved cross.

Where was the cross from? Up and down the beach, it was impossible to recognize what might have been a church. She looked up the bluff where nothing was left. She saw, instead, under a ledge, a cave. She remembered hearing that the Germans had defended the harbor here at Le Havre from a cave.

She walked and soon found the Chaplain's Quonset hut.

Chaplain Kirkemo stood to greet her warmly when he saw her standing in his office doorway. "It's good to see you, Kathy. I've remembered you in my prayers." His handshake was as vigorous as ever. His cheeks as rosy and his eyes as full of goodwill mixed with concern. "You're looking tanned and healthy."

"The sun shone every day in Biarritz in Southern France. It's hard to imagine that here."

"Nice of you to come visit an old man."

She didn't think of him as old. His eyes were young. Yet his hair was white, and the smile wrinkles around his eyes were deeply etched. "You've seen this war, and you haven't hardened. How have you withstood it?"

He smiled gently, "I believe in God."

That was all he said. He seemed to think that was as all he needed to say.

"Would you like to see my chapel? Did I write you about it?" He put on his trench coat and pulled on his four-buckle overshoes. "You may have noticed, it's muddy here."

They climbed the bluff to the cave. Kathy wondered, "You built a chapel in this cave?"

"Christianity in a cave? Why not? Christianity was begun in a cave." Chaplain Kirkemo folded back the cotton black-out curtain from the opening, and tied it back, inviting Kathy's entrance.

The cave was cold and damp with a hard stone floor. The walls were rough planes of chiseled rock. At the back of the cave, on a small box, was a plain wooden cross made of two crossed boards.

"Simple, isn't it? Christianity is simple." The Chaplain knelt.

Kathy knelt beside him, feeling reverence and awe. She wanted to pray, yet didn't know what to say. She was empty, with an emptiness that had nothing to offer. She was alone, with an aloneness to which no one spoke.

"Your chapel is magnificent," Kathy said. "But I must get back to my duties." Chaplain Kirkemo again thanked her for coming, and said he would continue to pray for her.

Kathy worked long hours for a month. She was assigned to ship after ship, five in total, but each time she was pulled off at the last minute. She noticed that nurses who had arrived after her had already left.

Kathy enjoyed the work and the chance to know the French workers and their families. They continued to be cold and hungry, but no longer freezing and starving. She heard of their wartime struggles when she visited them in bomb-shattered remnants of houses.

The work was a diversion from the waiting lives the nurses lived. They were awaiting their return to the States. They were waiting in line to wash their faces in the latrine, waiting in line three times a day for chow, waiting in line to turn in their gas masks, waiting to sign papers. They were waiting at the end of a war, hoping and waiting to begin another life.

One gray April afternoon Lt. Hill came in and announced. "Kathy, I have your orders." Kathy had worked frequently with him, a nice-looking boy, in the headquarters office during the last month. She was to be an Interpreter on the *Zebulon B Vance*.

Kathy read the orders. "What kind of ship?" she asked.

"The *Zebulon B. Vance* is a bride ship. You will be with 452 French mademoiselles that will be joining their new American husbands, along with 173 children. Starting new lives in the States. Some call it 'Operation Diaper Run.'"

"Yeah. Thanks." Always an interpreter, never a bride she thought. Always a midwife, never a mother.

"The Colonel worried about a French war bride that decided to have a baby. I said you were a good interpreter, so there you are. I thought you'd like that. You're always seeking new experiences."

"Thanks," Kathy said.

"Now, would you do something for me?" He grinned appealingly. "Come with me to the party tonight?"

Kathy had lost interest in parties and men. She didn't want to drink, and she didn't want a man to touch her. "No thanks."

"This is a station party. You know most of us."

"I like you. I just don't want any more parties."

Lt. Hill's grin faded to a sad look. "What fun is a party without a girl?"

She felt sympathy for his loneliness. "All right. I'll come."

"Can you get some of the nurses to come?" he asked. "A party together should be merrier for all of us."

At each of the five Quonset huts, Kathy stood inside the doorway and asked the girls, lounging on their bunk beds, if they'd like to help the station have a happy party. The girls looked up from their cards, paused only a moment, and didn't bother to answer.

In the fifth hut, one USO girl agreed to go. With a towel over her shoulder, and bottles of shampoo and hair dye in hand, the USO girl sauntered out to wash her hair.

The nurse on the bunk by the door disdainfully looked after the USO girl. She said, "She'll come back with a camera, or radio, or jewelry."

"How does she do it?" asked Kathy. "No one gives me expensive presents."

"She *earns* them."

When Lt. Hill called for Kathy at 2100, he explained that the other girl would go in a different car. He led her to a Jeep covered with a canvas top that kept out the rain, and opened the door for her. Kathy climbed in. A Major sat in the driver's seat, so Kathy moved over to make room for Lt. Hill to sit beside her. Lt. Hill poked his head in under the cover. "Major Baxter, this is Lt. Kathy Collens. Kathy, I'll see you there."

The Major drove off as the Lieutenant shut the door. Before Kathy fully realized that she was riding alone with a strange man, they were on their way. There was nothing she could do but ride along, and not judge the Major until he was proven guilty.

He took her to a bawdy bistro in the downtown area of Le Havre. They stepped from the fresh rain-washed air into thick air that reeked of wet wool and alcohol and cheap perfume. Gls and officers were dancing with French girls to the music of a battered piano. Half a dozen sailors leaned their elbows on the bar, drinking and watching the dancers.

The Major took off his cap and hung it on a wooden hook on the wall. His head was bald, with a fringe of brown hair. He took off his trench coat and hung it up. His stomach was a bulging paunch.

He gripped Kathy's forearm in his hand to lead her to a wooden table grooved with cigarette burns. On the way, Kathy stiffened when he gave her arm three little squeezes.

She looked around the tables, and recognized no one. They must be early.

"What would you like to drink?" The Major sat without bothering to hold Kathy's chair for her, and beckoned to the waiter.

"Ginger ale," replied Kathy, seating herself, and draping her coat over the back of the chair.

"You can't have a good time on ginger ale. Don't be a party pooper. Have brandy."

"I can't stand the taste of brandy. I'll order my own." She spoke to the waiter, "*Apportez-moi le jus de raisin; pas du vin, je veux seulement du jus, s'il vous plait.*"

As she hoped, the Major didn't understand a word she said. "What wine is that?" he asked when the waiter brought her a glass of red grape juice.

Why be cowardly about not drinking. "You might as well know, I don't drink with strangers. Matter of fact, I just don't drink, except this nice, tart grape juice."

"Try this." He held his brandy up to her mouth, not believing anyone could resist. "You can't have a good time without a few drinks."

She turned her head away. "I can. Maybe you can't, but I won't drink just because you can't have a good time without getting drunk."

They sat there for some time. It was obvious that as a drinking partner, Kathy was a failure. "Let's dance," said the Major.

While he danced, he wouldn't drink, so Kathy stood up. The Major held her hand in his puffy palm, and wrapped his flabby arm across her shoulder, pulling her tightly over his bulging stomach. He danced, holding her head beside his, swinging her back and forth on his repulsive fat paunch. She stiffened, trying to hold her head up, wanting to dance a little apart, to get away from that shifting stomach. He would not let her go. His grip was powerful. He bounced with the music, his stomach bouncing almost independently after him, and Kathy unhappily bouncing against him. He held her head against his, so her cheek rubbed against his scratchy, brandy-smelling cheek.

At the end of the song, Kathy, now released, returned to their table without explanation. They sat there, fumbling with conversation for some time.

What to do? This situation was tricky. A wrong move could be dangerous. Her dislike for him probably showed, and that could be hazardous.

Kathy's problem was to get back to Camp Home Run. She looked around at the soldiers sitting with their girls at the tables, and at the sailors at the bar, and saw only strange faces. Taxis had not yet returned to Le Havre. The Major was not sufficiently threatening to call a French policeman, and that would cause an international incident.

Could she call the staging area for transportation? The civilian telephone lines probably were not connected with the military lines, but it was worth a try. When he brought the next brandy, she asked the waiter in French if there was a telephone. There was no phone in this grubby bistro.

There were no MPs inside. She could not walk the streets outside looking for one.

What to do? Could she demand that he drive her home now before he got drunker? Did she want to ride with him? Yet how else could she leave? Her safest course was to assume this was a trusted date. In another ten minutes, she would have stayed long enough to fulfil any normal dating obligation, and could suggest they go back.

A French girl wiggled past the table and signaled a hip at the Major. The Major smiled. She smiled. She wiggled on. He followed the girl to another table. She smoked his cigarettes, drank his liquor and wrapped her curves around him as they danced. Their laughter rose above the murmur of other voices.

It was the most welcome jilt Kathy had ever received. Still, there was the problem of getting back to Camp Home Run. The bistro was full of drinking strangers. She would wait until a solution presented itself.

By midnight the crowd had grown noisy and rowdy. The Major was now hopelessly drunk. She wouldn't ride back with him if he did happen to remember her, which wasn't likely. His attentions were devoted to embracing the French girl.

Some Army soldiers were sitting quietly at tables, taking only occasional drinks. Surely one of these could be relied on to escort her, driving or walking. Which one? Were the sailors at the bar safer than the soldiers? Probably not, considering what the Navy thought of the Army. The most reliable might be one who had another date—but this would be interrupting his evening.

Which one? The quiet Captain with the girl in the tight black dress? He had a decent look around his eyes, and had only three empty glasses on the table before him. Yet his girl's dress made her look slinky. What did that mean?

A Lieutenant with a girl in a noisy pink dress had only one glass before him, but he laughed loudly and waved his arms around. How many glasses had the waiter removed? How to judge a man?

A Captain sitting with other officers curiously looked at her. She looked away. If he was thinking she was a barfly trying to pick up a date, he might or might not get her honorably back to Camp Home Run. She would have to trust someone. Him?

The door opened, letting in a gust of cold, fresh air. Two Sergeants came in, their faces washed clean by rain. If they had been drinking, the cold rain on their faces sobered them. Would they be the best risk for escorts? Was a sober man safer than a drunk man? Were two men safer than one?

The door opened again. The gust of fresh sea air was a delight in the room heavy with tobacco smoke. In came a huge man, followed by a shorter, broad-shouldered man. The huge man turned around. It was Mike! And Jim!

Kathy ran to him, threw her arms around him. With his long arms around her she was safe. "Jim! Take me home! I'm stranded...and...and...I sure need you!" He was revealed through his blue eyes, his feelings exposed. His caring, his concern was there. She could melt into this love.

He smiled and looked directly into Kathy's eyes. "I love you," he said. "I've thought of you," said his words, and his eyes added the depth of his thoughts. "I want to take care of you," he said. Before this, his eyes had been controlled, covered with a protection. Now the protection was gone. His vulnerable love was exposed, without reservation.

He looked around the bar at the raucous drinkers. The tight control returned around his eyes. "Looks like you need to be taken care of. How did you get into this dump?"

She nodded toward the Major, now with beads of sweat glistening on his bald head. His clumsy fingers were fumbling with the glass buttons on the French girl's red blouse. "He brought me."

"Who is he?"

"Let's get my coat and hat." She led the way back to her table.

"Who is he?" Jim stood at the table, facing her, arms crossed on his chest, intending to stand there until he received an answer.

Kathy stood opposite him. "I don't know. He was in the Jeep when I got in."

"You got into a Jeep with a strange man?"

"I didn't intend to."

"You didn't know you were getting in the Jeep?"

"I knew I was getting in the Jeep. I didn't know that Major was there. I got in and he drove away. My date was with a Lt. Hill. I've known him a month. When he opened the door..."

"Where is Lt. Hill?"

"I don't know. When he opened the door..."

Jim was no longer listening. He was glaring at the Major. Jim's frown was stern, his mouth grim and straight. "You came to this dump with that Major?" he accused.

The Major fumbled with the last button. Finally with a jerk he tore it off. The girl, without bothering to hold her blouse together, walked, chest high, towards a back hall. The Major followed.

"Please listen." Kathy leaned toward Jim, holding out her hands pleadingly. "I can explain. I had a date with..."

"No excuses and rationalizations." His eyes were accusing. His arms across his chest. "Just admit you did wrong."

"No." Kathy sat up straight, indignant. "I did not do anything wrong. Will you listen?"

"I can see you are here. I don't need to listen." His voice lowered to a gentler tone. "You do need someone to take care of you."

She put her shoulders back, and held her head high.

"Let a man take care of me? I considered it a moment ago, when I thought you loved me. I thought you were..., You're not. You're a mere man...and can you explain *your* coming here?"

"Don't change the subject." He smiled a condescending smile. "We were talking about your being here."

Kathy stood. "There's no use talking." She picked up her hat and slapped it onto the back of her head. Why bother to put it straight? She picked up her own coat and put it on without waiting for any assistance from Jim. "Take me back to Camp Home Run, if you please. It's north of the harbor, on top of the ridge."

Mike stayed in the bar. Jim and Kathy drove in an open Jeep through the April drizzle past shattered buildings and around bomb holes. The Jeep stopped in front of the Quonset huts, under a bare light bulb hanging from a high pole. The lone MP guarding the girls' five huts stood with water dripping from his white helmet onto his glistening rubber raincoat.

Jim put an arm around Kathy, and kissed her goodnight. His arm was strong, his kiss soft and warm and pleading, offering the passion and peace that had been theirs in Biarritz. Which could she believe, the warm peace of the love of Biarritz, or the cold harshness of the gray metal glistening in the reality of the electric light?

"Will I see you tomorrow?" he asked.

"No. I'm sailing in the morning. I'll be an interpreter on a bride's ship," she said. She'd be an independent, empty, frustrated old maid with a cold scientific career.

He jumped over to the door on her side of the Jeep. She opened her own door, and stepped into the mud. "I'll write," she said, knowing men didn't write.

"Sure. We'll write."

She stepped to the front door, and scraped the mud from her foot. "Goodbye."

"Goodbye." He jumped into the Jeep and drove away.

Though it was dark inside the hut, she knew just where the bag with toothbrush and soap was hanging on the bunk. She felt for it, and for the rough towel and washcloth hanging beside it. With them in hand, she stepped outside again, to walk past five Quonset huts to the last hut that was the latrine.

The MP walked beside her, a military escort to the latrine. "Nice evening, Lieutenant?"

"It's a miserable evening," she said. Yet it wasn't all miserable. It had the smell of spring. "Unless you remember April showers bring spring flowers," she added. Yet that was ridiculous statement in a land without flowers.

He stood waiting for her when she emerged from the latrine, and escorted her back past five huts to her door. "Lieutenant, could I talk to you?" Embarrassed, he spoke quickly, "I have to talk to someone."

"Of course. I don't feel like sleeping, anyway."

"Should I tell my wife?" His face was shadowed from the light by his helmet. His voice showed the depth of his concern. "I love my wife. You believe me, don't you? I love my wife."

His voice was desperately honest. She nodded, "Yes, I believe you."

"I was a good man. I went to church every Sunday. I taught Sunday School. I never drank, never had tasted alcohol. Never gambled, never played cards. Do you believe me?"

"Yes."

"Should I tell my wife?"

"Do you think she would understand?"

"Could she understand the loneliness? I wrote her. Every night I wrote her. One night I wrote her 64 pages. But letters don't help the loneliness."

"No. Letters are not enough."

He pushed his GI shoe into the mud, put his other big shoe beside it and watched the mud ooze up. "The other fellows drank beer. I didn't drink beer. They drank cognac. I didn't drink. The other fellows played poker. I didn't play. I wrote letters. They laughed at me."

Kathy shifted her weight from one foot to another, sought a clump of grass on which to stand to keep from sinking in the mud. There was none. "Oh," she said.

"They laughed at me. The fellows had girls. French girls that followed the camps. You know how it was."

"It was bad," Kathy said.

"Every GI in the outfit had "made it" with a girl or even girls. They talked about it. You know how they talked. There were two of us who had not. Two of us. And they all laughed at us. Then, when we fought through Germany, there were German girls. You know the girls that followed the soldiers. The other fellow made it with a German girl. He talked about it. Talked about all the details. Then the whole outfit laughed at me. Just me, alone. I was the only one."

He turned and took two steps. The rain drizzled silently on his sloping back, glistening in the harsh light of the bare bulb. There was no comforting patter of rain. The only sound was the squish of his feet in mud.

He turned again to face Kathy. "You know how it was, how the German girls were. One stepped in front of me, and held open her coat. She was naked under the coat. I followed her and...." He hung his head low and spoke low. "Should I tell my wife?"

Kathy, not knowing what to say, said nothing. He talked on, disgorging his war years, preparing to begin his life with his family again. There in the soundless April rain, a new outlook was revealed on an old life. Two years ago, both he and Kathy would have condemned his behavior—but now Kathy was understanding.

"Should I tell my wife?" His question sought an answer.

"If I were a wife, after living in this war, I would not judge. I would be thankful for the love that did not die. Do you think your wife could know how it was?"

"Maybe not. She's never been away from her hometown, her friends, her family. If I told her, I don't think she could understand, and would think I did not love her. I do love her. Do you believe that?"

"Yes. Surely you can show her you love her?"

"It would be harder if she knew of the German girls. I won't tell her right away. Maybe later she can love without understanding." His decision was finally made. He stood straight. "I had to tell someone. I'm glad I told you. Thanks. You helped."

"And you've helped me. Thanks, and good luck." She went inside the Quonset hut.

Kathy groped her way to her bunk, and hung her towel and bag on the frame. At the foot of the bed, she lifted the lid of her footlocker. She felt for her pajamas, for the softness of the flannel. She found her rough wool sweater, a slippery nylon slip, and her stiff combat suit. Then she touched the smoothly carved wooden folds of the sculpture, up to the broken arm and along the notches on the feathered wing. She touched the rounded curves of her face to feel the smile.

She left the damp air inside the cold aluminum hut to walk again in the April drizzle that had the fresh promise of spring. She walked along the path chiseled from the stone cliff overlooking the ocean. The buoys' bells clanged, one clang as a wave lifted and tilted the buoy, and another as the descending wave shifted it back.

When the drizzle turned to pouring rain, she sought refuge in the cave. She sat in the open entrance to the chapel. When the rain slackened, the lights in the harbor glowed. The lanterns hung over wrecked ships swung suspended in darkness.

She had a decision to make. She could choose to protect herself by becoming a career woman, so no man could hurt her again. She had the intelligence and ability for financial security and scientific achievement. That had been Vivienne's choice, and Mrs. Foster's path too. She could live where she chose, by herself—yet that sounded empty.

Or she could give herself in love, in marriage, to Jim, a man. That had been Mathilda's choice. Hooch might not return to Mathilda. What about Buntz – did she really know Tex? Jim might die, as Rhys had, or lust after another woman. Jim would be more likely to neglect her for his work. Could she love him when he looked, not at her, but at a book?

Again, black clouds covered the moon, and the blackness was darker than before, and the clanging bells sounded lonelier.

Tonight, Jim had refused to listen, and…he had not tried to understand. How could love exist then? Jim's sense of right and wrong was rigid, yet this was part of his tremendous attraction. Even this might be uncomfortable.

Kathy was asking that Jim love her. She expected from him more understanding than she had given him or anyone else. What had she known of Rhys's struggles? What had she done to pathetic Lt. Groot? She had chosen to believe that Rocky's marriage was over, and allowed her values to be compromised. How long had that taken for her to weaken – three months. What health could she promise Jim, as she herself had not tolerated the cold. She had sunk into despair and been saved by Charles. Didn't she expect the MP's wife to be understanding? Now she expected Jim to understand and love her, yet she was a mere woman. She wouldn't have survived without the help of many good people.

Clang. A wave rose. Clang. A wave descended. The bells on the sunken ships tolled a mournful warning, reminders of the hazards of war.

Kathy was afraid. Alone, without love, life was empty, unbearably lonely. Yet to give herself to a man was to invite pain. She would be hurt. As long as she thought of herself, she would be afraid. *I, I, I; me, me, me. As long as I put myself first, there is no solution.*

What could possibly happen to her that had not already happened in this war? She had experienced sickness and pain, had faced death, had lost her illusory true love. Yet she had endured. *Now none of it seemed unbearable.*

The crippled Major, with the angel, gave Kathy a gift, a way to relate to the world and accept her limitations. She had no obligation to change the world or achieve anything. She could love the world with all its disasters. She could relate to the world with love, and nothing and no one could daunt that relationship.

She wanted to love; she wanted to give herself in love to Jim.

The clouds over the ocean caught the red and gold colors of dawn. The light reflected into the recesses of the cave. The wet surfaces of chiseled stone caught the light, and the plain wooden cross glistened.

A waking bird twittered. She followed his song. Unable to build their nest in a tree because bombs had shattered all trees, two small birds were building a home. Kathy and Jim could too. She could not achieve a perfect love, yet she would try. With God's help, Jim and she would build a nest, if not in a tree, then on a rock. She would go to him as soon as she could, as soon as she was discharged and free of the Army.

In the harbor, white sails unfurled on the schooner's two masts. The sea wind puffed them out, tilting the ship with its force. As sheets and helm were adjusted, the keel leveled. The force of the wind sent the ship forward, past the ruined ships and clanging buoys onto the azure sea. Water, wind, sail and keel working in harmony.

There was Jim! Miraculously, Jim was walking the rock ledge towards Kathy. His face alight with the sunrise glow and with love. His blue eyes shone unmistakable love. "I had to see you before you sailed."

When Kathy stood with open arms, Jim wrapped his long arms around her. "I had to see you. I just couldn't leave you in misunderstandings. I had to tell you that the bistro and Major were not important."

"No. They're not important." His cheek was cool, his neck warm, his arms strong, and his passion peaceful.

Jim put his hand on her hair and held her head on his shoulder. "I went back to the Quonset huts at Camp Home Run and asked the MP to call you. He said you had walked down this ledge. So, I followed. I wondered what troubles you were getting yourself into here alone. Still haven't much sense, have you, walking a slippery ledge alone at night?"

"No, I haven't much sense, but I had to..."

"No explanations now. Because, you know, you won't be walking anywhere alone again."

# EPILOGUE

As voiced by Kathy (Nancy) in her original typed pages:
That was thirteen years ago, and I have never walked alone again.

Jack Munro, alias Jim Duncan, and I did return to Iowa State in June 1946. One adjustment problem remained; I still expected men to carry my packages, and I handed my grocery bags to whatever man happened to be walking beside me. Men looked bewildered, but carried them. I still did not trust any man out of sight; I simply would not let Jack out of my view for long. We were married in December 1946. Jim earned three degrees and became a teacher and then a professor of education. We started a family, and made our home in Missoula, Montana.

As a Head Start nutritionist, I did feed hungry children. Head Start, with supportive services by teachers, social workers, psychologists, nurses and nutritionists, made dramatic differences in the lives of disadvantaged people.

I was wrong not to have trusted Jack; he remained a totally good, caring, committed husband and father. Jack did not prevent a war, but he was an important part of teacher training in Montana. I regained faith in education, science, adjustment, honesty, and above all, love triumphant.

My army experience was the best of times and the worst of times. Particularly overseas, the Army provided us with the best facilities and services available. I'm grateful to the Army for shaping my life and providing a purpose that has guided me for many years.

Jack and I are proud to be veterans.

Gone but Not Forgotten
*Nancy Ewing Munro (1920-2005)*
*James Jackson Rutherford Munro (1913-1994)*

# PHOTOS

Nancy Ewing

"Jack" Munro

Lieutenant Ewing

Captain Munro

Mr. and Mrs. Jack Munro
Married December 1946

# ACKNOWLEDGMENTS

It all started when attending a meeting of the World War II (WW2) Battlefield Tour group, before joining their 20th tour. The leader was Colonel Don Patton who co-founded the Dr. Harold C. Deutsch World War II History Round Table (HRT) in 1987. I showed him the nearly four-inch-thick typed pages of my mother's story. The Colonel handed me a card, smiled, and said "Meet with this person."

Dutifully, I contacted the name shown: Connie Anderson, author, editor, and owner of Words and Deeds. Suddenly, the adventure began. Connie invited me to participate in her "Women of Words," or WOW, a local writer's group she co-founded 30 years ago. I was also introduced to my future publisher, the talented Ann Aubitz, co-owner of Kirk House Publishers.

Connie and the women of WOW provided much needed direction and support. Connie is not only a wizard with words, but she also suggested unforeseen opportunities for improvement. She is extremely responsive, has a delightful sense of humor, and is committed to helping her authors.

My husband Bill provided significant assistance. With a longtime interest in World War II, and a father that served in the Army, together we went on Don Patton's Battlefield Tours to different places in Europe, watched documentaries, and visited libraries and museums. We attended a 4th Fighter Group Association reunion and are members of the Eighth Air Force Historical Society of Minnesota.

A special thanks to the beta readers that provided a variety of feedback. In particular, Lonnie Dunbier, who immediately read the story two times, and provided trusted input throughout the review process. Helpful insights were received from members of the Berean Book Clubs—with extensive expert reviewing from Becky Brown, significant input from Cindy Nielsen, and perspectives from Anna Barnard and Fern Anderson. Valuable comments were also provided by Gretchen Wronka and Peggy Shepard.

Many thanks to David Geister, who shared his passion for history and artistic talents by providing eloquent sketches. Valuable expertise was provided by Damien Sadrant, French Instructor at Alliance Francaise, and Diane DeVere, Librarian at the Minnesota Military Museum.

Mostly, I am grateful to the veterans and others who stepped up to join the World War II war effort. In their words: "We just did what needed to be done."